Untouchable

Sibel Hodge

Untouchable
Sibel Hodge

Dedicated to survivors everywhere...

PART 1

THE BIG HOUSE

"There is something so very dreadful, so satanic in tormenting those who have never harmed us, and who cannot defend themselves, who are utterly in our power, who have weapons neither of offence nor defense, that none but very hardened persons can endure the thought of it."

~ Cardinal John Henry Newman

MAYA

Chapter 1

Today is going to be a great day.

That was the first thought I had when I woke up.

I stretched, listening to the sounds of Jamie clattering around downstairs. It had been six months since I'd moved in with him, and the excitement still hadn't worn off.

Today was our two-year anniversary, and Jamie had told me yesterday that he had a surprise for me. Something important he wanted to ask me. Well, we'd done the moving-in-together thing, so what else could there be? He was going to propose, I was sure of it. I grinned stupidly to myself as I imagined the scene later, just after I'd cooked a romantic dinner. Candles. Wine. Soft music. The works. Would he get down on one knee or hide the ring in a gift, cunningly disguised as something else so he could see the ecstatic surprise on my face when he thought he'd fooled me? Maybe it was clichéd, but I didn't care.

Jamie's footsteps plodded up the stairs and headed towards the bedroom. He pushed open the door with his elbow, a tray in his hand with a mug of tea and two slices of toast on it. Two little dishes held some strawberry jam and butter. A vase in the middle had one deliciously lush red rose in it.

All my life I'd been drawn to the wrong relationships, the bad boys who'd cheated on me or were only after one thing. Now I'd hit the jackpot, and I was lapping up the romance, clichéd or not. Jamie was the real deal. Sweet, gentle, caring, thoughtful. A fresh burst of love and happiness rippled through me.

A smile lit up his face when he realised I was awake. 'Hey, gorgeous.' He put the tray on the bedside table. 'Happy anniversary.' He sat on the edge of the bed and kissed me. Slow, soft, sexy. Even a kiss from Jamie made me melt.

'Maybe we should forget about breakfast. How much time have you got before you need to be at work?' I raised an eyebrow and patted his side of the bed.

He placed a hand on my cheek, a naughty half smile on his face. 'Don't tempt me. I'm already going to be late for a meeting this morning. But we'll have plenty of time after work to celebrate properly.' He nuzzled into my neck and kissed me lightly behind the ear.

It sent shockwaves detonating inside. I groaned and pulled him tighter. Kissed him harder.

'I love you, Maya,' he whispered.

'Love you, too.'

He pulled back.

I groaned again, but this time it was with frustration. 'You haven't got ten minutes to spare?' I ran my fingers down his shirted chest, lower to the buckle on his belt. 'It *is* our anniversary, after all.'

He chuckled, removed my hand, and kissed the palm. 'Seriously, I'm already late. We'll have all the time in the world later.'

I feigned pouty annoyance for a moment. 'And what time will you be back from work?'

'About six. What are you cooking?'

I shook my head. 'Not telling. It's a surprise. But I guarantee you'll love it.'

'You'll love what happens after dinner.' He grinned.

'Oh, I will, will I?' I joked. 'Why don't you tell me *your* surprise now?' That tingle of excited apprehension was back. I was going to say yes. Of course I was. I pictured myself squealing with delight at the ring. Throwing my arms around his neck. Planning the big day together.

'Nice try. Later.' He kissed me on the cheek and stood up.

I watched his retreating back as he walked to the door, wondering if this time tonight we would really be engaged.

As I ate my breakfast and got dressed for work, I gave Jamie's surname a test drive. Mrs Maya Taylor. Maya Taylor. Mrs Jamie Taylor. Any of them sounded pretty damn good to me.

I walked the fifteen minutes to work. Actually, I bounced. I smiled and said good morning to everyone I passed, breaking the stuffy British early morning rush hour etiquette. They gave me odd looks, probably thinking I was mad, but what did I care? I was in love. I was the happiest I'd been in a long time, and I wanted that to rub off on all the other grumpy-looking commuters walking to work or heading to the station.

When I arrived at Customer Solutions, I got in the lift with a woman in her early twenties who I'd seen before and who worked for a travel company on the next floor up. I wondered whether I should ask her where the most romantic honeymoon destinations were.

'I love your scarf,' I said to her with a grin.

She looked down at it. 'Thanks.'

'Where did you get it?'

'The market. There's a stall right at the end that sells them.'

'Yeah, it really suits you.' I smiled as the lift doors pinged open on my floor. 'Have a great day!' I breezed through the open-plan call centre floor, the steady hum of conversation and clattering keyboards in the air.

I'd worked there for eight years, and the company provided outsourced contact centre services for some of the UK's most successful companies and brands. If the office marketing brochures were to be believed, we provided award-winning people solutions that helped our clients provide number-one service and allowed them to expand their customer base. I'd worked my way up from being on the call centre floor to managing the department that was responsible for one of our biggest insurance clients, and now I looked after a team of twenty-five people. I said hello to all the staff who weren't on the phone, giving insurance quotes to customers or dealing with claims enquiries, and walked into my office. It was appraisal time, and I still had several to finish, so I pulled out a pile and got to work. Usually, I loved my job, but every ten minutes or so, I was watching the clock. I wanted today to be over so I could be at home. With Jamie. Planning our new life together.

My phone rang as I was staring out of the window, daydreaming about where we'd go for our honeymoon. Antigua or Barbados? Prague or Barcelona?

'Maya Morgan speaking,' I said.

'Hi, Maya,' Rachel, one of my team, said. 'I've got a someone on the line who wants to talk to a manager.'

'Okay, what's the problem?'

'He's received a letter regarding his insurance claim, and he wants to complain about it.'

'All right, bring it on.' I laughed. Ranting people definitely weren't going to spoil my good mood today.

A burst of music came on the line as she connected him.

'Hi, I'm Maya Morgan. How can I help you?'

'I've just received a letter about the accident I had, and I'm not happy. My car was legally parked before I reversed into the car behind! Why should I be penalised for that? The parking spaces shouldn't be there at all if you can't reverse! It's the council's fault.'

I tried not to laugh, but some of the excuses people used for insurance claims were priceless. Ten minutes later, I'd talked him around and put the phone down. Crisis averted. Another satisfied customer.

Despite my clock watching, the day whizzed by, and at 5.00 p.m. I headed into town to pick up the bits and pieces for dinner. I was cheating slightly and not making it all from scratch, but the crispy Peking duck from Marks & Spencer was to die for. All I had to do was pop it in the oven, heat up the little pancake thingies in the microwave, and chop up some spring onions and cucumber. Marks & Spencer were so thoughtful that they even included a generous helping of hoisin sauce. How handy was that? And it was Jamie's favourite so…no contest. I grabbed another couple of bottles of Prosecco—we obviously couldn't have too much of the stuff if it was going to turn into an even bigger celebration—and headed to the checkout before going home.

We lived in a two-bedroomed detached house in a quiet cul-de-sac with eight other houses that backed onto a park. Three on one side of the road, four on the other, and our house at the dead end. Actually, it was Jamie's house. It had made sense for me to move from my poky flat into his place. There was more room, for starters. Plus, it was cosy and homely. And a big bonus was that Jamie had already paid the mortgage off.

Twenty minutes later, as I slid my key into the front door and opened it, I was struck by a weird sensation.

The house was quiet and still. Jamie wasn't back yet because his Jeep wasn't on the drive. But there was…I didn't know what it was exactly. Something felt odd, as if the air had changed somehow. I could smell something different. Out of place. I sniffed and got a vague hint of cigarettes—that stale smell I got when I'd been in the company of smokers and the scent lingered on my clothes. Neither Jamie nor I smoked, but maybe he'd been back here with a colleague during the day. Or had one of the neighbours been having a bonfire?

I shook my head, kicked off my shoes by the front door, and carried the bags of shopping into the kitchen.

After a quick shower, I changed into a vintage tea dress. It was low on the cleavage, cinched in at the waist, and sleeveless. I whacked the heating up to compensate for the lack of clothing—it was January, after all—but I knew Jamie loved the outfit so, hey, why not suffer a little chill? It wasn't every day I got proposed to, and I'd want to remember in years to come that I'd worn something special. Hopefully, I wouldn't be wearing it that long, anyway, if things went to plan.

I went downstairs to start on dinner, barely containing my excitement. He'd be here soon. I turned on my iPod and picked out something smooth and romantic. Might as well get into the theme of things, even if I was there on my own.

I looked at the clock as I slid the duck into the oven. It was dead on six thirty. He was late.

I sang loudly along with the music as I chopped spring onions and cucumber. At seven, I poured a glass of chilled Prosecco and put the pancakes onto a plate, ready to zap in the microwave. I sipped slowly, staring at the clock, until I forced myself to stop watching it and set the table in the kitchen-slash-diner. I rattled off a quick text to Jamie: *Are you nearly home? Dinner won't be long! Love you xx.*

I lit strawberry-scented candles and put the vase with the rose Jamie had given me in the centre of the kitchen table, then straightened the tablecloth and cutlery again, even though I'd already done it several times. I was trying to make everything look nice and neat, not my forte usually. I was the sloppy, messy one. Jamie was the neat freak. He said it had been instilled in him during his eight years in the army. I couldn't imagine him in the army at all. He wasn't what I pictured when I thought of huge, muscly guys wading through trenches, weapons strapped to their backs. He'd joined the military, the Royal Signals, as a sixteen-year-old apprentice and spent two years learning his trade before getting posted to his regiment, where he dealt with communications and information technology, so he wasn't the front-line hand-to-hand-combat kind of soldier. Jamie was…not quiet exactly but happy to sit back and watch, whereas I was the loud one, especially when I got drunk and wanted to sing karaoke. He liked his own company and never seemed to get lonely. Another throwback to his army days, he'd told me. After bunking with so many different guys for so long, he loved his own space. I liked long chats with my mates and being with people. We were total opposites in a lot of ways. But then, didn't they say opposites attracted?

I sat at the table, sipping wine and staring into the small rear garden, with a smile on my face as I thought about how we'd met. Jamie was an IT buff, and the company he worked for had been designing an upgraded computer software system for Customer Solutions. It was his job to teach me and the other female supervisors how to use it so we could train our call centre staff. The first day he'd turned up in our training suite, I was sitting in the front row, having a laugh with one of the other girls about some customer who'd blamed the car accident he'd had on the bus driver because the bus was ten minutes early that morning. As I saw Jamie enter the room, I literally stopped talking mid-word. Now, *I* could talk. My old school reports all said the same thing. *Maya is intelligent, but she needs to stop talking so much and listen!* I couldn't recall anything stopping me from finishing a sentence before. But Jamie did.

He wasn't even what you'd call gorgeous. He wasn't a Tom Hardy or Channing Tatum lookalike. Nothing like that. Nothing like the type of obviously good-looking guys I usually went for, which my mum would point out had to be a good thing. I'd had my fair share of broken hearts and men who were unfaithful. The bad-boy syndrome.

Jamie was tall. Not packed full of the type of muscles I usually found attractive but lean and solid, with broad shoulders and a lot of definition. He had sandy hair. In some lights, it was more strawberry blond. And he had green eyes with fair lashes. But there was just *something* about him. I didn't know what it was. Maybe the slightly anxious way he'd held himself. The hesitant smile on his face as he took in the women already sitting there waiting. The way he'd dropped a stack of information folders he was balancing in one arm as he carried a laptop in the other. Or maybe the way he actually *blushed* when he'd dropped the folders—although he *swore* he didn't blush when I brought it up after we'd started dating.

Naturally, since I was in the front row, I'd jumped up to help him pick them up and flashed him a big smile. It was a flirty smile, I couldn't help myself. The blushing thing had done something to me, though. By the time he'd cleared his throat, adjusted his tie—even though it was already perfect—and introduced himself, I was thinking that a boring software upgrade was about to get a hell of a lot more interesting.

I was the one who'd asked him out for a drink. I didn't buy into all this 'women shouldn't do the asking' idea. Those who didn't ask didn't get, and I suspected he was shy around women and probably wouldn't ask me. On the last day of the training, he was either going to walk out of my life forever or not. As it turned out, it had been a very definite not.

I swallowed the last of my wine and checked the clock again.

Where was he? He hadn't texted back.

I turned the oven down. I knew the duck was supposed to be crispy, but at this rate it would be cremated.

I phoned his mobile and listened to it ringing. I tapped my fingers on the table before sending another text: *Hey, sexy! Are you on your way? I'm cooking dinner naked! XOXO*

I poured some more wine and stared at my phone, waiting for it to signal a reply.

Nothing happened.

By eight, I'd phoned twice more and sent another text. I was not usually the neurotic type. I was usually laid back. I didn't care if Jamie wanted to go out with his friends or did what he wanted without me. It worked both ways, didn't it? Everyone needed some kind of freedom in their relationship. But the thing was, Jamie didn't actually have many friends. He didn't go out and do many things without me except go to the leisure centre to swim a gazillion lengths or head out to the countryside to hike at weekends. He liked his own company. And he'd never once been late in all the time we'd been dating. In fact, he was a stickler for being on time. If anything, he got slightly panicky at the thought of being late.

That was when the thought first hit me that something had happened to him. There'd been an accident. Or—oh God—maybe he'd been mugged or attacked!

I phoned him again, and it just rang and rang. I chewed on my bottom lip, wondering what to do. Should I phone the police? Ask if his car had been in an accident? Was it too early for that?

I waited another half an hour then looked up the number for our local police station. It just wasn't like Jamie not to contact me. I paced up and down in the kitchen, waiting what seemed like an eternity for someone to answer. Then I was put through to someone else. And someone else, who eventually told me that no, there had been no incidents reported locally involving Jamie's car. That should've been a good sign, at least, but I still couldn't shake the feeling something was wrong.

Where had he been working today? Had he even said? As well as designing computer software systems, he was also responsible for training company employees all over the South East how to use them. He could have been anywhere.

I went into the lounge to find my laptop. I could do an Internet search to see if there was any breaking news somewhere that might mean he was delayed. Maybe there was a pile-up on a motorway and he was stuck in traffic. But that still didn't explain why he wasn't answering his phone. Unless he'd left it somewhere. Or lost it. Or the battery was dead. But he had a car phone charger, so why wasn't he using that? Maybe he'd broken down *and* the battery was flat.

The odd sensation I'd experienced when I'd walked in the front door hit me again in the lounge. Something was different about the room, but I couldn't work out what. Everything looked in the same place. The TV was still there. The expensive stereo.

I frowned when I spied Jamie's laptop on the coffee table next to mine. He always took it to work with him—for presentations and training. Why was it still here? Had he forgotten it?

I turned his laptop on instead of mine since it was far quicker. The first thing I noticed was that his background wallpaper picture was missing. It was a photo of the two of us, taken in Scotland where we'd been away for a romantic weekend about six months after we'd met. Then I realised there were no icons, either. It was just a blank black screen. How weird.

I frowned, wondering if it had crashed. Maybe it had caught a virus. Jamie's voice popped into my head, then, telling me that a computer couldn't 'catch' a virus, as I'd mentioned to him one day. He'd laughed his head off. But anyway, the most likely conclusion was that he'd left it here because it had died for some reason.

I turned it off, put it back on the coffee table, and reached for mine, balancing it on my knee as I waited impatiently for it to boot up.

I searched on Google for any traffic problems in the South East, but I couldn't see anything that might explain why Jamie had been delayed.

My mobile phone ringing in the kitchen made me jump. I put the laptop back on the coffee table and rushed to answer it, but when I picked it up, it was 'Ava,' my sister's name, that showed on the display.

'Hiya, Maya!' Ava sang down the phone. She always thought that was funny for some reason. Not that I hadn't heard it about a million times before. 'How's it going? You'll never guess what happened to me to—'

'Hi, sis. Look, I can't talk now. I'm trying to get hold of Jamie,' I butted in. Ava and I usually spoke to each other every day, but it would have to wait until tomorrow now.

'Oh, okay. Where is he?'

'I don't know. He's not answering the phone, and he was supposed to be home hours ago.'

'Oh, yeah! It's your anniversary, isn't it? Two years. Sorry I phoned. I totally forgot about it. Well, I'm sure everything's okay. Maybe he's just stuck in traffic or something.'

'Yeah, I hope so.' A burning smell hit me, and I stared at the oven. 'Shit! I've burnt the dinner now. Look, I've got to go.' I opened the oven door. Smoke and heat blasted me in the face. I wafted my hand around, trying to disperse it.

'All right. Well, I'm sure he'll be fine. He'll probably turn up in a minute. Speak soon, yeah?'

I tossed my phone on the kitchen worktop, removed the

annihilated duck, and felt tears springing into my eyes. Bugger! I plonked the useless meal on top of the oven and glanced at the clock again. It read 8.30 p.m.

Paul! That's it. Phone Jamie's boss. He'll know where Jamie was working today.

Except I didn't have Paul's mobile number and the office would be closed now. Jamie didn't have an address book. All his numbers were stored in his phone so how could I…

His phone bills. Jamie always had detailed itemised calls. If I checked through them, I'd find Paul's mobile number.

I ran up the stairs into the spare bedroom. In the cupboard, Jamie had a large cardboard box where he kept folders of everything important. Bank statements, credit card bills, household receipts, insurance papers, and vehicle documents. He kept trying to talk me into being more organised like that, but my bills usually went straight in the bin when I'd paid them. I always joked with him that he was a bit anal in the organisational department, but now I was glad. I scooped out some plastic A4 envelope-style wallets and looked at the first one on the pile. Credit card bills. The next had household receipts. The third one was his mobile phone bills. I slid out the first bill on top and scanned it. It took me a few minutes to work out that it was dated four months ago, which was strange. I knew he'd had a new bill a week before, and he would always put the latest on top, but that one, and those from several previous months, seemed to be missing. I didn't have time to think about that, though, as I checked through the numbers and names listed on the October bill, looking for Paul Porter.

At the bottom of the page, I found it. Punching in his number, I tried to breathe slowly as I held my mobile to my ear.

Come on! Answer!

Paul picked up on the tenth ring. Loud music sang out in the background, along with sounds of people talking and a fruit machine pinging. That was it. Paul must be at the pub with Jamie. Had Jamie forgotten it was our anniversary? Lost track of time? No, he wouldn't.

'Hello?' Paul answered.

'Hi, it's Maya Morgan. Is Jamie with you?'

He paused for a second, probably registering who I was. I'd met him only a couple of times at Jamie's work do's. 'Oh, hi, Maya. Um…no. He's not with me. Why?'

'He hasn't come home yet. He's really late, and he's not answering his phone. I'm worried that maybe he's been in a car accident or something.'

'I haven't seen him for a week. Not since he took his annual leave.'

'What?' I said, thinking I'd misheard. Jamie couldn't have been on annual leave. He'd been going to work every day, as usual. 'You must have him mixed up with someone else. He hasn't taken any time off.'

There was another pause on the other end of the line. 'I'm not getting mixed up, Maya. He booked a couple of weeks off work. He hasn't been in the office for a week, and he's got another week of it left.'

I blinked, trying to make sense of that. 'But I don't understand. He's been…he's been leaving for work.'

'I can assure you he hasn't. He said he needed some time off for personal reasons.'

'But…' I trailed off, listening to a woman laughing in the background on the other end.

'When was the last time you saw him?' Paul asked, sounding confused. 'I'm sure he'll be—'

A terrible fear danced its way up my spine. 'He was supposed to be here hours ago. It's our anniversary.'

'Maybe he's stuck in traffic. He'll be back soon, I'm sure. It's probably all a misunderstanding.'

I stared at the carpet. 'Why would he pretend he was going to work?'

'Did he actually *tell* you he was going to work?'

I thought back to what Jamie had said that morning. He was late for a 'meeting'. But if it wasn't a work-related meeting, what had he been talking about? 'Well…no, but he's been leaving in a suit and tie every day at the same time, just like always.'

A female voice called Paul's name. 'Look, sorry, I've got to go. He's probably just running late.'

'Yeah,' I said, ending the call, confusion swirling in my head as I prayed that was true.

I'd just put the folders back in the box when someone knocked on the front door. The apprehension vanished, and my face broke into a huge grin. Here he was. There was nothing to worry about after all.

I swung the door open. 'Have you forgotten your key? I thought—' The words died in my throat as I saw two police officers standing on the doorstep. A woman in her late twenties with an older man. Both of them had solemn expressions.

'Oh no.' My hands flew to my cheeks. 'Something's happened to Jamie, hasn't it?'

'Are you Mrs Taylor?' the woman asked.

'Um…no. Is this about Jamie?' I looked from one to the other frantically. 'I'm his girlfriend.'

'Can we come in, please?' the policeman said.

'Yes.' I stood back to let them into the hallway. 'Please, just tell me what's happened. Is he okay? Is he injured?'

'I think you might want to sit down,' the female officer said. I could tell by the expressions on their faces that this was something bad. Really bad.

'I don't want to sit down! What's happened?' I shrieked.

Just tell me!

The policeman cleared his throat uncomfortably. 'I'm afraid that a few hours ago, we had a report of a dead body being found in a wood near Tyttenhanger.'

I gasped. 'What does that have to do with…' I glanced from one to the other.

'I'm sorry to tell you this, but when we arrived at the scene, we found a deceased male who had hanged himself from one of the trees.'

'No.' I shook my head, blinking rapidly. 'Why are you telling me?'

'In his pocket, we found a wallet with credit cards and a driving license for James Taylor at this address.'

Cold horror slammed into me. I think I let out some kind of noise as the world tilted and stopped. Everything stood still for what seemed like years as I stared at him. And then it speeded up again, hurtling around too fast, making me dizzy as the words sank in. 'N-No. That's not possible. It must be someone else. It's our anniversary, you see. He's just late, isn't he?' I looked between them as if they were mad. They'd made a huge mistake. They must've done. 'He wouldn't have hanged himself, don't you understand? He wouldn't have done that. It must be someone else. Maybe that person stole Jamie's wallet and that's why he's late. Maybe he's at a hospital somewhere, or…or his car's crashed. Have you checked that? Have you checked?' A rising wave of hysteria welled up inside. I leant against the wall to steady myself.

'I know this is a terrible shock,' the female said. 'Do you want to sit down?'

I blinked rapidly, trying to make sense of what they were saying. She put her arm around me and guided me into the kitchen, gently settling me in a chair.

'I'm very sorry, but the photo on the driving license matches the deceased,' the male officer said. 'But we will need someone to do a formal identification. Are you James's next of kin?'

My throat constricted as their words stung.

No. They're wrong! It's not Jamie. It's not! It can't be!

I swallowed, trying to think through the shrieking in my head. 'Um…yes. His parents died years ago. He doesn't have any family.'

'Do you have anyone we can call for you?'

I shook my head, as if trying to shake away the image that bounced around the inside of my skull of Jamie in the mortuary. I opened my mouth to say something, but nothing came out.

'Are you sure?' the female said. 'A friend or relative? It's probably not a good idea for you to be alone at the moment.'

The room swam in and out of focus. 'It can't be Jamie,' I whispered. 'He'd never do…'

'We're very sorry,' the man said, but I could barely hear it over the rushing sounds in my ears.

I wrapped my arms around myself, rocking back and forth in the chair. I felt a hand on my shoulder. More words that I couldn't make out. Tears coming from somewhere. A glass of water being put on the table in front of me. Unsteady legs as the female helped me into my coat. Then I was in the back of their police car, trembling, looking out the window as the world passed by in slow motion, and it felt as if I was freezing from the inside out.

The female officer sat in the passenger seat, twisting around to face me. 'Are you sure you want to do this now? It can be done tomorrow.'

I shook my head. I had to see him. Had to prove it wasn't Jamie. Of course it wasn't. This was some kind of terrible case of mistaken identity.

She turned back around, and we drove to the hospital in silence as I dug my nails into my palms to stop my hands shaking.

We approached the brightly lit entrance and took a lift to the basement. Their rubber-soled heels squeaked on the linoleum as we headed up a long corridor. The smell of antiseptic and sickness permeated my nostrils, and my stomach lurched.

It's not Jamie. It's not Jamie.

We reached a door, and the male officer went inside. The female officer stood, awkwardly watching me. I turned away and looked up the corridor where we'd just come from. I wanted to run back. Get into the lift. Go home where I'd find Jamie waiting for me, a sheepish smile on his face. He'd lost his mobile phone and couldn't call me. He'd been stuck in traffic. There was a simple explanation. But I couldn't run because my feet were glued to the floor.

The door opened again, and the male officer stood there, his lips pressed together in a solemn line. The female placed a hand on my back and guided me inside the room. A male in blue hospital scrubs stood next to a trolley in the centre. A sheet was over it, and underneath the sheet was the indentation of a body.

It's not Jamie. It can't be.

'There are some injuries to his neck,' the man in the scrubs said.

I nodded blankly, but I just wanted him to hurry up and get it over with so I could go home and wait for Jamie to come back.

Slowly, he pulled back the sheet to reveal the person's face.

A stabbing pain hit me in the chest. I couldn't breathe. My legs wobbled.

It was Jamie.

'I…' I reached out to place a hand on Jamie's arm, to wake him up, and then stopped myself.

The man in the scrubs looked at me sympathetically.

'Can you confirm this is James Taylor?' the male police officer said.

I gulped back a strangled sob and nodded, before swaying forwards, bent double, gasping for air.

The female officer held me up to stop me collapsing to my knees. I had a form to sign. Instructions about the coroner's officer contacting me. Words I couldn't take in. Nodding numbly. The ride home. More offers to phone someone to stay with me. More condolences.

I couldn't take it in. Couldn't understand it all because Jamie was dead.

I walked into the kitchen and sat down blindly at the kitchen table. I didn't want to speak to anyone. Didn't want to call anyone. Not Ava, or my parents, or my friends. For once, I wanted my own company instead. Needed it.

I didn't know how long I stayed in that position. Frozen. Grief hitting me in between denials that it was really him. Thoughts flitting from one thing to the next. *Why did he do it? He was happy. He couldn't have done it. It doesn't make sense. Was he depressed? Had I missed some kind of signs? What about my anniversary surprise? A surprise I'd never get now. He loves me. I know he does.*

Loved *me. Past tense.*

Past. Finished. Dead.

'Oh, God,' I wailed, throwing my head in my hands as the tears I'd been holding back finally unleashed in an agonising torrent, and I felt as if I was plunging into darkness.

At some point, I dragged myself upstairs and got into bed, fully clothed. I hugged Jamie's pillow to my face, breathing in his scent, closing my eyes and imagining he was still here with me.

Today wasn't a great day at all. It was the worst day of my life.

JAMIE

Chapter 2

It had been a long time since I'd seen any of their faces. I'd successfully buried those memories deep. So deep they'd never resurface. Locked in a safe house in my head where they couldn't hurt me anymore. Or so I'd thought.

I'd never spoken about what happened. I'd become strong. The army helped with that. And I'd trained myself mentally to forget. Trained my body to become fit. I became adept at putting on a front. And lying. To others, of course, but to myself, mostly.

Despite that, I had problems forging relationships. I didn't trust easily. Sometimes I found it hard to handle emotions. I didn't want someone to guess there was something wrong with me. Something so sickeningly damaged. So even though I craved love and closeness, I pushed it away, never staying with a woman more than a few months. I was a loner. I didn't need anyone. Or so I thought until Maya came into my life. With her, the attraction was instant. She was so full of life. Energetic, bubbly. The way she livened up any room. Her witty one-liners. Her warmth and kindness. Her contagious laugh. And the way she was always so strong and positive. She didn't let anything faze her. She made me believe we could work.

She brought me to life again. Made me feel normal. So despite everything I'd trained myself not to do, I fell in love with her. Many times I'd wanted to confide in her, but I couldn't handle the thought she would leave me. I imagined her looking at me with disgust and revulsion, and I knew I could never tell. Not then.

I thought I was safe from the past. Safe in my new life with Maya. Safe in my job. My home. In a cocoon of happiness that I'd come to really believe I now deserved. But a few months ago, one of them invaded my home, and I wasn't safe anymore.

Maya had been out with Becca and Lynn, and I was watching a documentary on TV. The next minute the news was on, and there was a segment about a Member of Parliament who had now been appointed as the new children's minister. The memories hit me like the powerful force of an avalanche, knocking me to my knees. Pictures flooded into my head. I shook violently. My chest felt as if someone was squeezing the air from my lungs. I gulped for breath, suddenly a little boy again. This MP, Eamonn Colby, was a depraved, evil excuse for a human being, who preyed on the weak. Not only that, he was a murderer. And *he* was now the children's minister, in charge of protecting the vulnerable and innocent, keeping them safe, doing his utmost to look after their welfare. Nothing was more abhorrent or unjust.

I thought long and hard about what to do. I didn't want to drag up the memories from the past. I didn't want to put myself in that position, reliving what had happened. I'd spent enough time trying to forget and fix myself. I'd learned how to carefully hide the shadows and demons and shame for decades. It had been a long journey, but my life was now great, and I didn't want to do anything to jeopardise that.

The problem was, my head wouldn't let me forget. I had flashbacks and panic attacks sometimes. I found it hard to sleep again, hard to concentrate, and even harder still to keep up my pretence that I was a normal guy. I kept seeing what had happened all those years ago, and it wouldn't go away. Like a seed germinating in the ground, the anger started as a tiny little speck of life. Over the months, it grew until it blossomed into hatred and fury, and I knew there was only one thing I could do. My conscience wouldn't allow me another way. I wasn't that skinny, terrified little boy now. I was a man who'd fought to survive. I couldn't run away from it all any longer. And I wasn't going to stay silent anymore and let them get away with it. I was going to write a record of everything to get it straight in my head first.

Then I was going to finally tell my story.

MAYA

Chapter 3

Somehow, I fell asleep. I didn't know when or how, but I drifted off eventually, only to jerk awake to that sinking feeling that I knew something was wrong but couldn't work out what until it hit me like a wrecking ball.

My eyelids were swollen shut, stuck together with caked tears, and it took me a moment to open them and focus on the bedroom. Our bedroom. Except it wouldn't be *our* bedroom anymore.

A suffocating squeezing in my chest almost crushed me. I pulled Jamie's pillow tighter towards me. How could he really be gone? It wasn't possible. Twenty-four hours before, he was telling me he loved me. He was laughing. Looking forward to celebrating our anniversary with me. He was happy. There was no hint he was about to kill himself. Nothing. How could that be? How could it?

I wanted to lie there forever, smelling his lingering scent of soap and masculinity and...just Jamie. *The man I love. Will always love.* Not *loved.* I wanted to slip into oblivion, and when I woke, it would all be a horrific dream.

I was so hollow and empty that no more tears came, only the painful ache of tears that wouldn't flow anymore.

Why would he do it? How could he leave me like that?

I turned onto my side, staring at my bedside unit at the black-and-white photo of Jamie and me. A selfie I'd taken during a picnic in a field near Codicote. We'd rambled around the picturesque area before Jamie had led me to a river snaking through some woods. He'd said it was one of his favourite local places to sit and think and get away from everything. It had been a scorching July day in a deserted spot in the middle of nowhere, and after eating, we'd made love with the heat of the sun on our skin.

I reached over and picked up the photo, tracing his face with my fingertips. His eyes were sparkling. Alive and ecstatic. The left side of his lip curled up higher than the right, as it did when he smiled.

A strangled groan escaped my lips.

He wouldn't do it. Not Jamie. No.

And yet he had.

'Why?' I cried, my croaky voice echoing in the silence.

What was so bad that he'd felt he had to take his own life? We could've talked about things. Sorted out any problems he had. Made plans. I'd thought we *were* making plans for our future.

But surely there should've been a sign. Had I missed it somehow? Was this my fault because I hadn't noticed something was wrong?

I tried to think back to the last few weeks. He'd acted just as he always did. What had we done last week? We'd been out for a midweek curry because neither of us could be bothered to cook after work. We'd met up with my friends Becca and Lynn and their boyfriends on Friday night. We'd stumbled home, drunk, and had sex on the kitchen table. Jamie hadn't been acting weird. He was a little quieter than usual, I supposed. A few times, I'd caught him staring into space with a pensive look on his face, but he'd said he had a lot on at work and was a bit stressed. And he had been having a few nightmares lately, but other than that, he seemed okay.

It didn't make sense.

I remembered the phone call with Jamie's boss, Paul, last night. If Jamie hadn't been going to work, where had he really been going? What 'personal things' did he need to sort out? Was that something to do with why he'd killed himself?

Thinking about Paul reminded me I had things to do. People to phone.

Not yet, though. I couldn't cope with that yet. I needed help. I needed Ava.

It was 6.30 a.m. when I phoned her. I knew she'd already be up by now giving Jackson his morning feed.

'Wow, you're phoning early!' Ava gushed down the phone. 'You've got something exciting to tell me, haven't you? He proposed last night, didn't he, like you thought he would? Oh my God, I'm so happy for—'

'Ava, Jamie's dead.' As I spoke the words, they still didn't feel real. It was as if I was playing a role in a film. An actress stiffly saying lines she hadn't rehearsed. They sounded alien on my tongue. Alien and terrifying.

'What?' She gasped.

'He…last night…the…he hanged himself. In a wood nearby.' My hand flew to my mouth, as if somehow I could stuff the words back in. Never let them out.

Another gasp. 'No! What? Why would he do that?'

'I don't know. I don't know anything. I can't think straight. He was happy. He *was*. Why would he do it? Why? I don't understand.'

'Hanged himself? Oh, hon, I'm so sorry. So, so sorry.' She was silent for a while, apparently thinking of something to say. What should she say in these circumstances? 'I…shit, I'm shocked.'

'I don't know what to do.' My voice sounded small, like a child's. 'I think I need you to help me. There are people to tell. Things to…I don't want to…'

'Look, don't worry about anything, okay? I'll just finish feeding Jackson, then we'll be round. I'll take care of things. You just do what you need to do. Feel what you need to feel.'

'Thank you.'

'Do you want me to get you anything? Food or…anything else?'

'No. We've got food here.' I thought about the ruined anniversary dinner, and a sob lodged in my throat. 'I can't face food, anyway.'

'All right. I'll be there in about forty-five minutes. Love you, sis.'

'Love you, too.'

I stripped out of my rumpled tea dress and opened the wardrobe, staring at Jamie's clothes neatly staring back at me from the left half. I trailed my fingers along the fabric then recoiled at them lifelessly hanging there.

Lifeless. Hanging.

My mouth watered. Sweat broke out on my forehead. Acid rose in my throat.

I ran to the en suite bathroom and vomited violently. When I was spent, I wiped my mouth with toilet paper, curled up on the freezing cold floor, naked, and howled.

A knocking at the door sometime later jolted me out of my desperate thoughts. I grabbed Jamie's dressing gown from the peg behind the door and pulled it on. It was miles too long for me, the arms coming way past my hands, the hem dragging on the carpet.

I walked down the stairs on legs that threatened to buckle with every movement, feeling as if I had a bad case of the flu. Wobbly. Disorientated. Empty.

If only it was flu. If only Jamie was here. If only.

Ava's silhouette was visible through the obscured double-glazed panels on the front door. I took a deep breath and opened it.

She'd been crying, too, her eyes red and shiny. In the crook of her arm, she held a sleeping Jackson in his car seat.

'Oh, Maya.' Her upper lip quivered. She put Jackson down in the hallway and pulled me towards her.

I fell against her, and we clung on tight to each other, crying, our chests rising and falling with each sob.

'I can't believe it.' I sniffed, trying to breathe through my blocked nose.

'I can't, either. Can you tell me what happened?'

I closed my eyes, pressing the lids together firmly, not wanting to ever open them again to a world without him.

'It's okay. You don't need to talk if you don't want to. How about I make you a cup of tea? Something to eat? Take your time.' She released me and placed a soft hand to my cheek, her face twisting with anguish.

'Coffee,' I mumbled. 'Coffee. With some brandy.'

'You've got it.' She squeezed my arm, picked up Jackson, and walked through the hallway into the kitchen.

I stumbled behind her, holding onto the wall for support. Sitting at the kitchen table, I watched her pottering around, grabbing a couple of mugs, spooning in coffee granules, and adding a hefty dose of brandy to mine.

I tried to stop the turmoil of visions exploding in my head. Jamie in the mortuary. Jamie hanging from a tree. I wanted to block them, but they kept coming. Jamie laughing at his fortieth celebration in the pub three weeks ago. Me decorating the Christmas tree so badly Jamie laughed at it and had to take off all the decorations and redo it when I'd gone out. Jamie's eyes staring into mine intensely when we had sex. I blinked. Focused on Ava pressing a mug into my hands. Stared at the steam rising. Felt my heart splinter.

She sat next to me and shook her head. We were silent. The only sounds were the clock ticking on the wall and Jackson's snuffles and sighs of contentment in his sleep. I wiped my eyes with the cuff of

Jamie's dressing gown. A waft of his scent hit my nostrils, and a knife of grief stabbed me viciously.

'He's not coming back.' I shook my head. 'He's never coming back.'

She rubbed my back in soothing, circular motions. 'What happened?'

'I don't know.' I bent over and rested my head in my hands. 'I don't understand.' And the more I went over it, the less sense it made, but of course, I couldn't stop.

We'll have all the time in the world later.

You'll love what happens after dinner.

'He was fine. The last time I saw him was yesterday morning. He brought me breakfast in bed. We were talking about seeing each other later that night for our anniversary dinner. He talked about his surprise. He was happy, Ava. I thought he was going to propose, I really did. There wasn't anything…nothing. He wasn't depressed. He loved me, I know he did.'

'Of course he did. It was obvious.'

'He loved his life. He loved his job. I would've known if something was bothering him, wouldn't I? I would've noticed…' I trailed off, thinking about my conversation with Paul again. 'Except…'

'What?'

I shrugged. 'I don't know. His boss said he'd taken two weeks' annual leave to sort out some personal things. Jamie had only had a week of it before…before…he did this. And I didn't know that.' I sniffed again. 'Jamie didn't tell me about it.'

Ava stood and tore off a handful of kitchen roll. She handed it to me, and I blew my nose. Took a shuddering breath.

'Personal things? What does that mean?'

'I haven't got a clue. He was leaving for work as normal. He didn't say anything to me about it. I didn't think we had any secrets. But there must've been something that made him do it. Something that was going on in the last week I didn't know about. That's the only explanation, isn't it? Everything was good between us. Everything else was just as it usually was. Maybe he had some personal problem and it was...' I shook my head. 'I don't know. I can't even imagine what it was. His mortgage is paid off. He hasn't got any loans that I know of. It couldn't be anything financial. So, what?' I pleaded with her, even though she didn't know the answer. 'What could it mean?' I wailed.

'I have no idea. But it must've been pretty terrible for him to have taken his own life and leave you behind.'

'Terrible,' I repeated.

'Look, I'll organise things. Who do you want me to call first? Mum and Dad?'

I groaned. 'Mum will want to come over, but she's too busy looking after Dad at the moment. It's not fair on either of them. Tell her I'm okay, will you? Just that I don't want to talk to anyone yet.'

Mum and Dad had retired to Portugal three years ago, and Dad had just come out of hospital after having a hip replacement. He needed full-time care at the moment. 'I can't face telling people what's happened. Not yet. Not even Mum and Dad.'

'Of course. Whatever you want. And who else? Your boss? I can tell her you won't be in for a while. And does Jamie's boss know?'

'No. Jamie's boss is Paul Porter. His mobile number is on my phone.' I reached for it on the table and scrolled through the calls I'd made last night. Jamie's number was there, too, taunting me. I pressed the heel of my hand to the bridge of my nose, forcing the tears back down as I handed the phone to Ava.

'Anyone else?'

'I...um...I don't think so at the moment. I don't know. I've never done this before.'

'We'll just take it one step at a time. One day at a time.' She gave me an encouraging half smile and clasped both my hands in hers. 'You'll get through this, hon.'

'Will I? It just feels like…someone has scooped out my insides and set them on fire, and I'm burning from the inside out. It feels like the end of my life. How am I going to cope with never seeing him again?' My lips trembled. Tears filled my eyes. 'How can I ever stop missing him? Stop thinking about him? Knowing all the time that I'll never hear his laugh or touch him or talk to him? How, Ava? How do you do that?'

She pulled her chair closer and slid her arm around me, pulling me towards her so my head rested on her shoulder. 'Like I say, one day at a time. This is normal. This is grief. Gradually, it will get less acute.'

She held me for a while until I sat up and sipped at my coffee. The brandy burned my throat and stomach lining, but I didn't care. I wanted more of it. Maybe I could drink myself into unconsciousness. Numb the pain. At least for a while.

Ava went into the lounge to make the phone calls. Low mumbles echoed through the closed door, but I couldn't make out what she was saying. I stared at sleeping Jackson, clutching his blanket in his tiny fist, and felt a pang of jealousy. Jamie had wanted kids, and so did I. We'd talked about it before. He would make an amazing dad. *Would've.* Now there would be no chance.

I pulled my gaze away from Jackson, put my feet up on the edge of the chair, and hugged my knees. As Ava came back in, the phone in her hand rang.

She looked at me. 'Do you want me to answer it?'

I nodded.

'Hello? No, this is her sister, Ava. Oh. Right. Um…can you just hang on a second? She's very upset.' She pressed a hand over the mouthpiece. 'It's someone from the coroner's office. They want to come and talk to you today. Are you up to that?'

I ran my hands over my face. 'I suppose so. If I don't do it today, they'll just want to do it tomorrow or the next day. Maybe I should get it over with.'

'Sure?'

'No, but…' I trailed off, unsure how to end the sentence.

Ava removed her hand and spoke again. 'Yes, she'll be at home. What time?' She glanced at me and nodded. 'Okay. One o'clock. Bye.' She hung up and put the phone back on the table. 'Do you want me to be here when they come?'

'Would you?'

'Of course.'

'What did Mum and Dad say?'

'Mum started crying and said she wanted to come over, but I told her you weren't up to visitors just yet. And anyway, she can't leave Dad. He can't do anything for himself at the moment. She said to give you her love. They both do. They're in shock. I guess we all are. And they said to tell you they're very sorry and thinking of you. I spoke to your boss, too, and she said take as much time as you need, and if there's anything she can do, you can contact her.'

'What did Paul say?'

'He was completely shocked, too. He said to pass on his condolences.'

'Did he say anything else about what Jamie could've been doing on his time off?'

'No. He said to ring him when you felt up to it.'

I nodded vaguely.

'Do you want something to eat?'

The thought of food made me feel nauseous again. 'No, thanks.'

'Another coffee?'

'Maybe just brandy.'

She bit her lip for a moment then poured a hefty measure into the mug.

~ ~ ~ ~

I didn't know how I got through the morning, but somehow I was still living. Still breathing. My heart was still beating. Even if Jamie's wasn't.

At 1.00 p.m. on the dot, someone knocked on the door.

I looked at Ava. She looked at me.

'Are you up to this?'

I shrugged helplessly.

'I'll let them in.'

We sat in the lounge, me on the corner sofa with Ava next to me, clutching my hand tightly. The coroner's officer introduced himself as Tony Williams. He sat in the armchair opposite, placed a briefcase on the floor, and opened it, then he retrieved a clipboard with some papers on it and a pen. He was thickset, red-faced with a grey beard and bushy grey hair and eyebrows. He had kind eyes. Like Jamie. Jamie's eyes had a softness behind them when he looked at me.

'I'm very sorry about James,' Tony said.

'Jamie,' I corrected him. No one called him James. It was wrong. This whole thing was wrong. Couldn't he see that?

'Jamie.' He gave me a sympathetic smile. 'In these circumstances of sudden deaths, it's my job to investigate what happened to Jamie. To establish the circumstances leading up to his death and how it came about. So I'll be making enquiries with various people, and there will be an inquest.'

'Inquest,' I repeated stupidly.

'Yes. A post-mortem was carried out this morning,' he continued. An image of Jamie on a mortuary slab flashed in my head. I'd watched crime programmes on TV. *Silent Witness* and all that. I knew about the *Y* incision they would have made. The organs they would've examined and weighed. It was more than I could bear. I pressed my fingertips to my eyes until black-and-white dots appeared, trying to blot it out.

'I'm very sorry,' Tony said again. 'Unfortunately, these things have to be done.'

Ava squeezed my hand.

'Yes,' I said, because I didn't know what else to say.

'Cause of death has been listed as asphyxia due to suspension.'

My stomach contracted painfully, as if being squeezed by sharp claws.

'An interim death certificate will be issued, and the body will probably be released for burial in a few days. Have you thought about which undertaker you'll be using?'

I shook my head. *How can I think of that?*

'We have some time, so don't worry about that at the moment.' He clicked the top of his pen and adjusted his clipboard. 'I know this is very difficult for you, but as you know, we found Jamie in an area known as Bluebell Wood, yesterday evening. A dog walker reported it to the police, and they attended the scene. You then identified him last night. I want to look into what happened leading up to his death.'

My muscles stiffened. Ava squeezed my hand again.

'Can you go through everything that happened yesterday? I'll be making notes as I go, and then at the end, I'll prepare a witness statement and get you to sign it. Okay?'

No. It's not okay! None of this is okay!

He looked at me expectantly. I didn't want to speak. It would make it too real.

'Take your time.' He gave me an encouraging nod.

'Well...Jamie brought me breakfast in bed. I didn't start work until nine, so he was always up before me. Then he left.'

'And where did he work?'

'Porterhouse Systems and Solutions. They do software for companies. Jamie designed the software and trained personnel how to use them.'

'Where are they based?'

'At the business park.'

'Thank you.' He scribbled that down. 'Does his work involve a lot of stress?'

'Not usually, no. He loved his job. But the last few weeks, he said he had been a bit stressed about work. But what's really weird is that when I phoned his boss, Paul Porter, last night, trying to find Jamie, he said Jamie was on annual leave. That he'd booked two weeks off for personal reasons, and that Paul hadn't seen him for the last week.'

Tony made more notes. 'And he didn't tell you about the annual leave?'

'No.'

'Do you know what these personal reasons could've been? Was he having financial troubles?'

'No. Jamie never mentioned anything to me. He'd been leaving for work as usual, dressed as usual. Coming home at around the same time. In fact, I always asked him how his day was in the evenings, and he mentioned some software system he was designing and a training course he was doing, and some meetings he was having.'

'So he was stressed about work...did he seem worried about anything else recently?'

'No. I mean, last week, he was a bit quiet and distracted. He blamed something he was working on, but he wasn't upset or anything. But it couldn't have been to do with work, could it? If he wasn't even there?'

Tony made some more notes.

'It was our anniversary yesterday. We'd been dating for two years. I moved in here with him six months ago.' I played with the tassel on the hood of the sweatshirt I'd changed into, rolling the end into a ball then unravelling it. 'He'd been saying that he had a big surprise for me. I thought...' I looked at Ava. 'I thought he was going to propose.' My voice cracked, and I looked up at the ceiling, blinking back tears.

'What kind of mood was he in when he left?'

We'll have all the time in the world later.

You'll love what happens after dinner.

'He was happy. That's why I don't understand how he could've done this. He was excited. Looking forward to the evening when we were going to celebrate. I was cooking him dinner, and he was due back at six.'

'What did he say before he left the house?'

'He said he...was late for a meeting. I assumed it was something to do with work. And then he said...he said he loved me.' I wiped my eyes with the heel of my hand.

'Apart from that, was there anything else that might've been out of character leading up to yesterday?'

'No. Nothing.'

'No arguments?'

'No.'

'And you're sure about no financial problems?'

'As sure as I can be.'

'Did he have a history of depression?'

'No.' I shook my head vehemently.

'Who was his GP?'

'Dr Lattimer. Grove House Surgery.'

'Had he visited Dr Lattimer recently?'

'Um...he had tonsillitis about six months ago and got some antibiotics for it.'

'And he hadn't visited him for anything else?'

'Not that I know of.'

'You mentioned to the officers last night that Jamie doesn't have any other family, is that correct?'

'Yes. His parents died in a car accident when he was sixteen. There's no one else.'

'How would you describe his personality and frame of mind?'

'Um…he was a homebody, really. He liked doing things round the house, DIY, reading. He wasn't the life and soul of the party, but he was fun. He had a tendency to sit back and watch rather than being in the midst of things. Like, if we were out with friends, he felt more comfortable with just a few people there rather than in a big group. He had his quiet times, like we all do, I guess. But he wasn't moody or anything. He was happy. He worked hard. He was kind and caring. Generous. He was organised and dependable and focused. He had a dry sense of humour. He liked swimming and walking. Sometimes at the weekends, we'd head out to the countryside and walk for a few hours, then stop off at a country pub for lunch. He was just Jamie.' I stopped, wondering what else he wanted me to say.

'Had he been out with any friends recently? Perhaps he mentioned some kind of worries to them.'

'We usually went out once a week on Friday nights with my friends Becca and Lynn and their boyfriends.'

'Can you give me their contact details, please?'

I told him, and Tony wrote it all down.

'But Jamie didn't really have many close friends. Just acquaintances, I suppose. Colleagues he worked with. Sometimes he met up with his old army buddies, though.'

'Do you know who they are?'

'No, I never went with him. It was a guy's thing. The last time he

37

met up with them must've been about a year ago when he went to a reunion organised by a guy called Lee who Jamie had worked with. I don't know his surname, though.'

'Do you have a contact number for him?'

'Um…hang on, I'll need to look through Jamie's phone bills.' I made my way upstairs, feeling like a thick fog held me under water. I pulled out Jamie's itemised bills and searched through them, looking for Lee's name, but it wasn't there. I trudged back downstairs again. 'It's not listed anywhere. Maybe Jamie spoke to Lee at work, or maybe they emailed each other to arrange the reunion.' I handed Tony the plastic file of bills. 'Do you want to look through these? I'm not sure how they can help because the last few months aren't there.'

'No, that's okay for now. If I need to, I'll come back to them. You mentioned you went out walking with Jamie. Did you ever visit Bluebell Wood together?'

'Yes,' I said, my voice a whisper. 'Once. We were at Tyttenhanger Gravel Pits, walking around the lake there, watching the birds, and then we went to the woods.'

'Did they seem to have any special significance to him?'

I swallowed hard. 'Not that I know of.'

Tony made more notes. 'Okay. So you said he seemed happy yesterday when he told you he was leaving for some kind of meeting that you assumed was work-related. Do you know where he might've gone? The post-mortem puts his time of death at around five thirty.'

'I've got no idea.' I fiddled with my necklace, a silver Tiffany heart that Jamie had bought me out of the blue one day. He was always doing things like that. Little romantic gestures to let me know he was thinking of me. That I was special.

'His car was parked in a side street nearby. His wallet and keys were in his pocket. It would seem as though he parked up after it got dark, took some rope that he'd brought with him, and took his own life. The rope is a common type found in any DIY store. Do you know if he had any rope around the house?'

My hand instinctively went to my throat. 'Um…I don't think so, but if he did, it would be in the shed.'

'Can I have a look inside?'

'Yes.' I stood up on unsteady legs and held onto Ava's shoulder before I keeled over.

'Do you want me to show him?' Ava offered.

'No, it's okay,' I said to her, then to Tony, 'Follow me. I'll get the key.'

I retrieved the key from a drawer in the kitchen, and we left through the back door into the small garden, Tony carrying his briefcase. We walked up a slate path Jamie had laid when he'd first moved into the house twelve years ago. It led to the wooden shed he'd built at the end. I reached for the padlock and unlocked it.

I stood back to let Tony inside. Watched as he inspected items and nosed around. Some hooks were along one wall of the shed with various tools hanging on them, neatly lined up. On the end hook hung a coil of rope.

I turned away, unable to stand the sight of it. I stared at the fence along the neighbouring detached property until my eyes smarted. Behind me, I heard the snapping sound of Tony's briefcase opening. Plastic rustling. Then his footsteps creaking on the wooden floor of the shed as he moved around in there.

'I need to take the rope with me,' he called out.

More plastic sounds filled my ear. I stared at a robin pecking at a worm and wondered for the millionth time, *Why? What could've been so bad, Jamie? Was it me? Was it something I did? Something I didn't do? Was it us?*

When I turned around, Tony held a plastic bag in his hand, tied with a cable tie. Inside was the rope.

'Does it…does it look the same kind that he…?' Ava asked.

He nodded gravely. 'It looks like it, yes.'

'What happens now?'

'I'll write up a witness statement for you to sign. Then I'll be making other enquiries. With his colleagues, his doctor, that kind of thing. I have some leaflets I can leave about grief and grief counselling. It may help to talk to someone when you're ready. I'll contact you when we release the body, and you can decide on which undertaker to use. And I'll send the death certificate to you in the post so you can start making arrangements.'

I imagined Jamie's coffin being lowered into the ground. His body being eaten by insects. Did he want to be buried or cremated? How the hell was I supposed to know things like that? We hadn't talked about death. We were still in the honeymoon stages of our relationship.

It wasn't right. Nothing about this was right.

JAMIE

Chapter 4

I was six years old when they came and took me away. One minute my mum was there, lively and vibrant. The next, she'd died from a ruptured brain aneurysm. She had no other family to take me in, and my dad had died when I was two. Before her body had even been taken away from the tiny council flat we lived in, I was bundled into a car and driven to Denby Hall Children's Home by a social worker and left to their care.

I was alone and scared, confused and grieving for my mum, for a life that was now lost, and even though the other kids were in the same situation, I didn't make many friends. The place was so overcrowded and short-staffed, children came and went frequently, and it was better not to get attached to them. I couldn't help them. They couldn't help me.

A social worker was assigned to me, a young woman called Mary. In the beginning she did her best to find me a foster family, but there were too many kids and not enough places, and although she was kind and tried to reassure me everything would be okay, it wasn't. No one wanted me. Slowly Mary visited less and less, and I became like the rest of them, a neglected, forgotten child, just another face blurred in amongst hundreds of other faces. Little more than a number lost in a system.

I'd been in Denby Hall four years when we were told the home was closing. Excited whispers spread around the place, wondering where we'd be sent now. I fantasised about my future. How I'd be spotted and adopted in the new place. How I'd finally find a forever home with parents who doted on me, their new son, because they couldn't have children of their own and were looking for a boy to pour out all their love onto.

Little did I know I was being sent straight to hell.

Crossfield Children's Home was a large, imposing Victorian building with an oppressive gloom hanging over it. The first thing I noticed was its high brick wall with metal spikes on top, and tall iron gates that separated it from the world beyond. Inside, long dark corridors and wooden floors were everywhere. On arrival, I was marched by a new social worker straight to the head's office.

'This is James Taylor.' The social worker introduced me to a powerfully built man sitting behind a desk in a large office with a window that overlooked the grounds.

The man's thin lips lifted in a gentle smile. 'Nice to meet you, James. I'm Mr Barker. I'm sure you're going to enjoy Crossfield.'

The social worker handed Barker some paperwork, and I studied him as he read it. He had receding ginger hair kept short at the sides, an aquiline nose, and watery pale blue eyes.

Barker scrawled his signature on the papers and handed them back to the social worker, who was gone in a flash.

'So.' Barker sat back in his chair and steepled his fingers, his eyes appraising me. 'I run a tight ship here. There's to be no messing about. No stepping out of line. You do what you're told, when you're told. Understand?'

I glanced down at my shoes. 'Yes.'

'Look at me when I'm talking to you.' He said the words softly. 'Yes, what?'

'Yes, sir.'

He smiled again. 'Good. If you follow my rules, I'm sure we'll get along just fine. Now, let me show you around.' He stood up and walked towards me. Compared to my small frame, he seemed like a giant. He slung an arm around my shoulder and walked me along an empty corridor. 'The other boys are out at school at the moment, but you'll meet them at teatime.'

He showed me the refectory with three long tables where we'd eat our meals. The kitchen, where I'd be expected to do washing up and vegetable preparation. There was a common room that didn't hold many games, mostly shelves upon shelves of books. Upstairs were three dormitories that housed two rows of fifteen beds on either side. Apart from the beds, the dorms were almost bare, just a rickety chair next to each one. No cabinets or bedside tables. Nowhere to store any personal possessions. I'd learnt that we never actually owned anything in the homes. Clothes were handed down and around. Nothing was actually ours.

Barker pointed at a bed with a pile of clothes on top nearest the door. 'That one's yours.' He looked me up and down. 'There are some clean clothes for you, but first we need to get you into the shower. Can't have a dirty boy in clean clothes, can we?'

'No, sir,' I mumbled.

He led me through a doorway at the opposite end of the dorm, where there were sinks, urinals, toilet cubicles, and a long wooden bench with hooks in the wall above. Past the toilets was a row of open communal showers.

I glanced around, trying to get my bearings and take everything in.

'Come on. Let's get you into the shower.' He did a gentle ushering gesture with his hands, sat down on the bench, and crossed one leg over the other.

I froze for a moment. In Denby Hall, we'd never had to undress in front of the staff. They always left us to it, and there was something different about the way Barker was watching me that made me uneasy.

'Get undressed, boy. There's some soap in there already.' His thin lips formed into a smile, but there was an underlying authority in his voice. A voice I didn't want to challenge.

Don't panic. Don't answer back. Do what he wants.

I fumbled with the buttons of my shirt and removed it, carefully folding it as I'd been taught in the last place and putting it on the bench, all the while feeling Barker's eyes on me. Next came my trousers and pants. I didn't dare look at him as I walked into the shower block. I turned the water on, and it was cold. That was nothing new. They didn't like to waste hot water on us. A bar of carbolic soap was on the floor. We'd used that in Denby Hall, and it made our skin burn. I quickly lathered myself up and began washing with my back to Barker.

'Turn around,' he ordered. A glint of something in his eyes looked like excitement. 'I want to make sure you wash properly.'

I did what he said, my head down, trying to get on with the task at hand and get it over with as quickly as possible so he'd leave. I rinsed away the fiery soap and turned off the tap.

'Here.' He held out a towel that had been hanging on one of the hooks. His hand was extended only a little way, so I had to come close to him. So close I could smell his stale breath laced with cigarettes and see white specks of dandruff on the shoulders of his jumper.

I took the towel and dried my skin as he watched, all the while singing a song in my head to distract myself from the embarrassment of his unwavering gaze.

'Put the towel back on the hook and get dressed.' He stood up, waited for me to pull on my clothes, then put his arm on the back of my neck and led me back to the dormitory with his fingers stroking up and down my hairline.

A chill broke over my already cold skin, and goose bumps rose on my arms and legs. In Denby Hall, none of the staff had ever touched me. There were no hugs or kisses like Mum used to give me, and I missed being cuddled. Missed the warmth of someone holding me tight and whispering not to worry, not to be scared, that they loved me. So even though I was frightened and bewildered, it felt quite nice, calming, even. Caring. Maybe this place really would be better than Denby Hall.

'Good. Now you can wait in here until the others come back from school.'

I sat on the bed when he left and glanced around me in the spartan, unwelcoming dormitory with grey walls. At the window nearest my bed was a thick ledge big enough to sit on, and I whiled away the lonely hours looking out the window, worrying what this place was going to be like. Worrying about the other kids. About when someone would adopt me. How I was going to survive another six years until they let me out of the care system.

It was getting dark when I heard footsteps on the stairs outside the dormitory. Then I heard an adult shout, 'Oi, you! Stop running! How many times have I told you!'

There was a yelp and the sound of something hard hitting the floor or the wall.

'No, please!' a tiny, scared voice cried.

The door burst open, and a tall, wiry man with greasy black hair, ruddy cheeks, and spiteful eyes dragged a boy into the room by his ear, the boy's legs hardly touching the floor. The man's face was sweaty as he pushed the boy towards a bed in the middle of the room.

'No dinner for you. You can get into your pyjamas and stay in here for the rest of the day. I won't stand for any running or back-chatting,' the man said, breathing hard with his exertion.

A few other boys filed in, silently took their places next to their beds, and began changing out of their school uniforms into some clothes piled neatly on top of the thin, measly blanket. They didn't dare look at the boy trying desperately not to cry.

I sank back into the window seat, hoping the man wouldn't notice me there, wanting to turn my eyes away but unable to at the same time.

The man folded his arms, his eyes flashing darkly as he made sure the boy stripped completely. 'Jump up and down with your hands on your head,' he ordered.

The boy closed his eyes. Tears and snot streamed silently down his face. He placed his hands on his head and started jumping.

'Everyone look at Billy!' The man glanced around the room, a wicked smile turning up the corners of his mouth. 'What a pathetic excuse for a boy!' he mocked, before catching sight of me and glaring. 'Who are you?'

'J-Jamie, sir,' I whispered.

He cupped a hand to his ear. 'What? I can't hear you. Speak up.'

'Jamie, sir,' I said, louder.

'Well, Jamie, what do you think of Billy here?'

I didn't understand the question. I'd never met Billy, so how did I know how to answer? And I was pretty sure he didn't want me to tell him that I thought Billy was in pain and humiliated and upset. He could see that perfectly well himself.

'Answer me when I speak to you!' the man yelled across the room. One of the other kids flinched as he pulled on his trousers.

I bit my lip. If I gave the wrong answer, I'd end up like poor Billy. 'Um…'

'Come on. Spit it out!'

Billy carried on, jumping up and down, naked, his eyes squeezed tightly shut.

'I…I don't know, sir.'

'Look at Billy, everyone,' the man said slowly. 'Not good for much, are you, Billy?' Billy didn't answer. I didn't know whether the man was expecting an answer. 'Are you?' he yelled in Billy's ear.

'N-no, sir,' Billy stuttered.

'I can't hear you!' the man said in a sing-song voice.

'No, sir,' Billy said.

'Say it then!'

'I'm not…good for m-m-much,' Billy said.

The man glared. 'Idiots! The lot of you. What did I do to deserve such a bunch of degenerate lowlifes?' He ordered Billy to stop jumping and told him to put his pyjamas on and get to bed. Then he gave me one last look as he walked towards the door, pointing a finger in my direction. 'I'm watching you, boy. You're in my house now, and you'd better behave.'

I nodded frantically.

He slammed the door shut behind him, and the other kids exhaled with obvious relief.

'Billy, you okay?' a tall, skinny boy whispered from where he stood at the next bed to Billy's.

Billy grabbed his pyjama bottoms and hurriedly pulled them on before clutching his blond head in his hands, his shoulders heaving up and down.

'Billy?' the skinny guy said again.

'Leave me alone!' Billy got under his thin sheet and blanket and turned on his side, his eyes squeezed tightly shut, still clutching his head.

A boy approached me at the window seat. He was also blond, with huge brown eyes and very long eyelashes. 'Hi. I'm Dave.'

'Jamie,' I said.

'Where did you come from?'

'Denby Hall.'

He turned to look at some of the other boys. 'Oi, come over here and meet Jamie.'

I was introduced to the others. The skinny boy who'd asked Billy if he was okay was called Trevor. The other boy with a mop of curly light brown hair was called Sean.

'What's this place like?' I asked.

Sean didn't answer. Instead he asked a question of his own. 'Are your mum and dad still alive? You got any family?'

'No,' I replied and noticed a furtive glance pass between them.

'They're worse to the ones with no family left. They know there's no one we can complain to,' Dave said.

'Who was that man?' I asked.

'Mr Scholes. He's the deputy here. You don't want to get on the wrong side of him or Barker. They're nasty,' Dave said.

The others agreed.

Some more boys filed in and got changed, then a bell rang.

'It's dinner time,' Trevor said to me. 'Well, they call it dinner, but it's disgusting.'

They headed out of the room, and I went with them. In the refectory, I followed what they did, taking a plate from a hatch at the end of the room and holding it out to the cook, a sour-faced man with a tattoo of an eagle on his forearm. He dished some sort of stew onto it, and I took a seat in between Dave and Trevor at one of the long tables. Sean sat opposite. I stared at the watery brown mess on my plate. Potatoes, carrots, cabbage, and some kind of gristly-looking meat on the bone floating around.

'If you don't eat it, they'll just serve it back to you for breakfast,' Dave whispered.

I picked up a fork and started eating, trying to chew the gristle and swallow it without breathing. Scholes came in and wandered up and down the tables, his hands clasped behind his back, watching us with those cold eyes.

I kept my head down. I heard a clatter of something hitting the wooden floor, and Scholes strode towards Sean, who'd dropped his fork.

'Pick it up!' Scholes yelled.

Sean bent down quickly and retrieved the fork. 'Sorry, sir.'

'If you want to eat off the floor, that can be arranged.' Scholes tipped Sean's dinner onto the floor and pointed at it. 'Go on.' He sneered.

Sean looked at the food. He looked back at Scholes, his eyes wide and blinking.

'I'm not going to tell you again!'

Sean picked up a chunk of potato and put it in his mouth, grimacing.

'Not with your hands. Lick it up!'

I looked back down at my plate and concentrated hard on swallowing my own food. A little while later I risked another glance at Sean, who was being made to lick the floor like a dog.

'What are you looking at?' Scholes said to me. 'Do you want some of this, too?'

'No, sir.' I averted my gaze, shovelling food in my mouth before he could throw it on the floor.

He made Sean eat up every dirty scrap and then told him to get a mop and bucket and clean it up. The rest of us were ordered outside into the grounds for our free time. I stayed with Trevor and Dave, who filled me in on the rules of the place. No talking, no laughing, no running, no answering back. Try not to be left alone at any time. Try not to draw attention to yourself.

After free time, another bell rang, and it was bedtime. I got undressed and placed my clothes on the chair next to my bed. A pair of tatty, thin pyjamas were underneath my pillow, and I quickly stripped and put them on before cleaning my teeth under the watchful eyes of Barker. We were then ordered to bed.

'No talking and go straight to sleep,' Barker said before turning off the lights and closing the door.

I lay there, my stomach churning with anxiety, freezing cold. I listened to the soft snores of others, the creak of the metal beds as people turned in their sleep, unable to escape my worries and sink into oblivion. It must've been hours later when I heard the door open. My eyes had adjusted to the darkness, and I saw a figure creep across the room. It was Scholes. I kept my eyes partially closed, watching through my lashes to make it seem as if I was asleep.

He crept over to one of the beds across from me and put a hand over the mouth of one of the boys I'd met briefly, pressing the boy's head into the pillow with his elbow. I heard a muffled sob as the boy was pulled out of bed and dragged across the floor, his heels scuffing against the wooden boards. And then they were gone.

The next morning, the bed was empty. I never saw the boy again.

MAYA

Chapter 5

It took all my strength to get through the seconds. Somehow they merged into minutes and hours and days. Life was going on around me—birds singing, neighbours leaving their houses, dogs barking, but I was frozen inside. I wandered the house late at night, never settling in one place, picking up Jamie's things or reminders of our time together. Things we'd bought each other. Snippets of our life flashing into my head, all stabbing reminders that our home was now filled with torturous silence where once there was fun and laughter.

Alcohol became my friend and my tormenter. I drank to numb the agony, to sleep, to make the world go away. But then it would rip me restlessly from slumber a few hours later with a sinking sensation, and the raw pain hit me as he disappeared from my life all over again.

Jamie was gone. Forever.

The phone rang, but I couldn't answer it. People left messages I couldn't bear to listen to. Ava offered for me to stay with her, but I wanted to be here, close to him. I wore his clothes, used his deodorant and aftershave and toothbrush, as if somehow that could bring him back to life. Soon I would no longer be able to smell him or sense his presence, and I wanted to grasp on to it for as long as I could. Instead, Ava would spend hours at my house. Jamie's house. Trying to get me to eat, to sleep, to talk.

After Ava had left one afternoon for a health visitor's appointment for Jackson, the house was silent once more. I was alone again. I'd have to get used to being alone now.

The phone rang. I waited until it had finished before picking up. An automated female voice told me I had fifty-seven messages. I deleted all of them, then my fingers hovered over the numbers for a while before I called my parents.

'Hi, it's me,' I told Mum hoarsely when she picked up.

She let out a cross between a wail and a gasp. 'Oh, love, I'm so sorry. It's the most awful thing. I've been calling you. I left messages. How are you bearing up?'

'I don't know.' I sat on the cold floor, my knees hugging into my chest. 'I…' My eyes smarted with tears. 'It's just really hard. I'm trying to work out how to get through this.'

'Do you want me to come back? I could stay with you for a bit. I feel so useless being here.'

'No. It's okay. I need to be alone at the moment. And besides, Dad needs you.'

'I could get a friend to come in and check on him. Do him some food and whatnot.'

'No, really. Don't worry about me.'

'How can I not?'

'Ava's helping me.'

'Yes, I know. She's been keeping me in the loop.'

'But she's got enough on her plate with Jackson. Especially since Craig's not due home for a month.' Ava's husband worked away on the oil rigs, one month on, one month off. I'd always admired how Ava coped with that. It was like having a part-time relationship. I would've missed Jamie too much if he'd still been in the army. A twinge of irrational jealousy burned inside. Now I'd settle for a part-time relationship over this.

Mum sobbed on the other end of the line. 'It's just awful. I can't believe it. Did you know he was depressed?'

'He wasn't depressed,' I snapped.

'Oh, love, he must've been. What other reason could there be for him ha—doing it?' She couldn't say the word. I didn't want to say it either.

'He wasn't,' I said forcefully, wiping at the tears spilling down my cheeks. 'I knew him. He was happy. He wasn't depressed.'

She blew her nose. 'But we never really know people, do we? We don't know what goes on in someone else's head. Some people hide it well.'

'I just want to know why, Mum. Why did he do it? I keep thinking I should've seen it coming. I should've seen *something*. Some clue. But there was nothing. We were in love. He had everything to live for.'

She was silent for a moment. 'I don't think you can second-guess depression. People do desperate things sometimes.'

'But he wasn't depressed!' I shouted, wiping my nose on the cuff of Jamie's hoodie I wore. 'Don't you think I would've noticed that?'

'All right, calm down, love. I know it's hard to deal with.' There was another silent pause. 'When's the funeral?'

'In a few days. Ava's been arranging it for me. I can't...I couldn't...'

'I'll come back for that.'

'How are you going to do that? You're scared of flying, and you can't drive. And Dad certainly can't drive at the moment.' I spat out the words then took a deep breath, running my hand through my hair, feeling guilty. It wasn't her fault.

She ignored my outburst and said gently, 'I don't know. I'll think of something.'

'Like what?'

'I want to be there for you. I feel helpless over here, knowing you're going through something like this.'

'I know. I'm sorry.'

'It's normal to get angry.'

'It's not normal for your boyfriend to kill himself, though, is it?'

'Maybe I'm not saying the right things. It's difficult to know *what* to say.'

'There are no right things to say,' I said, an overwhelming tiredness sinking into my bones, as if they were going to crumble. 'I've got to go. I've got an appointment with Jamie's lawyer about his will. I'll ring you again.' I hung up before she could say anything else. I felt terrible for being bitter, but I couldn't control my emotions.

Bundling myself up in my parka, I fumbled with the buttons so hard I ripped one away from the fabric. It fell off and bounced to the floor. I ignored it and headed outside, desperately needing fresh air.

It was a short walk into town to Jamie's lawyer's office. My legs were heavy weights, dragging an unwilling body up the hill. The wind whipped my unwashed, greasy hair around my face. It flew into my eyes, making them sting. Or maybe it was the tears again. Ava had offered to go with me, but I'd said no. She was already doing so much for me. I had to get used to doing some things on my own. I had to try to be strong again.

St Peter's Street was busy with the regular market. Crowds of people browsing or wandering from one stall to the next got in my way, jostling me. I wanted to barge into them. Scream at them for being so inconsiderate. How dare they shop when Jamie was dead! How fucking dare they!

Outside the lawyer's office, I rested a hand on the brick façade of the building to steady myself. After one final glance back the way I'd come, I stepped inside.

I was led into the office of Graham Dunn, who was younger than I'd thought he'd be, probably only thirty-five, then I wondered why I was even thinking about his age. What the hell did that matter?

'I'm so sorry for your loss.' After shaking my hand, he sat behind his neat desk.

I wanted to laugh. Tell him he didn't even *know* Jamie as I did so what was he sorry for, but I mumbled the standard 'Thank you' instead and wiped my clammy palms on the knees of my jeans.

'I know this must be very difficult for you, but these matters have to be sorted out.' He reached for a slim green file without waiting for my response and took out some paperwork. 'Are you happy for me to read the will to you now?'

Happy? Are you joking? I nodded, balling my hands into fists, biting down hard on my bottom lip.

He recited words, legal jargon that hit me like a scalpel drawing blood. *Executor. Probate. Deceased. Bequeathed.* At the end he summarised everything for me, nice and neatly.

'So, basically, Jamie left you his house, which was mortgage-free, along with all his possessions, including the contents of his bank accounts. Everything seems pretty straightforward. It shouldn't be too lengthy to sort matters out. I've prepared a letter for you stating your legal position as next of kin, in case you need this when sorting out any of his affairs. Do you have any questions for me?'

I couldn't think straight. Too many things were going round in my head. Too many emotions threatening to drown me. Jamie had had the will drawn up six months ago, around the time I'd moved in with him. Had he known then that he was going to kill himself? Had he thought being so organised about it would make things 'straightforward' for me? And if he had, why had he ever suggested us living together?

I stuffed the letter in my bag, thanked him for his time, and he said he'd be in touch in due course. Back on the street, I found that the crowds had increased. Someone's shoulder bumped into me as I pushed my way through, making me trip. I stumbled forwards, falling to my knees with a bang. A searing pain shot through my kneecaps. My eyes watered.

'Hey, are you all right, love?' An elderly man perusing the stall next to where I landed helped me up by my elbow.

I blinked back tears and looked down at my scuffed jeans. 'I'm fine. Thanks,' I said, torn between wanting to cry and scream.

I hurried off down the road and was almost at the end of St Peter's Street when I saw him.

He was tall, with sandy hair, that familiar width to his shoulders through the jacket he wore. Swimmer's shoulders.

Jamie.

My heart stopped for a second as I stood, frozen to the spot, shoppers bustling around me. Into me.

Then I ran after him.

I knew it. Knew it was all some kind of horrible mistake. I'd catch up with him and there would be a rational explanation for everything.

'Jamie! Wait!' I yelled, losing sight of him in the crowds.

I stopped. Turned in a three-hundred-sixty-degree rotation. *Where did you go?*

I spotted him again, heading down the hill towards the cathedral. 'Jamie!' What was wrong with him? Couldn't he hear me? I carried on running, passing blurs of faces.

And then I was within touching distance.

I reached out and grabbed the sleeve of his jacket. 'Jamie! Oh my God. Didn't you hear me?'

He swung around, a surprised look on his face.

And it wasn't him. It wasn't Jamie at all. Of course it wasn't.

All the blood seemed to drain from my body. I stared at him, my lips hanging limply open.

'Do I know you?' The man frowned at me and retrieved his arm from my clutches.

'Sorry,' I managed to mumble. 'I thought you were someone…I thought…'

'No worries.' He shrugged and walked off.

I didn't know how long I stood there afterwards, watching the man who wasn't Jamie until he disappeared. Somehow, perhaps on autopilot, I ended up back at home, stomping around in the kitchen, grabbing a mug, and banging the cupboard doors. I tried to unscrew the jar of coffee, and it wouldn't work with my hands shaking. I released the yell I'd been holding deep inside, throwing the jar across the room, where the glass smashed into shards on the tiles. I stared at the glass and brown granules all over the floor and slid down the kitchen units in a crumpled heap, sobbing into my hands.

Eventually, I pulled myself together and cleaned up the mess. I made a cup of tea, ignoring the rumbling in my stomach. I hadn't eaten properly since I'd heard the news, and I didn't want to. Eating would just prolong the agony of being alive.

I took my tea into the lounge and curled up on the sofa, my eyes resting on a photo of Jamie and me on the wooden bookshelf. It was taken at Jamie's work's Christmas party the year before. Both of us dressed up to the nines. My head resting against his shoulder, a stupidly happy, tipsy smile on my face. His eyes crinkled up at the corners, looking down at me. I stared at it until I couldn't take it anymore. Then I dragged my gaze away, and it rested on the shelves below. There were three rows of books. All Jamie's. He was the reader. I was the one who watched movies and listened to music. He could lose himself for hours in non-fiction books. Maybe I should try to read something. Try to take my mind off things. Try to lose myself for a while. Anything was better than this constant torment of thoughts and questions with no answers.

I put my mug down on the coffee table next to Jamie's laptop and walked across to the books, scanning along the top shelf. He always put everything in alphabetical order. No, not just alphabetical order. They were in order of genre, too. On the top left-hand side were political books—Nelson Mandela, Winston Churchill, Ghandi, Martin Luther King—then came the books about the military—Damien Lewis, Chris Ryan, Mark Urban. His biographies and memoirs also ran alphabetically on the shelf below, with self-help books underneath. I'd always joked with Jamie about it. My CDs and DVDs were lobbed in the drawer underneath the TV any old how. Sometimes they weren't even in the right covers. But Jamie liked having things in order.

I scanned the books. I didn't want to read about war or death. Where was a romantic comedy when I needed one? I was just going through the autobiographies when my gaze darted back up to the previous shelf. The books were out of their usual A-to-Z order. The Mandela book should've been at the end, not the beginning. I picked up the Mandela book, flicked through it, then put it back in the right place where Jamie would've wanted it. Finally, I pulled out one of the self-help books, *Quantum Healing* by Deepak Chopra, and took it back to the sofa with me. I tried to concentrate on the words, but they seemed to run together on the page and didn't make sense. I rubbed my eyes to clear my vision and started again. This time I read the same line over and over again, so I gave up.

I put the book back on the shelf and noticed that, actually, the photo of us wasn't in the right place, either. It usually sat in the middle of the bookshelf, but now it was on the right-hand corner.

I thought back to the night Jamie had died. That weird sensation when I'd come in the house. The vague hint of cigarettes. Had someone been in here? Moved things around? The TV was still here. So was Jamie's expensive laptop and top-of-the-range stereo. There were no signs of a break-in.

No, I was just being stupid. Maybe Jamie had moved those things. It wasn't like him, but then he clearly hadn't been thinking straight, had he? I usually did the dusting, and I definitely hadn't cleaned anything since Jamie had gone, but had I moved things absentmindedly and put them back in the wrong place when I'd been wandering the house late at night, drunk, out of mind with grief?

I picked up Jamie's laptop and turned it on, frowning when the blank black page greeted me again instead of his screensaver. I clicked on the start button and then the 'documents' to check if they were still there, but nothing came up. No folders, no files, no photos, no work presentations that I knew had been on there. I tried to search for Word, but the programme wasn't there. Tried Excel, but that wasn't there either. The day Jamie had died, I thought maybe the laptop had crashed, but it seemed to be working okay. It was just that things had been deleted. Everything important had disappeared.

Why? Was there something on it he hadn't wanted me to find? *Personal things.*

'What fucking personal things?' I screamed. 'What were you doing, Jamie? Why weren't you at work? Why couldn't you just talk to me?'

I chewed on my lip until I tasted the metallic tang of blood.

Obviously, Jamie had been hiding something from me, and it was bad enough to make him take his own life.

I needed to know what it was. Had to know.

I decided then that I wasn't going to sit around and wallow and cry and drink myself into a black hole. I was going to find out exactly what Jamie was doing when he'd left the house, pretending he was going to work.

I was going to find out what it was that had led to his death.

JAMIE

Chapter 6

It didn't take long to be initiated into the regimented and disciplined way of life that was so different from Denby Hall. Awoken by a screaming bell at 6.00 a.m. Washing and teeth cleaning at ten past. Breakfast at 6.30. We were allowed to speak to each other only on the way to school or after dinner, when we had a couple of hours of free time. Slop served for meals. Chores of cleaning and laundry duties. Kicks, punches, slaps, being forced to eat soap, and more punishments if we didn't do a good job, or for any misdemeanour the staff felt like. Not answering them back quickly enough, answering too quickly. Not eating our food, eating too quickly. Not polishing or mopping fast enough, or leaving specks of dust around. It was hard to keep up with all the rules because they were constantly changing. Sometimes we were punished just for daring to be alive. I quickly learned not to cry. No one would take any notice, and it just seemed to make the staff angrier and more inclined to focus on me.

Instead, I watched and listened, attempting to work out the situation before I could get punished. I tried to read the staff to know who were worse than the others, sensing what mood they were in and when they'd strike. I kept my mouth shut and tried to be invisible, which worked for a while.

At first, I loved the new school I attended. Leaving Crossfield every day and going there was my one escape, and no matter how bad things were, for six hours a day I could get away from it and immerse myself in exciting new worlds of history and English and geography, maths equations and sums that stopped me thinking about my life. Even though the other pupils bullied us because they thought Crossfield kids were dirty or troublemakers or stupid, and called us 'Bastards', it was far better than being in the home. My form teacher, Miss Percival, was always warm and kind. I constantly looked forward to seeing her, and her smiles or words of encouragement became the highlight of my days. But as the months passed, for some reason I constantly felt the wrath of Scholes. No matter what I did, he seemed to hate me, but I didn't know what I was doing wrong or how I could make him leave me alone. I thought so much about the problem that my schoolwork began to suffer, and I lost interest in everything. I was so busy trying to keep out of trouble at Crossfield that I couldn't concentrate on anything else. Miss Percival noticed something was wrong and called me into her classroom one day at lunchtime.

She sat me down in the corner of the room and gave me one of her smiles. I couldn't smile back, though. There was nothing much to smile about.

'How are things, Jamie?' she asked.

I lowered my eyes, willing the tears not to fall, mumbling something.

She put her hand on my shoulder. 'Jamie?'

I didn't look up. Just stared at my hands.

'When you first started here, you were really enthusiastic. But lately you seem to be very down, and your work's suffering as a result.

Is there anything you want to talk to me about? Are you not happy at Crossfield?'

I felt the tears burn behind my eyelids.

'You can tell me anything that's troubling you. Maybe I can help.' She lowered her head so it was in my sight line, and I had no choice but to look at her.

It was her kindness that did it. That made the tears burst through the tight shell I'd tried to force them behind. And when they started, the weight of them cracked splinters inside, until everything came rushing out, a tsunami of sadness about what life was like at Crossfield. How Scholes bullied me and the other kids. How I was scared and frightened and very, very alone. How I didn't know how to be me anymore because no one wanted me as I was, and none of the staff seemed to like me, either. How I didn't know what to do.

She listened carefully, squeezing my hand, giving me tissues to mop away the tears. She hugged me, and I clung on to her so hard she had to prise my fingers away from her cardigan eventually.

'Okay, here's what I'm going to do.' She leant back and gave me a reassuring smile. 'I'm going to talk to the head of Crossfield and find out what's going on, okay? I don't want you to worry anymore. We'll get all this sorted out.'

I choked back another sob and nodded. 'Thank you.'

She ruffled my hair and told me to run along to lunch. As the rest of the day passed, I felt a horrible weight lifting from my shoulders. Miss Percival would stop the bullying at Crossfield, I was sure of it.

The next day was Saturday, and since there was no school, we all had to do chores in the mornings. I was assigned to sweeping and mopping the refectory with Trevor. We'd been at work for about an hour when Scholes appeared, leaning on the door frame, his arms folded, watching us with a look of hatred in his eyes. I sensed him there before I saw him, then I turned my head briefly before fixing my gaze steadily on my mop sliding across the cold, wooden floor.

Please go away. Please go away. Leave me alone.

'Taylor!' he barked. 'Come with me.'

Trevor shot me a look of sympathy before I silently walked up to Scholes. I hadn't done anything wrong that I knew of, so I couldn't imagine what he wanted with me. But then that didn't matter. Just being alive was considered wrong by him. He put an arm around my shoulders, his fingers kneading painfully into the flesh. I wanted to ask him where we were going as he led me down a warren of dreary corridors that all looked the same, but I knew I would be punished for speaking. We went down a flight of stairs at the end of one. It had no windows, and it was dark. A wooden doorway was at the bottom, and he pulled a bunch of keys out of his pocket and unlocked it. There were more stairs going down, and then we were in a cellar. Inside was various junk, and a huge boiler stood in one corner. Along the back wall, next to a dirty sink, was an ancient-looking, rusty bath filled with water.

I looked at the bath with trepidation, fear igniting in the pit of my stomach. 'What have I done, sir?' I asked quietly.

Smack! The back of his hand caught my cheek and sent me stumbling backwards.

'Don't speak until you're spoken to!'

I reached up and touched my burning flesh, staring at the broken tiles on the ground, wanting to be sucked underneath them. Anywhere away from here. Tears welled in my eyes, but I wouldn't cry. Wouldn't give him the satisfaction. The only time I allowed them to come was in the darkness, alone, at night. I wouldn't show any weakness.

I couldn't look at him, but I heard his breath coming in short, jagged rasps. I sensed something animalistic and violent rolling off him. A lion patiently stalking its prey before coming in for the kill.

'You like telling tales, don't you, boy?' He circled around me. 'You like shooting your mouth off to namby-pamby teachers who know nothing about how to keep reprobates like you under control.'

'I...I didn't mean to—'

'Shut up!' he barked in my face.

I flinched.

'Imagine if the hundred boys in here were able to run around wild, doing exactly what they pleased! It would mean chaos and anarchy, and we can't let that happen at Crossfield. We can't let that happen at all. Boys *need* discipline to keep them on the straight and narrow! They need it to teach them to be responsible young men. To save them from themselves.' He stopped circling and stood in front of me. 'Don't they?'

I was too scared to answer.

'Don't they?' he yelled.

'Y-Yes.'

'Yes, what?'

'Yes, sir.'

'Kneel down in front of the bath.'

I didn't dare to question him. I knew the punishment would be far worse.

I did as he asked, my bony knees painfully pressing onto the uneven, hard surface. I bit my lip and squeezed my eyelids shut, as if that could somehow make me invisible and transport me far away.

He panted in my ear as he pressed me against the bath with one hand on my neck. 'Do you know what happens to boys who tell tales?'

I mumbled something, but it was just a terrified sound that came out.

'No one would notice if you disappeared, would they? No one cares about you. No one's coming for you. Which means you're mine. My property. You understand? You do what *I* tell you.'

My whole body heaved up and down, trying to get enough oxygen in my lungs to stop the panic, coughing, spluttering, snot flying from my nose.

'You going to be a good boy now? You going to stop making up stories?'

I nodded vigorously.

'Tell me.'

'I…I'll…be good,' I managed to gasp. 'I won't say anything to anyone!'

He pulled his hand back, as if to hit me, and I pressed my small body against the bath, trying to get away. 'Good choice, Taylor. You keep your mouth shut, and I think you and I are going to get along fine, aren't we?'

I nodded vigorously, but it didn't stop his hand forcing my head into the water.

~~~~

After he'd finally left the room and locked the door with a sickening turn of the key, I curled up into a shaking ball and let the tears fall. I had a lot of time to think in that dark hole that smelt of mould and shit and fear, with only rats for company, talking to my mum in my head, pleading with her to come back and get me, even though I knew she never could. I forced my mind to picture happy times I'd spent with her before she died. How every weekend she'd pick a different place to visit and spend hours baking cakes and scones, before packing a picnic. Then we'd hop in the car and head away from London, out into the countryside. *Just because we don't have much money doesn't mean we can't experience the world,* she'd tell me. She always loved the great outdoors—the simplicity and complexity of nature. In my mind, I saw a lavender field we'd visited in Norfolk one weekend, the explosion of purple colours in my head replacing, for just a tiny moment, all the jagged blackness.

Scholes kept me in that place, coming back now and then with water and slices of stale bread that had a meagre scraping of margarine. He watched me forcing the food down my swollen throat, saying things like, 'Don't even think about telling anyone. They'll never believe you. No one gives a shit about scum like you.'

On the second day, Scholes returned again. I was cold and hurt all over from sleeping on the floor and where he'd dunked me in the bath, holding my head down until my arms flailed and panic hit, desperately sucking in water through my nose and mouth until I thought I'd die.

I had pins and needles in my legs, and my body wouldn't obey me when I tried to stand up. When I couldn't get up quick enough, he yanked me to my feet and marched me out of the cellar to Barker's office. He opened the door, deposited me in front of Barker, and left.

I stood trembling as Barker finished the paperwork he was writing, leant back in his chair, and smiled. But it wasn't a warm smile, like Miss Percival's. There was something cold and unemotional behind it.

'I'm very saddened to hear about an unfortunate incident where your teacher felt the need to contact us about your fabrications, James.' He folded his arms. 'Of course, I've explained to her how you have a tendency to make up stories and exaggerate things to get extra attention. And that your particular emotional and behavioural issues are very challenging to rectify, especially your difficulty in accepting authority. I also explained that running a boys' home is a very complex task, which requires a certain amount of discipline and control; otherwise we'd have a riot on our hands. We have to protect you from yourselves. I think Mr Scholes has already explained that to you, hasn't he?'

I nodded numbly.

'And what you must realise, James, is that disciplining our charges hurts us a lot more than them. We have to have a set of rigid rules to follow, and we wouldn't be doing our job if we didn't adhere to those rules.'

I tried to swallow away the hard knot in my throat.

He leant forward on his elbows. 'I'm sure you'd like to be adopted one day, wouldn't you?'

'Y-Yes, sir.'

'Well, who do you think some prospective adoptive parents would choose, hmmm? A good boy, one who gets his head down and follows the rules, or one who is unruly, undisciplined, and prone to telling lies?'

'A good boy,' I whispered.

He gave a pleased nod. 'Exactly. And who do you think chooses which boys these prospective parents get to see?'

'I don't know, sir.'

'Me.' He paused for a moment. 'You can see what I'm getting at here, can't you?' He carried on without waiting for an answer. 'Not only do good boys at Crossfield get the chance to meet possible new parents, but I also like to reward good behaviour with special privileges, like day trips.' He flashed me another smile. 'Next week I'm taking a group of well-behaved lads on a trip to the country. We'll be swimming in the river and playing games and taking a packed lunch. If you follow the rules here, if you're good, you too can get to do things like that.' He paused again. 'Do I make myself clear?'

I could only nod mutely as the weight of his words crushed me.

'Good. Now go back to the dorm and think on your behaviour.' He picked up his pen and turned his attention back to his paperwork.

I rushed upstairs as fast as I could. The dorm was empty when I got there, and I sat on the windowsill, watching the other boys outside during free time, my arms wrapped around my knees for comfort.

I thought about running away, but where would I go? I was ten years old with no family and no money. Trevor had run away a couple of weeks ago and was brought back by the police when they found him stealing apples from a greengrocer. Billy saw him dragged into Barker's office, but no one saw him again for two days. There were whispers that he was down there in the cellar with Scholes. When Trevor finally reappeared at dinner time, he was walking like a hunched, broken old man, and he couldn't sit down properly for a week. He didn't say a word to anyone for days, and even when he did finally speak, he never let on what had happened.

I was so lost in my worries that I didn't see Billy enter the dorm until he was right beside me.

'Are you okay?' he asked, his eyes not quite meeting mine.

I dug my fingers into my palms to stop the tears coming.

'Did Scholes put you in the cellar?'

I nodded. 'He dunked me in the bath. I thought he was…going to kill me.'

He stared out of the window, his voice a quavering whisper. 'You're lucky that's all he did. When he does the other things, you'll wish you were already dead.'

I wanted to ask what he meant, but I was too late. He'd already turned and walked away, his head down, his shoulders slumped.

When I arrived at school on Monday morning, Miss Percival called me into her classroom before school started.

'I had a very long chat with Mr Barker, and he assured me there have been some misunderstandings,' she said. 'I wanted to make sure that what he said was correct. Have you been making things up to get attention? Or as an excuse not to do your schoolwork?' She looked down at me, and I couldn't meet her eyes.

'Yes,' I said, because I knew Scholes and Barker controlled everything. No one would adopt me if I didn't keep quiet and do what they wanted. No one would take me away from there. No matter how nice someone seemed, I couldn't trust them to help me. If Scholes or Barker found out I'd spoken about what happened there, they'd make things a million times worse for me.

So I was trapped, with no one to talk to and nowhere to run. This was my life. My prison. And the only thing I'd done wrong was being born.

MAYA

Chapter 7

I grabbed Jamie's box of files from the spare room. If he was having some kind of 'personal' problems, then that could surely mean only a few things. Financial. Emotional. Relationship problems. Work. Well, he hadn't been depressed, and we weren't having any relationship issues, unless...had Jamie been having an affair? Is that what he'd been so secretive about?

No. I pushed the thought away. He wouldn't do that to me. I knew he wouldn't. So that left work and something financial.

I flicked through the A4 folders, reading the labels written in his neat, precise handwriting: *Mobile Phone, Credit Card, Household Receipts, Insurance, Vehicle Documents, Bank Statements.*

But something was wrong with that. The mobile phone bills were on top because I'd had them out to look at them, but the credit card bills were next, in the exact same place where I'd found them the night I was searching for Paul's number. In fact, none of them were in alphabetical order anymore, how Jamie always kept them.

What did that mean? Anything? Nothing?

And why were the last three months' itemised mobile phone bills missing, even though I'd seen them arrive? Had he thrown them away? Was there something he didn't want me to see on them? Someone he'd been calling that he didn't want me to know about? Was there really another woman?

Again, I dismissed the possibility.

I flicked through the rest of the monthly phone bills. All the other months' bills were there, going back to two years ago. I'd already checked through them when I was looking for Lee's number, but I scanned the numbers and names again and didn't notice anything odd. There were lots of calls between Jamie and me and Jamie and Paul. He'd spoken to the leisure centre, his bank, his insurance company, British Gas, and a telemarketing company who were probably selling something. Just ordinary, everyday calls. No weird names or numbers were listed that I couldn't account for, but had there been on the bills that were missing?

Then I went through his bank statements and credit card bills. Before I'd moved in with him, we'd agreed I would pay half of the bills, and that's exactly what they revealed. Debit card payments for petrol and Amazon for his books, his council tax. Other bits and bobs that were everyday items. He hadn't taken out any big loans and hadn't had any debts. In fact, his savings account was in credit by twenty thousand pounds.

I went into our bedroom and opened the wardrobe. The sight of his clothes crushed my insides, but I had to keep looking. Had to find an answer.

I went through his pockets, but nothing was in any of them except a few pieces of fluff. My gaze scanned his work shoes, his trainers, and his walking boots caked in dried, muddy clay.

I sat on Jamie's side of the bed, going through his bedside drawers. The first one just had socks and boxers in it, but I pulled them all out and spread them on the bed. His socks were paired, the tops folded down, turned into a neat ball. I unfolded every pair to check for...I didn't really know what, but nothing was hidden inside. The second drawer held neatly folded T-shirts.

I tried the bottom drawer.

The first thing my eyes homed in on was a small jewellery box. It was a deep green and had the words *Freyer Jewellers* on it. My hand hovered over it before I plucked up the courage to look inside.

I flipped it open. It was stiff. New. And inside was a white-gold ring with a row of stones, alternating blue topaz and amethyst.

My breath caught in my throat.

Just before I'd moved in with Jamie six months ago, we were out shopping on a lazy Saturday afternoon, our arms round each other, leisurely wandering around town, and he'd stopped outside Freyer Jewellers. He pretended to be looking at men's watches while I examined the ladies' rings. I could see him watching me out of the corner of his eye before he stood behind me, wrapping his arms around my waist and resting his chin on my shoulder, peering through the window.

'Which kind of stones do you like?' he asked, and something in his voice made me just know why he was asking.

My heart fluttered with excitement. I met his gaze in the reflection of the window, my face lighting up with a smile to match his.

'Diamonds? Isn't every woman supposed to like them?'

I laughed. 'I'm not every woman.'

'So what's your favourite?' He squeezed me tighter.

I pointed at a ring. 'That one. It's beautiful.'

I stared at the box in my hand now as a sense of despair and loneliness seeped into every fibre. He'd bought it for me. This was the surprise he'd been talking about. I hadn't been imagining things, had I? He really had intended to propose.

You'll love what happens after dinner.

Except…*You don't do that, do you? You don't buy the ring. You don't talk about a surprise on our anniversary. You don't do that and then kill yourself eight hours later. You don't plan on having a future with someone when at the same time you're planning on having no future at all.*

Again, I thought of the unusual scent in the house that day when I'd returned. The things that were out of place. They were subtle movements. Things that probably no one else would have noticed. I only did because of how ordered Jamie was about everything. What if someone else had been in here and searched through things, replacing a few items in the wrong way? But why? Were they looking for something Jamie had?

I thought of the laptop. What if it hadn't crashed or had a virus? What if it had been wiped clean for some reason? Had Jamie deleted everything on there or had someone else?

Or was I just being paranoid?

JAMIE

Chapter 8

We were eating lunch one weekend with Scholes patrolling up and down the refectory with an angry scowl when Barker came in. He stood in the centre of the room and clapped his hands together loudly over the din of scraping plates.

He looked around the room, that smile of his in place, making sure he had our attention before speaking. 'After lunch you will all carry out your cleaning duties as quickly as possible and come into the common room.' And with that, he left, giving us no further information.

'What do you think's going on?' Trevor whispered to me as we dried the dishes.

'I don't know. It can't be anything good, can it?' I snapped. I'd given up hoping for good news of any kind. It hurt too much.

Eventually, we filed into the common room, where other boys were already waiting, a whisper of nervous tension filling the air as we lined up at the front. Then Barker arrived, closely followed by Scholes, who was carrying a clipboard.

'This afternoon we have a couple arriving who want to adopt a boy.' Barker walked up and down in front of us, his hands clasped behind his back, not looking at anyone. 'It's up to me to direct these prospective parents to those of you who've obeyed the rules and who've shown exemplary behaviour.' He stopped, his gaze sweeping over us. 'I will be calling out the names of a select group of ten boys I think will interest this couple. If you hear your name, stand next to Mr Scholes, and you will be taken to meet them. They will spend some time chatting to you, getting to know you a little better, before making a choice of who they wish to spend further time with prior to starting the adoption process.'

A ripple of excitement in the air was palpable. My heart pattered in my chest. The thought of meeting prospective adoptive parents—the possibility of being chosen, of getting away—was almost too much. For the first time in a long time, there was hope. I nudged Sean and Trevor, who stood next to me. Their smiling faces and sparkling eyes matched mine.

Barker took the clipboard from Scholes and began reading names, pausing between each one. My stomach lurched as I willed my name to be the next one, or the next, or the next. One after the other, the boys called out broke away from the group, ecstatic smiles on their faces.

When nine boys had been chosen, Barker walked up and down in front of us again slowly. He stopped in front of me, grinning.

My pulse thumped in my ears, and sweat pricked on my palms.

Say it's me! Say my name! It must be me!

I swallowed hard as Barker's gaze drilled into me.

I stopped breathing. My heart threatened to explode in my chest.

Then he looked at the boy behind me and said his name.

The food curdled in my stomach. I swallowed to keep it inside, a sudden dizziness making me wobble on the spot.

'For those who haven't been chosen, better luck next time, eh?' Barker said. Then he led the lucky few out of the room, oblivious to the crushing pain in my heart, the devastation hitting painfully, destroying me from the inside out.

I hated those other boys then. Hated them for being given a chance in this Russian roulette. Hated their smiles of joy and their pathetic hope. Hated myself, too, for being me and not one of them.

~~~~

A week after that, Barker came for me. I was with Billy, Sean, Trevor, and Dave outside in the grounds of Crossfield during free time. They were rambling on about superheroes and who was the best one. Would Superman beat Batman in a fight? Who had the best superpowers? I sat on the sidelines, unwilling to join in. It was a stupid, pointless conversation. I'd become even quieter and more insular during my time at Crossfield, hardly speaking much. Instead, I buried my head in the books I found in the common room. It was one of the few times I could escape my life. Escape who I was. And I dreamt a lot about running away. Even though I knew it was futile, it was the only little piece of hope I could cling to. But I liked our little group of friends, and I didn't want to be alone. I hoped there was safety in numbers, but that was just wishful thinking.

'Barker's coming,' Dave whispered as I used a stick to draw a picture of a bird in the dust.

I didn't look up. Better not to draw attention to myself. Instead, I carried on perfecting the bird's wings. I didn't know what kind it was. It didn't matter to me. I just wanted to be that bird. Fly far away from here and never come back.

'Ah, Taylor.' Barker's feet appeared in front of me. 'I've got something to show you. Come with me,' he said gently.

I tried to block out his voice and carried on with my creation. If I ignored him, maybe he would go away. I wanted to press my hands to my ears and close my eyes so it wouldn't be happening. 'I'm okay, sir. I don't want to see anything,' I mumbled.

He laughed. 'I don't think you understand, Taylor. It wasn't a request.' He held out his hand. 'Come on. You'll like this.'

But I wouldn't. I knew I wouldn't.

I took his hand, and he pulled me up as terror shook my insides. He placed a hand around my neck, guiding me to his quarters, which was a small red-bricked house to the left of the main building. All the while, his thumb caressed my skin.

It was dark inside. Heavy brown curtains at the windows, a brown carpet, oppressive green-painted walls. The sofa was green corduroy, sagging in the middle. The furniture wooden, shiny with age. The smell of cigarettes and musty sweat was stifling.

'Now, I bet you'd like to watch a film, wouldn't you?' He smiled at me.

I glanced at him uneasily. We only got to watch a film on a Sunday afternoon in the common room. For a while I could immerse myself in them, pretending I was one of the characters—a cowboy, a detective, a boy with a dog called Lassie. Anyone who wasn't me. So for a moment, I thought maybe Barker was just being kind, and I relaxed and nodded.

'Good.' He smiled down at me. 'How about a drink first?'

'Thank you, sir.'

He left me in the lounge, and my eyes darted to the front door. I wanted to escape, knowing something was about to happen but not sure what.

When he returned, he had two glasses of amber-coloured liquid. He sat down on the sofa and patted the material next to him. 'Come on, then. Sit yourself down.' He pressed a remote control, and the TV sprang to life.

I sat down, and he handed me a glass. He moved closer, watching me intently. I took a sip and wriggled a little further away from him.

The taste was bitter, and I scrunched up my face. I'd never had anything like it before.

'It's beer.' He leant over and whispered in my ear cheerfully, 'I bet you've never had beer, have you, lad?'

'No, sir.'

'Well, drink up. You'll enjoy it.' He patted my thigh. 'So, how are you settling in now after that nonsense with your teacher?'

I want to die. I hate it here. Please leave me alone.

'Answer me, then.' His hand inched along the back of the sofa towards me. I stared at it. Imagined myself breaking the glass I held and stabbing him with it. Imagined the blood spurting out, hoping he'd bleed to death.

'It's…nice here.' I almost choked on the words and gulped some more beer as he asked more questions. I didn't like the taste, but I liked how it made me feel, calmer, more relaxed, more blurred.

He unwrapped a bar of chocolate. My mouth watered in anticipation. I'd never had chocolate or sweets since being in my real home, and I craved the sugar on my tongue.

'Would you like some?'

'Yes, sir.'

He broke a square off and put it in my mouth. I sucked on it greedily.

He got me another drink as the film carried on, but I couldn't tell what I was watching. I couldn't concentrate. I drank the next beer quicker. The room swam, and I suddenly wanted to go to sleep. He told me how much he liked me. How he could single me out for special treatment. How I could get nice things if I carried on behaving well. How I could be chosen to meet the next set of adoptive parents.

Then the room was spinning a lot more. Barker stood up and moved to the front door. He locked it then slowly walked towards me. 'Now, James, I think you should prove just what a good boy you can really be.' He sat down next to me and slid closer.

I didn't resist. What was the point? I would have to do what they wanted, when they wanted, because there was no way out. And if I tried to fight it, they would just make it more painful. I was powerless to stop them.

When he finally let me go, I limped away from his house, even more broken than before. Back at the dorm, Sean, Billy, Trevor, and Dave were changing into their pyjamas. They didn't meet my eyes. I didn't know how to put into words the disgusting things he'd done to me. I didn't have the vocabulary to explain. I didn't really understand it myself. I just knew it was wrong. And it hurt. I was used to the physical bullying now. I could handle the pain. I just didn't know whether I could handle this new kind of abuse.

I stayed silent, just as all my friends did, but I think they knew anyway.

I think they all knew.

MAYA

Chapter 9

There was one other place I could think of to look, where Jamie might've left some sort of clue as to what he'd been doing, where he'd been going, during the week before he died, and it was probably somewhere no one else would think of.

In the garden was a border covered with gravel. Dotted around were plant pots filled with lavender, rosemary, and a miniature olive tree. In the centre of the border was a statue of Buddha. It was huge, almost four foot tall, a heavy thing that made it seem solid, but it wasn't. And below the hollow Buddha, hidden underneath the gravel, was a metal tin that Jamie used to hide any money in, instead of keeping it around the house, just in case we ever got broken into and burglars found it.

I stepped into the garden, the gold ring feeling both alien and soothing on my finger. It shone in the sunlight, and a sob rose in my chest. I pushed it back down. Stared at the Buddha and fought back the tears yet again. I reached out my hand and rested it on Buddha's head. It was cold beneath my touch, and I shivered involuntarily. Gently, I tipped the statue to one side and bent down, separating the gravel with my fingers. There was the lid of the metal box. I pulled out more gravel from the box-sized hole Jamie had sunk it into and lifted it out, then put the gravel and statue back in place and took the box into the kitchen with me.

I sat at the table, staring at it. An unnerving feeling settled over me as I removed the lid.

Inside was a cheap Motorola mobile phone and a small bundle of money. I turned the phone on and checked through it. There were no numbers called or received in the call log, no text-message history, and no numbers in the contacts file. I lifted out the pound notes—three hundred pounds in total—and found beneath them a folded sheet of A4 lined white paper. I unfolded it slowly, smoothed it out against the table, and began reading Jamie's handwriting.

10 Crompton Place, London
Moses Abraham, 16 Dean Street, London
Billy Pearce, 43 Scarborough Ave, London
Sean Davidson, Flat 28, Derby Towers, Enfield X
Trevor Carter, 2 Dalton Terrace, Surrey
Dave Groom, 91 Ridge Street, Watford X

My first thought was that the list was something to do with Jamie's job. Was it a list of people who worked for Porterhouse Systems and Solutions? Or some of their clients? No. It couldn't be connected with his job, because he hadn't even been going to work, and I'd never heard him mention those names before. Obviously, if he'd taken the trouble to hide it underneath the Buddha, it had meant something important to him, though. Something he was trying to keep hidden from me. Was this list to do with why he'd been leaving the house every day as normal?

I took the list into the lounge and turned on my laptop. When I connected to Google, I typed in the first address. Nothing interesting came up

Next I typed in the name Moses Abraham, but I couldn't find anything. I checked through the rest of the names, but again, I didn't find any kind of clue that might help me.

Were they old army mates of Jamie's? I tried to recall names he'd mentioned in the past, but he didn't talk about them much. I definitely remembered the name Lee, who'd organised some kind of reunion about a year ago. Was there a Dave who Jamie had spoken about, too? Possibly. I hadn't seen any of these names in Jamie's phone bills when I'd been looking through them, and Jamie didn't have an address book of contacts because he kept everything stored on his phone, which would've been on him when he'd died. I made a mental note to contact Tony, the coroner's officer, and ask what had happened to Jamie's belongings.

I sat back on the sofa and stared at the laptop until someone knocking at the door made me jump. It was probably Ava, I thought as I closed the lid and walked to the front door, but when I got there, I saw a man's silhouette behind the obscured privacy glass. I stopped where I was, frozen. Whoever it was could see me hovering there, but I was spooked by the discovery of Jamie's list and the knowledge that Jamie had been hiding something.

The man knocked again.

I didn't move.

The letter box opened, and a voice said, 'Maya, are you there? It's Tony Williams, the coroner's officer.'

My shoulders relaxed, and I moved the last few metres down the hall and opened the door.

'Hello,' he said.

'Hi.' I glanced at his left hand, which was holding some clear plastic bags.

'I'm sorry I didn't call first, but I was in the area and just wanted to return Jamie's belongings that were found with him.' He held up the bags. In one I saw Jamie's wallet and briefcase. In a bigger bag were some folded clothes that I recognised as the ones Jamie was wearing the last day I saw him. Another contained a pair of black shoes that he usually wore for work. They were now caked in dry, brown mud. 'I'll need you to sign for them.'

A hand flew to my mouth as I stared at the items.

'We can do this another time, if you like,' Tony said.

'Um…' I tore my gaze away from the items. 'No, I…come in. I was…I was just wondering what had happened to them all, actually.' I stood back and let him in before leading him to the lounge.

'How are you doing?' His bushy eyebrows furrowed with concern.

'Not too good.' I sat on the sofa and waved a hand in the direction of the armchair. 'Have a seat.'

He perched on the edge and placed the bags on the coffee table. He opened the first bag and pulled out Jamie's wallet and slid it across to me before removing the briefcase. 'The wallet was found in his trousers.' He pulled two forms out of his pocket and handed one to me. 'The contents are listed there. Along with the contents of the briefcase.'

I read through the list:

1 black leather wallet
1 Barclays Bank debit card in the name of James Taylor
1 HSBC Visa credit card in the name of James Taylor
2 x £50 notes
1 x £5 note
1 receipt from Freyer Jewellers

1 black briefcase
1 Casio calculator
2 Bic biros

1 notepad
1 Computer World magazine

1 white shirt
1 pair of black trousers
1 red tie
1 pair of black boxer shorts
1 pair of black socks
1 pair of black shoes

'This form is your copy, but I need you to sign mine to say you've received them back.'

So that was it. The sum of Jamie's existence.

I frowned. 'Didn't he have his phone with him?'

'No. There was no phone. His car was recovered to a garage we use.' He handed me a business card with the name, address, and number of the garage. 'You can pick it up anytime. The keys will be there.'

'Right.' I fiddled with the card before looking up at him. 'But he would've had his phone with him. And what about his jacket? He was wearing a black one when he left for work. Wasn't that with him, either?'

'Everything we found in his possession is in those bags.'

I shook my head. 'So where are they, then? I mean, he would've been cold without his jacket. And he always had his phone.'

'I'm sorry, I don't know. He may have lost them before he went to the woods. Or he may have thrown them away. Perhaps he didn't want you to try to contact him after he'd made up his mind about what he was going to do.'

I shook my head. 'And why wasn't there a suicide note?' My voice rose. 'Look, I don't think…I don't…Jamie can't have killed himself.'

A look flitted across his face. A look that said he'd heard it all before. Denial. 'I'm very sorry, Maya. I know this is difficult, and often people don't want to believe that a loved one would do something like this, but the enquiries I've made so far all point to suicide, without a shadow of a doubt. A lot of people don't leave notes.'

'What enquiries?'

He watched me for a moment before taking a breath. 'The rope I took away matches the rope Jamie used in the woods. I spoke to Dr. Lattimer, and he confirmed Jamie had been treated for depression in the past.'

'What?' I stared at him blankly. 'When?'

'Eighteen years ago. Jamie was prescribed antidepressants and recommended counselling.'

'What for? I mean, what was he depressed about?'

'That is unclear but possibly related to the time he spent in the army. There are no records that indicate he sought any counselling, and he took the course of antidepressants for six months. The doctor's notes indicate that he was satisfied Jamie needed no further treatment at that time. However, depression can return, and people don't always seek treatment for it.'

'But even if that's true, it was almost twenty years ago. I mean, how many people have taken antidepressants in their lives? Thousands. Probably millions. Isn't Prozac one of the most prescribed drugs? But they don't all go on to kill themselves, do they?'

'No, but nevertheless, there's an established history of it,' he said calmly.

'And he wasn't depressed. He wasn't!' My voice was shrill, heat detonating through my insides. 'I would know, wouldn't I? I lived with him.'

'Often, people who are considering ending their lives don't

85

mention it to their loved ones. They want to spare them the pain and anguish. Outwardly they can appear happy and going about life as normal to hide what they're really feeling. I've seen it time and time again.' He shook his head in what was supposed to be a sympathetic gesture, but it just seemed patronising to me.

So what if he'd seen it all before. I still didn't believe it. He didn't understand. He didn't know Jamie. I wanted to punch him.

'I've spoken to his colleagues and his boss.'

'So you know Jamie had taken time off work for some personal reasons? If he was taking time to sort out some kind of personal things, why would he have killed himself?' I jutted my chin in the air, challenging him.

'Again, often people who are considering suicide get their affairs in order before they go. It's very common. I believe that's what Jamie was doing in his last days.'

'What affairs? He didn't have anything to sort out!'

'We may never know exactly what he was doing. Maybe he was leaving the house and going somewhere to think, to get things straight in his head. The reason for suicide is very rarely clear-cut. But I'm confident that he was troubled and depressed, and he hid it very well.' Tony paused for a moment. 'I know you want to believe that Jamie didn't take his own life. It's a hard thing to accept, I understand that, but I can assure you, that is what happened.' He spoke very slowly, enunciating every word clearly. 'Are you suggesting there's something suspicious about Jamie's death?' His forehead crinkled with what looked like surprise.

'No, I…' Was I? 'I'm just trying to make sense of it all. I mean, what about the—' I broke off abruptly. I was going to tell him about the list of names and addresses I'd found. The laptop. The things out of place. The engagement ring. But something stopped me. It sounded mad now when I thought about it that someone had come into the house, moved things around for no apparent reason, but not actually stolen anything. And the laptop could've just had a virus and died. And maybe Jamie *did* buy the ring six months ago, before he was even contemplating suicide.

Tony tilted his head with a patient look on his face, waiting for me to finish.

'Nothing,' I said. 'It's nothing.'

'I can assure you that I've investigated thoroughly, and I'm very sorry, but as sad and hard as it is to deal with, the reality is that Jamie did take his own life. We are completely satisfied there are no suspicious circumstances surrounding his death.'

I shivered and wrapped my arms around myself.

'Did you have time to look at the leaflets I left? Grief counselling can be very helpful to people.'

'No.'

'Well, it's something to think about.' He handed me a pen to sign his form. I scrawled my signature on it, and he stood up. 'The inquest isn't likely to be held for several months yet, but I'll keep you updated.' His sympathetic frown was back again, fixed firmly in place.

I nodded and showed him out. Then I pushed the door closed and leant my back against it, taking some calming breaths.

Tony was right. I *was* in denial. I was clutching at straws, seeing things that weren't really there, trying to find excuses for what Jamie had done, because then I'd have to admit that he didn't love me enough to stay.

JAMIE

Chapter 10

After breakfast one day, Scholes picked me and Sean to clean our dormitory.

'Dusting, sweeping, polishing, and mopping. And if it's not done properly, I'll make you do it all over again,' Scholes barked out. 'And no talking!' he said as he left the room.

We'd been at it for about two hours when he returned. I could tell by the weight of his footsteps on the floor and the way he flung the door open that he wasn't going to be happy with what we'd done. I carried on dusting the metal bed frames with my back to him, silently praying he would go away.

'What do you call this?' he yelled at Sean.

I froze, not wanting to turn around and look.

Make it go away. Make him go away. Please, I'll do anything.

'S-Sorry,' Sean spluttered.

'Sorry, what?'

'Sorry, s-sir.'

Sean's fear and mine were almost palpable, like the electric static before a storm. My stomach twisted at the thought of what was about to happen.

Sean screamed, and I turned around then. Scholes had lifted him up by the scruff of his shirt, suspending him in the air.

I gulped back my own scream as Scholes dragged Sean out of the room.

I started shaking then, scared that Sean would be taken to the cellar. I could hear Sean's cries out in the hallway and all the way down the stairs. Then I heard a strange noise, like *thump, thump, thump.* And Sean wasn't crying anymore.

It took a long time for the trembling to stop. I was cold. The kind of cold that seeped right inside my bones and I thought I'd never get warm again. In the empty room, the tears came. I tried to fight them, but I couldn't hold them in any longer. I had to snap into action, though. If Scholes came back and the room wasn't finished, I'd get the same treatment. Or worse. My survival instinct kicked in, and I frantically finished cleaning the room.

When I caught up with Billy, Trevor, and Dave at lunchtime, I wanted to ask them if they'd seen Sean as we ate some kind of soup that tasted as if it was made from boiled PE kits. Barker was on lunch supervision, so there was no chance of breaking the 'no talking' rule, and I didn't dare ask. It wasn't until we were all outside for some free time that I could properly talk to them.

'I saw Sean being thrown down the stairs.' Billy's eyes welled up as he spoke. 'He…he…his head hit the floor with a hell of a crack, and then…then he wasn't moving. I hope he's okay.' He wiped at the tears with the cuff of his frayed jumper.

'Stop crying!' Dave spat at him. 'Don't show your weakness to them. Haven't you learned anything yet?'

But that made Billy cry even more, his shoulders shaking, snot dripping from his nose.

Trevor looked down at the ground, mumbling words I couldn't hear.

'And what are you doing?' Dave snapped at him.

'Praying,' Trevor said.

'What for? God's not going to help us. No one's going to help us!'

Billy ran off towards a thicket of trees in front of the perimeter wall. He sat down and bunched his knees up, resting his head on them and curling his arms around his legs.

'What if he's d-dead?' Trevor stuttered.

I stared at the house of horror behind him. I was praying, too, but it wasn't to God. I didn't know who I was praying to.

'Well, at least it's not us.' Dave flopped to the ground with a thud, his face bright red with anger.

'How can you say that?' Trevor asked. 'He's our friend.'

'Yeah? There are no friends in here. We can't help each other. We can't look out for each other. We've got too much to do trying to look after number one.'

I watched their exchange and wondered what kind of a world we were living in where we'd rather wish that something bad happened to one of our friends because it meant it wasn't happening to us. I'd felt that, too. At night when they came for one of us, I'd lie awake, unable to fall into sleep because I didn't want to be the one taken to the cellar or Barker's quarters. I'd listen for every tiny little sound. Every creak of the floorboards. Watch for every shadow creeping across the room. I'd hold my breath and hope that I really was invisible so they wouldn't choose me. Then, when the dark figure walked past my bed and went to someone else's, I was glad. Glad it was them and not me. And when they'd been removed, I could finally fall asleep, dreaming about the bird with big wings, soaring over woods and fields and deserts, catching thermals and flying higher and higher.

The whispers started that afternoon. Sean was in the sick bay and still unconscious. We listened to them all but didn't talk about it again. Four days later, Sean returned to the dorm, but something about him wasn't right. He was listless and sleepy, and it took him a long time to get any words out. He spoke in slow sentences, his voice devoid of its usual cadence. There was a vacant look about his eyes.

The old Sean was gone, and in his place was someone we didn't recognise.

MAYA

Chapter 11

I took a taxi to the garage listed on the card Tony had given me. I didn't have a car because it was a useless expense. I walked to work and didn't really leave St Albans that often. I was born and bred here, and there was always plenty going on. I'd drive Jamie's Jeep sometimes when we went to the countryside for walks at the weekends, and occasionally I'd get the train into London with Jamie or Becca and Lynn. But I'd need to use Jamie's now if I was going to visit the list of addresses I'd found to see if it had anything to do with why Jamie had killed himself.

I had to pay a storage fee to get the car released. There were more forms to sign, and then I was directed to a row of cars and handed the keys.

Jamie's black Jeep Cherokee was the third vehicle from the end of the last row. I pressed the remote control, and the doors unlocked. I slid behind the wheel and closed the door. A waft of his aftershave hit me again, and a ball of grief punched its angry fist inside my stomach. I rested my head back against the headrest and pressed my fingers to my eyes to push the tears back inside. Crying wouldn't do any good. Crying wouldn't find out the truth about what had happened to Jamie.

I stayed like that for a while, wallowing in self-pity, trying to get myself together, until a horn blasted somewhere and jerked me back to the present. Another smell filtered through my consciousness. Was it cigarette smoke? As I thought I'd smelt in the house the day Jamie died? Or was I just imagining things?

I looked around the car, opened the glove box, and pulled out the vehicle documents: log book, insurance, service history. There was a pen and an ordinance survey map of Hertfordshire. A cardboard air freshener wrapped in cellophane. I checked under the front seats and found a couple of coins and an umbrella. I checked the rear, but nothing was there, so I opened the boot and found a red breakdown-warning triangle, a first aid kit, and a cool bag we'd got from Lidls one day when we'd bought some frozen food. I lifted the material from the flooring and found the spare tyre, a jack, and a small tool kit.

Nothing that told me anything useful.

I got back in the driver's seat, pulled out the list from my pocket, and turned on the vehicle's digital display. I selected the satnav option and typed in the first address from Jamie's list: 10 Crompton Place, London.

I drove on autopilot, and the scenery passed in a haze as I headed out of St Albans, listening to the chirpy automated female voice directing me to London. There were queues and road works, and it seemed to take forever. I didn't know what I was expecting to find when I arrived, but it certainly wasn't the well-to-do street lined with big mansions.

Number 10 had a tall brick wall around it and closed wrought-iron gates. Yellow lines on the street marked the parking restrictions, so I drove around, searching for a side street where I could park. I left the car and walked back to the house, spotting some CCTV cameras on the top of the gates and an intercom system on the wall.

Now what? What was I actually going to say now I'd arrived? Had Jamie been here in the days leading up to his death? And if so, why?

I stood there for a few minutes, a biting wind permeating my bones, shuffling from foot to foot. The quiet street had hardly any traffic. What I could see of the mansion over the tops of the gates and wall looked cold and imposing, spooky even, or maybe that was just my imagination.

I pressed the intercom and waited.

A few seconds passed. I looked up and down the street. In the distance, a woman was walking along, pushing a buggy. No one else was around.

I pressed again and heard a burst of crackly static before a male voice said, 'Hello?'

'Um…hello, is it possible to speak to the owner of the house, please?'

'Yes, you're speaking to the owner. I'm not buying anything, so please go away,' a well-spoken male voice said impatiently.

The CCTV camera moved with a whirring noise, pointing directly at me. I gave it a wobbly smile.

'Oh no. I'm not selling anything.'

'Then what do you want?'

I was struck dumb for a moment. What did I want? I didn't really know. 'I'm sorry to disturb you, but I was wondering if you knew someone called Jamie Taylor.'

'No. I don't know any Jamie Taylor. Goodbye.'

Another crackle and then there was silence.

I chewed on the inside of my cheek, wondering what to do next before pressing the button again.

'Yes?' the voice said, more clipped and impatient this time.

'He might've visited you recently? He…um…he's…he died, you see, and I found this—'

'I don't know any Jamie Taylor, and he's never visited me, okay? Thank you very much. *Goodbye.*' The 'goodbye' was very final.

The woman with the buggy had almost reached me as I turned away from the gates. She was dressed in designer clothes. Her hair was perfectly smoothed into an updo, and her makeup was flawless.

'Excuse me,' I said.

She narrowed her eyes suspiciously. 'Yes?'

I detected an accent. Russian, maybe, or Eastern European.

'Do you know who lives here?' I pointed at the house behind me.

She shrugged and carried on walking, her high-heeled boots clacking on the pavement.

I looked up and down the street but no one else was around, so I walked back to the car and got out the list, staring at it again, wishing it could tell me something.

10 Crompton Place, London
Moses Abraham, 16 Dean Street, London
Billy Pearce, 43 Scarborough Ave, London
Sean Davidson, Flat 28, Derby Towers, Enfield X
Trevor Carter, 2 Dalton Terrace, Surrey
Dave Groom, 91 Ridge Street, Watford X

What did the *X*'s mean at the end of some of the addresses? And why wasn't there a name listed with Crompton Place as there was with the others? I didn't have a clue.

Since I was in London already, I decided to work my way down the list and followed Miss Chirpy's directions to the address for Moses Abraham.

In terms of geography, the house was only a few streets away, but it couldn't have been further from it in terms of affluence. At 16 Dean Street was a tiny terraced house in the middle of identical houses in a street lined with cars parked on either side. I had to drive up and down a few times before I finally found a parking space five minutes away. I got out and walked back.

A flutter of nerves danced in my stomach as I rang the bell. I could hear a TV inside, so at least someone was home.

A biracial woman opened the door. She had tired eyes and grey hair, and her face was lined with deep-set wrinkles.

'Hi.' I forced a smile. 'Could I speak to Moses Abraham, please?'

Her eyes widened, her lips falling open, as if she was upset or scared, but she didn't speak.

'Is Moses here?'

She looked shocked. 'Why are you looking for Moses?'

'Well, um…this is going to sound weird, but I'm wondering if Moses knows someone called Jamie Taylor. I think he may have come here recently.'

She frowned. 'Who?'

'Jamie Taylor.' I blew out a breath. 'I'm sorry to bother you, but he was my boyfriend, and he's just…died. I found this list of names and addresses, you see, and it had the name Moses Abraham on there at this address. Does Moses live here? Maybe I could talk to him and see if Jamie knew him. He might be able to help me.'

She looked past me, up and down the street, before settling her gaze back on me. 'Are you a reporter?'

'No, nothing like that. Like I said, I think my boyfriend might've known Moses. Jamie might've come to see him.'

'He can't have done.' She started to close the door, but I put a hand out to stop her.

'*Please.* I just need to find out what Jamie was doing before he died. He had this address. Why would he have it? Can I just speak to Moses?' I pleaded.

Something in my tone made her stop pushing the door. She

poked her head round it and studied me for a moment.

I spoke quickly before she shut me out. 'I've got a picture of him. Maybe you might recognise him.' I fumbled in my handbag, pulled out my purse, and opened it to show her a photo of Jamie I always kept in there. 'This is Jamie. Did he come here?'

She looked at it briefly and then back at me. Her gaze darted up and down the street again. I recognised her expression for certain now, because I'd become immersed in it. Consumed with it. It was pain.

'How did he die?' she asked.

'He…he hanged himself.'

She shook her head. 'I'm sorry about that, but I don't know how I can help you. He wouldn't have been here to see Moses. You've made a mistake.' She closed the door in my face.

Tears of frustration pricked at my eyes as I stood there, transfixed to the door, wondering what to do. There was nothing I could do. I put my purse back in my bag and was about to leave when she opened the door again.

She studied my face for what seemed like hours. 'Your friend really died?'

'My boyfriend. I really need to know why. What made him do it.'

She swung the door fully open. 'You'd better come in. I'm Moses's mum.'

After leading me into a tiny lounge, she stood with her back to the bay window and told me to take a seat on a two-seater sofa covered with a brightly coloured throw.

She folded her arms and watched me warily, as if wondering what to say. 'What do you know about Moses?'

'I don't know anything. That's why I'm here.'

'What *do* you know, then?'

'All I know is that I found this list Jamie left, and it must've been significant to him somehow. He'd taken some time off work before he died, and I think maybe it was to do with the list. I was hoping Moses could tell me why his name was on it. Maybe Jamie spoke to him about something.'

She stared at the ceiling for a moment. 'When did he die?'

I swallowed down a lump of glass in my throat. 'A week ago.'

'And when do you think he would've come here?'

'The week before that, probably.'

'God.' She ran a hand over her forehead and stared at some photos resting on top of a mantelpiece above a gas fire with fake logs. One was of a biracial boy and girl, both smiling, both around mid-thirties. At the opposite end was a photo of a smaller boy, maybe around eight or nine. She picked up the photo and handed it to me. 'This is Moses.'

He was gorgeous. Green eyes, light brown skin, a cheeky, glowing smile. 'He's beautiful.'

'Was.'

'I'm sorry?'

'He *was* beautiful.' She flopped down heavily next to me on the sofa, as if all the air had been sucked out of her.

I frowned. 'I don't understand.'

'He's missing. Never been found.'

'Oh, how terrible. I'm so sorry.'

She took the photo from me and traced a fingertip over Moses's face. 'He disappeared in 1984. He was ten years old. I sent him up to the corner shop to get some sweets, and he never came back.' She sighed deeply, placed the photo on her knee, and looked into my eyes. 'I can recognise your anguish because it's one I still have. The need to know. To find out what happened. Believe me, I know all about that.'

'The police never found him?'

She made a snorting sound, her shoulders stiffening. 'Bloody police.' Her lips flattened into a hard line. 'I reported it at the time, obviously. It was awful. They took a statement and things, but nothing happened. They said they were investigating, but I don't think they really did. I kept calling this policeman to get updates, and he kept saying they were doing all they could, but it seemed as though Moses had just vanished without a trace. I mean, how can that happen? We live in the middle of London! Someone must've seen something!' She stared at the threadbare navy carpet with its pattern of huge seventies-yellow flowers. Her eyes were distant. 'I've never had any answers in all this time.'

'That's awful.'

'There's not a day that goes by when I don't think about him. Wonder if he's still alive. Or…no. I don't know. Deep down, I don't think he's alive. In my head, I think he's dead. But in here'—she patted her heart—'there's always that hope, still.'

I reached out and touched her arm, trying to comfort her.

'I don't think I'm ever going to find out. Not now. Not thirty-odd years later. Someone knows something, though. Someone is hiding something.'

'Did Jamie come and talk to you about Moses?'

'No. I've never seen your boyfriend before. I've been away for a couple of weeks, staying at my sister's place in Manchester. I only got back yesterday.'

Questions tumbled around my tongue. 'Maybe Jamie tried to come here, looking for Moses because he didn't know he was missing, but you were away at the time.' Then a thought struck me. 'Actually, Jamie used to live in London when he was a kid. Maybe Jamie knew Moses from back then. Maybe they used to play together and he was looking up an old friend?'

'Let me see your picture again.'

I retrieved my purse, slid the photo of Jamie out of the plastic cover, and handed it to her.

She studied it with a frown of concentration then shook her head. 'No. I don't recognise him, but then kids change so much. But I don't remember any Jamies around here, and I've lived here all my life.'

'How about James?'

'No, I don't think so.'

She handed me the photo back. I carefully replaced it in my purse.

'The not knowing is the worst thing,' she said softly, the emotional wavering of her voice unmistakable. 'It gets easier to bear, but still…I keep hoping that one day he'll turn up on the doorstep as if nothing's happened.' She turned to me, her eyes moist and haunted.

'I'm so sorry,' I said again.

'Do you think your boyfriend knew something about Moses disappearing?'

Her words hit me like a slap in the face. 'I…God, no. He couldn't have.' Could he? No, of course not.

'Why would he have Moses's name on this list, then?'

'I have no idea.'

'Maybe it would explain why he killed himself. Guilt is a good reason for suicide.' She twisted in her seat then, the pain etched on her face giving way to suspicion.

'No. No, I…' I trailed off. 'I mean, Jamie would've been about Moses's age when he went missing, so he couldn't have known anything.' I shook my head.

'So why was my son's name written down, then?' She narrowed her eyes. 'What possible reason could there be? Unless he was trying to write an article about it? Or he knew something.'

'I...God, I really don't know. Jamie wasn't a journalist. He worked in IT. Like I said, they must've been friends when they were kids, or maybe they went to school together at one time and Jamie was trying to reconnect—that's the only explanation.'

'Which school did Jamie go to?'

I tried to think if Jamie had ever mentioned the name of it before. After we'd met, I'd talked a lot about growing up, stories from school, my teenage years, drunken holidays with my girlfriends, the usual kind of past things shared with a partner. Jamie had told me the same kinds of stories about his childhood, too, but he'd never mentioned which school he went to. 'Um...I don't know.'

This time her eyes were wet and imploring. 'If you know something about Moses, you have to tell me!' She grabbed my arm with surprising strength.

'I don't! I really don't know anything. I'm sorry for upsetting you. Look, maybe I shouldn't have come here and stirred all this up for you.' I stood and rushed to the front door. 'Thank you for talking to me.'

But as I opened it, another question filtered into my head. 'You said you've lived here all your life? One of the other addresses on Jamie's list was 10 Crompton Place. It's not far from here. Do you recognise that address?'

Confusion spread across her face. 'Crompton Place? The big mansions?'

'Yes. Do you know who lives at number ten?'

'Not my kind of people. There are a lot of bigwigs up there. MPs, judges, businessmen, showbiz types.'

'Right. Well, thank you, again.'

'If you find out why your boyfriend had Moses's name written down, promise you'll let me know?'

'Of course.'

With more questions than answers, I walked down the tiny path, feeling her eyes boring into the back of me.

MPs. Judges. Important people. A missing boy.

What were you mixed up in, Jamie? What secrets were you hiding?

JAMIE

Chapter 12

The months passed, and the abuse continued, Scholes ruling with terror and brutality and Barker ruling with veiled kindness and treats. The good cop and the bad cop of the paedophile world. But both of them instilled fear, punishment, pain, degradation, and humiliation.

I didn't think things could get worse, but I had no idea.

It was my birthday. I thought about the birthdays I'd had when I was still at home with Mum. The jelly and ice cream, pass the parcel, pin the tail on the donkey, the presents. Most of all, the cuddles and laughter. The only way birthdays at Crossfield differentiated from every other day was it meant we got a present. One present. Except we weren't allowed to keep it. We weren't allowed to keep anything. Nothing was ours. Not even our bodies and minds. Usually, we got a book. Barker believed we should read a lot. But whereas I'd immersed myself in books when I'd first arrived, as a means to escape my existence, now I was jealous of the characters in the books because they could go anywhere and do anything and be anyone, and it just made an anger fester away inside because I couldn't.

At breakfast, I was given my present by Barker. *Stig of the Dump.* I thanked him profusely, knowing full well it would be taken away at the end of the day and put in the common room with all the rest of the books I couldn't bring myself to read anymore.

After we'd finished eating, Barker made me stay behind while the others cleared the plates and washed up.

'You're going to have a party tonight.' He winked at me. 'After dinner, you'll be coming to my quarters. Your friends can come, too.'

Despite everything, a ray of happiness sparked inside. I desperately wanted to believe something good would finally happen to me. And I thought that if my friends were there, he wouldn't touch me if everyone else was watching.

'And there will be sweets and cakes and beer. What do you think of that?'

'Thank you, sir.'

At school, I could barely contain my excitement. I was going to have a real birthday party again. Nothing could upset me that day. Not the pushes and taunts from the other kids in class who hated us Crossfield boys or the sarcastic remarks and rapped knuckles from one of the teachers who told me I'd never amount to anything.

I walked back to Crossfield at the end of the day with Billy, Sean, Trevor, and Dave, my excitement rubbing off on them as we wondered what kind of cake we'd have, what party games there would be. Only Dave didn't join in the speculation.

'Don't get too excited. They'll want something in return,' Dave warned.

But I didn't let his doubts affect me. I was trying to hold onto the happiness for as long as I could.

After dinner, Barker told me, Billy, Sean, Trevor, and Dave to go with him. We followed him in silence to his quarters, sneaking goofy looks at each other. All except Dave, who had a face like thunder. I thought he was just jealous that Barker had never thrown him a party.

When we got inside the lounge, there was a table laid with drinks and snacks. Cans of beer. Popcorn, crisps, chocolate biscuits.

'Let me get you boys some drinks.' Barker clapped his hands together and poured beer into plastic cups before handing them out. He sat on the sofa, crossed one leg over the other, and stretched his arm casually along the headrest.

We boys didn't need to be asked twice. We drank quickly and munched on the snacks. More drinks were handed out. Barker put music on, and we danced around stupidly while he watched and smiled and laughed. He encouraged us to mess about, take off our tops, and show him our puny muscles. And we didn't care how he was looking at us because we were having a good time. Everything was funnier, happier, lighter in our fucked-up world. For just a few moments, we grasped onto a sliver of enjoyment while we could, knowing there would be a price to pay in the end.

Then more men arrived. An older man with swept-back dark hair and a neat beard, dressed in a suit; a fat man with bulging eyes; a tall man with a side parting; and a short ferrety-looking man with round glasses. They watched us, encouraging us to muck about while they clapped and drank more alcohol. When one of them suggested we take off our trousers, it suddenly seemed hilarious, so we did.

They were talking about us, but I caught only snippets because I was having such a good time with my friends: 'Pretty', 'Cute', 'They'll be pleased', 'Party', 'Up for anything'.

Sean was giggling, with that constantly vacant, indifferent look he always wore now. Trevor spun around and around in circles, seeing how many times he could do it without falling over, finally collapsing in a fit of laughter on the floor. Dave poured himself more alcohol and gulped it down. The short man with glasses stood up and poured me yet another drink. A look passed between the men, as if it was a cue.

And then I was being led by the tall man into a small bedroom upstairs, and his hot, sour breath was in my ear as he told me to behave and I'd enjoy it and we were going to have fun.

MAYA

Chapter 13

My phone rang as I was driving. It was Ava, checking up on me. I pulled over in a lay-by and answered.

'Where are you? Did you forget I was coming round? Are you all right?' she asked.

'Oh, damn. Sorry. I had some things to do.'

'You haven't been out for days—I was worried about you when you didn't answer.'

'I'm okay.' Except I wasn't. I couldn't get Moses's face out of my head. Couldn't get Jamie's out of my head, either.

'Where are you?'

'London.'

'London?' she shrieked. 'What are you doing there?'

I pinched the bridge of my nose, trying to get rid of a tension headache building in my forehead. 'I...I don't really know.'

'You're acting weird.'

'How am I supposed to act when my boyfriend's dead?' I snapped, instantly regretting it. 'I'm sorry.'

'No, it's okay. I can't even begin to think how I'd feel if Craig was gone. You have my permission to get angry. Are you sure you're all right, though? Sorry, that's a stupid question, isn't it? When are you coming back?'

'Soon.' My gaze strayed to the list resting on the passenger seat.

'Do you want to come round to mine instead? I'll head back there now. We could get a takeaway. Have a bottle of wine. Talk, if you want.'

Suddenly, I wanted that more than anything. Something normal, comforting. 'Yes. Thanks. I've just got one more stop. I'll probably be there in a couple of hours.'

'All right. See you then.'

I turned off my phone, put it in my bag, then followed the directions to the next London address on the list I'd programmed in.

It was getting dark by the time I pulled up outside 43 Scarborough Avenue. The house was right at the end of a dingy road, the windows boarded up with panels of wood behind grey metal shutters. High weeds grew in the front garden, and graffiti adorned the wooden front door that was peeling paint. I didn't know whether the place was abandoned or if it was a squat.

I checked the address again. Yes, it was definitely Number 43.

Apprehension prickled at me as I got out of the car, warning bells clanging loudly.

The front door opened, and a woman in her late teens with long, messy purple hair came out. She wore a black flowing skirt and a tight white vest top, even though the air was chilly, showing off a tattoo winding up her right arm. She sat on the step, lit a roll-up cigarette, and took a deep puff.

'Hi,' I said as I approached.

She took another puff and blew smoke in my direction. Up close, I noticed her nose and lip were pierced. 'Who are you?' She looked me up and down.

'I'm looking for Billy Pearce.'

She removed a blob of tobacco from her tongue and rolled it between her thumb and forefinger. 'What, are you a copper or something?'

'No, no, nothing like that. I'm a…friend of a friend. I just wanted to ask Billy something.'

'Nah, you don't look like a copper.' She looked me up and down. 'You'll have to speak to Neal about Billy.'

'Neal?'

'Neal Pearce. Billy's brother.' She stood up. 'I'll show you if you like.' She turned her back on me and pushed the front door open.

I hesitated nervously on the doorstep, not knowing what I'd find inside. What the hell was I doing here?

She turned back to look at me. 'You coming or what?'

I thought about going back to the car. Starting it up and driving away. But then I'd never know why Jamie had this address written down. I bit back my trepidation and followed her.

Inside the hallway it was dark, with candles and oil lamps dotted around, giving off an eerie glow. A smell of rotten rubbish, sewage, and body odour hit the back of my throat. We walked past a room on our right with no door on it. Sleeping bags lay on bare floorboards that were littered with cans and empty packets of food. Some of the sleeping bags were occupied by shapes. A white guy with dreadlocks was lying down, one arm resting behind his head, a joint in his other hand, and a can of cider on the floor next to him. His spaced-out red eyes followed us as we walked by.

She led me into a filthy kitchen at the back of the house. Most of the units had been removed, and the few that remained had no doors on them. A limescale-stained sink hung half off the wall in one corner, along with a plastic table that had probably started life white but was now ingrained with dirt and had cigarette burns all over it. At the table sat a scruffy guy with long, greasy hair pulled into a ponytail. His bushy beard and patchy sideburns made him look older than he was. He could've been anywhere from early thirties to late forties. He used a teaspoon to eat baked beans from a can, but he stopped eating when he saw me, his spoon stuck in his mouth.

'She wants to see you, Neal,' Pierced Girl said, leaning against the door frame, watching.

Neal licked the spoon slowly, weighing me up. He took it out of his mouth. 'You're not from the bloody council, are you?'

'No.'

'What do you want, then?'

'I'm looking for Billy Pearce. Does he live here?'

His eyebrows raised a fraction, but he didn't answer.

'Do you know where I can find him? I just need to talk to him.' I glanced at Pierced Girl. She inhaled on the roll-up and blew smoke at me, an intrigued look on her face.

'What do you want with Billy?' Neal asked gruffly.

'I think he might've known my boyfriend, Jamie Taylor.'

Something flashed in his eyes briefly before it disappeared too quickly for me to register what it meant.

'Jamie died recently, and I found a list with names and addresses. Billy's name and this place were on it. I'm trying to find out what it means. If he spoke to Jamie recently. If he knew what was going on with Jamie before he—'

'Get lost.' Neal glared at Pierced Girl. She shrugged and disappeared. He opened a small tin box on the table, pulled out cigarette papers and tobacco, and began rolling, his eyes downward. 'I've got no idea what the fuck you're on about. Never heard of no Jamie Taylor.'

'Well, maybe I can ask Billy?'

He licked the edge of the paper, smoothed it down, and lit the cigarette. 'Billy don't live here no more.'

'I can show you a photo of Jamie if you like.'

'I don't need to see a photo. I told you, I've never heard of him.'

'So he didn't come here recently? To speak to Billy?'

He took a drag and blew some smoke rings in the air before answering. 'No.'

I adjusted the strap of my bag on my shoulder, wondering what to ask next. I was pretty sure he was lying.

'Is that it?' He nodded down at his half-finished tin of beans. 'Only you're interrupting my dinner.'

'Are you sure—'

'Don't you understand the word no?' His dark eyes mocked me. 'Shut the door on the way out. You don't know who might come in.' He laughed.

I gave him one last fleeting look, but he was swigging from a can of lager and ignored me.

I walked down the dark hallway, half expecting Neal to jump me from behind. My heart was in my throat by the time I got out of the front door and up the path. I'd just unlocked the car door when I heard Pierced Girl say, 'Hey, wait up.'

I swung around.

She glanced behind her at the house before walking up the path. 'That guy you mentioned. Jamie. He was here.'

The breath hitched in my throat. 'Really? When?'

She licked her lips and put a hand on her hip. 'I can tell you, but I want some money for it.'

'How much?'

She scrunched up her nose, thinking. 'Forty quid.'

'How do I know you're going to tell me anything if I give it to you?'

She shrugged again. 'You don't.' She held her hand out.

I weighed that up for a moment. I didn't trust her, but I didn't think I had much choice. 'If Jamie came here, then you'll be able to describe him, won't you?'

She shrugged. 'Tall, green eyes, sort of blondish-sandy hair.'

That sounded like Jamie. 'Twenty,' I said.

'Thirty.'

'Okay.' I got thirty pounds out of my purse and handed it over. She stuffed it down the centre of her bra.

'When did Jamie come here?'

'Dunno exactly—it was about ten days ago. He spoke to Neal. He was looking for Billy, too.'

'Did Jamie say why he was looking for Billy?'

'Nope.'

'Did he mention someone called Moses?'

'No.'

'What did Jamie say, then?'

'He just asked Neal where he could find Billy.'

I waited for her to elaborate, but she didn't, so I asked, 'And what did Neal say?'

'He told him Billy was dead. He killed himself.'

A chill settled over me that had nothing to do with the wind. 'How did he kill himself?'

'He jumped in front of a train. It happened about a year ago, not long after Billy got here. He managed to trace Neal after he got out of prison and bunked here for a while.'

'What do you mean "trace Neal"? If they were brothers, didn't they know where each other was?'

'Well, Billy and Neal were in different children's homes when they were kids, so I don't think they were that close. And Billy was in and out of prison all the time so…' She shrugged casually, as if that was all normal.

'Right.' I tried to process all that. 'Was Billy ever in the army?'

'No.' She snorted.

'How old was he?'

Another shrug. 'About forty.'

So that meant Moses, Billy, and Jamie would all have been the same age if they were still alive. Was that relevant somehow? Had they all been school friends?

'Oh, yeah, I just remembered your man said something about a house.'

'A house? What house? Where?'

'Dunno.' She played with the hooped ring in her lip, twisting it round and round for a moment. 'But he called it the Big House. They had an argument. Neal told him to fuck off and not to come back. Never saw your man again.' She turned on her heels and went back inside. Conversation over.

A memory ignited in my brain. Jamie had been having nightmares for a few weeks before he died. He'd been thrashing around in bed, sweating, talking in his sleep, and repeating the same things over and over. I'd wake him up, hold him, comfort him, until his panting returned to normal and he fell asleep again with us wrapped tightly in each other's arms.

When I'd asked him about it, he said he couldn't remember what the dreams were about. Said it must be something to do with being stressed about work projects.

But I remembered clearly the words he screamed out in the dead of night:

Don't take me to the Big House!

JAMIE

Chapter 14

I didn't realise it then, but that was some kind of scouting party. A few weeks later, on a Friday night, Barker drove us to somewhere in London in his car. Sean sat in the front, staring out the window, mesmerised by all the real life going on around us. Billy, Trevor, Dave, and I sat in the back, watching the world speed past. An outing should have been a huge adventure in our sad lives, but I now knew exactly what Barker's 'special treatment' entailed, and I could taste the fear like poison in my mouth.

We pulled up outside a big house with an intercom and camera system on the front gate, and we all suddenly fell silent, staring up at what looked to us like an opulent palace. Barker spoke into the intercom, saying he had a delivery for the party, and a male voice on the other end laughed. Then the gates swung open, Barker stopped the car on a large driveway, and we got out.

'Come along, boys.' He ushered us up the front steps with ornate white pillars on either side, and the door opened.

We were pushed into a large hallway, and then Barker was gone. Standing in front of us was the fat man from Barker's party, with a glass of whisky in his hand and that look on his face I could now read so well.

'This is a fancy dress party.' The Fat Man chuckled. 'Come with me, and we'll get your costumes sorted out.' He led us along the corridor into a room with huge sofas and a desk and paintings along the whole of one wall. On the desk were bottles of alcohol—whisky, vodka, gin—and cans of beer. On top of one sofa were piles of costumes.

'When I come back, I want to see you all in your costumes.' He said it with a grin on his face, but it wasn't a request, it was an order. 'Help yourself to drinks while you get changed. I'll be back in a little while.' The Fat Man shut the heavy wooden door and locked it with a turn of the key.

Dave headed straight for the drinks. He opened a bottle of vodka and swigged it straight out of the bottle before coughing and spluttering and wiping his mouth with the back of his hand.

'Blimey, what's this?' I picked up a costume. The glittery white ballerina outfit had a tight top and flared tutu. A glittery tiara went with it.

'I'm not wearing that!' Trevor gawped at it, rummaging through the other clothes, pulling out a pair of very short leather shorts with some kind of leather braces.

Sean sat on the floor with a leopard print loincloth, rubbing the soft, shiny material over his face.

'Here.' Dave handed us some drinks, his eyes haunted with fear. 'We're going to need some more of this.'

We knocked back the drinks and pulled faces as the hard alcohol burned our throats.

'Someone's going to have to wear the girly thing. There are only five costumes here,' Dave said.

'I'm not,' Trevor said through a mouthful of drink, which sprayed all over Sean, who didn't seem to notice. Sean didn't seem to notice much since his head injury.

'Me, neither.' I picked up a different costume, which was also a girl's one—a tight pink dress with lacy wings stitched on the back and a flared, raggedy skirt.

'Ha ha! You've got a fairy costume.' Dave punched my shoulder playfully.

I glanced around at the others, unable to decide which was really worse. Sean had the loincloth on his head and was stuffing crisps into his mouth between gulps of gin and lemonade. I heard music and deep male laughter booming from somewhere outside the door.

We got dressed into our respective clothes, drinking more and laughing at each other to push away the terror that gripped our insides. Except the laughter wasn't funny. It was nervous, with an underlying nausea. I looked down at the fairy costume I had on, embarrassed, desperately hoping that wearing a bunch of stupid clothes was the worst we'd have to endure that night and knowing at the same time that this was just the precursor for something much, much worse.

When the door unlocked, we were all pretty tipsy, but it didn't stop my heart pounding and my mouth losing all moisture as we followed the Fat Man down the corridor. He was dressed up now, too, wearing a judge's costume of long, flowing robes and a fancy grey wig.

'Come along. We're going to have some fun now.' He grinned at each of us, but behind the grin was the hint of a hundred kinds of threats.

He led us to a very large room with wood-panelled walls and fancy high-backed furniture with plump cushions.

The other men who'd been to the Crossfield party were also there. The short man with glasses poured himself a large whisky from a fancy trolley of drinks in the corner. He was dressed in a pinstriped navy suit. The tall man with the gaunt face and side parting sat on an uncomfortable-looking sofa with a drink already in hand. He was dressed in a policeman's uniform. The other man with the neatly trimmed beard and swept-back hair with a widow's peak, also dressed in a posh suit, licked his lips as he rested one elbow on the ornately carved mantelpiece, studying us all carefully. And there was another man I hadn't seen before. He was old, with thick grey-white hair and bushy eyebrows.

The old man poured us drinks as we stood nervously in the centre of the room, trying not to catch any of the men's eyes. The room was already swaying around me as he pressed a large vodka and Coke into my hand. When everyone was served, he told us to line up in front of them, and he sat down in an armchair.

Our gazes darted into our drinks, at the floor, at each other. Wanting to look anywhere other than at those men.

The judge picked up a wooden gavel, banged it on a block of wood on the table next to him, and said, 'The Friday Club is now in session,' which made all the men chuckle. 'I believe it's my prerogative to pick first.' He leant forward, looking down the row of seated men.

'You always get to pick,' the policeman said.

The judge licked his lips repulsively. 'My house, my rules.'

'Oh, go on, then, you old bugger!' the man with the beard said, leering at me.

I tried to swallow more drink, but my throat had constricted.

They examined us with predatory, appraising eyes as they sipped their drinks slowly. We were nothing more than pieces of meat lined up for their entertainment.

The judge beckoned Billy towards him. Billy looked at us, the cold, hard fear evident in his eyes.

'Come on! Come over here. I've got something for you.' The judge picked up a bowl of sweets on the table next to his gavel and held them out. 'I bet you like these, don't you?'

Billy's eyes lit up. He walked towards the outstretched bowl, but the judge whipped the bowl away before Billy could take any. Billy stared at the sweets with longing, unaware of the man's gaze roaming Billy's body with a different kind of hungry look.

'Here, take them.' The judge thrust the bowl at Billy, who shovelled them in his mouth so fast he didn't notice anything else.

'You,' the policeman said to Dave. 'Come and sit with me.' He patted a seat next to him, and Dave walked towards him, his head bowed, his shoulders rigid.

The bearded man picked me. 'I *love* fairies,' he said, which made the other men cackle hilariously.

The old man picked Sean. And the man with glasses picked Trevor.

More drinks were pressed into our small hands, and we were passed funny-smelling cigarettes that we were told to inhale. I coughed and spluttered through the smoke, and the men laughed and joked with each other.

We were made to act according to the costumes we were dressed in. Sean pretended he was in the jungle, and the judge told him to holler like Tarzan, but we had no idea who Tarzan was, which started to seem funny to us, too. I was instructed to dance and prance around the room on my tiptoes.

When it came to Trevor's time, he could hardly stand, he was so out of it with the drink and marijuana. He got up from the sofa and tumbled to the floor, lying there, his eyes closed. The man with the glasses said something to the other men that I could no longer understand. I was tired, and the room spun out of control, and nothing was funny anymore. Everything was hazy and tilting, and a blackness hovered on the edge of my vision. Then suddenly the room was empty apart from the bearded man, who took hold of my hand

and led me into a large bedroom.

There were flashes of light and the click of a camera, and my eyelids were heavy. So heavy.

Then he stopped playing with the camera, and he started his new game.

MAYA

Chapter 15

'Hiya, Maya.' Ava gave me a half smile when she opened her door.

I attempted a smile, too, but my mouth wouldn't cooperate.

She pulled me into an embrace. 'How are you? Or is that another stupid question?'

I inhaled her familiar perfume. Hugged her tightly and didn't let go.

'Don't be nice to me,' I finally said. 'If you're nice, it's going to set me off again.'

'Okay, I'll be a complete bitch.' She drew back, her worried eyes examining my face closely. 'Want a glass of wine?'

I nodded.

'Get it yourself then.' She gave me a fake glare.

Despite myself, it made me smile. 'Have you put Jackson down?'

'Yes.'

'Can I go and see him?'

'Of course. But don't wake him up—he's grouchy at the moment. It's taken me ages to get him settled.'

I crept up the stairs to Jackson's bedroom, painted in a delicate, warm yellow. He lay on his back, his chest gently rising and falling, his plump lips puffed out, his eyelashes fluttering against his smooth, creamy skin. I kissed his cheek, inhaling the intoxicating aroma of clean baby and talc, feeling an overwhelming rush of love for this beautiful little boy.

When I went downstairs into the lounge, Ava sat on the sofa with her legs curled up underneath her, sipping a glass of wine. An opened bottle of Chilean red was on the coffee table, and a spare glass.

'I'm only having the one since I'm still breastfeeding, but you go ahead and drink the whole lot if you like. You could stay here tonight.'

'Maybe.' I still wanted to be at Jamie's so I could feel his lingering presence close to me. Maybe it was stupid, but that was how I felt. I poured myself a glass and sank down next to her.

'So.' She adjusted in her seat to face me. 'What did you have to do in London?'

I hesitated for a moment, rubbing a finger round the edge of the glass, wondering what to say. I didn't even know myself what was going on. What *had* been going on. Would it sound crazy? Ridiculous?

'What is it?' She placed a hand on my arm.

I took a large gulp of wine. 'I think there's something weird about Jamie's death.'

'Weird, how?'

I told her about Jamie's laptop having been wiped. The bizarre things moved around in the house. The smell of cigarettes that day and the same smell in Jamie's car. How a few things were missing, like his last three months' phone bills and his mobile phone and jacket. 'And look.' I held my hand out to her, showing her the ring. 'He bought this for me. We were in town about six months ago, looking in a jeweller's window. And he was asking me questions about what I liked. Then, when I was going through his things, I found it in his bedside drawer. There was a receipt for it in his wallet dated four months ago. I'm *sure* he was going to propose on our anniversary. He said he had something important to ask me. He told me before he left that morning that we'd have all the time in the world later on. So why would he say that? Why would he be about to propose if he was going to kill himself? Why would he buy it?' I glanced up and met her gaze. A gaze that softened and looked at me the same way Tony had. With sympathy and pity. I was getting sick of that look.

'Oh, hon, there could be perfectly reasonable explanations for the laptop. It might've had a virus and Jamie wiped everything off himself to repair it. He was an IT expert, after all. And if Jamie wasn't thinking straight before he went up to those woods, he could've gone back to the house and moved those things around himself.' She frowned with concern. 'And you don't know it was an engagement ring. It could've been a birthday present for you. Your birthday's in three months.'

I stared down at the ring. 'No, I'm sure it was meant to be an engagement ring, so why, Ava? You don't buy it and then kill yourself, do you?'

'I've bought Jackson's birthday presents already, and his birthday isn't for months. Jamie was an organised kind of guy. When he bought it, whatever it was for, he probably wasn't thinking about ending things.'

I spun the ring on my finger one way, then the other. 'But why would he have seemed so happy that day? If he was going to do it, he would've been upset and depressed, wouldn't he?'

She thought for a moment and then said softly, 'It's possible he was happy because he'd made his mind up and it was a relief. You told me yourself that Tony said Jamie had suffered from depression in the past.'

'That was years ago!'

She took a sip of wine and looked at me with a frown of worry. 'Do you remember when I was at uni and one of my friends there killed himself?'

'Vaguely.'

'You'd never have known it was going to happen. He was always the lively, funny, loud one. Always joking around. He was out with us in the pub the night before, too. I was having a really good laugh with him, just like usual, and the next day he was found after taking an overdose of tranquillisers.' She shook her head sadly. 'He would've been the last person I thought would ever do something like that. So, what I'm trying to say is that you don't know what's going on in someone else's head. You can never know. Jamie was obviously good at hiding how he was feeling from you.'

I finished my glass of wine and poured another as her words hung in the air and permeated my head. Was I looking for things that weren't there because I didn't want it to be true? Didn't want to think Jamie had done this intentionally? Had left me?

'I found a list of names and addresses that Jamie hid. And Paul said Jamie had been off work, but Jamie was leaving the house every day just like normal. That's why I was in London. I think he'd been going round to see the people on this list.' I told her about Moses's mum and about the squat and the house in Crompton Place.

'He probably took time off work because he was trying to get things clear in his head. Maybe he needed time to think about things before he…' She trailed off and bit her lip. 'You don't even know Jamie went to see Moses's mum. And how do you know that girl at the squat was even telling the truth? She'd probably say anything for a few quid.'

I took another sip of wine and swirled it round in my mouth. 'Maybe, but why would he have the name and address of someone who lived in a squat, anyway? Or the name of a boy who went missing thirty years ago? Why would the other names and addresses be on there? It means something important, I'm sure of it.'

'That list could be really old. You don't know when Jamie put it there. Maybe it was something to do with work. People who had bought software from his company, or maybe it was a list for his colleagues or something. Maybe they were old army mates.'

'That girl at the squat said she didn't think Billy had ever been in the army.'

She raised her eyebrows in an *aren't-you-listening-to-me* kind of way. 'Well, then, maybe Jamie knew them when they were kids, like you suggested. Maybe they did all go to school together.'

'But why would he go looking for them now, after all this time, when Jamie's never mentioned them before? And don't you think it's suspicious that if they did know each other all those years ago, that one disappeared and two committed suicide?'

'I think it's tragic, but Moses disappeared thirty years ago, and Billy committed suicide a year ago, if you can even believe anything that girl said, so I can't see how it has anything to do with anything. And I also think you're looking too deeply into things, looking for a reason to justify what Jamie did, which is normal when someone you love kills themself. But it's not healthy. You'll just go mad thinking about it because you'll probably never find a reason to justify it to yourself. He was obviously depressed and not thinking straight. And you can't second-guess his actions leading up to that point. You're never going to know the exact reasons why he did what he did, and it's just going to stress you out and upset you, even more than you already are. The most important thing you need to concentrate on is trying to cope with the grief so you can eventually move on.' She reached out and stroked my hair. 'I know it's hard to admit to yourself that he did it, but denial is a perfectly normal stage of grief.

Why don't you speak to someone? Call one of those counsellors in the leaflets Tony gave you?'

'I don't want to talk to anyone,' I muttered, downing some more wine. Talking wouldn't bring him back. It wouldn't change the fact there was a huge, gaping hole in my life. I'd been ripped inside out and scattered into a million pieces that I could never get back.

'It might help.'

'No!'

'Okay, calm down, it's okay.'

'I am bloody calm!' I said in a grating voice I didn't recognise.

She smiled gently, unflapped by my angry bellow. 'You can always do it later if you change your mind.' She dropped her hand.

A tic fluttered at the corner of my right eye. I pressed my fingertip to it.

'Everything is arranged for the funeral, so you don't have to worry about anything.'

Don't have to worry about anything? I almost wanted to burst out into bitter, hysterical laughter.

Out of the corner of my eye, I saw her watching me as I poured some more wine. Half the bottle had gone already, and I was going to drink the whole lot to try to stop thinking. 'Thanks. I don't think I could bring myself to do it all.'

'You don't have to thank me. What are sisters for?'

'I don't know how I'm going to get through it.' Tears prickled in my eyes again. 'I'm not ready to say goodbye to him yet. I don't want to see his coffin being put into the ground.'

She put her wine on the table and shuffled closer, then rested her head against mine. 'I know. It will get easier. At some point, it will.'

But I didn't want it to get easier. If it got easier, it would mean I'd forget him, and I didn't want to forget. Unexplainable as it was, I wanted to carry on feeling the sharp, jagged pain in my heart. It made me seem closer to him, somehow, as if we were still connected.

Jackson's scream wailed through the baby monitor on the floor in the corner of the room, and Ava stood. 'Better go and see to him. Then we'll order some food, yeah? What do you fancy?'

The thought of food made my stomach contract. I didn't need food. I needed more wine. 'Whatever. I don't care. You choose.'

As Ava left the room, my mobile phone rang in my bag. I picked it up and saw that it was Mum and Dad's number. I hesitated for a moment before answering.

'Oh, hi, love. How are you?' she asked.

I wished people would stop asking me that. *I'm fucking awful! How do you think I am? I want Jamie back! I want our life back!*

I gave the standard answer. 'I'm okay. How's Dad?'

'Oh, he's got an infection, and he's in quite a bit of pain. He's on antibiotics at the moment, though, which seem to be working. The doctors think he'll be okay soon.'

'Oh no, I'm sorry to hear that. Give him my love.'

'I will.'

'And how are you?'

'I'm all right. Just a few aches and pains. The joys of getting old. Still, the sun's wonderful for my arthritis, so I mustn't complain.' She sighed, suddenly sounding old. 'Are you eating properly?'

'Yes,' I lied.

'Have you managed to get any sleep?'

'Yes.' Another lie.

'Did Ava chat with you about talking to someone? A counsellor? We've been discussing it, and we think it's a good idea.'

A ball of anger welled up inside. I didn't want to be talked about as if I was a little child who couldn't take care of herself. But then I pushed it back down. They were only trying to help. It was just that they couldn't. No one could.

'Yeah, maybe I'll do that,' I said so she wouldn't talk about it anymore.

'Good. We think that will be good for you.'

'Uh-huh.' The room spun slightly as I zoned out. I didn't want to listen to useless words that wouldn't make a difference.

'Maya? Are you still there?' Mum said a while later.

'What? Yes, I'm here.'

'Oh, I thought you'd been cut off. Anyway, I was saying that Ava told me everything's all set for the funeral. You're having the wake at her house, aren't you?'

'Yes. I don't want people in the house. Not yet. It would seem wrong.'

'I think it's a good idea. Your friends Lynn and Becca are going to help out with the food and things. And Craig will be back then.'

'Yeah. Ava told me yesterday.' I hadn't even spoken to Lynn and Becca yet since it had happened. I couldn't face the questions and the sympathy and the meaningless chat that wouldn't solve anything. They couldn't understand what I was going through. And I couldn't trust myself not to break down or blurt out something bitter and jealous.

'And people from Jamie's work are coming, Ava said.'

'Yes. I haven't been able to get in touch with any of his old army mates—I haven't found any contact numbers for them.' I stared at the now empty wine bottle. How did that happen? I went into the kitchen, rummaged around in Ava's alcohol cupboard, and pulled out another bottle, balancing the phone between the crook of my neck and my ear while I unscrewed the cap. Mum was talking again, but I wasn't listening. Instead, I just gave yeses and noes every now and then.

'Well, phone me if you need to talk, all right? Anytime, it doesn't matter. I don't sleep much these days, anyway.'

I leant back on the sofa with exhaustion, closed my eyes, and gave another yes.

JAMIE

Chapter 16

I awoke in the same bedroom the next morning with every part of me throbbing or burning or aching. It took a while for my eyes to focus on the room, but the pounding in my head made it hard. The only good thing about the situation was that I was alone.

I sat up, dizzy and nauseous, and rested my head in my hands for a moment to stop the spinning. A glass of water was by the bed, and it was gone in seconds as I gulped greedily. I was naked, and bruises were all over me. I listened to the sounds of the house to see if anyone was around, but I couldn't hear a thing. My own clothes were on a chair by my bed, and I dressed slowly, wincing at even the fabric touching my sore skin.

I tried the door, but it was locked. I went to the window and lifted the thick red-and-gold curtains, staring into a huge rear garden that was completely private from any neighbours, with tall trees and high walls. I tried to lift the window, but it wouldn't open. Some kind of lock was on the bottom of it. What would I do if it did open? Where would I go? Who would I tell?

I spied on a table in the corner a framed photo of the Fat Man dressed in the same judge's costume. He was with an important-looking couple, accepting an award, and the realisation dawned on me that the men's costumes weren't fancy dress at all. One of them was really a judge, and one was a policeman. God only knew who the others were. I wouldn't be allowed to tell. And no one would believe me anyway.

The sound of a key turning in the door made me jump half out of my skin.

Please, not again. Please leave me alone.

The door swung open, and Barker was there, a jovial smile in place. 'Come on, then.' He jerked his head in the direction of the corridor. 'Let's go.'

Gingerly, I got up and followed him to the front door, where Trevor, Billy, Dave, and Sean were waiting in silence, their heads hung low, looking as pale and hurt and hopeless as I felt.

We never spoke about it between ourselves. We just noticed the bruises on each other as we undressed that night. Noticed the haunted look in the others' eyes and kept quiet.

A few days later, we were outside during free time when Dave plucked a silver cigarette case from his pocket with the initials *HS* engraved on the front.

'What do you think of this?' He held it up to us. 'I reckon it might be worth something. It's going into my running-away fund.'

'Where did you get it?' Trevor asked, taking it from Dave and examining it.

'Stole it from the Big House.' Dave's chin jutted defiantly in the air. 'There was so much stuff in there, I bet they don't notice it missing.'

'You're running away?' I asked.

'Yeah.'

'Don't be stupid,' Trevor scoffed. 'Where are you going to run to? There's nowhere to go.'

I nodded, wishing I was braver so I could go with Dave, but I knew it was useless. 'He's right. There's nowhere to go.'

Dave shrugged. 'I'll live on the streets. Anywhere has got to be better than being here.'

'You're eleven years old. How are you going to live on the streets? Where are you going to get money for food from?' Trevor asked.

Sean stared at Dave with glassy eyes.

'I'll just steal it.'

'They'll find you,' I said. 'They'll just bring you back.'

'At least I'm going to try. You lot are pathetic! I'm sick of it. I can't wait another five years until I'm sixteen and they let me out of this place.' Dave jumped to his feet, his nostrils flared, his face flushed, and he ran to his favourite spot under the trees to be alone.

~ ~ ~

Our nightmare carried on, and Dave didn't run away. He became angrier, though, choosing to spend more time on his own. I became even more introverted. Sean became more vacant. Billy and Trevor became more scared, jumping at every little sound. Scholes and Barker carried on abusing us, and the parties happened every Friday night. Sometimes there were 'special guests', other men who came to take their turns. A particularly sadistic one, with a wide mouth and thinning hair, had been there for the last few weeks running, taking his turn with me, Sean, and Trevor.

One Saturday night following Billy's turn with him, when we were back at Crossfield, I was asleep in bed. Usually, after one of their parties, I was so tired the next day it was the only time I fell into a deep sleep. But that night, I was woken suddenly by the familiar silhouette of Scholes creeping into the room, his footsteps creaking on the floorboards. I watched through my lashes, praying it wasn't going to be me again. My pulse clanged in my ears. My chest tightened. I fought to take a breath.

He walked to Billy's bed. I saw him lean over. Heard Billy whimpering. Heard Scholes whisper, 'If you make a sound, I'm going to kill you.'

I pressed my hands over my ears and squeezed my eyes shut. Somehow I must've fallen asleep again, and I was awoken later by Billy's muffled sobs.

At least he's come back, I thought, remembering all those boys who didn't. I tried not to think about them. I knew all too well by now what happened in the cellar. I heard Scholes's voice in my head telling me no one cared about what happened to us and how they could do anything to us. And he was right.

Again I drifted off to sleep, only to be woken by shouts in the corridor outside our dormitory. I sat up in bed along with the other boys.

'Get him down!' Barker shouted, his voice higher than usual and sounding urgent.

'Take his weight,' Scholes said. 'I'll undo the sheet.'

I crept towards the door and opened it an inch, but I couldn't see anything.

'Come on!' Barker shouted.

'The knot's too tight. I'm trying!' Scholes replied.

I opened the door wider, and that was when I saw Billy, hanging from the banisters, with his sheet tied around his neck, his battered body jerking, spittle on his mouth, his eyes bulging. Barker stood on the landing below, trying to take Billy's weight and hold him up to slacken off the sheet. Scholes fumbled with the knot Billy had tied around the banister as he and Barker shouted to each other.

Finally, Scholes untied Billy, who dropped limply into Barker's arms, a rasping sound coming from his mouth as he gasped for air.

'I'll take him to the sick bay.' Barker hurried down the next flight of stairs and disappeared.

I found myself wishing Billy were dead. At least that way, he could escape it all. But he came back four days later with a necklace of bruises on his skin. He didn't speak for weeks. I didn't know whether that was because his throat was too painful or because there was nothing left to say. He couldn't take anymore. And the horrific irony was that the men he was trying to get away from were the very ones who found him and stopped him succeeding. He didn't try to kill himself again.

Not then, anyway.

MAYA

Chapter 17

I woke up early the next morning on the sofa in Ava's lounge with a single duvet over me and a cushion under my head. My head throbbed. My stomach grumbled loudly. Had I eaten anything last night? I couldn't remember.

I reached for my mobile phone on the coffee table to check the time. Five thirty. Ava would be up soon with Jackson, and I wanted to leave before she surfaced. I had things to do. Despite Ava's reasonable explanations for what I'd told her, I couldn't just forget things and get on with my life. My brain refused to let go of the questions surrounding Jamie's death.

I drove back home, feeling light-headed and weak and nauseous. I needed to eat something. After stopping off at the all-night garage, I put a loaf of bread, some peanut butter, cheese, milk, soup, and four bottles of wine in a basket.

The Asian guy behind the till laughed as he rang up my purchases. 'You having a party for breakfast?' He wiggled a bottle of wine at me.

I glared at him.

He shrugged and put them in a bag.

As I walked back to my car on the forecourt, the bag split. It was just about the last straw.

I let out a loud cry, bending down and stuffing everything back inside, clutching the split as I marched to the Jeep. When I got inside, I caught sight of a bald man with tattoos, filling up with petrol, watching me with a look of pity.

I arrived home, let myself into the silent house, and put two slices of bread in the toaster before I unpacked the rest of the bags. I stared at a bottle of wine. Was it really too early to carry on drinking?

I made a coffee instead, with three heaped teaspoons of instant and two sugars. Sitting at the kitchen table, I forced myself to chew and swallow the toast lathered with a thick mound of peanut butter. All the time, I stared at the list, knowing it meant something crucial. Had the girl in the squat been lying? Or had Jamie really been trying to visit Billy, asking Neal about him and talking about a Big House? Something Jamie had been having troubled nightmares about? Did Jamie know something about Moses's disappearance? And if so, surely he knew Moses had never been found. Or was he trying to tell Moses's mum something? Was Jamie involved in something illegal?

There was only one way to find out, and that was to work through the rest of the list.

At 9.00 a.m., I phoned Paul Porter.

'Hi, it's Maya.'

'Oh, hi.' There was an uncomfortable pause as he probably wondered what to say. 'Um…how are you?'

Confused. Angry. Devastated. Feeling like my world has imploded. Take your pick. 'Yeah, I'm…' I stared at the list. 'I wanted to ask you something.'

'Oh, right. Okay.'

'Before Jamie took time off, what was he working on?'

'Uh, let me think. Hang on a sec.' Another pause. 'He was designing some new software for Levenson Accounting.'

'Where are they based?'

'In Bedfordshire.'

'Did he tell you he was stressed out about it?'

'About the project? No. It was something he could've done with his eyes closed. Why?'

It was the answer I'd been expecting. I was pretty sure by now that Jamie had told me a lie about work being the reason he'd been having nightmares and was distracted. I ignored his question and asked one of my own. 'I found some notes when I was looking through his things, and I didn't know if they were to do with work. Do you recognise these names?' I read them out from the list, one by one.

'Not off the top of my head. Let me just check our client list. Hang on.' I heard the clatter of a keyboard as he checked them all, each time saying no, he'd never heard of those people.

'Is it important, do you think?' he asked.

I thought about telling him what I'd told Ava, but he would just find a way to explain it in a logical, rational manner, too. Plus, how did I know I could trust him? I'd only met him a few times, and while he seemed very nice, a thought was worming its way into my brain. What if the list was to do with work after all? If Jamie dealt with IT, people's computers, maybe he'd discovered something on the computer of a colleague or one of their clients' employees? Something that related to Moses's disappearance? 'No, I'm sure it's nothing. Thanks, anyway.'

'I'll see you at the funeral, then.'

A lump rose in my throat. 'Yes.'

'If you need anything, if I can do anything…you know, just, um, call me,' he said in a voice that really hoped I wouldn't in case things became awkward.

I hung up and stared at the next address on the list. Enfield wasn't that far. It would probably take me an hour to get to Sean Davidson's address. Then an idea struck me that would prove whether Jamie had really gone to see all these people.

I got into the Jeep and looked up the history of recent journeys on the satnav, expecting it to confirm my suspicions, but according to the screen, the only recorded journeys were the ones I'd programmed in yesterday. So what did that mean? That Jamie had deleted the history, just as his laptop had been wiped?

I drove through rush-hour traffic, so lost in dark thoughts that I ran through a red light, narrowly missing an oncoming Mini who slammed on the horn. By the time I'd pulled up outside a tower block of dilapidated flats, my hammering heartbeat had returned to normal. I parked the car next to an abandoned old Fiesta with a smashed-in wing.

I got out of the car and found the lifts. They had graffiti on the doors, and when I pressed the button, nothing happened. Probably a good thing, I thought, climbing the stairs to the seventh floor and walking along the outer balcony that ran the length of the flats.

Number 28 had a front door that probably used to be white but was now a filthy kind of beige. Next to the door was a small window with a grimy net curtain. I forced my trepidation back down and knocked on the door.

No answer.

I knocked again, louder this time.

Nothing.

I bent down and flipped open the letter box. 'Hello? Mr Davidson? Are you in there?' What I could make out of the narrow hallway was dark. I smelt greasy fat and cigarettes. I stood up again and knocked once more.

When no one came, I stood with my back to the door. I could go and find a café somewhere and come back later. With that decided, I was about to leave when I saw a woman with brittle-looking bleached-blonde hair and black roots looking at me from the identical window of the flat next to Sean's. She pointed towards her front door then disappeared for a moment before opening it.

'Are you looking for Sean?'

'Yes.'

'Are you from social services?'

'No, I'm...a friend of a friend.'

She put a hand on her hip. 'Well, they've taken him off to hospital again. He's in the Kingfisher Unit.'

'Is he ill?'

'Mental health problems.' She rolled her eyes. 'I wish they'd rehouse him. I'm sick of his carrying on. He's in and out of the hospital all the time. They should just bloody-well keep him in there. I keep complaining to the council, and they don't do anything. There are kids round here. He's a friggin' danger.'

'What happened?'

'Barricaded himself in and wouldn't come out this time. His community nurse arrived, and Sean was shouting and screaming about people coming to get him.' She blew out a frustrated breath. 'Honestly, he was screaming the place down. My little girl couldn't get any sleep! Paranoid, he is. Schizophrenic.'

'Oh, how awful.'

'Awful for us, too.' She clicked her tongue against the roof of her mouth.

'Was he sectioned?'

'Nah. He went voluntarily in the end. He prefers to be in hospital, I think, but they keep letting him out again. Care in the community, they call it. Then he forgets to take his medication and he ends up back in there again. It's a joke.'

'Do you recognise this person?' I got out the picture of Jamie from my purse and showed it to her. 'I think he might've been to see Sean recently.'

She took it, squinting closely. 'Hang on. I'll get my reading glasses.' She disappeared back inside, and I glanced around me. The place was deserted, except for a group of teenagers on what I assumed passed for a play area, the swings rusty and decrepit, the see-saw broken in two. She returned with the glasses perched on the end of her nose. 'Actually, yeah. I was coming back with some shopping and saw him talking to Sean on the doorstep. It was just before Sean's latest episode. Before they carted him off to hospital.' She handed it back to me.

'Okay, thanks.'

She nodded towards the photo. 'Is he a bloody nutter, as well? Not that I've seen Sean with many friends.' She tilted her head. 'Come to think of it, I don't think anyone's visited him for years, apart from the community mental health nurse.'

'No. Nothing like that.'

'I think it's outrageous they leave them to just get on with things, don't you? What if we're not safe? You hear about it all the time, these people they let out and then they go round chopping people up with machetes. He's probably dangerous!' She leant on the door frame, in full flow now. 'And then if—'

'Well, thanks for your help,' I said again, interrupting her and hurrying back to the car.

~~~~

The Kingfisher Unit was a separate block at the back of the main hospital site. I asked the young lady on reception if I could visit Sean, and she looked something up on the computer before directing me to the wards. Outside the unit was an intercom that I had to use to gain access, so I pressed it and repeated my request.

A tall, harassed-looking man in a nurse's uniform eventually came and buzzed open the security doors.

'You want to see Sean Davidson?'

'Yes, is that possible?'

'Are you a friend or relative?'

'A friend.' The lie rolled off my tongue easily. 'Is he okay?'

'He's calmed down a lot now. He's back on his medication. He's in the day room. Follow me.' He led the way past some four-bed cubicles and private side rooms towards another door at the end. The day room was a bright, open space with views of the grounds. A TV was mounted high up on the wall, and plastic chairs dotted the edge of the room. Books stood on a shelf in one corner, and in the other was a large table. Only one person was in there, and he sat with his back to us, staring out the window, jigging his knee up and down repeatedly.

'Sean, you've got a visitor.' The nurse stood beside him and smiled.

Sean carried on staring out of the window.

'Sean? Here's a friend of yours to see you.' Sean didn't respond, so the nurse said, 'Have a seat. I'll go off and get a cup of tea for you both.' He disappeared out the door.

I stepped closer into Sean's sight line. He was rail-thin, with sallow skin stretched over gaunt cheeks, and bloodshot eyes. 'Hi, Sean.'

He turned his head quickly, then just as quickly back to the window, avoiding my eyes. 'Don't know you. Who are you? What are you doing here? Did you follow me?' As he spoke, I noticed that what teeth he still had left were stained a dark brown.

'No,' I said gently. 'How are you feeling?' I asked, then I realised that was that same ridiculous question people kept asking me.

He didn't look at me as he said, 'What do you want? Don't know you. Don't know you. Not talking to police. Mouth doesn't work.' His words came out in a jumbled rush.

'I'm not from the police.'

'The other lot. Not the other lot.' He bounced his leg up and down frantically and chewed on the skin around his thumb, which was already jagged and red raw. 'I told them. I told them.'

'What other lot?'

'Leave me alone. I didn't see the stars. They weren't out.' He scratched at his forearm.

'I'm a friend of Jamie's. Jamie Taylor. He came to see you, didn't he? Your neighbour saw him.' I pulled a chair from the wall and moved it towards him, sitting down.

'No way! There's no face.'

'Sorry?'

'No face. They don't have a face. They stare at you with those eyes, but they don't have a face. They don't have a soul.'

'Look, I'm really sorry to bother you, but Jamie's dead, and I—'

'Don't know you. Don't know you.' His head whipped around to face me, his eyes wide and terrified. 'Leave us alone. Mouth don't work. Mouth don't work. Nothing to no one. Nothing to no one. I'm not going back!'

'Going back where? Home?'

'Fuck off. Fuck off. Fuck off. Fuck off,' he spat, jigging his leg faster.

I jerked back at the anger in his words.

He jumped to his feet and stormed out the door just before the nurse entered, holding two cups of tea.

The nurse didn't even look surprised or flustered. I guessed this was just a normal day's work for him. He put the teas on the table and gave me a tight smile. 'Sometimes it's a good thing for the patients to have visitors. It can be a positive part of their recovery, but sometimes it can also be an agitation. Maybe you should leave it a little while before trying again.' He pointed at the tea. 'You can finish it before you leave, if you like.'

'Thanks, but I'm okay.'

He shrugged. 'I'll show you out, then.' He escorted me back up the corridor. Someone in one of the side rooms was shouting about a worm under their skin. I flinched and gave the nurse a sideways look, but he appeared to be concentrating on the corridor ahead.

As I walked back to the car, Sean's words rang in my ears, and I wondered what they meant. Did he know something about Jamie, or was he just confused and delusional?

JAMIE

Chapter 18

They controlled every part of our lives. We were toys. Playthings. Mindless bodies to use in their depravity. Fear penetrated every waking moment, and even in broken sleep, we had no release. If I wasn't being taken in the middle of the night, then I dreamt that I was. Day in and day out, it was all the same. I didn't question them. Didn't fight back. Didn't hesitate to do the things they wanted. I'd learned the hard way that refusing would mean severe and horrific punishments.

The men at the Big House didn't try to hide who they were. Some of them spoke openly in front of us, calling each other by name, sometimes making reference to their professions. They had no qualms about being caught. Why should they? As we'd discovered the first time, the owner of 10 Crompton Place, the Fat Man, was a high court judge who sat at the Old Bailey. We later discovered the policeman was a senior officer of a nearby police force. The Bearded Man was an MP. The Short Man was some kind of financial person, a banker in the city. The Sadistic Man was also an MP, who had now been rewarded for his heinous abuse and vile predilections by becoming a cabinet minister—the new children's minister, no less!

The rest we didn't know yet, but these people were leaders of the Establishment. The elite. Peers of society. That much was clear. So they could do anything they wanted with impunity. They wouldn't be caught and forced to stop. They wouldn't be punished for what they were doing. They were untouchable.

Sometimes other boys we didn't know would be there with us at the Big House, and the parties all started out the same. We were given drinks and made to smoke their cigarettes. Sometimes there were different themes. One night a boy was there who looked only about seven or eight. He had pale, freckled skin, huge brown eyes, and curly hair. When we entered the lounge, he wore a studded dog collar around his neck with a chain tied to it. The banker walked him around the room, telling him to act like a dog.

'Do it,' the children's minister ordered the boy.

He looked up at the man through teary lashes, whimpering, his eyes wide and terrified. 'I want to go home. Please, I just want to go home to my mummy.'

'Come on! What are you waiting for?' the children's minister sneered.

The other men laughed and jeered and suggested things for the boy to do. 'Get down on all fours and cock your leg like a dog', 'Pant like a dog', 'Bark!'

I turned away and dragged heavily on the marijuana and gulped vodka, trying to ignore the sickness in my stomach, in my head, and the hand on my shoulder dancing its way down my back.

Through his choking tears, the trembling little boy did as he was ordered with jerky, uncoordinated movements while a camera was passed around. A Polaroid that spewed out the photo within a few seconds. The judge had a video camera, too.

We tried to get as drunk and drugged up as quickly as we could so it wouldn't matter as much. If we were spaced out, it could mask the pain and the horror.

The judge laughed hysterically as he filmed the boy acting like a dog. 'Make him wear my wig!'

The children's minister forced it onto the boy's head and removed the dog collar, tears of laughter streaming down his cheeks. 'Get up, boy!'

The boy cried out, his own tears falling in fat pellets on the fancy patterned carpet. 'Please, n-no. Don't make me, p-please,' he whimpered, his eyes bulging with terror.

'Get up!'

The boy curled himself into a quivering ball.

Just do it. It will only make it worse. The warning words were on the tip of my tongue, but I just stared silently, helplessly, like the rest of my friends.

The children's minister grabbed an empty whisky bottle from the table in the corner of the room and strode towards the boy. 'Hold him down,' he said to the banker.

The banker kneeled on the boy's back, pushing his head into the carpet. The boy struggled, crying, pleading.

I turned towards the door, wanting to escape but frozen in place with shaking legs. The boy's screams were louder but muffled by the carpet. And then there was an agonising cry, and I knew what was happening, as he'd done it to me and the others before. My guts churned. I was light-headed, floating. I huddled down on the floor, my knees drawn into my body, and buried my face into my thighs, pressing my hands over my ears to block it all out, but I could still hear it.

Gradually the screams stopped and were replaced by a thumping sound on the floor. Inexplicably, I was drawn back to look at him. The boy was sprawled on his back with the children's minister straddling his chest, a demonic look in his eyes. His hands were round the boy's throat, and the boy's arms and legs slapped the carpet, terror in every gasped breath. He struggled as he fought for his life, his eyes bulging, before sinking back into his head, staring blankly, and his body slackened into stillness.

A scream caught in my throat, unable to come out, the pressure of it making it hard to breathe. An uncontrollable shaking wracked every muscle in my body. I squeezed my eyelids closed, pressing my hands over my head, trying to crush my skull.

Trying to crush away what I'd seen.

MAYA

Chapter 19

I had two more names and addresses left, and I still didn't understand what Jamie could've been doing.

Trevor Carter's house was a modern semi-detached in a large housing estate. A girl of about eighteen opened the door to my knock.

'Hi. Can I speak to Trevor Carter, please?'

She immediately turned around and yelled back inside the house, 'Mum! Someone's looking for that Trevor guy again.'

A harassed-looking older woman approached the door, wiping her hands on a tea towel, and the teenager disappeared with an energetic bounce.

'You're looking for Trevor Carter?'

'Yes, does he live here?'

She shook her head. 'No, we bought the house off him a couple of years ago.'

'Do you have a forwarding address for him?'

'No. I think he went to America.'

'Has someone else been here looking for him recently?'

'Yes. There was a man round here about ten days ago.'

I showed her the photo of Jamie. 'Is this the person?'

She leant forward and gave it a brief glance. 'That's him. I told him the same. Does Trevor owe you money or something? We're always getting post for him still, but I just put it back in the post box and mark it "no longer at this address".'

'No, nothing like that,' I said, disappointment welling up inside. 'Thanks for your help, anyway.'

I got back into the Jeep and punched in the final address in the satnav. As I drove, all I could think was, *Please let me find some kind of an answer here.*

The house was a large detached mock Tudor on a fairly new estate. A Ford Focus with a private number plate AG1 was parked on the gravel drive. I rang the doorbell, and an echoing chime reverberated behind the door.

An elderly woman's face appeared at the front window and looked at me for a moment. She disappeared and then opened the door.

'Can I help you?'

'I'm looking for Dave Groom.'

A hand flew to the centre of her chest. The muscles in her neck rose and fell as she swallowed hard. 'Dave passed away.'

Her words buzzed in my ear as the shock registered. 'Um...oh, how terrible. I'm so sorry for your loss. What...um...what happened?'

She glanced over her shoulder briefly back inside the house before stepping out and closing the front door behind her. 'There was a hit-and-run accident. We only had the funeral yesterday, so Anita's obviously still upset. She's not seeing anyone at the moment.'

'That's awful. When...I mean, when did it happen?' She told me, and I calculated back through the days. The hit-and-run was the day after Jamie was found hanged. A horrible sensation slammed behind my ribcage. 'Anita's his wife?'

'My daughter, yes.'

I stared at the ground as the world swam in and out of focus at the edge of my vision. 'So, the police haven't caught anyone for the accident?'

'No. No witnesses have come forward yet.'

'Um...I think my boyfriend came to see Dave about something. His name was Jamie Taylor. Jamie was found hanged the day before Dave would've died.'

'Oh, dear. Sorry for your loss, too. It's a terrible thing. Were they friends?'

'Yes,' I said, even though I didn't have the first idea whether that was true. 'Could I just ask Anita whether Jamie came here to see Dave? It's really important. I'm trying to find out...' I looked back up at her. I didn't know *what* I was trying to find out at all. Didn't have a clue what the hell Jamie had been mixed up in. 'Um...I just need to know if Jamie visited and spoke to Dave before he died. And if...if maybe Anita knew what it was about.'

She pursed her lips together. 'Anita doesn't want to see anyone. I'm sorry to hear about your boyfriend, too, but I don't think Anita's in any frame of mind to talk right now.' She stepped back inside, and the door began to close. 'I can't help you, I'm afraid.'

'Please!' My voice came out like a yelp. 'Could you just ask her for me?' I fumbled in my bag for the photo of Jamie and handed it to her. 'This is my boyfriend. Could you just ask Anita if he came to see Dave recently?'

She glanced at the photo in my outstretched hand, and for a moment, I thought she was going to say no. She took in the expression on my face, and then the photo was in her hand.

'Hang on a minute. I'll go and have a quick word with her.' She closed the door.

I waited, shuffling from foot to foot, chewing on the inside of my cheek, my mind reeling.

Five minutes later, she returned and handed me back the photo. 'Sorry, dear, but Anita doesn't recognise your boyfriend.'

I just nodded because I didn't know what else to ask. 'Please give Anita my condolences.'

'Thank you.' She closed the door.

~ ~ ~ ~

The first thing I did when I got home was pour a large glass of wine. I sat at the kitchen table and stared at the list. That was all I seemed to be doing lately. I stared and stared as I drank until the letters blurred on the page, trying to get my jumble of thoughts to form a coherent pattern. What did it all mean, and how did it all relate to Jamie?

10 Crompton Place, London
Moses Abraham, 16 Dean Street, London
Billy Pearce, 43 Scarborough Ave, London
Sean Davidson, Flat 28, Derby Towers, Enfield X
Trevor Carter, 2 Dalton Terrace, Surrey
Dave Groom, 91 Ridge Street, Watford X

Moses had disappeared thirty years ago. Why was Jamie interested in something that happened so long ago? If I could believe what Pierced Girl from the squat had said, Billy killed himself a year ago. Sean Davidson was suffering from mental health problems. Trevor Carter was supposedly in America, or had he disappeared, too, like Moses? And Dave Groom had been killed in a hit-and-run accident the day after Jamie died. Did the X's mean people Jamie had actually spoken to? I had confirmation from Sean's neighbour that Jamie was there shortly before he began barricading himself in his flat. But what about Dave? Anita apparently hadn't recognised the photo, but Jamie could've met him when Anita wasn't around. Or did the *X*'s mean something completely different? The person I spoke to at 10 Crompton Place said Jamie hadn't been there, but was he lying for some reason?

How did it all connect together? The only central strand was Jamie. And the common theme was people dying or disappearing.

A sliver of cold, hard fear curled up my spine. My mind wandered to Jamie's laptop, the things moved in the house, the cigarette smells, the missing phone bills and Jamie's phone, the empty satnav history, the engagement ring Jamie had bought, Jamie's nightmares about the Big House, and Pierced Girl's words: *He called it the Big House.*

People dying.

One boy missing for thirty years. Two suicides. One accident.

A fatal hit-and-run and a hanging within two days of each other. Surely, it was too much of a coincidence.

We'll have all the time in the world later.

You'll love what happens after dinner.

And that was the first time I thought that Jamie hadn't taken his own life after all. Whatever Jamie had been doing before he died had got him killed. No, not killed.

Murdered.

I rolled the word around in my head. A stabbing sensation shot through me. If Jamie hadn't taken his own life, it was the only explanation. But a murder made to look like suicide? Who would do that? It sounded ridiculous. Insane. But it was the only thing that made sense to me.

So, who?

The same kind of person who would make a child disappear?

Someone with a very important secret to hide. Maybe someone who knew what had happened to Moses and didn't want Jamie to find out.

A tingle of fear squeezed at my scalp as the thought sunk in.

Had Jamie discovered something about Moses's disappearance, after all these years?

I grabbed my laptop, brought it into the kitchen, and fired it up. Then I did a land registry search of 10 Crompton Place. The owners were listed as Mark and Elaine Bowyer, and they'd bought the house four years ago. Why hadn't Jamie written a name next to that address on his list as there was on all the others? Why was it underlined? Was 10 Crompton Place *the Big House?*

I Googled their names and found hits for a website offering genealogy services, mention of a Mark Bowyer in a military history book, and a Facebook page for an Elaine Bowyer. The website didn't seem to relate to anyone called Bowyer, so I clicked on the Facebook link, but the woman was a teenager, probably no more than fourteen or fifteen. She couldn't be the owner of the house. So that left the military history book. Was Jamie trying to get in touch with some old friends from his army days for some reason? Pierced Girl said Billy hadn't been in the military, but she could easily have been wrong. Or lying. But how did Moses figure into everything? I clicked on the book's link, but it referred to a book on the Rhodesian war, between 1964 and 1979, when Jamie was just a kid. I shook my head. Surely, that couldn't have anything to do with Jamie's death.

Going back to the land registry search, I checked the previous owner of 10 Crompton Place, a man named Howard Sebastian. I Googled that name and found out that the Sebastian family was one of Britain's eminent aristocratic families, whose hereditary titles dated back to the fifteenth century and included dukedoms and earldoms. Howard Sebastian was a descendant of Nicholas Sebastian, the Seventh Earl of Jersey. Another website described how Sir Howard Sebastian had been a high court judge who'd sat at the Old Bailey until he retired in 1999. He'd died just before the house had been sold to the Bowyers.

I rubbed at the mass of knotted tension in my shoulders, wondering if this Sebastian person had any significance, and poured some more wine. It grew dark outside my window. I turned on the lights, put my elbows in on the table, and rested my head in my hands.

Tell me, Jamie. What was going on?

I had nowhere to go now. No more addresses to check. No more avenues to follow.

Whatever secret Jamie had been hiding from me would be buried with him tomorrow.

JAMIE

Chapter 20

A care assistant called Miss Davey, but who let us call her Rose, had been working at Crossfield about three months or so. She didn't work on Fridays or Saturday mornings, so she never witnessed us being taken to the Big House and returned. But she was different to Barker and Scholes and all the others. Apart from the fact she was the first female to work there, she was younger than them and had a warm, sunny smile that reminded me of Miss Percival, who had long since left our school after she'd had a baby. Rose didn't look at us with hatred, like Scholes, or twisted depravity masquerading as fake jovial kindness, like Barker. Or the uncaring indifference of the other staff, who, if they didn't participate, turned a blind eye.

All the boys loved Rose. They all wanted to talk to her, be near her, hold her hand, all fighting for her attention. When she was supervising meal times, we were allowed to talk quietly. If she was outside during free time with us, she'd join in some of our games. She was a sparkling ray of light in our wretched lives. I watched her observing Barker and Scholes carefully, and I thought she must've known what was going on and had become suspicious of their dirty, dark secrets.

One Saturday afternoon when she started her shift, I was ill in bed because I couldn't stop being sick—an effect of the alcohol and drugs I'd been given at the party the night before. It felt as if my soul was sick, too, dying a little more each day.

She entered the dorm, a cup of soup in her hand and a sympathetic smile on her face. 'How are you feeling, sweetie?'

With shaky arms, I lifted myself to a seated position. 'I think I've got a stomach bug.'

She put the mug on the floor and felt my clammy head with her palm. 'You are hot. Do you think you can eat something now?'

I looked at the soup, and my stomach flipped. Maybe I could just go on hunger strike, never eat anything again, and slowly waste away. 'I don't feel like it, sorry.'

'You don't have anything to apologise for.' She plumped up the thin, hard pillow behind me then seemed to notice a large bruise above my elbow from where I'd been held in position by those men. She lifted the arm of my T-shirt up higher to get a better look, her eyes narrowing, then her eyes met mine. 'Is there something going on, Jamie? Something with Mr Scholes or Mr Barker?'

I blinked hard and shook my head, making the room spin nauseously.

She pursed her lips, frowning. Then she glanced over her shoulder, at the closed door, before looking back at me again. 'I think there is, Jamie. Something's not right here.'

I couldn't look at her.

'Some children disappear suddenly, far too quickly for them to have found a foster placement or transfer without notification. Some boys have too many bruises and marks on them for it to be the normal rough and tumble of playing.' She rested her hand on mine. 'Are they beating you?'

I made an unintelligible sound, like a squeak. If only that were *all* it was.

'You can tell me what's going on, Jamie. I can help you. But I need to know exactly what's happening.'

I thought about how I'd told Miss Percival. Now things were even worse, there was no way I could tell Rose. Scholes really would kill me this time, or one of the other men from the parties.

I fiddled with the sheet, not daring to look at her. 'Could you take me home with you?'

'Awww, sweetie, I wish I could.' She gathered me towards her in a hug.

I rested my head on her shoulder, squeezing my eyes shut, clutching on tight and never wanting to let her go.

'I've got two children of my own,' she said. 'I'd love to take you home, but I just can't. I'm so sorry, Jamie.'

Of course she couldn't take me anywhere. I knew it was a pathetic and ridiculous idea as soon as I'd said it. 'Nothing's going on, miss.'

She held me for a while, stroking my back, then she let me go, resting her hands on my shoulders and staring deep into my eyes. 'Are you absolutely certain?'

I nodded and reached down for my soup to stop the questions. 'I think I can manage a bit of this now.'

She opened her mouth, as if to say something more, then apparently changed her mind, patted my shoulder, and left.

As the weeks passed, Rose seemed increasingly more watchful of Barker and Scholes with the other boys. Whenever we were on our own, she'd ask me the same questions. Was I okay? Was there something going on? Were they physically abusive? At first, I answered in the way I'd learned to. 'Everything's fine. Nothing's going on here.' But then I began to trust her. I could tell by her expressions when she looked at the other staff that she didn't like them. Could tell she was one of the few people who'd ever actually *cared* for the people in care. Could she really help me? It was different this time than Miss Percival, because Rose actually worked here. She suspected first-hand something was going on, and she knew us boys, she knew we wouldn't lie.

'I can't help you unless you tell me exactly what they're doing,' Rose said to me one day during free time when we were on our own. She held my hand tightly. 'You can trust me, Jamie. I can take this further. But I need to know. I need you to tell me.' I glanced over her shoulder and spotted Barker walking towards us, a smile on his face.

'It's nothing, miss.' I slid my hand from hers and walked away.

But Rose didn't let up, and as the time passed, I convinced myself she could be the one person I could tell about the horrors going on here and at the Big House.

The day I finally plucked up the courage to tell her everything was a Sunday. We had free time, and I sat in the grounds, alone, waiting for her to arrive and start her shift, my palms sweaty, my heart racing, hardly daring to breathe.

And I waited. And waited. But she didn't come. She'd just disappeared without saying goodbye, and I never saw her again. She didn't care after all.

But the desperate urge to tell had taken hold again now and refused to go away. It consumed me. I was thirteen. How could I survive another three years in here? I just didn't know how, though, or who would listen and actually help. But about six months later, we were informed there was going to be a children's home inspection of Crossfield, and I decided I would try to tell the inspector instead. I didn't know whether the inspector would speak to us all individually or whether we would be supervised by Barker and Scholes at all times. I suspected we would be, but then I had the idea of writing the inspector a letter. Maybe I could put it in his pocket when he came round. Maybe I could leave it under the windscreen wipers on his car. I would make the letter anonymous so it could never fall back on me. That was better. Much better than telling someone face-to-face. If they didn't know it was me, they couldn't punish me, and he'd still have to do something. Wouldn't he?

I didn't tell the others. I couldn't face the negativity when they would tell me it wouldn't work, that no one would listen; no one would do anything. I'd heard it so many times. But I still had to try. Like Billy, I didn't know how much more I could take.

We were all on extra cleaning duty before the inspector arrived. Barker wanted the place spotless, and I was assigned to cleaning the kitchen with Dave. And as we wiped and polished and mopped, Dave whispered his usual crazy ideas of running away.

'I'll go into the centre of London,' he said as he shined the steel worktops. 'It's massive. No one will be able to find me.'

I nodded and tried to shut him out as I swept the floor. I was still trying to work out in my head the right things to put in the letter.

'You could come with me.'

I swept harder and ignored him.

'Eventually, I'll get a job and a place to stay.'

'You're thirteen,' I snapped. 'How are you going to get a job? As soon as they know who you are, they'll send you straight back.' My plan was much better.

'So I'll just live on the streets for three years. Then they can't touch me, can they? I've got to get out of here.'

I stopped sweeping and leant my elbow on the brush. 'You've been talking about it for years, so either shut up about it or go and do it!' I spat. I didn't know why I was angry at Dave. It wasn't his fault, but at that moment, I couldn't help it. The anger had to go somewhere, or it would consume me. Drag me down into a big, blank nothingness.

Dave glared at me. 'No wonder you're always the fairy. You stupid little girl!'

Something exploded inside me, and I launched myself across the room, diving into Dave. We fell to the hard tiled floor in a writhing heap, our fists and legs flying. It didn't last long. The next minute, I was being pulled off Dave by Scholes.

He gripped each of us by the scruff of our jumpers, holding us apart. Dave's right eye was already swelling. My lip was cut, blood dripping onto my jumper.

'What are you doing, you animals!' Scholes yelled

I laughed uncontrollably then. I was the animal?

Scholes dragged us up by our collars and pulled us both along the corridor by our ears. I was thrown into the cleaning cupboard, and the door was locked behind me. I didn't know where Dave was put. It was only because Scholes was busy organising everything for the inspector that he didn't beat or abuse us further.

I sat on the floor in the dark, the smell of bleach scratching at my throat and nostrils, and all the time I was still desperately thinking of the right things to write in my letter. I'd show Scholes and Barker. I'd show those sick excuses for human beings in the Big House. Someone *would* come when they read it. Someone *would* do something to get us out of hell.

A couple of hours later, Scholes dragged me by my ear back downstairs to the common room to mop the floor.

'If I hear one peep out of you, you'll be spending the night in the cellar,' he warned before turning on his heels and leaving me to it.

A couple of hours later, he came back. He walked casually around the room, his arms folded, scrutinising the floor. 'It still looks filthy.' He kicked the bucket of water over on the floor so it ran out in a dirty river over the newly cleaned floorboards. 'Do it again. And you'll get no dinner tonight.'

It took another two hours. The bell went for dinner, but I ignored the rumbling in my stomach. We were always hungry—there was never enough to eat, and I was used to the pangs gnawing at me by now. Hunger pangs were the easy part. I carried on mopping and watched the other boys through the window as they filed out for free time. Carefully, I rinsed out the mop and bucket, put them back in the cleaning cupboard, and stole upstairs to the dorm.

I took one of my school notebooks and tore a sheet out of the back. Then I began writing.

I should've slept well that night because no one crept into our room to take a child. Maybe they were too busy with the finishing touches for the inspection. But my mind raced uncontrollably as I imagined the inspector reading my letter. The horrified expression on his face when he knew what went on at Crossfield. When he discovered the parties where we'd seen another boy's life snuffed out for their sick pleasure without a second thought. I pictured people coming to rescue us, storming the house, taking us to safety. Somewhere. Anywhere that wasn't here. A place people would give us the love and attention we needed. Where our bellies would be full and the sexual and physical abuse would be over. A letter was the only way we would be getting out of here.

I was dressed before the alarm bell went off that morning, sitting on my bed, fidgeting, waiting for the others so we could descend the stairs in silent single file. I forced myself to swallow watery porridge, even though it was hard to get it past my throat, which was tight with the anxiety and excitement that we'd soon be leaving the house of horrors, because if I didn't eat, I'd be made to eat it from the floor, or it would be back there for me at lunchtime or dinner time, congealed and hard, probably with a cigarette butt or lump of dirt or fluff added by Scholes.

We heard whispers as we finished breakfast that the inspector had arrived and was talking to Barker in his office. Scholes made us clear and wash the breakfast things and then told us to line up in the common room, glaring at us all with hateful, narrowed eyes. It was the first time I'd ever seen him look nervous or worried.

'The inspector is going to speak to each of you in turn. Just make sure you tell him what a nice place this is and how lucky you are to be here. Anyone who steps out of line will be in for some severe punishment. I don't want you bunch of ungrateful bastards telling tales!'

Butterflies danced in my chest as I fingered the letter in my pocket. If Scholes stood at the entrance to the common room, he wouldn't be able to see me slip it into the inspector's pocket.

We lined up as ordered. I glanced down the row at my friends, who were staring at the floor. Barker swung open the door to the common room with a beaming smile on his face, closely followed by another man.

The butterflies turned to snakes, writhing and biting my insides with their venomous teeth as the horrible realisation took hold.

The inspector wouldn't help us.

The inspector was the grey-haired old man from Crompton Place.

MAYA

Chapter 21

In those few moments when I did eventually fall asleep, I kept having the same dream. It was dark, just the full moon lighting the way. I was in some woods, running, the branches scratching at my nightdress. In the distance, I saw Jamie. He walked through the trees slowly, without a care in the world. I called out to him, but he couldn't hear me. I called again, telling him to stop. To wait. To wait for me. But he still couldn't hear. I ran faster, my hair whipping around my face, sharp twigs and branches digging and slicing into my bare feet. But I wasn't moving forwards. It was as if I was stuck behind an invisible wall, and Jamie was getting further and further away from me. I glanced at my feet, and there was so much blood oozing out from the cuts. I looked behind me and noticed a trail of it, sticky and glistening and bright, bright red, where I'd been. I screamed out his name frantically, but no sound came out, and he still couldn't hear me. Wild with fear, I put all my effort into a last burst of energy. I had to get to him. Make him stop. I yelled as hard as I could, and this time he did hear. He was so far away that his features were blurred, apart from maggots writhing around in his empty eye sockets. He raised a hand, waving. And then he turned away from me and walked off, disappearing into the trees that swallowed him whole.

I screamed myself awake, my breath coming in jagged bursts, convinced I could hear Jamie saying, *Maya, I'm leaving now.*

My pillow was wet with tears and cold sweat, the sheets in a tangle around my legs. I wanted to pull the covers over my head and never get out of bed. Wanted to rewind my life to before Jamie was killed. Do something differently. Maybe I could've stopped it happening somehow. If only Jamie had talked to me. We could've dealt with whatever was going on together. I could've kept him safe. Why hadn't he trusted me enough to tell me what was going on?

My mobile phone rang on my bedside table. It was Ava.

'Hiya, Maya,' she said sombrely. 'I'm not going to be nice to you, so don't panic.'

I sighed, rubbing a hand over my sweaty face. How much wine had I drunk last night? I had to stop drinking, but I couldn't. 'I don't think I can do this today. I don't want to go.'

'You can. You have to say goodbye.'

'I don't want to remember him in a coffin.' I blinked up at the ceiling. A waft of stale sweat hit me from the sheets. I wasn't about to wash them. Not when I could still smell him. I couldn't wash away all traces of him. Not yet. 'It's not that I don't care, of course it's not. God, anything but that. It's because I still love him so much, I can't face seeing it. It means it's really final. Would it look bad if I didn't go? I don't think I can handle it.'

She paused. 'I know how you feel. I'm not going to force you to do anything, but I think it will actually help the grieving process. This is a way to say your goodbyes. It is final because it has to be. If there's no finality, you can't start to rebuild your life.'

I wiped the tears streaming down my cheeks. 'I don't want to rebuild my life without him.'

'Oh, hon, you say that now, and that's completely understandable.'

'Just because funerals are expected, who says they're right for everyone that's left behind? I'm not ready. I can't go.'

'I don't know what to say.' Then she added, 'Bitch,' trying to lighten the mood and make a joke.

It didn't work. 'I mean, really, why do we have to have funerals? Why can't we say goodbye in our own time?'

'People will expect you to be there. It's all arranged. Your friends are coming. Jamie's colleagues. They'll be saying goodbye, too.'

'But would they really care if I wasn't there? And what happens after, at the wake, when they're all standing around talking about him as if they knew him, when no one knew him like me. And making stupid comments and offering condolences that aren't going to bring him back!'

'Everyone's going to understand that you'll be upset. And I'm going to be there to support you. I'll be holding your hand every step of the way. Say the word and I'll take you back home on your own.'

I sniffed. 'You promise?'

'With all my heart. I'm dropping Jackson off at Craig's parents' at twelve, and I'll collect him after the wake. I'll pick you up at half past, okay?'

I wiped my eyes again. I didn't know how I still had any tears left. I was exhausted with crying. With worrying. With struggling to find an answer. Exhausted with living. 'Sorry to be so difficult. I don't want to be like this, I just...'

'You're not at all. Of course you're not. I want to give you a hug.'

I stayed in bed, unable to will myself to get moving.

Finally, when I knew I couldn't delay the moment I'd have to get ready any longer, I dressed in black trousers and a black polo-neck jumper. My slow, shaky movements belonged to a ninety-year-old instead of a thirty-seven-year-old. Everything seemed impossible—

breathing, walking, standing—and yet somehow I put one foot in front of the other, even though my world crumbled a little more with each step.

I made it down the stairs. Sat in Ava's car next to her as Craig drove behind the hearse to the church. I said hello to Paul and Jamie's other colleagues. Accepted warm, sympathetic hugs from Becca and Lynn, and my other friends and people I worked with. Watched the vicar without listening to his words. He didn't know Jamie. I bet he said the same thing every time he held a funeral. I didn't bother mouthing the words to songs I didn't give a shit about. I stared at the flowers people had left. Numb. Frozen. As if it was happening to someone else. I watched the coffin disappearing into the freshly dug grave. Disappearing. And all the time I thought, *This isn't real.*

Then somehow Ava and Craig were guiding me away, and I was back at their house, where Ava pressed a glass of wine into my hand. People milled around, chatting in sombre voices, flicking sad looks in my direction as I sat in the kitchen. I couldn't stand. My legs wouldn't hold me up anymore. I didn't want to talk. Didn't want to be there. Becca and Lynn hovered beside me, tears in their eyes. People bustled in and out. Kissed me. Took hold of my hands and squeezed them. Gave condolences. Left cards on the table for me. Said what a lovely service it was and other inane things that made me want to strangle them. More wine. More chatter. Finger food that I couldn't touch. Everything was hazy around the edges, as if I was being sucked underground, somewhere I couldn't breathe, being buried alive. I was a spectator in my own life, hanging on by a strand of the finest silk. A scream was barely stifled beneath the surface.

And then suddenly it was dark outside, the house was empty, and Ava was sitting next to me, squeezing my hand, not saying anything.

We sat in silence for I didn't know how long before I stood up, clutching onto the table for support. 'I need to go home.'

'Do you want to stay here?'

'No. I need to be on my own.'

She opened her mouth to speak but then appeared to think better of it and pulled me into a tight hug. 'Just phone me if you need me.' She let me go, picked up the condolence cards people had left on the table, and shuffled them into a neat pile before walking me out to her car with them in her hand. She put them in the centre cubby box and drove back to my house. Jamie's house. She pulled up on the drive, and I got out.

'Thank you for today,' I said. 'I couldn't have done it without you.'

She waved my words away. 'I just wish I could make things better for you.' I turned to leave, and she said, 'Wait, take the cards. At some point, you'll want to look through them, I'm sure.'

I took them, knowing full well that I wouldn't. Could never bring myself to.

I opened the door to the cold, empty house and thought, *That's it. The end of everything. Jamie's life is really over.*

JAMIE

Chapter 22

There were more parties. More drink. More drugs. More themes. More games that always ended in rape and abuse.

One night the theme was hide and seek. The men gave us ten minutes to find a suitable hiding place, and as my friends ran in different directions, I headed down a corridor that led to the back of the house, finding myself in a room I'd never seen before. A library. Whole walls were lined with book-filled shelves. It had a couple of dark green leather chairs and an antique mahogany desk in the corner with photographs on top. I glanced briefly at images of the judge, pictured in his robes and wig with several important-looking people in fancy uniforms, before my eyes scanned the room for somewhere to go where they'd never, ever find me.

Footsteps came closer to the door. My heart beat wildly, threatening to explode in my chest. There was nowhere to hide that they wouldn't find me easily. I saw the deep green curtains and darted behind them, flattening myself against the wall and rearranging the fabric around me carefully. I looked at the sash window behind me and tried to lift it, but as always, it was locked.

The door creaked open. My pulse hammered in my ears so loud

I thought he would be able to hear it.

'Where are you?' the policeman said in a sing-song voice. 'I know someone's in here. I can smell you.' I could no longer hear where he was, as the thick carpet masked his steps. 'Under the desk, I wonder…no, not there. Hmm…well, there's only one place left to hide.'

I squeezed my eyes tighter. Pressed myself flatter against the wall and the edge of the windowsill.

I could dive through the glass. Drop to the ground and run. Run and run and just keep running. I could—

He pulled the curtain back, and an evil grin snaked up the corners of his lips. 'Looks like I've got my prize!' He held out his hand. 'Come on, then. Let's have a few drinks before we *really* get started.'

My gaze darted back to the window. *I could bash my head against the glass. I could kill myself. I could die, and it would all be over.*

'Let's go.' His voice hardened.

I couldn't do any of those things.

When we arrived back in the lounge, Billy, Sean, and Trevor were already there, along with a boy I'd never seen before. He was about eight years old, biracial with smooth cinnamon skin and green eyes. He was beautiful. A paedophile's dream. His eyelids drooped with the concoction of drink and drugs he'd obviously been given.

'Look what I've got. Special delivery!' The judge chuckled raucously, his eyes gleaming with excitement as he said to the other men, 'I bet you're all jealous.'

'Want to share?' The banker grinned greedily.

The judge looked down at the boy, who had now mercifully fallen into a drugged sleep on the sofa. 'Why not? There's plenty to go round.'

'Let's go to the dungeon.' The children's minister smirked.

They finished their drinks, and all the men disappeared with the boy. Billy, Trevor, Sean, Dave, and I darted scared looks at each other as we drank and drank in that locked room, trying to numb ourselves, because we'd all been in the dungeon before. It was downstairs in the basement. The walls were painted black, with chains, ropes, and whips hanging from them. A big wrought-iron bed was against the centre of the back wall with handcuffs attached to the head and footboard. It smelt of decay and dead things, and spots of dark purply-red were on the floor. A video camera was set up on a tripod in front of the bed. There had been another 'special guest' in the room with me and the other men. Someone who wore a long black cape with a hood, his face covered with a mask. And I'd thought they were going to kill me down there as they'd killed that other boy in front of my eyes.

Hours later, after Sean had been sick in a wastepaper basket, I'd passed out on the sofa and was woken by the door being unlocked. The bearded MP's hair was messed up, strands out of place and falling over his ears. The judge was red-faced. The policeman had a tiny speck of what looked like blood on his cheek. The children's minister was breathing heavily and sweating.

A cold knot of terror ripped through my insides. I knew what was going to happen next.

And I knew what had happened to that poor, helpless boy.

MAYA

Chapter 23

Jamie was the first thing I thought of when I woke up. The last thing at night. And all the hours in between. I couldn't shake the sadness. The emptiness. I couldn't face going back to work, even though Ava thought it would take my mind off things, but I also couldn't face being in the house any longer, alone. I knew I couldn't go on like this forever. I had to make a start on trying to get through this. Rebuild my life. Somehow.

And the questions in my head refused to go away. What was Jamie doing before he was snatched away from me? What did the list have to do with it? Had he been involved in something dangerous, criminal? Had he witnessed something? Were those men on the list friends of Jamie's? Friends I'd never known existed? Had someone really murdered Jamie? Or was I going mad?

No. I was convinced someone *had* killed Jamie, and somehow I was going to prove it. I just didn't know how. Didn't know where to look anymore.

Two weeks after the funeral, I forced myself to open the condolence cards Ava had given me and the ones that came through the post. They all said pretty much the same thing. *Sorry for your loss. My condolences. We'll miss him. Thinking of you. Sending our love.* All except the last one, which, according to the postmark, had been delivered a few days ago.

I slid my forefinger under the flap of the envelope and tore it open. It had a sepia-coloured photograph on the front. A man with his back to the camera, walking along a seashore, the sun shining over the ocean, the words *In Sympathy* in bold white at the centre. Something about the photo reminded me of Jamie. How he loved to walk in the country, in the woods. How he loved the outdoors and large open spaces. How he was a loner.

I put it down on the kitchen table. Poured yet another glass of wine. Stared at the photo. I took a sip of wine and picked up the card again. Inside it read:

Dear Maya,

You don't know me, but I knew Jamie. I'm sorry I missed the funeral. It must've been very difficult. I have some information about Jamie's death that you may want to hear. I've thought long and hard about whether to tell you or not. In the end, I decided you should know, then you can make up your own mind.

Call me on this number 07580 3657789, but don't call from your mobile or landline. Don't tell anyone or go to the police, either. You'll understand why after we speak, but your safety depends on it.

Mitchell

I sat rigid, reading the words again and again as they ricocheted around my head like bullets.

Who was this Mitchell person? I didn't know anyone of that name, and I'd never heard Jamie mention him. A thought flashed into my head that it was a trap. If the person who murdered Jamie suspected I knew something, were they intending to kill me, too, and make my death look like an accident or another suicide?

Your safety depends on it.

There was only one way to find out. I grabbed my bag and walked into town, stopping at the first phone box I found. I hadn't used one since I was a kid and realised that they didn't take coins anymore. I needed to buy a phone card, so I walked to the newsagents, purchased one, and walked back. I opened the door, stepping over a broken bottle. By the time I put the card in and dialled the mobile number, my heart was pounding, a pulse in my temple twitching, a nauseous feeling rising in my stomach.

The number rang in my ear. Once. Twice. Three times. On the fourth, a deep voice answered.

'Hello?'

I started to speak, but my tongue felt as though it was blocking my dry mouth.

'Hello?' the voice said again.

I panicked and put the phone down, my heart racing into overdrive.

I swallowed. Reached out a hand to the glass wall to steady myself. Swallowed again. Licked my cracked, dry lips.

I picked up the phone and dialled.

'Hello?' the voice answered.

'Hello. This is Maya,' I blurted out before I could change my mind again.

'Maya,' he said. 'Thanks for ringing me. You got the card, I take it?'

'Yes. Can you tell me what this is all about?'

'Not on the phone. Can we meet somewhere?'

I hesitated, thinking of some kind of trap again. 'Why can't you tell me on the phone?'

'Lots of reasons, but we really need to do this face-to-face. I've got something for you. Something of Jamie's you probably want to see.'

'What is it?'

'Again. Not on the phone.'

'Can't you post it to me?'

'It's not the kind of thing you'd want to fall into the wrong hands. Or to get lost. We can meet somewhere out in the open, where there are lots of people. You choose the place.'

'Where are you?'

'North London, but I can meet wherever you want.'

My mind suddenly went blank as I tried to think of somewhere. Did I want this person coming to St Albans? What if they followed me home? But then they'd posted the card, so they already knew where I lived. 'How about Molly's? It's a café on St Peter's Street in St Albans.'

'Okay. When and what time?'

'Can you make it today?'

'No, I'm afraid not. Tomorrow? I can get there by ten.'

'Okay,' I said breathlessly. 'Ten tomorrow.'

'I'll see you then. And Maya…I'm really sorry about Jamie.'

'Thank you.'

'It's very important that you don't tell anyone about this. Your safety is at risk if you do.'

'Why not? Is it—' But the dialling tone sounded in my ear then as Mitchell hung up, cutting me off.

I stared at the receiver, trying to work out how I was going to get through the next twenty-four hours. What did he have of Jamie's, and whose were the 'wrong hands' he didn't want it to fall into?

When I got back home, I wondered if I was safe there anymore. Someone had definitely been in here before, I was sure of it now. Someone who'd done a tidy search. Someone who'd probably wiped Jamie's laptop, his satnav. Someone who'd probably planted in the shed the rope that they'd strung Jamie up with. Would they come back for me? Should I go somewhere else? A friend's? Ava's? I didn't want to mention this to any of them because they wouldn't believe me. They'd say I was depressed, in denial, confused, seeing connections where there weren't any. I supposed I could tell Ava I didn't want to be in the house on my own anymore, but what if she and Jackson were dragged into this? Whatever *this* was. Something terrible was going on, something that had got Jamie killed, and I couldn't put them in danger, too.

I watched the clock. Paced the floor. Wrapped my cardigan tighter round me in the cold. Jumped at every creak in the house. I made myself eat a sandwich. Avoided alcohol for once so I could be clear-headed. That night I lay on the sofa with all the lights on in the house.

I waited. And waited. At some point, I fell into a restless sleep, then something jerked me awake. My heart thumped wildly. I strained my ears, listening for the sound of someone breaking in— the turn of a doorknob, footsteps creaking, a window shattering. I searched the room for something to use as a weapon and picked up a heavy vase.

But there was nothing. No sounds. No movement. The house was empty, except for Jamie's ghost and me. I lifted the corner of the curtain in the lounge that overlooked the front of the house and saw a fox rummaging around in the black rubbish bag a neighbour had left next to their overflowing wheelie bin. Then the corner of my eye caught movement further down the street, at the end of the cul-de-sac, but as soon as I turned my head, it was gone. Had someone been walking down the street? A friend of a neighbour who'd been visiting? Or something more sinister?

I let the curtain fall, my heart pounding, and clutched the vase. I watched the clock. Wondered. Thought. Terrified myself with possibilities. With questions.

I was a nervous wreck by the time I walked into Molly's twenty minutes early the next morning. I stood by the door, surveying the customers already inside. A young couple was at one of the tables, holding hands and laughing about something. In the corner, an elderly woman sipped a cup of tea and smiled at me. A man walked out of the toilets at the rear. He was in his thirties, with dark cropped hair and a thick beard. Was that him? He glanced at me briefly then sat at a table with a woman and a young girl who was licking the icing off a sticky bun.

I walked to the counter and ordered a double espresso. The door opened. A woman walked in and queued behind me. I took my drink and sat in a private corner away from everyone, where we could talk without being overheard, my gaze firmly fixed on the door as I fidgeted with my hands.

Ten minutes later, a man entered. He was medium height, stocky, broad-shouldered, probably late fifties, maybe older, but looked very fit for his age. He had a smoothly shaved head and a round face. He wore jeans and a white T-shirt, even though it was February and really cold. Sleeves of tattoos were visible up the length of both well-muscled arms. He had a small white plastic bag in a large meaty hand.

Our gazes met.

He smiled. It was warm, friendly. Not a psycho *I-killed-your-boyfriend-now-I'm-going-to-kill-you* smile. But it crossed my mind that he could easily kill me. Crush my windpipe in a second with those hands.

He walked towards my table. 'Maya.'

I swallowed and nodded.

'I'm Mitchell.'

'Hi.' I'd pictured him in my head, but he hadn't looked anything like this. And the more I looked at him, the more I thought I'd seen him before, but I couldn't place where.

'Can I get you another drink?'

I looked at my half-touched, now cold coffee, wanting to scream, *No! Just get on with it! Just tell me why you're here! What's going on?* Instead, I said, 'No, this is fine, thanks.'

'Okay. I'll be back in a minute.'

I observed him as he went to the counter and ordered. He came back, sat down with his back to the wall, placed the bag on the table in front of us, his gaze scanning around him, and that was when it hit me. The petrol station. He'd been filling his car up when my bag had split open.

A cold vibration washed over me. 'I've seen you before. You were at the petrol station.'

He looked at me but didn't say anything.

'Were you following me?'

Reluctantly, he nodded. 'Yes, but it's probably not what you think.'

'I don't even know *what* to think anymore,' I hissed, pins and needles jabbing into my skull. 'Why have you been following me?'

'I was following you to make sure no one else was.'

'Who? What's this about?' I leant forward. 'What happened to Jamie?' I asked, unable to wait any longer. 'You said you had some information. Please, just tell me what you know.'

He rested his elbows on the table, his voice deep and low. 'Like I said in the card, I didn't know whether to tell you or not. I thought maybe it was better for you not to know the truth. I thought eventually you'd be able to move on without ever finding out. And I have been watching you, but it was only to make sure that no one's after you. But...'

'But what?'

He tapped his paper coffee cup. 'In the end, I thought that it wasn't my judgement to make. I thought you should know what happened to Jamie. And where you've been going, what you've been doing, I realised you were looking for answers, anyway, and were going to get yourself in trouble. And if it was me, I'd want to know the truth. There have been too many lies.' He took a sip of his drink and watched me carefully over the rim.

I stared at him, blinking. 'What happened to Jamie? What was he involved in?'

His gaze searched mine for a moment. 'This is going to be a shock.'

'It can't be more of a shock than I've already had.'

He studied me hard. Shook his head. Ran his hands over his cheeks. Sighed. 'Shit. This was a bad idea. I've handled it all wrong. Maybe I shouldn't have told you. I'm sorry.' He stood up as if he was going to leave.

'You haven't told me anything!' I said. 'What is it? What happened to Jamie? I need to know.'

He sighed again, looking as if he was battling with some internal decision. Sat back down. 'Maybe you should just trust me on this one. I was wrong. You shouldn't get involved.'

'Trust you? Trust you?' I cried. 'I don't even know you! You tell me you've been watching me, for fuck's sake! Do you know how creepy that sounds?'

'It wasn't creepy. It was necessary. I was protecting you, like Jamie would've wanted.'

'Then tell me why. Explain! For all I know, you could've had something to do with Jamie's death yourself!'

'I had *nothing* to do with it.' His lips hardened into a thin line.

'You *have* to tell me what's going on. I need to know. I *deserve* to know. And I'm already involved. I found out some things. Jamie was going to see some people in the week before he was killed. But I don't know why. Can you give me any answers? Fill in the blanks? If you can, you have to help me. *Please.*' My eyes watered.

His hesitated, glancing around the café before leaning in towards me. 'Jamie got in touch with me before he died. He wanted some advice.'

'About what?'

He took a sip of coffee. 'About how to deal with something from his past. He thought I might be able to help him.'

I frowned. 'What kind of thing?' I wailed, clenching my fists.

The elderly woman glanced over at us then dropped her gaze when I caught her looking.

I lowered my voice. 'Look, I don't understand what's going on. Please, just tell me. I don't think he killed himself. What happened to him? Who did it? What was he involved in?'

His lips pursed into a thin line as he studied me again. 'Are you sure you really want to know? I'm certain they killed him because of it. They may come after you.'

I let out a bitter snort. 'Of course I want to know. I don't care about me. My life's not exactly a thrilling barrel of laughs at the moment, is it? I don't have anything to lose anymore. I have to know what happened to him. And whatever it was, I don't think it's just Jamie who was murdered. I found a list of names and addresses Jamie made, and I've been visiting them. One person, Dave, was killed the day after Jamie died. Another one, Billy, apparently also committed suicide a year ago. One has mental health problems. One is apparently in America. And the other one, Moses, disappeared thirty years ago. What the hell was going on, Mitchell?'

'Dave's dead, too? Shit.' A frown creased his brow, and he looked over my shoulder, apparently deep in thought. 'How?'

'A hit-and-run.'

'How convenient.' A flash of hatred burned in his piercing blue eyes.

'Just *tell me!*'

He dragged his gaze back to me, talking so quietly I had to lean closer, straining my ears to hear the words. 'Jamie knew things about...certain people. Very important people. Things that happened years ago. He'd tried to forget about them. Pushed them out of his mind for a long time, but he couldn't anymore. He was going to blow the lid off it, but he knew no one would believe him and that it would be his word against theirs. That's why he was talking to the other people involved.'

I pulled Jamie's list out of my bag and unfolded it on top of the table. 'These people? These are the other people involved?'

Mitchell picked up the list. 'Yes. Jamie needed corroboration. Other witnesses to come forward. Because it happened so long ago, there would be no evidence now, so he needed the others. He'd spent months locating them via the Internet and various other enquiries. In the week before he died, he was going round to talk to them, to see if they'd be willing to give their accounts, too, before Jamie made it official.'

I put a hand to my mouth. The espresso curdled in my stomach.

'But these people Jamie wanted to expose are powerful. Dangerous.' He folded the list back up and placed it on the table. 'If you really want to know what was going on, you need to read this first. Then decide what you're dealing with.' He opened the bag, pulled out a small black computer flash drive, and handed it to me.

'What's on here?'

'A diary. Kind of. There's an untraceable pay-as-you-go mobile phone in the bag, too. If you want to go further with this, call me with it when you've read what Jamie wrote. Then we'll talk.'

I pulled out an old Nokia from the bag. It was so old and big it felt like a brick in my hand.

'Is someone watching me? I think someone broke into our house the day Jamie was killed. I think they wiped his laptop and satnav and took his last few months' phone bills and his mobile phone for some reason. I found another phone I'd never seen before that Jamie had hidden with the list, too.'

'Yes, it's also an untraceable pay-as-you-go. He started using it when he became suspicious that they might be watching him. It looks like they're cleaning up loose ends. Getting rid of evidence.'

'But are they watching me?'

'I don't think so. I haven't spotted anyone. They probably bugged Jamie's house and his landline and mobile. Maybe his Jeep, too. Somehow they found out what Jamie was doing and then silenced him. The same as they've done with Dave—maybe Billy, too. But I suspect they think they've contained it. If they thought you knew something, you would've been taken out with Jamie in some kind of double accident. But you need to take precautions, just in case.'

I tried to take in the words.

Contained. Double accident. Bugged. Taken out.

They were just too bizarre. It sounded like something from a film. Some kind of conspiracy thriller. And I didn't know this guy. Didn't know whether I could trust him, but...something told me I was going to have to.

'This has to be kept a secret, Maya. You can't let anyone suspect you know something. If they find out, they *will* come after you. That's why you need to think carefully whether you want to open this can of worms.' He stood up, leaving his untouched coffee on the table, and walked to the doorway.

I shot up and followed him. 'Wait! Why you? Why did Jamie want advice from you? Who are you?'

'If you really want to know the truth, just read it. Read it and then phone me again.' And he slipped out the door and into the throng of people, leaving me staring at his back.

JAMIE

Chapter 24

When the bell startled me awake one Sunday morning, I blinked my eyes open to the sight of an empty bed. I shot upright as horrific thoughts whipped through my mind. Dave had been taken by Scholes or Barker and would be one of the boys who never came back. Then I noticed his bedclothes were missing, and terror welled up inside me.

He'd hanged himself as Billy had tried to.

I jumped out of bed and rushed to the dormitory door. Peering out, I checked the hallway and stairs, but there was no sign of Dave. I rushed into the shower and toilet block, but he wasn't there either. It was then I noticed the window behind his bed was open slightly. The other boys whispered, 'Where's Dave?' 'Has he killed himself?' 'He's better off if he has.'

'Look here!' I beckoned them to the window and opened it fully as we crowded round to get a good look. Just below us was the flat roof of a big storage room connected to the kitchen. It was an extension, built at a later date to the original building. From there it was an eight-metre drop to the grass below, and I saw a sheet tied to the metal guttering, flapping in the wind, that he'd used to climb down. I didn't know how he'd managed to scale the boundary wall, but somehow Dave had escaped.

We all pumped fists in the air and cheered for him, and we were so busy being happy for Dave, we didn't notice Scholes entering the room.

'Silence!' he shouted, making us all freeze. 'What's going on here? Why aren't you dressed?' He marched over to the window as we tried to disperse out of his way. The nearest person to him would get the brunt of his anger.

'Who was it?' Scholes thundered at us. 'Who got out?' His gaze darted all around, trying to work out who was missing. He grabbed Trevor by the ear, twisting it hard. 'Who got out? Where is he?'

Trevor turned his head, following the direction of Scholes's hand pulling him downwards. 'Argh!'

Scholes twisted harder. Tears trickled down Trevor's cheeks.

'It was Dave!' Trevor cried when he could take no more.

Scholes shoved Trevor away and rushed out.

There was no breakfast for anyone that morning as Barker and Scholes and the other staff rushed around, checking the grounds. Then the police were called. We were all locked in our dorms, but we saw their car bursting up the drive. Saw Barker's heated exchange then saw them depart again.

We all prayed for Dave in our own ways, willing him to be far away from there by then. I hoped we'd be talking about this for years to come. We'd tell the new kids who arrived how Dave had managed to escape. How he'd outwitted them all. And we'd invent stories about where he'd gone, which would become more outlandish with time. He was living in a palace. He'd stowed away on a boat to Australia. He'd hitched a ride to Scotland or was living on an island in the middle of nowhere. He'd been adopted by a rich family.

Two days passed, and Dave didn't return. Someone came to weld bars on the outside of the windows. We were locked in the refectory during meal times. Locked in the dorms at night. There was no free time outside. The staff kept an even closer eye on us.

On the third day, Dave was brought back. From the common room window, I saw him dragged from the rear of a police car and frogmarched up to the building. He didn't return to the dorm for another three days, and when he did, he was black and blue.

After lights out, we whispered questions to him. 'Where did you go?' 'How far did you get?' 'What did you eat?' 'Where did you sleep?'

But Dave didn't tell us. He ignored our questions and simmered away with anger and frustration.

Dave tried to run away three more times after that, and each time he was brought back. I wished I'd had his fight, but I didn't. I was damaged, destroyed, decayed.

Around that time, the parties stopped. We were fifteen, and I think we'd become too old for their twisted predilections. Every Friday instead, we watched a group of the younger boys being driven away with Barker, returning on Saturdays with that haunted, dead look in their eyes. I wanted to reach out to them, but what could I say? I couldn't comfort them or tell them everything would be okay. And I still couldn't speak the unspeakable.

Barker and Scholes also seemed to lose interest in us then, too. Younger boys were taken in the night, or often in broad daylight, only to return like mirror images of our younger selves. Although the sexual abuse had ended, the physical abuse continued right up until my sixteenth birthday, when I was ordered to Barker's office and presented with a ten-pound note and a letter releasing me from care. A social worker arrived and drove me to a hostel, where I would be spending the next two years. An appointment was set up at the job centre for me on Monday morning.

When I walked out of the hostel on Monday, I strolled into town, marvelling at my new freedom. I could go anywhere I wanted. Be anything I wanted. But I wasn't going to stick around in case they decided to take me back to that place. Instead of going to the job centre, I went straight to the nearest army recruitment office and signed up. I was going to make something of myself. Learn a trade while I was in there and never look back. I was going to bury deep all the years of my childhood, somewhere they'd never come out. I was going to forget. Jamie Taylor would be reinvented.

I wouldn't say the basic army training was easy. I was a skinny, undernourished teenager, but I'd had years of taking verbal and physical abuse, and compared to the previous eight years, initiation into army life was nothing. I joined the Royal Signals as an apprentice, and my desperation to put the past behind me and build a new life for myself was a huge motivator to get through it. It was that motivation and single-minded determinedness that made me stand out in the ranks of my fellow recruits. My grades in all elements of my training were at the high end, and as my recruit was nearing completion, I was in line for champion recruit, which brought me to the attention of various signals regiments recruitment teams, who persuaded me to apply for spec ops training. I spent the next six years in 299 Signal Squadron Special Communications, supporting the Foreign and Commonwealth Office operations in the UK and overseas. Being in spec ops suited me. It meant I was rarely in uniform as I was generally working abroad in various overseas embassies. We wore civvies most of the time, and there was none of the usual bullshit we had to put up with in the Green Army—no senior NCOs telling me what to do. With spec ops, we operated in a more grown-up fashion and were left to get on with it—a mutual trust and respect thing, which suited me perfectly. I really enjoyed the work, and I learnt a lot. However, after six years, it was time to move on to the next chapter in my life, so I resigned from the army and started my career in specialist IT with the skills I'd amassed.

I worked hard, saved money, made myself comfortable. Blocked out the horrors of the past. Until that day when he appeared on my TV, and I knew that I couldn't keep the secret any longer. I wanted justice. For me, for my friends, for all the boys they'd abused. For those they'd murdered. For all the innocence they'd stolen and crushed and turned into something worthless and warped.

So one by one, I found out who they were. I already knew some things about them, and it didn't take long for me to find out more.

The owner of 10 Crompton Place, the high court judge, was Howard Sebastian. He died four years ago.

The children's minister, well, I already had his name: Eamonn Colby.

The other MP, Douglas Talbot, was now the defence secretary.

The high-ranking police officer was Colin Reed, now the chief constable of Bedfordshire Police.

The children's home inspector was Ted Byron, now retired.

The banker turned out to be from an old banking family, owner of the largest privately owned bank in the UK: Felix Barron.

Keith Scholes was also retired.

Geoff Barker, thankfully, had died of lung cancer.

I still didn't know who the hooded man was in the dungeon. But I was getting closer.

PART 2

UNTOUCHABLE

"If you tell a lie big enough and keep repeating it, people will eventually come to believe it. The lie can be maintained only for such time as the State can shield the people from the political, economic, and/or military consequences of the lie. It thus becomes vitally important for the State to use all of its powers to repress dissent, for the truth is the mortal enemy of the lie, and thus by extension, the truth is the greatest enemy of the State."

~ Joseph Goebbels

MAYA

Chapter 25

After meeting Mitchell, I hurried back home with Jamie's flash drive safely in my bag, clutched tightly to my side. Did I want to know what was contained on it? How could I not find out? Could I trust Mitchell? I didn't know.

Mitchell's words echoed in my head. *Jamie knew things about certain people. Very important people. Things that happened years ago. If they find out, they* will *come after you.*

Someone had gone to great lengths to kill Jamie and cover things up. Someone didn't want me to find out what Jamie had wanted to expose.

So the question was, was I prepared to put myself in danger, too, if I read whatever was on the flash drive?

And the answer? I didn't know.

I closed the curtains, even though it was still broad daylight, and turned on a lamp. Pacing the lounge, I chewed the skin around my thumb until I drew blood, staring at the flash drive on the arm of the sofa.

The answer was: I *had* to know. Even if I put myself in danger, it didn't matter. Nothing mattered except finding out who had murdered Jamie and why.

I slid the flash drive into my laptop and opened up the only document on it.

Curled up on the sofa, I read what Jamie had written, my shoulders stiff, my cheeks streaked with tears, shivering. I read about the unimaginable horrors. The torture, the murders, the parties, the terrible abuse.

Jamie had lied to me about his past. His parents hadn't died in a car accident at sixteen, and that wasn't why he'd gone into the army. The childhood photos they'd taken of him when he was a kid hadn't got lost when they'd moved house. He hadn't lived in a middle-classed home in London growing up. He'd invented a new past. Hidden the truth because he couldn't bear to speak about it. Afraid I wouldn't love him anymore once I knew. But it just made me love him more. I couldn't begin to imagine what it had done to his psyche. He'd fought back. Dragged himself from those gates of hell and made a life for himself. He was so much stronger than he gave himself credit for, and I wished with all my shattered heart that he were here so I could tell him that.

You shouldn't have kept it all a secret from me, Jamie. I would've understood. I would've loved you anyway. I would've been there at your side. I would've had your back.

I shut my laptop. I didn't need to read it again. Jamie's words were etched permanently in my brain. I would need to hide the flash drive somewhere, though. The people who'd searched the house had probably been looking for it, too.

I walked into the kitchen on jellied legs, poured myself a brandy, and dropped onto a chair. I sipped slowly, thinking, wondering what the hell to do next, a paralysing chill gripping me.

The sun set behind the blinds and rose the next morning, and still my mind churned.

So now I knew the truth. Or most of it. Part of me wanted to curl into a ball and weep, or sleep and never wake up again. Never have to think about the awfulness of it all. It would be so easy. I could get some sleeping tablets from my GP. I could join Jamie. I'd never have to spend the rest of my life without him. But...

The suffocating, brutal grief that overwhelmed me was replaced by something else.

Anger.

A seething, writhing anger that eclipsed everything else. They'd stolen his childhood, and now they'd stolen his life to shut him up. My beautiful Jamie. How dare they? How fucking dare they?

I ignored the little voice in my head telling me how dangerous this would be. Ignored it when it told me to let the past stay in the past. That I might be next to befall some freak accident or staged suicide. Because I wasn't going to let them get away with it. I was going to finish what Jamie had started. I was going to expose them.

Somehow.

His death could not be for nothing.

I left the house, forgetting to put my coat on. As I walked along the street, my breath coiled around me in dragon-like vapour. I shivered and walked faster. And when I got to Veralamium Park, I sat on a bench overlooking the spires of St Albans Cathedral. I got the pay-as-you-go Nokia from my bag and turned it on. It was so old and basic, it had no Internet or GPS function. I didn't even know who Mitchell was, but if Jamie had trusted him with this, then I had to as well, so I dialled the only person I could.

'It's Maya.'

'You read it?'

'Yes.'

'So now you know.'

'I want to blow the lid off this.' My voice sounded hard as steel. 'I want them to pay for what they did.'

'Have you thought about what you'd be getting into? Who these people are? You already know what they're capable of.'

'I don't care! I can't live with this and not do anything. I think about all the lives they've ruined…how can I let them get away with that? What if they're still at it with other boys? Still abusing them? Murdering them? Somehow, I'm going to expose them.' I blew out a furious breath. 'I'm so bloody angry, Mitchell. Angry and sickened and devastated and repulsed and…so many things I can't even begin to name.'

'Believe me, I know exactly how you feel.' His voice was calm but had an undercurrent of something deadly in it.

'Then you understand I have to *do* something about it.'

'But how far are you prepared to go?'

I paused. I bit my lip.

'If they find out that you know, they will shut you down.'

'Or shut me up?'

'Same thing. So…what are you prepared to do about it? Because if this comes out, there's no going back.'

I knew what he was saying. The message in his words, his voice, was perfectly clear.

Was I prepared to die?

'There may be a way to expose them without revealing who you are or what you know,' Mitchell said before I could answer. 'I think we should meet. I'm sure you have a lot of questions, and you can decide where to go from here.'

'I do. When?'

'Can you come to London today?'

'Yes. Just tell me where and when and I'll be there.'

'How about Hyde Park? At noon? I'll meet you at the Diana Memorial Fountain.'

'Okay.'

'And Maya, they're assuming Jamie's secret died with him, otherwise they would've killed you already. But be careful. Watch out for people following you. Don't talk about this in the house. Don't talk about it on the landline or your own mobile. Only use the pay-as-you-go to phone me. And don't tell anyone else.' He hung up.

I didn't realise it was sleeting and I was bone-numbingly cold until I got back home. I hurriedly pulled on jeans, a thick black jumper, my black parka, and boots. I added a black beanie hat over my head and wore sunglasses so my face was obscured. Black for mourning. Now I had a purpose, I felt the strength lift me up, ignite in my stomach, and spread through every fibre of my body.

Watch out, you fuckers. I'm coming to get you.

Chapter 26

We sat on a bench in Hyde Park, probably looking like any regular couple out enjoying a rare sunny day in February.

Mitchell had a canvas backpack at his feet, which he nodded towards. 'I thought this might take a while, so I packed us some lunch.'

The thought of food hadn't even entered my head. A heavy nauseous sensation pressed against my stomach lining. I had so many questions they were tripping over themselves on my tongue.

'Why you?' I asked. 'Why did Jamie come to you? Are you a private investigator or something?'

He stared out at a family who were playing bat and ball on the grass in the distance. 'Several reasons. I met Jamie about a year ago at a squadron reunion in Hereford.'

'The reunion Lee organised?'

'Yes.'

'You were in the same regiment?'

'No. I started army life in the paras, but I spent most of my career down H, in Special Forces.'

'SAS?' My eyes widened.

'Yeah, 22 SAS to be precise. I was an A Squadron man for most of it.'

'I thought people who were in the SAS weren't meant to advertise that fact.'

'Well, normally I wouldn't. Because of the nature of what I did, it's obviously something I prefer to stay secret, but you're not just anyone, are you? This isn't exactly a normal situation.'

'So is your name really Mitchell?'

He gave me a wry smile.

'Or is it that if you tell me, you'll have to kill me?' I laughed, but it wasn't funny. 'Maybe you'll have to get in the queue now.'

'It doesn't matter what my name is. You just need to know I'm the good guy.'

I studied him for a moment. His face was inscrutable. 'I hope so.' I glanced down at my hands. 'Anyway, go on. You were saying how you met Jamie.'

'Well, like I said, I didn't cross paths with Jamie in the military. It was later, at the reunion. Jamie had worked with Lee in 299 Signal Squadron, then Lee was later recruited into 264 SAS Signal Squadron.'

'He never really spoke about his days in the army. It was so long ago by the time I met him. I knew he occasionally met up with some of the guys he served with, but he never said much about them.'

'Anyway, Jamie found out then that I'd...I'd lost my son.' Mitchell's jaw clenched. 'His name was Alex. He was seven years old and...he disappeared one day. It was 1985, and I was serving in Northern Ireland. My wife, Jo, couldn't contact me.' He leant forward, his elbows on his thighs, staring into the distance, a hard undercurrent to his voice. 'I didn't hear about it for two days. By the time I got special leave and came back, the police had found Alex's body.'

'Oh my God. I'm so sorry.' I reached out my hand to touch his, a gesture of sympathy, but unsure if that was the right thing to do, I let my hand just hover in the air.

He turned to look at me, his blue eyes full of pain, but with something else in there, too. Something fiery and dark.

I pulled my hand away.

'The last time Jo saw Alex, he was leaving the house to go to our local park. It was only two streets away. We lived in a nice neighbourhood. At that time, you didn't think about...those kinds of people living near you. Alex was tortured. Raped. And murdered. Dumped in a quiet country lane like a piece of rubbish.'

My hands flew to my cheeks and rested there a moment as his words stung my skin. And then I did touch his hand. Squeezed it. 'I'm so sorry.'

Mitchell glanced away and slid his hand from mine. 'He was obviously killed by a paedophile. But the police had no leads. No witnesses came forward. Forensic evidence wasn't advanced then. Alex had been washed and dressed in new clothes. Cheap trousers and a T-shirt you could buy in any Woolworth's at the time.' Mitchell delivered the lines calmly, in control, but there was a painful edge to his voice that was heartbreaking to hear. 'They never found who did it. I got involved myself. I spent hours knocking on doors, asking people who lived near the park and the lane where he was found if they'd seen or heard anything. But...' He pinched the bridge of his nose. 'Alex had just seemed to vanish. And when he came back to us, no one had seen a thing.

'Things hadn't been going well with Jo and me for a long time before that. Being a regiment wife, well, it takes its toll on relationships. We had Alex too young, and we were already at a strained point in our marriage, which was probably more my fault than hers. But even if we could've worked through our marital difficulties at the time, there was no way we were going to get through the murder of our child.'

I blinked back my own tears and cupped my hands around my mouth.

'She blamed me for not being there when it happened. I blamed her for not looking after him. I blamed myself for being away. Not being there to protect him. With so much blame and guilt and anger and sadness going around, we had no way to recover *us* from that.' He opened the backpack, took out a flask of tea, and handed me two plastic mugs. He poured steaming milky liquid into them and took one himself, then he sipped slowly before returning the flask to the hamper.

I pressed my cold hands around the warm mug.

'She never got over it, obviously. Eventually, we divorced. I threw myself into work as a way to forget, which worked for a long time. But then I started thinking about what I was doing for a living. Some of the things I had to do.'

'You mean…killing people?'

He took another sip. 'I mean, did it make it right that I was doing it in the name of Queen and country?' He shook his head bitterly. 'I couldn't justify it to myself anymore. All I kept seeing in my head was Alex. And I thought about the innocent casualties of war—the kids, the women, the civilians. I didn't want to be a part of it any longer.

'When I left the SAS, I went to work for a friend who'd set up a private military company.'

'*Private* military? What does that mean?'

'A private military company is very similar to government security, regular military, or the police. They carry out risk assessments for companies and provide VIP close protection, especially in hostile or high-risk territories. They do surveillance, due diligence, and other investigative work, train military or private security forces, test defence systems or government installations, and provide cyber security. And some of the more ruthless ones carry out a lot of other questionable things that would never be listed on a company's website.

'We were officially in Iraq to support the reconstruction initiative for the Big Boys, people like Recon5, which is what I wanted to do to feel like I was doing my part to bring some positive change to the country after all the destruction. But it didn't turn out like that. My company was providing private security for Recon5, who'd won a major government contract to rebuild infrastructure and provide services for the military, but all they did was scam the taxpayers.

'They were supposed to provide safe cleaning and cooking water for the troops, but it was all contaminated because they weren't spending the money on the water treatment plants that they were charging the government for. So those soldiers who didn't get a bullet would come home with pathogens in their blood that they didn't even know about.

'Then they were serving food to the troops only at certain times, instead of providing twenty-four-hour service, because it was cheaper. But that meant the enemy knew when the troops would be out of action and all congregated in the same place, so the mess halls got attacked. They were also overcharging the government for everything, even work already completed.

'The tents they provided to the military were mouldy, and soldiers were getting ill, but the Recon5 executives were staying in plush five-star hotels in Kuwait and driving round in fifty-thousand-dollar cars they didn't even need that they were leasing for two hundred fifty thousand dollars at a time.

'They brought new construction vehicles but didn't have any equipment to fix them when they went wrong because they couldn't charge for it. They didn't even have basic things like oil filters or spare tyres. What they'd do is set fire to a brand-new vehicle, which cost thousands, then bill the government and make more profit.'

'That's unbelievable!' I gasped. 'That's bloody fraud.'

'It's only the half of it. The list goes on and on. It was the *hugest* fraud, sanctioned by the government and paid for by the taxpayers, and they got away with it. All they were concerned with was making profits. They didn't give a shit about the soldiers on the ground or the Iraqi people.

'I made a lot of money doing it. More than I'll ever need. But what we did and the ethics of what Recon5 and the government were doing in Iraq affected me. I couldn't morally justify it anymore, so I resigned from the company. Of course, once I stopped working and it all settled down, I had time to think again, and Alex invaded every thought. I wondered what the hell I was doing with my life. Why wasn't I doing something to get those paedophiles off the street? Alex's life had to stand for something. So I became a paedophile hunter.'

'A what?' My forehead scrunched up, the blood draining from my face, my eyes wary and unblinking. 'You mean…you catch them and then…what? You kill them? You're a vigilante?'

He took a deep breath. 'No, I don't kill them. I'd like to, but after my career, I swore there would be no more killing.'

'So, what do you do, then?'

'I catch paedophiles. Not the VIP kind Jamie was involved with—the powerful public figures linked to the heart of the Establishment and beyond. The people I hunt are online predators. You wouldn't believe how many of them are out there.'

'So…God, I don't…this is a lot to take in. How do you…' I trailed off, not knowing what to ask. Not knowing if I wanted to know. 'Did Jamie want you to kill those…' I couldn't call them people. There was nothing about his abusers that made them human. They were inhumane. Evil. Sick. Psychopaths. 'Did he want you to kill those bastards?'

He glanced at me. Looked away. 'Like I said, I don't do that anymore. And anyway, if he'd wanted to, he could've killed them himself. He had combat skills.'

I chewed on my lip, glancing at a young mum pushing a small boy in a pushchair around the lake. He was bundled up in a red anorak and a fleecy bobble hat, one hand holding a toffee apple, one pointing with excited glee at the swans gliding across the water. 'But what if...what if you ever found out who'd murdered Alex? What would you do then?'

A flash of raw hatred flickered over his face, but he ignored the question. 'This wasn't about finding them and killing them,' Mitchell went on. 'Jamie wanted justice, not revenge. He wanted them exposed and convicted. He wanted the truth to come out. And he knew what I did now. He thought maybe I could help him with some contacts in the police who would see this through and not cover it up because of who was involved.'

I was consumed with an incandescent rage for what those men did to Jamie and the others, and I wondered briefly whether I could do it. Get hold of a gun, blow their brains out. Torture them. Run them over in the car. They had killed. Wasn't killing them a form of justice, too? How hard would it be? How easy? Could I live with myself? Would I get caught? Did I care?

I shook the thoughts away. Of course I couldn't kill anyone, no matter how much I fantasised about it.

'So how do you catch them, then?'

'I pretend to be a young girl or boy in chat rooms or on social media. Then I interact with the paedophiles online until they want to meet me. I record everything they say. Every stroke of their keyboard. All the disgusting, sick words. All the evidence of grooming. Then I hand everything over to the police and let them deal with it. It's a crime to befriend a child on the net or other means with the intention of abusing them. There are also new orders prohibiting adults from engaging in behaviour like sexual conversations with children online.'

'And the police actually use your evidence to convict them?'

Mitchell nodded. 'Preserved evidence is permissible to use.'

I was stunned, momentarily lost for words.

'Most of the time, they lie through their teeth when they're caught, denying they knew they were talking to an underage boy or girl. Deny the disgusting suggestions, the photos they send, the grooming, why they want to meet. They make ridiculous denials, but the evidence is always there. I never initiate contact with them online. I wait for them to come to me. I'm not trying to entrap them. They manage to do that very well themselves.'

'I can understand why you're doing it, but why not let the police deal with it?' As soon as the question was out of my mouth, I knew the answer. Some of the police were involved in it. I took a sip of tea, hoping the warm liquid would settle my stomach.

'Firstly, because they can't cope with the amount of people out there. They don't have the manpower or funding. And I know what you're thinking, after reading what Jamie wrote, and you'd be right. Some of the people involved are the police. They come from all walks of life.'

I blinked back the tears blurring my vision.

'The money I made when I was doing private military work means nothing. It's just a means that allows me to do this. And if I can get one sick bastard off the streets, then it helps to fill the void for a while. I can't sit there and just do nothing when I know it's going on all over the place.'

I shook my head. 'I want to get them, Mitchell.'

'You know this is going to get ugly and probably dangerous. Getting the truth to come out won't be easy. There will be cover-ups, enquiries will be quashed. These people are powerful. The elite. They have links to Westminster. To influential families. They will protect the Establishment—the System—at all costs. And they will stop at nothing to keep the truth from coming out.'

'I don't care. Like I said before, I don't have much to live for anymore. You of all people will understand that.'

He looked at me, studying the determination on my face.

'Will you help me? You obviously have some experience.'

'Yes, but not with the people involved here. And that's what I told Jamie. I warned him, too. I told him my contacts weren't high up enough to deal with the kind of person he was trying to expose, but he was determined to get the truth out there.'

'But will you?' I gripped his arm, holding on tight.

He paused, his biceps stiffening beneath my touch. 'All those kids…they were abused and tortured and treated as if their lives were nothing—they were like some disposable commodity—and they were just fucking kids! Just like Alex. I don't understand how we can breed the kind of people who do that.' He paused for a moment, grinding his teeth. 'So of course I'm going to help you. I couldn't live with myself if I didn't.'

'Thank you.' I released my grip and wiped my eyes. 'Was Jamie ever going to tell me what he was doing?'

'He was trying to work out *how* to tell you. It's not just something you can bring up casually at the dinner table, is it? He'd kept this secret for a long time. Become a different person. He was agonising about what this would do to you.'

Jamie had been going through all this alone, and he was worried about *me*? I stroked the ring on my left hand, a weight of unbearable misery crushing me.

'At first, he was trying to get the other lads who were with him at Crossfield to come forward, too. With cases of historic child abuse, you're talking about years that have gone by, which means there's no evidence. The only way to even get a hope of some heads rolling is with corroboration from other people. It wasn't too hard for Jamie to find out where these people were. He's an IT expert, after all.'

'Was,' I whispered, the word stinging my tongue like acid.

'Sorry.'

I gave him a brief flick of my head. 'How did they do it? How could they have hung him? I mean, he was in the military. He had training. He could look after himself.'

Mitchell pursed his lips. 'It doesn't mean he was infallible or didn't make a mistake. They could've surprised him, overpowered him, threatened him with a gun, threatened him with you.'

'Me?'

'They could've threatened to kill you. Or worse. Cripple, maim, mutilate you.'

A wave of dizziness hit me, as though I was falling. 'Oh God.' One hand clutched my stomach. 'So…he could've sacrificed his life to save me?'

Mitchell didn't answer. He just looked at me, but the answer was written in his eyes.

It took me a while to get my head round that. We sat in silence while I tried not to cry.

Eventually, I said, 'Remember I showed you the list Jamie had written? I went to see the people on it. I found Billy's brother, but apparently Billy committed suicide a year ago. Sean is now suffering from schizophrenia and is in and out of hospital, but I think, under his strange ramblings, he managed to tell me that he wasn't going to talk. Trevor moved to America somewhere, apparently, and like I said before, Dave was killed the day after Jamie in a hit-and-run accident.' I wiped away a tangle of hair that the wind blew in my face. 'There was another address for someone called Moses. I spoke to his mum, who said he disappeared in 1984. I saw a photo of him. He was biracial, beautiful. He was the second unknown boy who was at the party, wasn't he?'

'Yeah. The one who disappeared with all the men into the dungeon but was never seen by Jamie again. They obviously killed him, like the other boy who was strangled by Eamonn Colby.'

I rubbed at the tension in my forehead, trying to knead away tiny knots. 'So, there's no one who can or will corroborate anything?'

'Actually, in the end…Jamie had found a way to expose them that wouldn't point back to him. He phoned me the day before he died and said he'd got hold of something explosive. Something that wouldn't need corroboration from other witnesses. He didn't want to tell me what it was over the phone, but I'm guessing it was a film or photos. I was going away with Lee to climb Aconcagua the next day, so I arranged to call Jamie when I got back so we could meet and try to come up with a plan about who he could trust to pass it on to. But I never got that far. I was away for three and a half weeks, and when I got back, I found out he'd been killed.' He drew in a deep breath. 'Lee sends his condolences, by the way.'

'Thanks.' I nodded slowly, trying to get my head around everything. 'Where did Jamie get this "explosive" stuff?'

'From Dave. After every party at Crompton Place, Dave always used to steal something from the house. Usually something small that he could hide in his clothes. Jamie didn't tell me what Dave gave him, just that it was something no one could deny once they'd seen it. Dave had kept it all these years. It was his insurance.'

I thought about Dave's poor wife, Anita, who probably was blissfully unaware of what had happened in Dave's childhood, as I'd been about Jamie's. 'And then he was murdered, too.'

'Looks like it.'

'But how did they know what Jamie had found or what he was

doing? How did they know he was going to try to expose these people?'

'Maybe certain Internet searches were being monitored, or Jamie ended up speaking to the wrong person, who then tipped off someone high up. Someone with authority. Someone who could arrange the death of a whistle-blower. Or some kind of other intelligence led back to Jamie and they were tracking his movements. His phones and house are more than likely bugged, so you need to be really careful about what you say at home now.'

I thought back to what I'd said on the landline at home since Jamie had died. The conversations I'd had with Ava and Tony in the house. Were they listening to me, trying to find out what I knew? And had I said anything incriminating that revealed I suspected something?

No, I didn't think so. Those conversations were just grief talking. A heartbroken spouse trying to find answers to the unanswerable. And I'd called Mitchell from outside on the pay-as-you-go phone.

'But Jamie was an IT expert. Surely he'd know how to look for things on the Internet without getting caught, especially with something as potentially dangerous as this.'

'There's software you can use to make yourself anonymous online. I use it myself, and I'm sure Jamie would've probably been using it, too, so he didn't set off any flags. It's very likely he set up his laptop to wipe itself clean if anyone unauthorised started looking at it. But these people are professionals. They have thousands of ways and resources to get information.'

'But who are "these people"? Who do you think killed him?'

'People who can't risk any of this getting out. People who protect the highest echelons of the Establishment and matters of national security. Special branch? MI5? Or a deniable operator who works for the security services.'

I thought about my conversation with Sean. He'd mentioned *the other lot*. Had he been talking about the national security services?

'They broke into our house. They were looking for something. I thought it must've been the diary, and maybe that was part of it. Maybe they knew Jamie was writing it down, but they would've also been looking for the evidence Dave gave Jamie.'

'But did they find it? That's the question.'

'How can we know? I suppose we can't at the moment. We just have to assume they didn't and try to find it ourselves.'

'They've already killed Jamie. It's highly likely they killed Dave and possibly Billy, or if not, at the very least they were responsible for his suicide. If this evidence is still out there and was, like Jamie said, something explosive—something that needed no other corroboration—then you can use it, too.' He twisted in his seat to face me. 'But even if you *can* use it, there's still a chance they might find out that you know. Are you sure you want to do this? You have to be absolutely one-hundred-percent certain, because there will be no going back.'

I looked out at a family in the park, laughing, having fun, being happy, being alive. That would've been Jamie and me in the future. Married with a couple of children. But that had all been viciously snatched away from me. Bloody right I wanted to do this.

'Yes. I have to. For Jamie.'

'Okay. Assuming they didn't find this evidence, then, where would Jamie hide it? You know him better than anyone.'

'I searched the house after he died, because I was trying to find answers about why he'd taken his life. All I found was the list with the names and addresses of the other guys who were at Crossfield with him. They, whoever *they* are, didn't find that. It was hidden under some gravel in the garden, where Jamie often kept things in case the house ever got broken into. So there's nothing at home, I'm sure.'

'But did you look under carpets and floorboards? In the loft? Any other nook and cranny?'

'No.'

'Do you think the killers did? Did you notice a corner of a carpet or a piece of flooring was disturbed? Things like that?'

'No.'

'Well, you need to thoroughly scrutinise it again. Check for a change in dust patches anywhere. Do a thorough search of the house and garden, and I mean everywhere. If you have bifold doors on the wardrobes, check behind them. He could've hidden things behind the doors where most people wouldn't think to look.'

I wanted to ask him how far he was prepared to go, too. For me, who he didn't know. For Jamie, who he'd met briefly and with whom he'd shared only a vague connection of past military life and the terrible effects of predatory paedophiles. Would Mitchell kill those animals? For me? Would he? He was in the SAS. He could probably take out someone fifty different ways with a toothpick. Could I even ask that of him? I wondered if I was going crazy just contemplating asking him.

I pushed those dark thoughts to the corner of my brain. 'Jamie's laptop had been wiped, so if there were digital photos or videos on it, they would've been destroyed.'

'This happened in the early eighties, so I think the evidence would've been physical photos, probably Polaroids.'

'Yes, he mentioned Polaroids in the diary.'

'Did he?'

'You didn't read it?'

'I didn't need to. Jamie told me most of it himself. If it was a film Dave gave him, it would've been an actual videotape or cine film.'

'If you were going to hide something like that, where would *you* put it?'

Mitchell thought for a while. 'If he put it in his Jeep, then they would've already checked it when it was left at the murder scene.'

'You're right. It's probably clean, but there's no harm in checking it again, just in case they missed something.'

'What about at his work?'

'His boss said he hadn't seen him that week. Jamie was on annual leave, and if Dave gave it to him the day before Jamie died, then he couldn't have hidden it there.'

'Maybe his boss didn't know. Did Jamie have keys to the office?'

'Yes.'

'He could've gone back there when the place was closed. Also, did he have a storage unit anywhere?'

'Not that I know of.'

'That's something to check. I know he had no family left, but he might've left a copy with friends. I asked Lee and some of the other guys Jamie served with, but he didn't contact them and ask them to keep something safe for him.'

'He didn't have any other close friends, just the colleagues at work. No one I think he would've trusted with something so important.' I paused, remembering the words in the document he'd written. No wonder he had trust issues. Had trouble letting himself get close to people. It made me even more honoured that he'd chosen me as the one person he wanted in his life.

'He could've opened a safety deposit box. Or left them in a locker somewhere.'

'The leisure centre! Maybe he left it in his locker. He was always down there. Exercise was like an obsession with him. I can understand why now. He wanted to transform himself from that helpless little boy into someone strong and fit.'

'Or it could be in a bus or train station locker at the other end of the country. It could be anywhere.'

'No, don't say that. I have to believe we'll find it, whatever it is.'

'Then let's take it one step at a time.' He placed a warm hand over mine and squeezed it. 'I would suggest me helping you, but I just think we should keep my involvement hidden for now. I could be more helpful later, especially if they don't know about me. I think you should do this on your own. For now. If they are watching you, it's going to look suspicious if I'm with you. Are you all right with that?'

I wasn't okay with anything. Suddenly I wanted Mitchell with me as some kind of security blanket, but he was right. It would look suspicious. I pulled out the flash drive of Jamie's diary from my pocket and handed it to him. 'I think you should keep this again. Just in case they come back and find it.'

He nodded, took it, and slid it into his pocket.

'I have one more question.' I fiddled with the ring again. 'Did Jamie tell you he was going to propose to me?'

His eyebrows crinkled up slightly. A brief look of pity crossed his face before it was gone, replaced by an expressionless neutrality. 'Yes. He thought that if you said yes, when things came out later, he had a better chance of making you stay.'

I brought the ring to my lips. 'I would've stayed anyway,' I whispered. 'I loved him.'

'I know.' He opened the hamper, pulled out some shop-bought sandwiches wrapped in plastic packets, and put them on the bench between us. 'Whatever you do, keep your eyes open. Stay safe, okay?'

But I wasn't sure I'd ever feel safe again. Not now.

Chapter 27

I sat on the train on the way back to St Albans, my gaze flitting across the other passengers. Were 'they' watching me, or did they think Jamie had taken his secrets with him? Was the man in the suit sitting opposite, tapping on his laptop, an innocent commuter or was he more sinister? Was the woman reading *Cosmo* next to me a spy, working for MI5? Was the young guy who'd wheeled his bike on board, leaning against the doors, out to get me?

By the time I arrived home, I was looking at everyone, my eyes roaming them to check for something suspicious. I kept looking back over my shoulder to see if anyone was following me, but no one was.

Ava was on my doorstep when I returned, ringing the bell. Jackson was in his car seat, happily sleeping by her feet. A plastic supermarket bag was on the front step.

'Did you forget I was coming round again?' She gave me a worried frown.

I slapped a hand to my forehead. 'Sorry. It completely slipped my mind.' I tried to force a smile. Even though I loved them both, I had more important things to deal with now.

She hugged me then stepped back, holding me at arm's length, looking me up and down. 'You look awful. I bet you haven't been eating, have you? Or sleeping.'

I stared at her shoes. 'It's been hard.'

'Have you been at work? Have you gone back?'

'Not yet. I had four weeks annual leave owing to me, so I took it all. But I can't face going back.' And now, even if I wanted to, I couldn't. I had to do this. I was going to finish what Jamie had started, and I had no idea how long that would take.

She gave me that sympathetic, pitiful smile I was getting used to. 'It might be better to go back to work. It might take your mind off things. It's not healthy to just be on your own all the time, thinking, shutting yourself away.'

'It's only been a month. I'm entitled to mope around.'

'There's a difference between grief and depression.'

'Have you been reading those bloody leaflets again?' I picked at my thumbnail.

'I'm worried about you. You're acting really—'

'Really what?' I snapped.

'Well…distant and…weird. Talk to me! Tell me what you're thinking, what you're going through. I want to help. Talking can help.'

I wanted to tell her about everything. Wanted to so badly. The words were in my mouth, waiting to explode, but I had to think about her and Jackson's safety. These people were capable of murder. I couldn't have their deaths on my conscience if they thought Ava knew something. So the words evaporated, died right there. Like Jamie.

I forced a wobbly smile. 'Let's not talk out here. Are you coming in?' I said, but secretly I was willing her to go away so I could get on with searching the house.

'Of course I'm coming in. I'm going to cook you dinner.'

I picked up Jackson, holding his car seat in the crook of my elbow as I opened the door. My eyes scanned the hallway, looking for signs of anything untoward, any clue that someone had been inside again, but there was nothing. I wondered if I should change the locks. Had they broken in using Jamie's own key? Or were they expert enough to be able to break in without leaving a trace, anyway?

Special Branch. MI5.

Yes, they were experts, so surely any extra security measures would be pointless. If they wanted to get in, nothing would stop them.

I set Jackson down next to the kitchen table and stroked his cheek. Ava went round opening curtains, lifting blinds, and opening the kitchen window to get rid of the stuffy, stale, oppressive air that had built up. Then she pulled out items from the carrier bag onto the worktop.

'I bet you've got no food in the house, have you?' She peered in my fridge at the lone cucumber, mushy with furry mould growing on one side, a bottle of white wine, half opened, a bottle of vodka, and a bottle of Diet Coke. She swung around to face me, her hand on her hip. 'You've got to start taking more care of yourself.'

I sat at the table, fidgeting with my hands, and nodded, as if she was the parent and I was the incapable little girl. 'Yes, Mum.'

'Good.' That seemed to satisfy her, and she set about preparing roast chicken with roast potatoes and vegetables. She chattered away as she worked, about Mum and Dad, about Jackson and Craig, the weather, in an attempt to distract me from my insular thoughts about Jamie. I gave one-syllable answers in reply, all the while my eyes darting around the room.

Could it be taped underneath the dishwasher? In the microwave? Behind the white plinth at the bottom of the kitchen cupboards? What about behind the bath panel? Under the carpets? Hidden in a photo frame underneath another picture? Is that why the photo of us in the lounge had been moved out of place?

It could be anywhere.

It could be nowhere.

Ava whipped her head round suddenly. 'I can't hear you, what?'

'Huh?'

'You were mumbling about something.'

Had I said all that out loud? Shit! Had 'they' heard me on any bugs they were listening to?

'Um…what did I say?'

She stared at me as if I'd just sprouted a new head. 'You mean you don't know what you were just talking about?'

I waved a hand vaguely. 'Um…I'm just…just tired.'

She studied me for a long time before eventually rummaging around in her bag. She pulled out a box of tablets and put them on the table in front of me. 'These are natural sleeping tablets. Why don't you give them a try? I know you're not sleeping well, understandably.'

I picked them up, turning the packet over and over in my hand, staring at them as the silence filled the room. 'Did you hear what I said just now?'

'No.' She shook her head and chewed on her lip anxiously. 'Will you try them?'

'Okay,' I said in an effort to placate her.

Apparently satisfied, she went back to preparing the dinner, and an hour later, she finally put a piled-high plate in front of me.

'Eat!' She sat opposite, shook some salt and pepper onto hers, and tucked in, keeping an eye on Jackson, who was due for a feed soon and would be waking up.

Dutifully, I chewed and swallowed like a robot, hardly tasting anything, pushing away the plate when it was half finished.

Ava looked at my plate and glared at me. 'You didn't eat very much.'

'I'm not a horse! That plate was huge.'

'Well, you can have the rest tomorrow, can't you? Put it in the microwave.' She gave me a decisive smile.

The thoughts chased around in my head as I half listened to her with a rising impatience. I sat on my fingers to stop myself from picking them. Jigged my leg up and down. And finally, *finally*, Jackson woke up, and she suggested leaving.

'Now, make sure you eat that tomorrow, and if you want to come round, just do it, okay? And I'll phone you to check in. I'm keeping my eye on you.' She wagged a finger at me playfully, and I wondered just who else was keeping an eye on me.

I waved them off in the car, closed the door behind her, and stood with my back against it.

Right. To work.

I made sure all the doors and windows were locked. Then I closed the curtains, turned on lights, cranked the stereo up loud, and started searching. I moved furniture and pulled up the carpets, running my hands along the floorboards to check for any loose ones. I checked for loose skirting, behind pictures and photos, and in between the pages of books and CD and DVD covers. I went through my laptop, searching through every file I could find to see if there were digitised versions of photos or film on there. I checked in the DVD player, stereo, printer, microwave, behind the kitchen plinths, in the curtain hems. I checked under, in, and behind furniture, cushions, and drawers, pulled the washing machine and dishwasher out and felt underneath them, looked behind them, inside. I checked the wardrobes, my hands hovering over Jamie's clothes, that familiar ball of anguish detonating inside me again. I checked his pockets, trousers, jackets, shirts. I looked inside his shoes. The browny-orangey clay mud on his hiking boots was dried now, and bits fell off onto the floor of the wardrobe. Nothing was inside them. Nor in any other boots, bags, suitcases. I checked all my clothes, too, just in case

Jamie had hidden something there. I stood inside the wardrobe and closed the sliding mirrored doors, searching for something taped to the back.

Leave no stone unturned.

I looked in boxes of teabags and in the freezer. In Tupperware boxes, between the stack of baking trays. Searched through all Jamie's document folders again. All the boxes in the loft, sifting through mostly my stuff that I'd had when I moved in and hadn't unpacked yet because there was no room. I looked behind the cobwebbed water tank and felt inside the insulation jacket of the immersion tank, in toilet cisterns. Sifted through piles of towels and bedding in the airing cupboard.

I searched the garden, looking for patches of grass that had recently been disturbed. I checked under the whole border of gravel this time. Beneath the patio table and chairs. In plant pots. I rifled through the shed, lifting lids of half-used paint and in toolboxes, in the middle of folded dust sheets.

Everywhere.

I looked everywhere one could possibly hide something, but I didn't find any photos or videos or even a flash drive that could hold any digitised versions of them. Nor did I find anything that looked like a bug or camera.

It was getting dark the next day by the time I finally finished in the shed, a film of perspiration on my forehead, the armpits of my hoodie and between my shoulder blades damp. I needed a shower. I blew away the hair stuck to my sweaty forehead and stared back at the house, wishing the bricks and mortar could tell me what I needed to know.

Where did you put it, Jamie? Where?

Chapter 28

Car? Workplace? Storage unit? Safety deposit box? Gym locker? Somewhere else in the whole world?

I downed a cup of coffee early the next morning, grabbed my bag, and checked up the street before exiting the house. Neighbours were leaving their houses, going to work. Cars passed by on the main road at the end of the cul-de-sac. Life was going on as normal for everyone.

Everyone except for me.

A clattering sound to my left made me jump. My head whipped round to see one of my neighbours dumping a rubbish bag in his wheelie bin inside his front gate. I put a hand to my chest with relief.

He turned away quickly and avoided my gaze, probably not knowing what to say to me anymore. Death made people jittery and uncomfortable. He'd put a condolence card through the door several weeks ago, but I'd thrown it in the bin, where I'd put all the rest, unable to stand the sight of them staring at me.

I got into Jamie's Jeep, not knowing where I was going. I just had to make sure no one followed me.

I kept one eye on the rear-view mirror and drove around randomly, taking turns without signalling, which resulted in a few angry blasts of horns. I pulled up in a quiet street, where I'd be able to see someone coming, and turned off the engine. I checked the glove box again. I felt underneath the front seats and behind the visors. I got out, opened the doors, and felt along the fabric to see if something were somehow hidden inside them. I opened the boot, peeled back the carpet, and lifted out the spare wheel, which I inspected before checking every inch inside. I opened the rear light covers, looked in the first aid kit, in the box where the emergency red triangle was kept. Pulled off the cover to the fuses.

Nothing.

I groaned to myself, but I wasn't beaten yet.

I drove back into town, parked, and went into Costa Coffee. There were more commuters, suited and booted, stopping in for their caffeine fix before they started their day. I had half an hour to kill before anyone would be starting work at Porterhouse Solutions, so I nursed a latte with three sugars and watched people hurrying up and down the street as everything spun around inside my head, ramming against my skull.

My coffee was cold when I took the last sip. My hands shook, but I didn't know whether that was from the caffeine, lack of food, fear, anger, or frustration. My stomach grumbled, and I ignored it.

I drove out to the business park, and as I was getting out of my car, Paul pulled up in the spot reserved for the managing director. I licked my dry lips and got out, walking towards him.

'Hi, Paul.'

He swung around, surprise registering in his eyes before he smiled. 'Maya. How are you?' He stood up straighter, briefcase in hand.

'I've been better.'

'Of course. Stupid question, I suppose, but I bet everyone else keeps saying it.' An awkward smile flitted across his lips. 'What are you doing here?'

'I've just been going through Jamie's stuff, trying to sort out his estate for the lawyer, and I think Jamie might've kept some of his personal things at the office, because I can't find them.' The lie rolled quickly off my tongue. 'Is it possible to check his desk?'

Paul's face flushed. 'Actually, someone else is using Jamie's desk now.'

'Oh.' I took a step back, surprised Jamie's life had been erased so quickly when he'd been a loyal employee for years. But then it had been four weeks. How long were people supposed to wait before moving on with their lives? A stab of anger penetrated my gut. Not long, obviously.

'I was going to call you, actually, because there were a few non-work-related things in his drawers I thought you might want.' He tilted his head towards the entrance. 'Shall we go inside?'

I followed him past the reception, where a smart young woman with lashings of makeup filtered calls. We got into the empty lift, and a silence descended between us. Before Jamie died, I would've been making lively small talk, laughing and joking, finding something to say. Now I didn't care if it felt uncomfortable. Laughter and jokes were meaningless. Conversation was overrated, which was why I couldn't speak to Becca and Lynn anymore. Why I let their messages go unanswered. How could I talk to them about normal things? Shopping, fashion, which pub we were going to hit on Friday night, what was happening in *Emmerdale*, who'd been voted off *X Factor*. Who gave a shit about that anymore? Nothing was normal now I'd been plunged into this surreal nightmare. Except I could wake up from a nightmare, couldn't I? This was far, far worse. And pretty soon, they would stop calling altogether, which was fine with me. I was so far removed from them, from what I'd once been, I didn't have anything to say anymore that didn't involve paedophiles and murderous thoughts. I hated them for being able to carry on with their lives while I couldn't.

Paul shifted from foot to foot until the doors opened. He said good morning to his staff in their cubicles and led me to his office at the back of the open-plan space. He put his briefcase on his desk and picked up a large cardboard box from underneath the window in the corner of the room. 'This is everything personal.' His lips flattened into a sympathetic smile, which, inexplicably, made me want to punch him. I was sick of people looking at me like that.

I took the box from his outstretched hands. 'Thanks. Is it…would it be possible to look at his desk? Just to sit at it for a moment?'

He gave me an odd look.

'I just want to…you know, feel close to him. Where he worked.' I blinked rapidly. *I will not cry. I will not cry.*

'Um…yes, I suppose so.' He led me to an office down the hallway.

The door still had a plaque with Jamie's name on it. The breath hitched in my throat. I reached out and fingered the words.

'Bob's out training today, so he won't be using it. Take your time.' He leant against the door frame for a moment, watching me as I sat down in Jamie's old chair. He pointed back towards his office. 'I'll just be…er…I've got some urgent work to do.' He shut the door and scurried away.

I put the box on the floor and looked through the drawers, underneath them, inside folders of notes. I checked the filing cabinets, which were empty. Jamie's replacement obviously hadn't spent enough time here yet to accumulate more paperwork. I felt underneath the drawers and chair. There was no computer on the desk because all employees used their own company laptops. At some point, Paul would probably ask for Jamie's back.

Satisfied nothing was in the office, I picked up the box and left, the cardboard burning a hole in my skin.

I drove home erratically again, watching out for someone

following me, itching to open the box. Once inside, I dumped the box on the kitchen table and checked the door locks and windows. Everything was as I'd left it. Everything secure. Nothing looked out of place or disturbed.

I snatched off the lid from the box and rummaged around, but it contained only the usual detritus left from years of working at the same place: An old Christmas card from Paul, ancient copies of *Smart Computing* and *Wired*, a Parker pen I'd bought him for Christmas last year, a framed photo of me when we'd been in Scotland for that first romantic weekend away, a spare phone charger for his missing iPhone, a silver flask to keep his water chilled, a pocket-sized pack of tissues, a Tupperware box with some cashews and raisins in it, a can of deodorant, and a pair of goggles. There was no Filofax or diary or address book that might've held a clue, as Jamie always used the organiser app on his phone.

I ran a despairing hand through my knotted hair. I needed to wash it. I needed to start eating, instead of surviving on coffee and alcohol. Take care of myself. Do normal things. Put washing on. Go food shopping. Normal? Who was I kidding? Nothing would be normal again.

My mobile rang then, breaking the silence that seemed to be closing in around me. It was my iPhone, not the Nokia. I looked at the screen, which showed my boss calling.

'Hi, Maya.'

'Hi, how are things at work?' I asked, deflecting the conversation before she could ask how I was.

'It's a bit hectic at the moment. The appraisals are all due, and we've taken on a few more big clients. You know how it is.'

'Yes.' I stared out the window into the garden. Stared at the shed where Tony had found the rope that ended Jamie's life.

'Um…how are you doing?'

*I'm angry and bitter and I want to kill them. And I'm scared. And hopeless. And alone. And...*I settled for, 'Tired. I'm exhausted.'

'Look, I know how awful this is, but I just wanted to know if you were coming back. If not, we need to recruit someone else. I'm sorry to have to bring it up when you're going through this, but...well, we really need to know where we are so we can plan.'

I don't care about my job! I wanted to yell at her. I couldn't go back to the real world now. Couldn't go to work with a bounce in my step and supervise the girls and talk to stupid, annoying, complaining customers all day long. Couldn't go home at the end of the day feeling happy and satisfied. Couldn't cook dinner, singing along to the radio. Run myself a leisurely bath with candles dotted around the room, relaxing. Nothing would ever be the same again. I knew too much, and I couldn't unknow it.

I rubbed at my forehead and turned away from the shed. 'No. I...I'm sorry, but I won't be coming back.'

'Ah. I'm sorry, too. I'll be very sad to lose you. We're all going to miss you. But I understand.'

You don't! No one does. No one except for those other boys and Mitchell.

She carried on talking, but her words weren't penetrating. 'Sorry, I have to go now.' I stabbed the *off* button with my finger and hurled my phone across the kitchen worktop.

Chapter 29

Next stop was the leisure centre. I'd discovered Jamie's locker key was missing. He used to keep it on the same ring as his car keys, but it wasn't there now. Had the people who'd killed him taken it? Had they got there first?

I was sure a member of staff would be able to open it for me with a master key, though, so I entered reception, the cloying smell of chlorine and ammonia hitting the back of my throat, the heat steaming the glass panels to the swimming pool behind.

I asked the young, spotty guy on reception if I could talk to the manager, and he called her to reception. I was flicking through some membership brochures, pretending to read them, when a gangly woman appeared next to me.

'You wanted to talk to me? I'm Sally, the duty manager.' She tilted her head with a big smile, and I wished everyone would just stop fucking smiling at me!

'Yes. My boyfriend has just died, and he used to have a locker here. I'm his next of kin, and I'm trying to sort out his estate for the lawyer. I think he may have left some personal items in there.'

That made the smile slide straight off her face. 'Oh, my condolences. I'm very sorry to hear that.'

'Thank you.' I reached into my bag. 'I have his death certificate here if you need to verify it, and a letter from his lawyer.'

She glanced me up and down briefly. Probably taking in a gaunt woman with bloodshot eyes and dark bags underneath, messy hair that smelt stale, who'd thrown on any old clothes that no longer fit, and surmised I must be who I said I was. A woman on the edge of hysteria. A woman trying desperately not to crack into a million scattered pieces. 'No, that won't be necessary. Do you have his key?'

'No, I think he lost it.'

'Okay, what was his name?'

'Jamie Taylor.'

She walked back to the reception desk and typed on the computer. She nodded to herself, then produced a bundle of master keys from one of the drawers and asked me to follow her. We headed into a unisex changing area, past private cubicles, to a row of lockers, which were situated next to a block of showers.

'Here we are.' She inserted a key into one of them, unlocked it, and stepped back so I could open it.

I waited, my fingers poised on the handle, hoping she'd go away, but she just stood there with that pitying look I'd come to recognise so well.

Thankfully, an employee came over then and asked the duty manager to return to reception.

'I've just got to deal with something. I'll be back in a moment.'

I waited until she disappeared and then opened the door. Inside, I found a can of deodorant, a bottle of shampoo, and shower gel. I saw one of Jamie's ties, another pair of goggles, some socks rolled into a ball, and nothing else.

I picked out the tie, bringing it to my nose, trying to inhale his lingering scent, but all I could smell was chlorine. I threw the toiletries into a nearby bin, put the tie and socks and goggles in my bag, and took Sally's keys from the door, then handed them back to the reception with a thank you.

~ ~ ~ ~

I drove home, a weariness in my bones making it hard to concentrate on the road. I hadn't slept properly since Jamie was killed; the nightmares were too real, and the lack of food was taking its toll. My eyelids drooped closed. My wheels hitting the kerb jerked me awake again.

I wound the window down, blasting fresh air on my face, thinking again how easy it would be to just let go. I could drive into a wall. Off a cliff. I could go to the coast, step into the freezing waters, and never come out. Jump in front of a train, like Billy. There were so many ways to escape all this horror. The unending pain of grief and despair. The molten hatred and fury. It was tempting. Very tempting. The nothingness. The end of the loneliness. The end of the pictures of Jamie and those men that were now in my head, unable to go away. But then I would've let Jamie down, and I'd already failed him by not being the person he felt he could've leant on and confided in about what he was doing before he died. If I had been, he wouldn't have been out there on his own when they got to him and strung him up and murdered him. If I had been, maybe he'd still be alive.

So. I was his only hope now to get his story told. To get justice. To assuage the guilt that had mushroomed inside me like a mini Hiroshima. It was all down to me, because if I didn't do it, who would?

I stopped at the supermarket, grabbed a trolley, and filled it with things. I turned into one aisle and stood there in the middle, my mind a sudden blank. What was I doing here? People tried to get past me, giving me odd looks. Someone's trolley hit the back of my heel. I think they did it on purpose to get me to move.

'Hey!' I yelled, anger bubbling to the surface, making the

offending woman rush off further down the aisle to get away from the dishevelled nutter.

It wasn't until I got home that I found I'd purchased tins of cat food instead of baked beans, and a packet of frozen raspberries, which I was allergic to.

I was throwing some of it in the bin when my iPhone rang from inside my bag. It was Mum. I kept meaning to call her so she wouldn't call me, but I'd forgotten. Again.

'Hi, love. How are—'

'How's Dad?' I cut in before she could ask the dreaded words that made my head scream.

'Oh, he's improving. The infection's cleared up nicely. He can limp along now, but he's still in quite a lot of pain. I do hope these doctors out here know what they're doing.'

'Is he still moaning about being incapacitated?' I forced words out of my mouth, anything to deflect the conversation away from me and stop her worrying.

She tutted. 'You know what he's like. He keeps talking about what he's going to do in the garden as soon as he can bend down properly. I've told him he should take it easy. You know, get back into his routine slowly, but he says he'll be dead before long so he needs to make the most of it.' She chuckled, then she stopped abruptly when she realised she'd mentioned the D-word. 'Oh, I'm sorry!'

'It's okay. And how are you?'

'You know me, I'm struggling on,' she said cheerfully. 'But I was ringing to see if you wanted to pop out for a holiday. I'm sure that your work will extend your time off, won't they, under the circumstances?'

I mumbled something but didn't tell her I'd just quit. That would only give her something else to worry about.

'So, how about it? You could come over for a while and just get away from everything. A break will do you the world of good. And I'd love to fuss over you. I don't see you nearly often enough.'

'I don't think so, Mum. I've got too many things to sort out here.'

'What things? The lawyer can handle Jamie's estate. It's not like you've got—' Again she stopped and checked herself. 'I'm making a right pickle of this, aren't I? But the trouble is, love, I don't really know what to say. Ava is really worried about you, and so am I.'

I imagined the conversations they'd had about me. 'She's not eating.' 'She's depressed.' 'I'm worried she'll do something stupid.' 'She doesn't want to talk to her friends anymore.' 'She's not getting on with her life.'

'We think you might be depressed. Why don't you speak to someone about it? One of those grief counsellors. Or get some of that Prozac, love.'

I bit my lip. I didn't need a counsellor. Talking to someone would be like putting a Band-Aid on a shark bite. What I needed was an AK-47 or a grenade to blast the people who'd killed Jamie to smithereens. Could I get a prescription for that? 'I'm fine, Mum. Stop worrying.' I was stifled by her concern.

'I can't help it. No matter how old your children get, you still can't stop worrying.'

'Well, I'll never know now, will I?' I said bitterly.

I heard her breathing, probably wondering what to say next that wasn't going to upset me. 'It would be really good to see you. Oh, hang on, Dad wants a word.' She handed the phone to him.

'Don't listen to your mum,' he said.

I heard Mum's mumbled protests in the background.

'You have to do what's right for you at a time like this. We miss you, though, and we're thinking of you.'

His voice wrapped me in a warm embrace. 'Thanks, Dad.'

'And we're here for you. Any time. If you want to come out and stay, we'd love to see you. You just say the word.'

'I know.'

'All right, then. Make sure you take care of yourself. You know what your mum's like. She's a worrier. I've told her when you're ready to get yourself together, you will. You can't rush these things. It's not the same for everyone.'

At that moment, I wanted to hug him. Hug them both. Book the next flight to Portugal, get on a plane, and forget everything.

But that was impossible now.

Chapter 30

Before I passed out from hunger, I heated up a can of tomato soup and thickly buttered two slices of bread. Why had I bought wholemeal? I hated the stuff. I ate too quickly, the soup burning my throat. I dunked in some bread and brought it to my lips. Red soup dripped onto the table. Red. Like blood.

And then the little I'd eaten threatened to come back up, vomit rising in my throat, burning.

Blood. Death.

I couldn't bear to look at it anymore, so I poured the soup down the sink and left the empty bowl there with all the other overflowing dirty coffee cups and wine glasses I hadn't bothered putting in the dishwasher.

I poured a glass of vodka and Coke instead and found the Yellow Pages. There was definitely no sign in Jamie's paperwork files at home that he'd opened a safety deposit box or rented a storage unit anywhere, but *they* could've taken that when they'd searched the house.

Some fifty storage units were in the St Albans and surrounding area, and I called each one, giving them the same spiel. My boyfriend had died, I was his next of kin, I thought he'd opened a unit before his death, and could they confirm it.

No one had any records for Jamie.

I did the same with the banks, starting with HSBC and Barclays, where he had accounts, but they wanted to see proof of his death and my status as next of kin before they'd tell me whether he'd opened a deposit box, so I spent the next few days trawling round them with the letter from his lawyer and his death certificate.

It was useless, though. He hadn't opened a safety deposit box with anyone locally.

I sat on a bench and called Mitchell on the pay-as-you-go Nokia. I hadn't found anything that looked like a bug or listening device when I'd searched the house, but I'd watched a few spy movies before—in fact, it felt as if I was starring in my own episode of one—and I knew it was possible to hide those tiny things anywhere these days, wasn't it?

Mitchell was the only one who didn't ask me how I was. He didn't need to. From his own experience, he already knew.

'I've got no more ideas,' I told Mitchell. 'It could be anywhere. It would help if his satnav history hadn't been deleted. Maybe the evidence doesn't even exist anymore. Maybe they already took it and destroyed it.' I worked my neck from side to side, trying to disperse the burning knots of tension. 'What can I do now?'

'I'm thinking.'

'I've got to expose them.'

'I want that, too. They don't deserve to get away with this. They've got away with it for too long already.' He paused for a moment. 'Was there anywhere that Jamie had a special connection with? Anywhere he liked to go? A place you went on holiday together, maybe. Somewhere he was happy?'

I chewed on my lip, thinking of the screensaver photo of us Jamie had had on his laptop, before it had been wiped. 'We drove up to Scotland once and stayed near Loch Ness. We hired this log cabin and did some walking and hiking, and he loved it there. He said when he retired, he'd like to move there. But he was still coming home at the end of the day, pretending he'd been to work. He wouldn't have had time to get there and back after he'd seen Dave that day.'

'Anywhere else?'

'I'm thinking.' I gnawed on my lower lip.

'What did he like doing in his spare time?'

'Swimming, but I checked his locker. There was nothing there. He liked walking in the countryside. We went together at weekends.'

'Okay. Was there anywhere he particularly liked?'

I thought about Bluebell Wood, where he was found. A picture of Jamie writhing at the end of a rope, his eyes bulging, his face turning red, flashed behind my eyes. A noise which sounded like a cross between a sob and a gulp flew from my mouth.

'Maya? Maya, what's happening?'

I pressed the heel of my hand to each eye, trying to stop it. 'He...there was somewhere he loved locally.'

I told Mitchell about the photo next to my bed. The selfie I'd taken when Jamie and I went out to those woods near Codicote for a picnic in the summer. Jamie said he used to go there before he met me, whenever he needed to sit and think about things. Clear his head. I thought about the fresh mud I'd seen on his walking boots a few days after he'd been killed when I was searching through his things. Mud and clay. Of course! Jamie would never have usually put away his boots in the cupboard in that state. He would've cleaned them first. Unless...unless he was in a hurry or had been distracted.

'I found fresh mud on his boots just after he died. I didn't think anything about it at the time, but the soil is full of clay up there. He could've gone straight there after Dave gave whatever it was to him and hidden it somewhere. I'll go and have a look.' I rose to my feet, adrenaline and a sudden burst of energy pulsing through my veins.

'Let me know if you find anything.'
'Don't worry. You'll be the first to know.'

～～～～

I arrived home after an anxious journey, looking regularly over my shoulder. I only stopped to grab the framed photo of Jamie and me at the picnic: me smiling, my head on Jamie's shoulder as I held the phone at arm's length, snapping the photo. So happy. So in love. I shoved it in my bag, put my trainers on, and left again.

I drove from St Albans to Wheathampstead then took the road to Codicote. Masses of fields were on either side, and I couldn't remember exactly where the woods were. I drove the length of the road and found myself in Codicote village. I didn't recognise where Jamie had pulled off the road and parked on that day, but I turned around in the village and drove back the way I'd come, checking again. There was a lay-by somewhere along here where we'd left the car.

I drove at 30 mph, and a young guy in a BMW came up behind me, sitting practically on my rear bumper. Was he one of them? Was he following me? My chest tightened as I tried to keep one eye on the road and one on the rear-view mirror. I spotted a garden centre further up and turned into the car park. As I pulled off the main road, he treated me to a blast of his horn and sped off.

I waited in the car a few minutes, trying to calm myself, then I pulled back out onto the empty main road and concentrated on looking for the lay-by.

A little way along, I found it and pulled over. The lay-by was really a patch of gravel big enough for three cars. It was quiet and deserted. I got out of the car and stared at the fields, the hill of long grass ahead of me leading up into the woods.

I was hit with an overwhelming sensation of being watched. I spun around, a cold bead of sweat sliding down my back, but I saw no one. Was there someone in the woods, though, watching for me? Waiting?

I didn't care.

But that was a lie. I did care. I was scared to death. More scared than I'd ever been in my life. In five minutes, ten, half an hour, I could end up like Jamie. My only insurance would be to find what Dave had given him before he died.

I ignored the prickling sensation on my skin and the tingling of my scalp as I clicked the remote control to lock the Jeep. I put my hands in my pockets, wondering why I hadn't thought to bring a weapon with me. I should buy some pepper spray. A stun gun. Could I even get those in England? At the very least, I should have a knife.

I kept my eyes open, scanning the hill for signs of life. At the top, I paused at the entrance to the woods. It felt as if there was an invisible brick wall in front of me, stopping me from going any further, as in my recurrent dream. I drowned out the warning voice in my head, telling me to go back, and stepped under the canopy of trees. It was darker under here. Eerie. Creepy. Decaying leaves crunched under my feet. At least I'd hear someone coming if they were following me. I walked on through, alert to the slightest sound. A raven cawed. I flinched, my pulse skyrocketing. The trees became denser. I stepped over fallen logs and the carcass of a dead fox. Rabbits scurried away from me down into their dens. It seemed as though I was walking forever. Seemed as though the woods were closing in on me, squeezing the breath from my lungs. Eventually I emerged out of the trees into the low sunlight. Down there, somewhere by the river was the spot where we'd picnicked.

I walked down a sloping hill towards the slow-flowing water and took the photo out of my bag. My smiling face stared back at me beside Jamie's as we sat in front of a large log with the picnic blanket spread out around us. On the blanket was a bottle of champagne, balancing precariously on the uneven ground, strawberries in an open Tupperware box, French bread, Brie, and vine-ripened tomatoes. I could taste them on my tongue as the memory lingered in my brain, and a jolt of grief kicked inside my sternum.

I found the log and held up the picture, moving it around until I was standing in the same spot as the blanket. Then I crouched down and examined the grass, looking for any signs that the earth had been disturbed recently.

The grass was six inches long, still wet with dew that the weak winter sunshine hadn't burnt off. I glanced up and down the riverbank but found no patches of mud that looked as if they had been dug up. I widened my search, walking around the area in increasing circles.

In my rush to get there, I hadn't even thought to bring a trowel or spade, but it didn't look as if I'd need one anyway. It all appeared untouched.

I sat on the log and cradled my head in my hands. I was wrong. There was nothing here.

The feeling of something touching my shoulder made me jump to my feet. I glanced around wildly, but no one was there.

Is that you, Jamie? Are you here?

A breeze whipped up. A sudden, inexplicable heat wrapped around me. And I knew it was him. His presence, his spirit. Something. He was here with me, I was sure of it. Or maybe it was just wishful thinking. Longing.

'I miss you,' I whispered over and over again, as if by saying it enough, it could bring him back. 'Are you here? Are you looking out for me?' I called out. I waited for an answer, but nothing happened. Of course it didn't. Maybe I was going mad.

A noise made me jump. Then a squirrel hurtled out of the log and darted away from me, running towards the cover of the woods. I put a hand to my chest with relief and waited for my breathing to calm down. I *was* going mad. My imagination was working overtime. Jamie wasn't here. He wasn't watching over me.

Even so, the hope that maybe he was there made me sit on the log again, waiting for him to come back to me.

I didn't know how long I sat there. Hours. The sun sank lower in the sky. Black clouds drifted overhead. I didn't want to be there when it got dark. I was halfway back up the hill when the thought hit me.

The squirrel. The log.

The log was hollow.

I ran back down, almost falling over my feet. Kneeling on the wet grass, I peered inside the log. It was dark inside, with spider's webs and patches of fungus. A few half-eaten acorns were scattered around. And there was something else…

I reached my hand in, my fingertips touching metal, pulling it towards me. It fell out of the opening onto the grass, and I recognised it instantly.

It was a rectangular metal box with a picture of a dog on it that had once been in our kitchen cupboard.

I looked around me, making sure once again no one was watching. Then I opened the lid.

Chapter 31

I vomited onto the grass, coughing, spluttering for air, choking.

I took a tissue from my bag and wiped my mouth, but that wasn't the end of it. Again I vomited. And again. Until there was nothing left except watery fluid.

With shaky hands, I closed the lid of the box, my mind registering the horror I'd seen while at the same time trying to reject it.

I shoved the box in my bag and ran through the woods. Running, running, my lungs burning, my calves aching, until I was out the other side and down the hill and in the car.

My tyres squealed on the road as I drove at full speed, all the while with my eyes checking my rear-view mirror. I pulled into the car park of a huge DIY superstore, where lots of other cars were around. People unloading shopping trolleys. Kids cutting through the car park on their way home from school, laughing and joking with each other.

I narrowly avoided an elderly man emerging between the cars, carrying a shopping bag. His shocked face passed by in a blur as I drove into a space. I snatched the Nokia from my bag and exited the car, walking with shaky legs to a corner of the car park where I could still see people but where no one would overhear me. I couldn't take the risk of talking in the Jeep in case it was bugged. With a shuddering finger I hit the *redial* button.

It rang and rang with no answer then clicked off.

I tried again. *Come on, come on. Pick up!*

Mitchell answered this time. 'Sorry, I was just talking to my niece on my other phone.'

'I found it. You were right. It was hidden there.'

'What is it?'

'There are photos. Lots of photos. Disgusting, vile things. Rape of boys. Oral sex. In some of them, the poor boys are tied up or restrained. And they're being...it's so awful, they're being tortured. I recognise Jamie. And I think it's Sean in some of them, too. And there's a videotape. It's got *The Friday Club* written on it.'

'Have you watched it?'

'No. I haven't been home yet. I want you to see it. I don't want to watch it alone.'

'You can't do it at your house. If the place is bugged, it will tip them off. Can you come to London?'

'Yes. Give me your address.'

He told me and I repeated it back. Then said, 'I'll be there in about an hour. Pour yourself a stiff drink. You're going to need it.'

I hung up and drove towards London. It wasn't until I was almost there that my breath started to reach normal levels.

I parked behind a Mitsubishi crew-cab pickup on the drive of a 1920s detached house with a bay window and porch.

Mitchell opened the front door, waiting for me to approach. He glanced up and down the street before ushering me inside.

He gestured for me to take a seat in the large kitchen, which had been modernised in a way that made it look cold and clinical, with lots of gleaming glass and polished granite surfaces. The coffee maker, kettle, oven, and hob were all shiny stainless steel, and all the utensils were arranged with complete precision. There were no photos or pictures or personal items around, as if a robot lived there. I could smell bleach and furniture polish.

'What do you want to drink?' he asked.

'Something that will make it all go away.'

'It's too late for that.'

'Have you got any vodka?'

He pulled out a bottle from a cupboard in the corner. It looked full, which was good. I'd need a whole bottle and more to blot out what I'd seen.

'Please make it a large one.'

'Slice of lemon?' He grabbed a tall glass and poured a hefty measure of Stolichnaya into it.

'Please. Do you have any Diet Coke?'

'Yes.' He topped up his own glass from a bottle of brandy already out on the granite worktop, added Coke and a couple of slices of lemon to both, and brought them to the table.

I slid the metal box towards him, brought the vodka to my lips, and didn't stop swallowing until I'd drunk half of it. My stomach burned in protest.

He took the photos out of the box and studied a few, his jaw flexing, before placing the pile to one side. 'I don't need to look at anymore.' His face had lost his mask of neutrality. His cheeks flushed, his eyes narrowing with pure hatred. He downed his drink, refilled our glasses, and sat down again. 'Did you look at all of them?'

'Yes,' I croaked, my gaze avoiding the pile. The vodka churned in my stomach. 'I recognised Eamonn Colby, the children's minister. And there was Howard Sebastian. I Googled him before, when I was looking at previous owners of 10 Crompton Place. And I saw Douglas Talbot, too, the defence secretary. I don't recognise the others, but they must be the same people Jamie wrote about. And there's another one…the one Jamie said was in the dungeon with

---

him—he's wearing a cloak and hood and mask like Jamie described. Who do you think he is?'

'A sick bastard, that's who. Someone who doesn't deserve to breathe the same air as us.' His nostrils flared as he reached for his glass. Swallowed a hefty gulp. Stared at the videotape. 'I've got an old VHS player in the loft somewhere. I'll go and get it. Help yourself to more drink.'

His footsteps disappeared up the stairs, and I heard him banging around. I'd polished off another vodka by the time he came back.

'Come into the lounge,' he called from the hallway. 'I'll set it up.'

I followed his voice towards a spacious room with patio doors that overlooked the garden. It was immaculately tidy and minimalist in there, too, with cream walls and a deep red feature wall behind the large sofa. Again, there were no photos or knick-knacks around. It screamed *functional* but not *homely* or *personal.*

I hesitated in the doorway, watching him connect the dusty video player to the large flat-screen TV via a SCART lead, then close the curtains and turn on the light.

I perched on the edge of the three-seater sofa, my knees pressed together, clutching my drink.

He picked up a remote control, turned the TV on, then sat next to me. He took my hand in his. Squeezed it. His eyes searched mine, as if asking permission to turn it on.

I nodded.

It was grainy blackness at first. Then came a room that looked like an old cellar or dungeon, and I knew instantly this was the place Jamie had described at 10 Crompton Place in his diary. A close-up shot showed a biracial boy secured to a bed by the handcuffs on his wrists. No doubt he was Moses. His eyes fluttered open and closed, and he moaned every now and then. He looked drugged, mumbling in slurry words, 'No, please don't hurt me! No, please! I want to go home. I want my mummy!' The camera panned out, and there were other men in the frame: Howard Sebastian, the judge; Douglas Talbot, the defence secretary; Eamonn Colby, the children's minister; a grey-haired old man, probably Ted Byron, the children's home inspector; a short man with glasses who must've been Felix Barron, the banker; a tall gaunt one, who was probably Colin Reed, the chief constable; and the one in the hooded robe.

I witnessed the brutal, repeated abuse, rape, and horrific torture of the poor boy over hours of footage. Even if I turned my head away and squeezed my eyes shut, I could still hear him screaming as the drugs wore off and the pain penetrated through his hazy mind. Begging for mercy. In the end, begging for his life. I forced myself to watch the sickening, sadistic evilness because I had to know everything that was on it so I could finish what Jamie had started. Through my tears, and the splintering of my heart, I witnessed his battered, bruised, cigarette-burned, mutilated body being strangled to death.

Strangled by the hooded man.

Chapter 32

It couldn't be real. Nothing that awful could be real. Except it was, and I'd seen it with my own eyes. It visualised everything Jamie had written about in his final days.

I was frozen in shock. I couldn't move. Couldn't speak. Could barely breathe. And then a sound escaped from deep inside. A howling scream.

I wrapped my arms around my shaking body, bent over double, rocking myself back and forth, wanting the images to go away. Knowing they never would.

My hot tears fell onto the carpet. And then Mitchell squeezed me towards him, his strong arms holding me tight, holding me upright, his quiet strength keeping me from disintegrating.

I'd never hated anyone before in my life, but I hated those people with an all-consuming viciousness. Hate. Hate. Hate. Even animals didn't act in such a ruthless, brutal manner, and we were supposed to be the civilised ones. There were no words to describe what they were.

They had to pay. For Jamie. For his friends. For Moses and the other boy Jamie described whose lives were so despicably and cruelly snuffed out. For the boys who'd disappeared from their beds at night, and all the others who might be out there.

'It brings it all back,' Mitchell said, his hot breath fanning against my hair. 'Alex. He was strangled, raped repeatedly before and after he was murdered. He was just nothing to them.'

I held him tighter, letting him know I understood. His muscles were rigid.

I took an almighty sniff, trying to clear my blocked nose. 'Does it ever get any easier?'

'The dead are never far away. It's like knives are repeatedly being stabbed into every part of your flesh. Especially when you know those bastards are still out there, getting away with it. People who say grief gets easier are liars. Grief is like a cancer.' He pulled back, and I rested my head on his shoulder, my eyes swollen with tears, breathing in erratic sobs.

I couldn't look at the TV, even though the tape had finished. I looked at the carpet instead, not really seeing anything. 'What are we going to do about this? Who can we trust with it? With the work you do catching online paedophiles, who do you hand your evidence to in the police?'

'I have a contact in the Paedophile Unit at Scotland Yard. He's a good guy, overworked, frustrated with the lack of convictions he and his team get when it goes to court, but he does everything he can to convict these sickos. But we can't go to the police with this, because the police are involved. It could've been Special Branch or the security services who killed Jamie so he wouldn't show this to the world. My contact's only a sergeant; he doesn't have enough power to stop this being squashed from up above when they know who's involved.'

'So who else? Who can we trust with something this big?'

Mitchell stood up and scrubbed his hands over his face, but not before I saw his eyes glistening with his own tears and the anger turning to hatred on his face. 'I need another drink.'

SIBEL HODGE

I followed him into the kitchen on weak and rubbery legs. I sat at the table, rested my feet on the edge of the chair, and curled my knees against my chest, hugging them tight.

We drank long into the night. Drank to try and forget. To block out the images we'd seen. Because if we didn't, there was no way we could get any sleep. Sometime in the early hours, my eyes drooped, but every time I allowed them to close, I could see Moses. Now I knew why Jamie had Moses's mum's address written on that list. He was probably going to finally tell her what had happened to her son. When I met her, I'd thought the worse thing was the not knowing, but I didn't believe that anymore. The agony of her knowing the truth was far, far worse. And I couldn't ever bring myself to tell her.

I poured myself a vodka from the now half-empty bottle on the table. 'Do you see Alex? When you fall asleep?' I slurred.

'I see him every day. In everything. I see his eyes whether I'm awake or asleep.' He stared into his drink and wrapped his fist around his glass, as if squeezing the life out of it.

'I don't know if I can get through this.'

'You're a lot stronger than you think.'

'But where does strong get you? Jamie was strong, and he's gone.'

He didn't answer, because after all, what was there to say?

Eventually, I must've succumbed to sleep, because the next thing I knew it was morning and I was on Mitchell's sofa with a thick duvet over me and a pillow underneath my head. Mitchell was asleep in the armchair across the room.

My head pounded. My mouth was an arid desert. My eyes were so puffy from crying, I could hardly open them.

I sat up, the room tilting around me. I stumbled into the kitchen for some water and downed two glasses in quick succession before splashing my face with it. I spied my bag on the table and retrieved a packet of Paracetamol. I took two. I needed to be clear-headed and think.

Mitchell had a fancy, complicated-looking coffee maker on the worktop, but by the time I figured out how to use it, it would be dinner time, so I rooted around in the cupboards, looking for instant.

I poured three heaped spoonfuls in, along with three sugars, and drank it boiling hot and black.

'Morning.' Mitchell strolled into the kitchen barefoot, wearing jeans and a black T-shirt. His eyes were just as swollen as mine, and the day-old stubble on his cheeks and head was peppered with grey.

'Morning.'

'The coffee maker does nicer coffee.' He tilted his head towards it.

'I'm not very technical. It's got too many buttons on it. I probably would've ended up breaking it. Jamie was the techie one.' I smiled sadly.

Mitchell nodded in acknowledgement.

'I've had an idea,' I said.

'What is it?' He got some kind of little pot out of the cupboard, placed it in the machine, and added water before pressing a few buttons.

'We've found irrefutable evidence against them now, so there is a way to expose this without revealing who *we* are, like you said. We can send it to the media—the newspapers and TV.'

Mitchell handed me a mug of frothy cappuccino. 'They won't publish it.'

'What? Why not? Of course they will!'

He repeated the coffee-making process with another mug then took a sip of it before answering. 'Who do you think controls the mainstream media?'

I shrugged. 'I don't know…the owners of the papers and TV stations.'

'No.' He sat down at the kitchen table, leant back, and scrubbed

2

22 SIBEL HODGE

his hands over his face. 'Do you think they report the truth?' He laughed, but it was devoid of humour. 'Mainstream media is a way to control the masses. They brainwash us with their own agendas to get public opinion swayed in a certain way. They're in the business of selling lies. Lies and cover-ups. And if you sell the lie, and keep selling it, people start to believe it, and then it becomes the truth, and the public don't question it because it's there, in black and white and colour in the papers, on the news! Come on. You're an intelligent woman. What do you think is going on?' He snorted.

I sat back, stunned at the vehemence in his voice but also the content of his words. I'd never thought about it before. Never had a need to. 'So, you're saying all the mainstream media is controlled by who? The politicians?'

'Not just politicians. Most of the time, they're the puppets behind the real powerhouses. There are hidden hands—puppetmasters—controlling everything.'

'Who, then?'

'The Big Boys. The money men. The banksters, hedge funds, Federal Reserve, Bank of England—those cartels who control the financial systems—along with the corporations, the industries, the lobby groups. The elite. People with more power and more money than you can even imagine. People whose only interest is greed and profit and control. The media's job is to operate on behalf of corporate and political agendas, which is exactly the same way politics works, so of course we never get to hear the real truth,' he spat. 'Here's a prime example of how it works. The public is sick of war, right? Sick to fucking death of it. The parents whose kids go off to fight and never come back. The innocent civilians. Women, kids, men who have nothing to do with it at all. We're causing problems all over the world, butting our noses into things that don't concern us, starting wars that aren't even legally sanctioned. But the death toll rises. And rises. Why?'

242

I shook my head, trying to keep up. 'Because of terrorism?'

'The war on terror! That's the biggest lie of all. The real war is the war on truth!'

'What?'

'Most of these so-called terrorist organisations or cells are funded by our own governments or security services in the first place. They instigate a regime change on bullshit pretexts founded on a pack of lies, because it suits their political agenda and foreign policy, without realising they're creating a monster by playing with jihadist groups. The West is sending their own countries' kids off to die, fighting the very same people their governments are secretly arming, and they're not only condoning it but actually writing their names on the fucking bullet! Because nobody loves a war like the Big Boys. They're hypocrites and parasites who are earning trillions from it. We're the biggest terrorists on the planet! And don't even get me started on 9/11.'

'So you're a conspiracy theorist?'

'It's very telling that anyone who dares to question the mainstream is automatically labelled a conspiracy theorist, don't you think? I'm not talking conspiracy theory. It's conspiracy fact. There is overwhelming evidence that needs investigation, but enquiries are mismanaged and quashed. They're just whitewashed.' He leant his elbows on his knees, shaking his head with disgust. 'I've seen it with my own eyes. Out there in the unforgiving desert, in the Balkans, on the streets of Northern Ireland. The bloodbaths. The unnecessary killing. Murder under the guise of war because of secret corporate agendas.' He breathed deeply. Closed his eyes. 'I've seen it all. You have no bloody idea. And this is just one example—the tip of the iceberg. There's so much brainwashing going on, people just don't realise.' He opened them again and stared at me, his deep blue eyes with so much pain and fire behind them. His usually controlled demeanour and calm mask were beginning to fall apart. 'And I was one of the brainwashed, too. But it's not until something drastic happens, like Alex, that makes you start to question what you *think* you know. What you've been bombarded with from an early age. And when you wake up and have that moment of clarity, you finally see through all the smoke and mirrors and become enlightened to what's really going on, you wonder how you could've ever fallen for it in the first place. It's the biggest con of all. Everything is just so fucked up.'

I cupped my hands tight around my coffee, confused, not knowing what to say.

'So, if people don't want a war—are totally opposed to a war—how do you get away with it? You change public opinion and manufacture consent, that's how. You construct a carefully organised deception. A well-crafted and perfectly executed lie. Stage false flag attacks, created by our own security services, blame it on terrorists, blow up British or US soldiers, bomb our buildings, fly planes into them, lie about weapons of mass destruction that can annihilate us in forty-five minutes flat. And bombard people with it in the media. Terrorists! Terrorism! Cells! Al-Qaeda! Isis! So *every* single time you turn on the news or read a paper, it's there. Despite the fact that statistically, you're more likely to be killed in a car accident or by your own bathtub than killed by a terrorist! And all the while, they're hiding the real reasons. Oil and gas. Gold. Regime change. Land. Power. Money. So they carry on until the public gets scared and angry, and yes, let's bomb those bastards! And how dare these people threaten and attack us! Then they *want* the war. The public are practically begging for it by then! Like George Orwell said, "The people believe what the media tells them". And if you control the media, the money, the politics, and the military, you control the whole system.'

He flexed his jaw, a muscle twitching under the surface. '*That's* how you sell the lie.' He slapped an open palm on the table, making me flinch. '*That's* how you manipulate the people.' Another loud slap. 'And *that's* why the mainstream media will not touch this.' A final slap. 'Because the people you're dealing with *are* the Big Boys. And they're going to protect each other at all costs and fake a truth that doesn't exist!' He jerked to his feet, yanked open the sliding patio door into the garden, and walked to the end of it. He paced up and down barefoot on the frosty flagstones, muttering words I couldn't hear, his hands on his head, leaving me staring in shock at his sudden outburst.

I'd never seen this side of Mitchell. But then what did I really know about him? Nothing.

Strangely, though, I wasn't scared of him. I'd rather take my chances with Mitchell than anyone else right now. And after what I'd discovered about the Establishment, the so-called peers of our society, there was a profound truth to what he was saying. I'd been living in a naïve bubble my entire life, where everything I thought I knew about how the world worked was just one big lie. Seeing what I wanted to see. Closing my eyes. But there was a hidden world out there, where people were participating in extreme brutality—abhorrent, bloodcurdling things. Keeping secrets which determined who lived and who died. And nothing would ever be the same again. It couldn't be after what I'd discovered.

But it wasn't fair of me to drag Mitchell into my problems. It was obviously sparking horrific heartbreak about Alex all over again and possibly bringing some kind of stress from combat to the surface.

I grabbed hold of my bag and then shovelled my phones and the metal box containing the video and photos inside it. I pulled my coat from the back of the chair and felt his hand squeezing my wrist, his fingers digging into my flesh.

I froze. Gasped.

He let go. 'I'm sorry about that.'

I turned around.

He ran his hands over his bristly head and left them there, his elbows sticking out to the side. He stared at me, his eyes shining. 'The world we're living in makes me so insane with anger.'

'No, I'm the one who should be sorry,' I said. 'I shouldn't have asked you for help. I...you've been through so much, too. With your job and Alex. Things I can't even imagine. And I...' I glanced towards the kitchen doorway. 'I should go. This isn't your problem. It's not your fight.'

'No!' His voice was loud but gentle now. 'Don't go. This is definitely my kind of fight. I want to get them off the streets as much as you.' He pointed at the chair I'd previously been sitting in. 'Please. Sit. I've had an idea.'

I swallowed and sat down, wondering if I should leave anyway. I was still thinking about it when he spoke.

'I follow an alternative, investigative news website called Truth.com. The guy who owns it writes most of the articles. He's very thorough, very professional. His name's Simon Wheelan, and the website covers things the mainstream media won't publish. They have a particular interest in uncovering the truth that goes on in the political arena.'

'Okay.'

'I think they would be very interested in publishing Jamie's story.'

'But then it would come out who Jamie is. Who I am.'

'They could do it without revealing his identity or yours. They vigorously protect their sources and whistle-blowers. But they can easily cover what happened at Crossfield and Crompton Place in a way that doesn't come back to you. There must've been hundreds, maybe thousands of kids through there over the years before it closed down.'

'Would they publish the names of the people who did this to the children?'

'No. For legal reasons.'

'But that's what we need to do, isn't it? Show these photos and video to the world? That's why I suggested the media. If they're published, then the police will have to take action against them. They won't be able to cover it up. There would be too much pressure from the public.'

Mitchell slumped in his chair. 'I don't think anyone would dare to publish the tape or photos. Apart from the fact they'd be sued and probably have injunctions and gagging orders slapped on them left, right, and centre, they wouldn't be able to because it would compromise any criminal investigation.' I opened my mouth to say how outrageous and offensive that was to me, but he carried on. 'But I think Simon *will* print the story with allegations, maybe name their professions. And I also think we need to show this evidence to someone else. The more people who see it, the more insurance we have.'

'Not if they can't tell anyone what's actually in it or show anyone.'

'Maybe.' Mitchell shrugged. 'But I still think it's in our best interests for someone else to see this. It's an offence for us just to have something like this in our possession.'

'So, what are you suggesting? That we just hand the tape and photos over to a journalist?'

'Yes.'

'No way! Like you said, this is our only insurance. And anyway, what good is an article that doesn't name them or expose what they've done? These people are sadistic murderers!'

'This isn't my area of expertise, obviously, but I think this is the first step in exposing them, because we don't know who else we can trust with this. Maybe other boys will come forward. Other witnesses. They can't go round killing everyone.'

'What if the evidence gets lost? Or stolen?'

'We make a copy of everything first and secure it somewhere safe.'

I thought about that as I swallowed the bittersweet dregs of coffee at the bottom of my mug. Thought about the powerful people involved. We couldn't go to the police on our own. It would go nowhere, and Mitchell and I would be exposed straight away. Exposed and probably killed, like Jamie and Dave. My head throbbed, and my jaw ached. 'I suppose it's the only thing we can do.'

He stood up decisively. 'I'm going to cook us breakfast, then we can make digital copies of everything and contact Simon. But we're going to use an alias for ourselves. Simon would probably do that anyway, for any story, but it's better to be safe than sorry.'

My stomach churned at the thought of food. 'I'm not hungry.'

'I'm not taking no for an answer. You need to eat something after what you polished off last night. You don't want to be flaking out in Simon's office, do you?'

I didn't say I agreed, but I let him take charge as he sliced paninis, filled them with cheese and tomato and fresh basil leaves from his fridge, then squashed them beneath a panini grill. He made me more coffee from the machine, and it tasted a million times better than instant.

'Thank you,' I said as I tucked in, not realizing until then how starving I was. Mitchell was right that I needed to eat. I was no good to Jamie if I didn't look after myself. No good to the others who could no longer speak for themselves. I'd never get justice then.

I just hoped he was right about everything else.

Chapter 33

While I scanned all the photos via Mitchell's laptop onto a flash drive, Mitchell converted and copied *The Friday Club* tape with his media equipment before adding that to the drive. Then Mitchell affixed false number plates to his pickup, and we drove into central London via a random route, Mitchell regularly doubling back and keeping a constant eye on his rear-view mirror for anyone tailing us. Eventually, we parked in an underground car park and walked another random route to the offices of Truth.com. Mitchell wore a baseball cap, the peak pulled down low, and sunglasses to obscure his face. He had the evidence secured inside his zipped-up bomber jacket. I also wore sunglasses and a hoodie that covered my head.

After we took a seat for a few minutes in reception, a guy who looked in his early forties appeared from the lift to our left and strode towards us. He was tall and thin, with a protruding Adam's apple. He had blond hair and grey eyes behind square, frameless glasses. He wore a smart, casual white-checked shirt with navy trousers.

He smiled at Mitchell and held a hand out to him before turning to me. 'Nice to meet you both. Let's go up to the conference room.'

We followed him into the lift and rode it to the fifth floor, then we stepped out into an open-plan space with cubicles containing desks, cabinets, and computers. The noise of keyboards and people talking and phones ringing brought me back to being at work in the call centre. It seemed like another lifetime away now. A past that belonged to someone else.

Glass-fronted offices were around the edge of the room, and we walked to one right at the end that overlooked the busy London street below. The Venetian blinds were tilted slightly, making the room private from any prying eyes in the office windows on the opposite side of the street.

'Have a seat. Can I get you something to drink? Tea? Coffee?' Simon gestured at the large oval conference table in the centre of the room. Various TV screens on the wall were set to different news channels, the volume muted. A projector screen was set up on the opposite wall. State-of-the-art equipment was hooked up to another TV.

I shook my head. I'd had enough coffee by then to keep me wired for days. 'No, thanks.'

'None for me, either.' Mitchell removed his sunglasses, and I did the same.

Simon sat at the head of one end of the oval. The padded chair made a *poofing* sound as he sat down. Mitchell sat next to him. I sat next to Mitchell, wringing my hands in my lap, trying to get my erratic heart rate back to normal.

Simon leant forward, his elbows on the table, his fingers locked together in front of him. 'So, you didn't go into too much detail on the phone, but you think you have an explosive story we might be interested in?'

'You never know who's listening,' Mitchell said.

Simon gave an acknowledging smile. 'I take it that Matt and Jane aren't your real names, then?'

Mitchell just gave him a wry smile in return and twisted in his chair to me. 'Do you want to tell him why we're here?'

I swallowed hard and sucked in some air, hesitating, gnawing on my lower lip.

Simon smiled again. It was warm and confident. 'Obviously you're using aliases, but I'd also like to assure you that we always vigorously protect our sources and whistle-blowers. If you've followed our website, then you'll know we have the utmost integrity in that area. You have my guarantee that anything you tell me will be confidential unless you specifically agree to it being published. And even then, we also give aliases to sources. If we do video interviews, the sources' faces are never revealed, and their voices are distorted.'

I glanced at Mitchell. He nodded his approval slowly.

'Okay, recently my boyfriend died.' Those words still felt wrong on my tongue, even though I couldn't deny them anymore. 'It was made to look like a suicide—a hanging—but I started to question it.' Once I began speaking, everything just poured out of me in a nervous vomit of words.

Simon angled his chair to face me, sat back, and listened carefully, occasionally nodding, occasionally shaking his head.

'The care system was rife with this kind of thing back then,' Simon said. 'It was a magnet for paedophiles and child abusers. The people in charge of the homes who had those predilections employed like-minded people, of course. It kept their circle close and avoided detection. It also isolated the kids because they had no one to talk to who wasn't involved. There were also a lot of staff who weren't trained or qualified, or were on minimum wage, which led to further abuse and neglect because employees didn't care about the kids—the same as instances of animal abuse in slaughterhouses and farms.'

Mitchell's jaw clenched.

I carried on with the story, finally getting to the part about finding the tape and photos Jamie had hidden.

Simon's eyes widened with horror. 'You have actual video evidence of Moses's murder?'

I blinked slowly, trying to erase the vision behind my eyes. 'Yes. And photos of the other unknown boy being murdered. Along with other photos that detail the vile abuse of more boys by these people.'

Simon swivelled in his chair, blowing out a deep breath. 'Whoa.' He steepled his fingers together, apparently thinking.

'There's also a diary that Jamie wrote before he died, detailing most of the events that happened. The things I've already told you.'

'If what you say is true, this is definitely going to be explosive.' Simon tapped the table, his lips pursed.

'I want this exposed, but if they find out I know about all this, they...' I trailed off.

'I can completely understand that, given the nature of the people you say are involved in this, and I reiterate that I always protect my sources. If you want me to publish this, then I'll give your boyfriend an alias. Now, obviously I need to verify what's in the evidence you have and try to make my own enquiries. Are you happy to leave it all with me temporarily, and I'll contact you when I've reviewed it?'

'I've brought the original photos and video, along with Jamie's diary, on a flash drive, but how do I know someone else won't be able to get hold of it all? Like I said, if anyone else reads this diary, it will lead them to me.'

'Everything will be seen by me only, and they'll be kept somewhere safe and secure until I return them back to you. We have the utmost security on our website, but all of the digital evidence you loan to me will be viewed on a system that's not linked to our servers, so there's no chance of someone hacking into it.'

I glanced at Mitchell. Mitchell glanced at me. I had to trust someone, and if Mitchell thought this guy could help us, then I had to go along with that.

'Okay.' I took a brown envelope containing everything out of my bag and slid it towards him.

'I'm not going to publish anything without contacting you first, you have my word on that. Your safety is obviously a huge priority here. Can you leave me a phone number?'

Mitchell wrote down a mobile phone number and handed it to Simon.

Simon pressed his hands on the table and pushed himself to a standing position. 'Thank you for taking the time to see me. I'll get onto this straight away so, hopefully, I can get in touch by the end of the day and return this all to you.' He held out his hand for us to shake again.

During the lift ride down Mitchell replaced his sunglasses and motioned for me to do the same. Back out on the street, he handed me another cheap mobile phone. This one was a Samsung.

'What's this for?' I asked.

'This is the pay-as-you-go number I gave Simon. Use it only for him. The other Nokia I gave you is for us to contact each other only. That way, if anyone hacks into Simon's phone records, they can't connect us to each other, and they won't know who you are.'

'Right.' So now I had three mobile phones, including my own. I just hoped I didn't mix them up inadvertently.

As if to remind me which phone was actually my personal one, my iPhone rang in my bag.

'Hiya, Maya!' Ava's cheery voice sang out. 'How are you? Do you want to go out for lunch? My treat?'

'Um…thanks, sis, but I'm kind of tied up at the moment.'

'Oh? What are you up to? I haven't seen you for ages. You must be really lonely rattling around at home all alone. You haven't even called me lately, and I just get your voicemail all the time.'

I pinched the bridge of my nose. 'Yeah, I'm sorry. It's just…' Just what? That I felt contaminated by murder and perverts and filth and evil, and I didn't want my family immersed in that darkness? That was hardly something I could tell Ava. 'Um…'

'Where are you? I can hear traffic. Are you in town? Shall I bring Jackson up and we can meet for something to eat?' I heard the worry in her voice again.

'No, it's okay. I'm not in town, anyway.'

'Well, where are you then? Why are you being so secretive all the time? I want to help you, but you never talk to me anymore, and I don't know what's going on with you since—' Ava broke off abruptly, not wanting to bring up Jamie's death.

I exhaled a huge breath. 'Look, I'm sorry, sis. I've got to go. Give Jackson a kiss from me. I'll see you soon, okay?' I hung up before she could ask anything else and the conversation became too awkward. As I put my phone back in my bag, I heard a loud bang, like an exhaust backfiring. I glanced around sharply, but it was just an old car heading down the road. When I looked at Mitchell, who'd walked a short distance away to give me privacy during the call, he was leaning against the wall of the next building, breathing hard, blinking rapidly, his shoulders stiff.

I walked towards him, and as I got closer, I noticed the sheen of sweat on his forehead, a vibrating, nervous energy oozing out of him, and he mumbled something to himself I couldn't make out.

And then I heard it clearly…

'It's not happening right now. It's not happening right now. It's not happening right now.'

I put my hand on his arm. 'Mitchell? Are you okay?'

It was as if he didn't see me at first. Didn't hear me.

'A bus, a street, a shop, a bike,' he said, his gaze darting around him.

I kept my hand there, unsure what to do. Was he having some kind of panic attack? A flashback?

'A bus. A street. A street. A shop,' he muttered.

'You're okay, Mitchell. You're okay.'

Slowly, he turned to me, his blank eyes suddenly seeming to refocus.

His breathing slowed down again. Then he shook his head and shoulders. Ran a hand over his bald scalp.

'Are you all right?' I asked.

'I'm fine.' He started walking away from me, down the road.

I followed.

'Do you want to talk about it?' I asked.

'No.'

'Fair enough.' I knew how it felt with Ava and my parents asking me that stupid question enough times, so I walked with him, not saying anything, moving through men and women in suits, bustling around carrying briefcases.

About ten minutes later, Mitchell looked at me. All the anxiety emanating from him so powerfully a moment ago seemed to have gone, as if nothing remotely odd had even happened. 'What do you want to do now?'

I looked around the busy London street, feeling totally and utterly lost. 'I don't know. I don't think I want to go home.'

'You're welcome to come back to my house. I have some work to do for a few hours, though. I need to catch up online.'

'Catching paedophiles?'

'Yes.'

'Will you show me what you do?'

His forehead furrowed into a frown. 'Are you sure you want to know?'

'It's not like I can forget about them, is it? Every moment is filled with thoughts about paedophiles now. And I'm only going to be looking at my phone every five minutes, waiting for Simon to call. Maybe this will distract me, and maybe I can learn something useful that might help you in return for helping me.'

'All right, then.'

~ ~ ~ ~

We sat on his sofa, Mitchell with an iPhone in his hand, me with his laptop. He'd logged me into one of the teen chat rooms he used, where he'd set up a profile as a twelve-year-old girl called Emma. Her photo showed she had long dark hair, wide eyes with long lashes, and full lips smiling cheekily to the camera. She was dressed in skinny jeans and a pink T-shirt with *Drama Queen* splashed across the front.

'Who is she?'

'No one.'

'What?'

'She's Photoshopped. The original photo is of my niece, Kelly, my sister's daughter. She's actually seventeen, not twelve. But I've altered her facial features so it looks nothing like her now.'

'And she doesn't mind?'

'No. She wants to help. So does my sister. They feel as strongly as I do about getting these people off the streets.'

'But she doesn't actually have to meet these men, does she?'

'Christ, no! She never comes into contact with them. The perverts online see her fake profile, her fake picture, and start chatting with her—or me. I don't instigate any sexual talk. In fact, I act immature and shy. I wait for them to rise to the bait, and with these guys, it doesn't take long. They start grooming the kids, flirting, becoming more and more suggestive. Often they send naked photos of themselves. They get more lewd about what they want to do to her, becoming bolder as time goes on. Eventually, they want to meet. The majority of the time, they blatantly say it's because they want to have sex, which is usually the time I hand everything over to my contact at the Met's Paedophile Unit.'

'And then what happens?'

'Most of the time, they deny it when they're confronted with the evidence I've collected. Deny knowing the kids are underage, even though it's a priority of mine to reiterate it to them many times. Or they're ashamed. Sometimes angry or even violent. Sometimes they say they're sorry.' His eyes narrowed with hatred. 'But what's sorry going to do? The only thing they're sorry for is getting caught. A lot of the time, when the police take their computers or search their houses, they're full of child porn. Sometimes even with babies. Sometimes snuff films like *The Friday Club* tape.'

'No!' I cupped my hands around my mouth, trying to hold back the disgust.

'People think that paedophilia is just a small minority of people, but it's prolific, believe me. There are so many of these sick shits out there. And the problem is, a lot of them don't think they're doing anything wrong. They actually believe they *love* children. They don't think they're hurting them in any way. Some even think that children should be sexually liberated and have the right to have sex.'

'What?' I scrunched my face up in horror.

'I know, it's in-fucking-sane! My contact at the paedo unit has had several convictions so far with the evidence I've provided, but one of the biggest problems is that the sentences are so lenient. A lot of the time, these people get off with just a slap on the wrist. The police who work in the unit are fuming about the punishment these judges dish out. They're sitting on their bench, removed from the real world, totally unwilling to make an example of these people. If you can even call them people.'

'Or they're involved in it all, too.'

'Exactly. That high court judge Jamie spoke about, Howard Sebastian, he sat at the Old Bailey. Do you know what the inscription is above the front doors? "Defend the children of the poor and punish the wrongdoer". It makes a mockery of everything, doesn't it? Often it takes months and months of painstaking work for dedicated police officers, putting a case together, only for it to be thrown out in court, or for a totally unjust punishment to be handed down. And I'm not just talking about possessing child porn, which feeds the whole industry in the first place. I'm also talking about terrible sexual assaults. Repeat offenders.' His fingers squeezed the iPhone he was holding so hard I was surprised it wasn't crushed in his meaty hand. 'It makes me so bloody angry because a lot of the time there's no justice for these children.'

I couldn't describe to him how terrible I thought it all was. The word *horrific* didn't even begin to vocalize it. 'So, what do I need to type?'

He signed into another chat room on his phone and sat closer, showing it to me. I curled my legs up beside me, leaning over his shoulder.

'This is a different profile I've set up. This girl I've made up is also twelve and called Lucy. Some guy has been chatting to me for the last week. Look at his photo.'

The man was about forty-five, with receding hair, trying to dress in a trendy way, wearing tight jeans that only accentuated his pot belly, and a long-sleeve T-shirt with writing all over it. He wore Converses and sat on the bonnet of a yellow Ferrari. His profile said his name was Nick.

I shook my head, a sickening sensation welling up inside. 'Whose photo are you using for Lucy?' The profile showed a different picture to the previous one.

'This is another Photoshopped picture. It fools them every time. That, along with the abbreviated text-speak of a young kid typing.'

Mitchell showed me what the man had just typed in the personal chat message.

Nick: You've got lovely tits in your photo!

I watched Mitchell's fingers move over the iPhone's keypad in return and waited for a reply. A minute later, his iPhone pinged, and he showed it to me, his eyebrows raised, shaking his head.

Lucy: LOL, im only 12!!!

Nick: You look a lot older. Very sexy.

Lucy: thx

Nick: Want to send me a photo of them?

*Lucy: *blush**

Nick: Have you ever had sex before?

Lucy: course not!!!

Nick: I bet you've got all the boys after you. You're gorgeous.

Lucy: maybe ;)

Nick: You're so sexy, of course they all fancy you. Who wouldn't!

Lucy: maybe some guys at school but theyre too immature.

I wondered how my life had come to this, passing the afternoon by trying to get sick perverts to reveal their true colours so we could try to put them away. It was disturbingly surreal. But I was starting to believe the same as Mitchell.

Did justice really exist? Or was that another lie?

Chapter 34

Mitchell phoned a local Indian restaurant at seven p.m., and we ordered a delivery. Surprisingly, I was starving. We moved the laptop and phone to the kitchen table as we ate, reading out the chat coming into each other's profiles and what our replies were as we typed.

'He's asking if we can meet up. He says he'll take me anywhere I want to go and wants to know my dress size so he can buy me something special!' Mitchell glared a venomous look at his phone and growled. 'Imagine if I was a real young girl being fooled by him?' He forked a mouthful of chicken tikka into his mouth.

The laptop pinged, and I read out the message from the guy chatting to me as 'Emma'. "Would you like to see some more photos of me?" he's asking.' I typed in as I said the words out loud. '"Okay. Smiley face".' I gasped when I saw the nude photo a guy called John had sent me. I turned the laptop round to face Mitchell. 'Dirty pervert!' I pushed my dinner away. 'That's completely put me off my food. Even *I* wouldn't want to see that at my age, so why does he think a twelve-year-old would?'

'Because he's not right in the head.'

One of my mobile phones rang then. It was my personal one, resting on the table, with Ava's number flashing at me. 'My sister again,' I said to Mitchell before picking up.

'Hi, I'm sorry about earlier. I probably sounded like a nosey, bossy sister, didn't I?' she gushed. 'But…look, are you at home yet? I was going to pop round. And before you say no again, you'll actually be doing me a favour. I've been stuck in the house all day, and I'm feeling antsy.'

'I'm…um…' I glanced at Mitchell. 'I'm not at home at the moment.'

'Oh. Where are you? Have you finally decided to go and see Lynn or Becca? Good, I'm really pleased you're getting out of the house again and trying to move on with things.'

I heard the relief in her voice, so I didn't bother to correct her. What would I say, anyway? I'm in a paedophile hunter's kitchen, chatting online to sickos, while I wait to see if a journalist will help me expose my boyfriend's killer after I watched a snuff movie involving a VIP child abuse ring?

'Well, I hope you're having a nice time.' The warmth in her voice filtered down the phone. 'I'll catch up with you soon, okay?'

'Okay.'

'Love you.'

'Love you, too, sis.' I hung up. 'She'll probably be straight on the phone to Mum and Dad now, telling them I seem to be feeling a bit better and am out with my friends. I think that's better than them knowing the truth. I want to protect them from anything bad happening to them all. And they would never believe it, anyway,' I said sadly. My Samsung rang then, which meant it was Simon. 'Hello?'

'Hi, it's Simon. I've just finished going through everything, and it's shocking. I've got to make some more enquiries, obviously, but I'm going to put a story together. I'm convinced the tape and photos are genuine, and I'd also like nothing better than to name these depraved individuals, but I won't be allowed to print their names.

One, for legal reasons. We can't name them unless they're arrested or interviewed by the police. And two, because we can't do anything to jeopardise any future police investigation. I know you don't want to contact the police yourselves at this stage, but we can act as an intermediary, if that's something you decide on later. That way your identity stays hidden. However, there is another way to initiate an official investigation.' He paused for a beat. 'This really needs to go to the top first, so I've been thinking about that, and I wanted to make a suggestion. There's an MP called Alistair Bromwyn. He was very outspoken about historical child abuse allegations that happened several years ago in another children's home, involving a prominent VIP network. Not quite in the same league as we're talking now, but they were still well-respected, influential men. He was very vigorous in campaigning for a public enquiry into it after a stalled police investigation seemed to be covering up what had happened. He came under a lot of pressure from all arenas over it, including members of his own party, but he didn't back down. And because of his tenacity, in the end, with Alistair's involvement, the victims managed to get the justice they deserved.

'I think Alistair will be sympathetic. I'm certain he won't let this get brushed under the carpet. He'll want to make sure there's no cover-up, the same as you. And even if no other witnesses come forward, the evidence you have is undeniable. Considering the high-profile nature of the people involved, you're going to need some influential help on your side, and Alistair is one of the few, genuine politicians who are actually in the game to do something good. Do you want me to arrange a meeting? I interviewed him several times when I was covering the children's home scandal, and I have a secure phone number for him.'

'Let me talk it over with Mitchell, and I'll get back to you.'

'Absolutely. I'll leave it with you. In the meantime, getting back to the story, I can reveal their professions—MP, judge, high-ranking police officer, cabinet minister, etcetera. And I'll put in an appeal for any witnesses with information to come forward. I'll show it to you before it goes to print to get your approval. Are you happy with all that?'

'Yes, that's very helpful.'

'I've seen a lot of terrible things in my career. You have to become hardened to the atrocities people inflict on each other. But what I saw on the tape...it's impossible to be hardened to something like that. I'm going to do everything I can to make sure this story is covered sensitively, *and* help in any way to bring the perpetrators to justice.'

'Thanks so much, Simon. Oh, and one other thing, just for the record. If anything happens to me as a result of this, you know where to look.'

We said our goodbyes, and I hung up and relayed the conversation to Mitchell, who was instantly dismissive of involving Alistair Bromwyn, calling all politicians lying bastards controlled by puppetmasters. But after spending hours researching him and his past, the more it seemed that Alistair was one of the good guys, as Simon had said. Everything we found out about him showed an MP who actually seemed to care. An avid social-justice activist who wanted to bring about positive and progressive change in areas like human rights, peace, and environmental issues. A straight-talker who didn't stoop to childish slurs or personal insults. Someone who seemed genuinely authentic and sincere, and willing to stand up for what he believed in with courage and conviction, regardless of whether it toed the party line or not. Back and forth Mitchell and I went, me trying to convince Mitchell that Alistair was exactly the right kind of person who had both the influence and integrity that we needed in our corner—the only person we could take a chance on—and him slowly acquiescing. In the end, I felt as if we didn't have a choice. It was Alistair or nothing.

Half of me felt grateful and almost happy there had been some good news. But the other half knew the journey had only just begun.

Chapter 35

I walked up the steps of the community centre with Mitchell at my side. When we reached the top, I stopped for a moment, trying to prepare myself to tell a story that didn't get any easier the more I told it.

We had an appointment to meet Alistair Bromwyn at one of his weekly constituency surgeries, arranged via Simon. My stomach turned to liquid with worry. Alistair couldn't deny what was in the photos and on tape, but did he really have the strength and integrity to take action against a serving government minister and the defence secretary? Members of his own political party? Or was this a waste of time? It could be like me holding up a big arrow and saying, 'Come and get me! I'm here. You can bump me off now, too!'

Mitchell gripped my arm before we went inside. 'Are you absolutely sure you want to do this?'

I nodded. 'If I want to finish what Jamie started, then I have to take a chance on Alistair.'

'Okay, then.'

We headed inside and were met by Alistair's secretary, who introduced himself as Damien Hammond and led us to an empty office down a corridor across from the main hall.

'He'll be with you shortly.' Damien gave us a curt nod, closing the door behind him.

I picked at my fingernails while we waited. I took a deep breath, trying to dampen the sickness churning away. I glanced at Mitchell, who sat back in the plastic chair next to me, his hands in his pockets, his gaze casually scanning the room as if he didn't have a care in the world.

'Aren't you nervous?' I asked.

'I've had years of practice at waiting. Anyway, either he's going to help or he's not. Being nervous isn't going to change that.'

'Yes, but if he doesn't help us, where do we go from here? We don't have many options, and they'll just get away with it,' I hissed, angry at his lack of worrying. 'Is that what you want?' I glared accusingly at him, my face so tense all my muscles ached.

'You know that's not what I want at all. Let's not think about it until it happens, okay?'

I had to sit on my hands in the end because I'd drawn blood on the skin around my fingers. After what seemed like an eternity, Alistair entered the room. He was short and nondescript but had an air of stature and solid strength about him.

I stood up so quickly to introduce myself that I knocked my chair over, and it went clattering to the floor. My face flushed with embarrassment, stupidity, and probably the fact that my blood pressure was about to hit top figures.

Mitchell picked up my chair as Alistair gave me what I thought was probably a well-practised politician's smile, holding out a manicured hand for me to shake before turning his attention to Mitchell.

'A pleasure to meet you both, Matt and Jane.' He sat behind the desk and rested his forearms on it, leaning forward, his thick salt-and-pepper eyebrows furrowed and a grave expression on his face. 'Simon Wheelan had some very disturbing news to tell me in relation to this meeting.'

'Yes,' I said and started at the beginning again, telling him everything I'd told Simon about what had happened. He interrupted me occasionally to clarify points, and although his face paled, he didn't give any indication that he believed what I was saying.

'My condolences to you. What a very tragic turn of events,' Alistair said when I'd finished. He glanced at the desk for a few moments, appearing deep in thought. 'Those are very serious allegations you've made.'

'Which is why we came to you,' Mitchell said. 'You're in a position to put pressure on the justice system to take this seriously. Obviously, because of the people involved, it's likely that if *we* went to the police, any investigation would be shut down in a political cover-up.'

He glanced between us. 'I take it Matt and Jane aren't your real names?'

'Of course not. Our involvement has to remain secret,' Mitchell said.

'Whoever killed my boyfriend may come after me.' I waved my forefinger between myself and Mitchell. 'Or both of us, if they find out what we know.' I sat back in the chair, feeling sick. I couldn't deny I was scared. I could end up kicking and screaming at the end of that rope, begging for my life. Or killed in an anonymous hit-and-run accident. But my anger overrode the fear. I didn't care much about my own life anymore. I just wanted those sadistic, evil people to pay. But what about Mitchell? I couldn't be responsible for anything happening to him.

Mitchell gave him a tight-lipped smile. 'You don't have to reveal where this came from. You can easily keep our involvement out of this because the evidence speaks for itself.'

Alistair tilted his head. 'Do you have the photographs and video evidence, along with the diary in question?'

'Yes.' I pulled out of my bag the brown envelope containing the originals we'd picked up from Simon on the way there. In Jamie's diary, we'd changed any reference of him to 'Ian', just as Simon was going to do in his forthcoming news report. And we'd changed the names of all the other innocent boys to protect their identities. We didn't tell him about the digital copies of everything Mitchell and I had made. They were safely hidden.

Alistair held his hand out for them.

I clutched the envelope in my hand tightly, unwilling to hand it over until we had assurances he was going to do something.

'How do we know you're going to take action about this?' Mitchell asked suspiciously, wanting the same assurances as me.

'I assume you know I was the only MP calling for an enquiry into the Litton Care Home child abuse scandal?' He glanced between us, and we nodded. It was one of the things we'd researched on Alistair. 'Some of the people involved were esteemed members of society. Priests, teachers, solicitors, and of course staff. Not quite as prominent and powerful as we're talking about in this case, but nevertheless, we were dealing with some well-respected people. I spoke to a lot of the victims, who were damaged irreparably by the actions of these predators, and I don't care whether the offender is a teacher or the Queen of England, I will not stand for the systematic abuse of children. The system failed them once, but I couldn't let it fail them a second time. I'm a father myself, and I couldn't sleep at night if I didn't do my utmost to uphold the law of our country so we can protect the most vulnerable in our society. So we can learn from past mistakes and stop it happening again, as well as obtain justice for those people who've been wronged in the most abhorrent ways.

'The children's home care system of the past cultivated, protected, and defended sexual abusers and predators, and we have a duty to stand up and say enough is enough. It can't be allowed to continue.' He placed his hands flat on the desk. 'Please believe me when I say that if what you've told me is correct, and I will need to review the evidence you're going to give me, then I will stop at nothing to press for a police investigation to be made at the highest levels. And I *will* make sure that there is no cover-up. You have my absolute word on that.

'I didn't go into politics to protect the wrongdoings of the Establishment. I did it to serve the people of my constituency and the general public. And while I'm still an elected MP, that's exactly what I'll be doing. Now, I understand the concerns for your safety, and you have my utmost assurance that your involvement will remain confidential.'

I glanced at Mitchell, who looked at me with a clear message in his eyes. *How can you believe the word of a politician?* And yes, most of them told lies for a living, after all. But Alistair's voice was sincere. His body language appeared sincere. He seemed genuinely shocked, upset, and disturbed by what we'd told him.

And we had to trust someone with influence.

I handed Alistair the envelope.

'I'll be in contact when I've gone through this in detail to discuss the next course of action.' Alistair placed it on the desk in front of him and opened it. He pulled out the tape and the flash drive with Jamie's diary on it. When he got to the photos, he flicked through them, his frown of deep concentration being replaced by one of pure disgust and horror. He shook his head slowly. 'Well,' he said, his voice choked with emotion. 'I can guarantee this is all going to explode now.'

269

Chapter 36

It was a waiting game, the days and nights blending into each other as I waited for Alistair to tell us the police were going to do something. Waited for Simon's story to progress as he contacted the people from Jamie's list who were still alive, and tried to trace any other witnesses. And waited to get through each day without thinking of Jamie for every second of it.

It had been four months now since Jamie had been murdered. That meant 120 days. Or 2,880 hours. Or 172,800 minutes away from him. The photo I kept of Jamie in my wallet was now dog-eared and cracked from me taking it out and kissing it all the time. I was worried I'd forget what he looked like eventually. That his face would vanish from my memory, just like the scent of him slowly disappearing from his clothes I wore around the house, and then there would be nothing left to remind me that he really had been here. I talked to him in my head all the time. Talked to him out loud when I was at home on my own. I no longer saw him in random men I passed in the street or spotted him from across the supermarket. I knew he was gone. I got that now. It still didn't make things any easier, and I didn't know whether it ever would. I was being dragged down into an overwhelming dark pit.

The only thing keeping me from going insane with all the waiting was helping Mitchell catch the men he chatted with online. After what I knew now, I wanted these people exposed and convicted as much as Mitchell did. I would chat to these paedophiles, pretending I was an underage girl or boy, and I became good at talking like a teenager or pre-teen, learning all the texty-chat abbreviations. Mitchell had discussed paying me for helping him out, making it an actual job. In one of the rare moments where my sense of humour returned briefly, I wondered what job title I would put on my CV. *Maya Morgan: Paedophile Hunter.* But Jamie's estate had been pretty straightforward, and I was living off the money he'd left me and my own savings. His house had no mortgage, so I was okay for a while. I couldn't think about getting a real job while this was hanging over me, and I told Mitchell to keep his money. For the time being, it was what I had to do. It was almost cathartic, knowing I was helping in some way to stand up for the children who couldn't speak out themselves, but who knew what would happen in the future? It was hard to think about next week, let alone next month or next year.

I often visited Jamie's grave, and as strange as it was, given what I'd found in the field by the river, I went there, too. It made me feel closer, more connected to him, knowing it was one of the last places he'd been before he was murdered. And it was a place Jamie had always loved. He was happy there. It meant something to him. *We* were happy there that day he took me for the picnic.

The weather had been terrible all week. The sky a painting of charcoal and slate and navy blue. Rain lashing down in sheets, leaving thick, dirty puddles on the ground. Wind whipping through the trees. But on Thursday the weather broke. It was cool, but the sun was out, shining weakly in the spring sky.

Today was the day.

I stopped at the supermarket and bought the same things we'd had on so many of our picnics. French bread, Brie, tomatoes, olives, and pâté. Easy things I could eat with my fingers. Instead of champagne, I bought a bottle of Buck's Fizz. After packing it all into Jamie's wicker picnic hamper, I drove on towards Codicote.

Again, the place was deserted, and my car was the only one in the gravel lay-by where I parked. I carried the hamper and picnic blanket up the hill, through the woods, and down the slope on the other side to the river. For once, I didn't think about how Jamie's life had been cruelly and mercilessly snatched away from me. Instead, with the birds and rabbits and squirrels as witnesses, I celebrated Jamie's life and allowed myself to remember our time together. I sat beside the flowing river, toasting him with the Buck's Fizz and eating slowly, savouring every mouthful, just as I'd done when I was with him, and feeling him close, so close he was like a blanket wrapping around me, holding me up.

I stayed there for hours, whiling away the afternoon, lost in my memories of happy times, twisting the engagement ring on my finger. Taking Jamie in and breathing him out again. Trying to not let everything twisted and bad taint everything that had been good, for just a little while.

And saying goodbye in a way I hadn't been ready to at the funeral.

Chapter 37

I hardly slept, which was nothing new anymore. But this time it was because of an excited flutter beating inside me instead of the weight of loss and anxiety swallowing me. Simon had phoned the night before to tell us the story would be on Truth.com's website at 7.00 a.m. the next morning. I phoned Mitchell, who invited me to his house to read it together. Simon had already emailed the proof version to Mitchell for us to read and give our approval prior to publication. Mitchell had some kind of software on his laptop that made him completely anonymous when using the Internet, courtesy of Lee, Jamie's old mate in the Signals Regiment who had worked with Mitchell and was a communications expert who now owned a cyber-intelligence company.

But it was going to be different seeing it in black and white, live on the screen. With the click of a button, it could be in millions of homes, worldwide. Even if the names of the offenders weren't revealed, people would be talking, speculating. People would be shocked and outraged and furious. And along with Alistair's involvement, that could only help drive a police investigation.

I drove to Mitchell's house impatiently in the pre-dawn darkness, speeding, huffing at red traffic lights, cursing people pulling out in front of me who I couldn't overtake.

'Have you looked at it yet?' I breathlessly asked Mitchell as soon as he opened the door.

'No. I said I'd wait, didn't I? Come in. The laptop's in the kitchen. Kettle's on.'

I stood in front of the laptop, looking at the home screen on Truth.com's website as a slideshow of news stories appeared with their headlines.

Why We'll Never Win the War on Terror

How to Bring Down a Global Economy

Who Really Owns the Federal Reserve and the Bank of England?

Cowspiracy and Racing Extinction: 2 Must-See Documentaries Showing the Environmental Catastrophe Governments Won't Talk About

And there it was…

Rich and Powerful Held Child Sex Abuse Parties

Truth.com has received explosive and shocking new information and evidence that highly respected members of society held child sex abuse parties at a London mansion.

According to one witness we will call 'Ian', these abuse parties took place every weekend during the early – late '80s. At the time, Ian was in the care of Crossfield, a London children's home, where he suffered frequent physical and sexual abuse by staff that he believed was designed to groom him.

Ian reports that he was a young boy when staff from Crossfield began to traffic him to a mansion he calls 'the Big House' for abuse parties. He describes how he was plied with alcohol and drugs and, along with other boys from the children's home, was repeatedly raped, tortured, and beaten.

In his disturbing account, Ian describes sadistic and sickening assaults by high-profile and powerful men, including two serving cabinet ministers, a high-ranking police officer and judge, an investment banker, a children's home inspector, and an unknown man who always remained hooded and masked.

Ian also describes the death of one child at 'the Big House' in front of himself and other witnesses, along with the connection of the VIPs to another child murder.

Because the allegations are linked to the Establishment and Westminster, we understand that other witnesses to the abuse parties may not trust the police enough to investigate, however, Truth.com has received and authenticated irrefutable and shocking proof of Ian's allegations of assault and murder.

Truth.com is in liaison with one highly placed official who has previously campaigned vehemently against historical child abuse, and who is taking an active role in ensuring this evidence is passed to the police for a criminal investigation to proceed.

If you have any information that might help our investigation, please contact us in the strictest confidence...

My mouth lifted into an unfamiliar smile. I looked at Mitchell, whose face was lit up like mine. And at that moment, I was happy. I was proud of myself. I was strong. I was invincible.

And they were going to pay.

Chapter 38

Mitchell had been right about the mainstream media. After Simon's story broke, not a single newspaper or TV station picked up on it.

Simon called one day to say that he'd spoken to some journalists, and there was a media blackout on the story. They'd been issued with Defence Advisory Notices by the government, warning them not to publish any intelligence that might damage national security. The Cabinet Office's Media Monitoring Unit would not let anyone else touch it. Simon explained how difficult it was to get someone to report it when their salary depended on *not* reporting it. Someone had also tried to hack into Truth.com's website and take it down, but they hadn't succeeded.

'There are rumbles that another "War on Terror" is imminent in the Middle East, and nothing buries an embarrassing and dangerous story more than directing the public's attention away from it and onto something else.' Simon blew out a frustrated breath as we sat in Truth.com's conference room for an update. 'But I thought you'd like to know a witness has contacted me about the story.'

'That's good. Who?' I asked.

'She was a care assistant at Crossfield. The same woman Jamie spoke about in his diary. She said she only worked there a short while. She became suspicious about the abuse that was going on and reported it.'

'So there's a record of it?'

'Unfortunately not. The person she reported it to was Ted Byron.'

An angry growl escaped from my throat. 'The children's home inspector? The one who was involved in it all?'

'Yes. She had some disturbing things to say. He became quite aggressive, telling her she didn't have a clue what she was talking about. And said that she was only a lowly assistant and didn't understand the type of discipline needed to keep control of an unruly home full of adolescent boys. She told me he made veiled threats about her own children. Basically, the gist was that if she didn't keep quiet about it all, she would find her own kids removed and taken into care themselves.'

'Oh my God!'

'She was obviously very scared. She quit working there and never went back. She's not willing to go on the record.'

I didn't blame her.

'And someone else contacted us,' Simon said. 'He wanted to tell his story, but he's too scared to go to the police or get involved.'

I could understand him being scared. Fear of being discovered was something that followed my every move. But the fear of not being able to expose them was worse. Yes, fear was my constant companion these days, along with spiking-hot rage and black sadness.

'When I spoke to him, he regaled a very similar version of events as Jamie did in his diary. The abuse at Crossfield. The parties at Crompton Place. He talked about how he'd left Crossfield at sixteen and tried to put his life together, but what happened had affected him so badly he'd turned to drugs to blot it all out. He's been a heroin addict for years.'

'Another life wasted and ruined.' Mitchell's nostrils flared as he spoke, his fists clenching and unclenching.

'He also spoke of some other boys at the parties who didn't seem to be from the children's homes, and I'm wondering if Moses and the other boy who was killed were kidnapped to order because they had a certain look that members of The Friday Club preferred.'

A shudder spasmed through me.

'I've tried to trace other residents of Crossfield and other members of staff, but the council's records were apparently lost in a fire after the home closed in the early nineties.' Simon carried on, raising his eyebrows in a gesture of disbelief.

'How convenient,' I said.

'Very,' Simon agreed. 'I've been unable to find Trevor Carter from Ian's list. Maybe he did go to America, or maybe he's just vanished.'

'Maybe he's *been* vanished,' Mitchell said.

'I wouldn't be at all surprised.' Simon pushed his glasses up his nose. 'And there's more terrible news. I tried to visit Sean Davidson at the psychiatric unit, but he'd been discharged after he was responding well to his treatment. He...' He glanced between Mitchell and me. 'His body was found yesterday, on an abandoned industrial estate not far from his flat. He'd been beaten to death.'

I opened my mouth to speak, but no words came out.

Mitchell stood up and paced the room. 'Shit.'

I forced my mouth to cooperate, but my voice was barely a whisper. 'It was my fault. They must've known I'd spoken to him.'

'Or they knew I was digging into previous residents of Crossfield or that Jamie had spoken to him. I very much doubt it was a random murder.' Simon shook his head sadly. 'Also, I've been doing some more digging into the people involved in The Friday Club, and I think this could possibly be about more than a VIP paedophile ring. Felix Barron isn't just the owner of Barron Private Banking Group, which is huge, by the way. He also owns four TV stations and eight major newspapers. Douglas Talbot, the defence secretary, was the former finance minister who brokered a deal to receive fifty million pounds in party political donations from hedge funds managed by Barron Private Banking Group, and in return, Talbot delivered one hundred fifty million pounds in tax breaks to the very same hedge funds! And Talbot, of course, has a direct part to play in the country's military budget.' He raised an eyebrow. 'Then you have Eamonn Colby, the children's minister, who is a shareholder of Petrogas, which is the seventh biggest oilfield services company in the world. They're based in London but operate out of thirty offices worldwide, with extensive interests in the Middle East. A subsidiary of Petrogas is a major international construction company called Recon5, which I'm sure you've heard of.' He glanced at Mitchell.

I recognised the name as the company Mitchell had told me about in Iraq.

'Heard of?' Mitchell's eyes narrowed. 'I was there in Iraq and had first-hand knowledge of their accounting scams.'

'Exactly,' Simon went on. 'It was the biggest legalised, government-sanctioned fraud, and although allegations were made against them, they were all brushed under the carpet.' Simon took a breath. 'And then we come to Chief Constable Colin Reed, whose wife just happens to be the director-general of one of Barron's TV stations.' He pursed his lips and waited for that to sink in. 'So you see the circle of power here. A revolving door that links them and their shared interests and common mentalities together. And that interest is oil, finance, and war. Which is worth trillions to them. So even though the child rape and murder they're also involved in is vile beyond belief, I think it's just the tip of the iceberg that connects them.'

I glanced over at Mitchell and caught his eye, thinking back to his previous impassioned outburst. *If you control the media, the money, the politics, and the military, you control the whole system.*

'The whores of war and power,' Mitchell spat.

'Are MPs and government ministers allowed to have businesses and financial interests in companies in which they have major conflicts of interest?' I asked incredulously. 'Surely that would affect their policy decisions.'

Simon leant his elbows on the table. 'Well, there are ways around everything. Legally, Douglas Talbot didn't do anything wrong. And Colby is the children's minister, not the minister for energy, so they're all avoiding a visible conflict of interest while at the same time being inextricably linked. God only knows who the hooded man is, but you can bet it's someone far more powerful than even these people. So yes, of course their private interests are going to affect political and decision-making policy which positively influences them, and that in turn affects every single member of the public by transferring money from the poor and the taxpayers to the financiers and super rich. That's the heart of Recon5's scam and why they got away with it. It's what the Establishment—the System—has become. It's not there for the *people's* needs, rather to serve the elite.'

Mitchell's lips thinned into a tight line. 'We're living in a perverted and twisted smokescreen of democracy that's nothing short of dictatorship, where the unelected actually rule. And behind it lurks a powerful and arrogant network of people who are raping us all and are totally unaccountable for their actions. It's a lose-lose situation for everyone except the elite few.'

I felt like giving up then as the magnitude of it all rained down on me. How could I beat these people? How could I win against them when all the power was on their side and they'd go to any lengths to silence this? Like Jamie had said in his diary, they really were untouchable. What did I think I was doing?

I was stupid. Crazy to think I could get justice. And part of me wanted to stop it right there. Just give up. Try to move on. Get on with my life. Try to be happy again. Maybe eventually I'd forget. It would take years, but it would stop at some point. Wouldn't it?

Of course it wouldn't. I could never forget.

'What's happening with Alistair's side of things?' Simon carried on, oblivious to the chaos exploding in my head.

I told him how Alistair had passed a dossier directly to the Home Secretary eight weeks ago, detailing the sexual abuse and murders, along with the photographic and video evidence, but minus Jamie's diary in case they pieced together who I was. 'But Alistair hasn't had any response yet,' I explained. 'I can't believe it's been two whole months and no one's accountable for anything.'

'It's ridiculous!' Mitchell finally stopped pacing and slammed his hand on the conference table. 'If you or I made an allegation of murder about Joe Bloggs who lived next door, they'd be onto it straight away.'

Simon shook his head slowly. 'Given the crimes and stature of people involved, I'm not at all surprised. But it totally rocks your faith in British justice, doesn't it?'

'I'm not sure there is such a thing,' I muttered.

'If I get anything else, I'll let you know, but I wanted to keep you in the loop so far.' Simon stood to shake our hands.

I stood up too quickly, and all the blood drained from my head. I saw black-and-white stars, felt dizzy, and sat down again.

'Are you okay?' Simon asked.

Despondently, I let him take my hand in his and nodded, trying to push away images of Sean, battered and broken and dead. 'I just need a moment.'

He enclosed my hand in both of his and patted it soothingly.

I stood again, more slowly, pulled the hood of my sweatshirt over my head, put my sunglasses on, and Mitchell and I exited from the rear of the building that led out onto a back alley. We made sure no one was watching before we cut through to a parallel street on the other side and joined the crowds. Now Simon's story had broken and Sean had been killed, things were getting more risky.

We went into a pub with two entrances on the corner of the road and stood at the bar, neither of us saying a word as we watched the doors and windows, searching for someone paying too much of an interest in us. Mitchell's shoulders were tense, his eyes alert, ignoring his pint on the bar. I gulped down my double vodka and Coke as if it was water.

When he was satisfied his counter-surveillance hadn't shown a tail, he said, 'Do you want to get some lunch? We should probably get some calories down us while we can.'

'Thanks, but I don't feel like eating.' I stared down into my empty glass. 'I can't believe they murdered Sean, too.'

Mitchell embraced me, almost crushing me in those hugely muscled arms of his. 'Don't give up. Don't let them win.'

'Sometimes I think it might be easier.' A lone tear slipped out and snaked down my cheek against his shoulder. 'How long will it be before they find out about my involvement and come after me?'

He pulled back, his face rigid. 'We've covered your tracks well. There's no reason for them to suspect you know anything. Jamie would've been so proud of you, you know.'

His words reverberated around my head until my Samsung rang, and Mitchell released me. It was Alistair, who was using the same pay-as-you-go number as Simon, contacting me to say that the dossier he'd put together, along with the evidence, which he'd previously passed directly to the Home Secretary, had now been forwarded to the Director of Public Prosecutions for them to assess it. Alistair was confident it would then be passed to the police for an official investigation to be launched.

Finally, we were one step closer.

I hoped.

Chapter 39

'He said his first word today.' Ava bent over Jackson's buggy, ruffling his hair as we walked around the park.

'What was it?'

'Flah.' She laughed.

'Is that an actual word?' I smiled despite the dark fog that had settled over me for weeks since I'd heard about Sean.

'Well, I think so,' she said proudly.

The weather had warmed up, although I'd hardly been outside. I knew it wasn't healthy to be cooped up at home or at Mitchell's, but I couldn't bring myself to care anymore.

I'd missed Ava, though. Before, we were so close and spent loads of time with each other. But now I couldn't tell her the things I wanted to. Not yet. Not until those men were behind bars and I knew for certain we'd all be safe. There was more waiting to be done. I was isolated and lonely and scared and disconnected from everyone, and a million other things. And it was taking every ounce of strength I had to hold it all together. I was living with a secret I couldn't share with anyone except Mitchell. It was just too horrible. Too dangerous to know what I knew.

'I'm glad I finally managed to coax you out. I've missed you.' She put a hand on my arm and stopped me. 'I thought things were getting better. You seemed a bit brighter for a little while. But now...' She trailed off.

'You need to start letting go and move on to the next chapter in your life with some kind of peace, rather than bitter turmoil, or anger and regret. I know Jamie would've wanted you to be happy again.'

I let out a mirthless laugh. If only she knew the half of it. The only thing keeping me just about sane was my effort at hanging on to reveal the truth. Nothing else would ever matter to me now. I couldn't fail Jamie and all the other kids who deserved better.

'Why don't you go and get a job? Concentrating on something else might help you get over Jamie.'

'I've got a job,' I said.

'Oh, wow! Doing what?'

I thought about what I did with Mitchell. The chat messages with the paedophiles, hunting for their latest victims. Last week a man had been convicted based on Mitchell's evidence, and that made it all worthwhile. For a few days after that, I'd been on a high. At least I was doing something to help protect the voiceless. But even the high didn't last long because nothing had changed for Jamie. His killers were still out there, walking around, living their lives, going to parties, laughing, working, spending time with families, pretending they were upstanding members of society, preaching to us about moral standards. Nothing had changed, and I was sick of it. Time was racing by, and there was no sign of any official investigation on the horizon. The hatred was eating away at me.

'I'm doing some admin work from home,' I told her vaguely.

'Oh, that's great! And then, maybe you could save up and go on holiday. We could all go! I've been thinking, actually, about going to see Mum and Dad now Jackson's a bit older. Yes, let's do it.' She beamed at me. 'That's a great idea, isn't it? We could both do with a break, and Mum and Dad keep on at me to meet Jackson. A change of scenery will be good for both of us for a while, and they want to see you, too. What do you say?'

'I'll think about it.'

She opened her mouth as if to say something else, try to talk me into it, but something changed her mind. 'Okay. Don't think too long, though.' She wagged a finger at me. 'Shall we walk up into town? Maybe a spot of retail therapy will cheer you up.'

I forced a smile. Anything to deflect the conversation away from me. 'If you like.'

We spent the afternoon traipsing round the shops while I pretended to be interested in the latest fashions and looked after Jackson when Ava tried on some clothes in the sales. I pretended to enjoy myself, be carefree, be happy. Smiled in the right places. Pretended I had a life again in a nice, safe, normal world.

Ava splashed out on a new pair of cut-off jeans, and while she was at the till with Jackson, paying, I headed towards the doors to wait for her outside where I could get some fresh air. It was one p.m., and the streets were busy with shoppers and workers running errands or whiling away their lunch hours. Just as I stepped out onto the pavement, a man walking past bumped into me, his shoulder colliding with mine, forcing me to stumble sideways.

He grabbed hold of my arm to stop me falling. 'Sorry.'

I glanced up at his face, startled. 'It's okay. It was just an accident,' I said automatically.

He stared into my eyes with a strange expression, a barely there smile on his face, and said in a tone that made the hairs on the back of my neck stand up, 'You should be careful. You're going to get hurt if you don't watch out.'

It all happened so fast, and before I could register what he'd said, he'd walked away again, leaving me standing there, staring after him.

Just fourteen innocuous words. Words that anyone would say in the same circumstances, but it was the *way* he'd said them, with a hint of some underlying message beneath them. A warning? Or a threat? I couldn't tell.

Goose bumps rose on my skin. My heartbeat cranked up. Was he a perfectly harmless man who'd genuinely bumped into me, and I was reading too much into it? Were anxiety and stress making me see things that weren't really there? Or was there something more sinister to it?

'Hey.' Ava tapped me on the shoulder from behind as I stood, still gawping after the man.

I jumped.

'Are you okay? You look a bit ill.' She frowned.

I shook my head, trying to shake the fear away. Of course it wasn't a threat. They didn't know who I was. My existence had been kept a secret by Alistair and Simon.

'Um…yeah, I'm okay,' I said.

Ava linked one arm with me as she pushed Jackson's buggy with the other. She smiled. 'All right, how about we go to New Look next?'

I spent the next two hours trying to convince myself there was no ambiguous message in what that man had said as Ava dragged me round more shops. When I got back home and peered in the fridge, I realised I'd forgotten to go food shopping yet again.

I was just about to walk up to the corner shop for some essentials when my Samsung rang. It was Alistair, finally announcing some good news. The Department of Public Prosecutions had passed the file over to the police for them to launch a criminal investigation. Operation Highland, they were going to call it.

After we hung up, I poured myself a glass of wine, picked up Jamie's photo from my bedside table, and kissed it, then I traced his face with my finger.

We're going to get them, Jamie. We're really going to get them. They thought the dead would stay silent.

They were wrong.

Chapter 40

But my high was replaced by frustration. There was no word from the police, despite Alistair's repeated pressure. One month passed. Then two. Then three. After four months, still no arrests. What were they waiting for?

I wanted to punch something. Or someone. I was livid. With the photos and the video, the police had everything they needed to arrest the people involved. The bloody proof was right in front of them! What *were* they doing? Filing their fucking nails?

I stomped about the house one day, screaming to myself. Or maybe I was screaming to Jamie to come and get me. Take me away from everything. I often felt as though I was going mad these days. As though everything was slipping away from me. I didn't know who I was anymore. So much murky darkness was in my head. The world no longer made sense. I drank too much. Hardly ate. Clothes hung off my bony frame. I was scared. Exhausted but wide awake, with nervous jangling and relentless energy at the same time. My mind hummed endlessly, but when I did manage to eventually fall asleep, I had nightmares, where images of what I'd seen wouldn't leave me alone. I was still drowning in grief. And consumed by anger and hopelessness and sadness.

I went through the motions of living, but I thought about ending it all more and more these days. I hated everyone else out there in the real world. In their safe little bubbles where I used to live. Their worlds were still spinning, but mine had stopped and shunted me off with brute force, and I was still scrabbling around, broken and scabby, trying to pick myself up.

Jamie, Moses, Billy, Sean, Dave, the anonymous boy at Crompton Place with the curly hair. How many innocent people had to die to keep them untouchable?

How had I ever thought I could expose them? Nothing was going to happen. Nothing would change. They could act with complete impunity to do whatever they wanted. And they would come after me. They were probably trying to find out from Alistair or others who had leaked everything to him. How long would it be? How much time did I have?

I slid a sharp knife from the drawer in the kitchen, running my finger along the blade. A bead of blood broke through my skin, stretching across the surface.

Should I give them a helping hand? Then at least everything would be over. All the waiting, worrying, the turmoil of emotions I couldn't control anymore. I was losing my mind, already in hell, just as Jamie had been. And I missed him so much it was unbearable. So, so much. His crooked smile. His touch. His kisses. His kindness. Everything. The way he looked at me, as though I was something special. As though I was his whole world. I ached to be with him again. Have him hold me in his arms. Tell me he loved me.

Could I do it? Not across my wrists but upwards, one smooth, sharp line. More blood loss that way.

I stared at the knife. It glinted back at me. Daring me. Taunting me.

You could leave now. You could be with Jamie. It would all be over. No more pain. No more being afraid. Oblivion. They're never going to let you live. They're going to find out, and they're going to get away with it.

I stood on the edge of an abyss, looking down into darkness. My head swam with images of Jamie hanging lifelessly from a tree, his eyes bulging, spit on his chin, having his last breath stolen from him. Had he pleaded for his life? For mine? Fought back? Struggled? Or had he accepted his fate with the same fierce bravery he'd lived his life? I saw Moses and the other boy being brutally killed, their deaths and abuse captured forever in photos and video. Imagined Sean's body beaten to a pulp to silence him. Dave battered and crushed from the hit-and-run.

My throat tightened, as if Jamie's noose were around my own neck.

I wasn't strong. I'd always thought I was, in the past, before anything like this happened. Mitchell said I was. But no, I wasn't strong. I wasn't strong at all.

I didn't know how long I stood there, contemplating the release of the knife, waiting for it all to end. I had no future.

But despite an overwhelming hopelessness, I wanted to survive. Stay alive. At least long enough to see this through. I had to hold on a little longer before I could let go.

I heard a voice that sounded like Jamie's whispering in my head. *Fear is a reaction. Courage is a decision.*

I pulled my mind away from the horrific images. I had to stay objective. Had to fight. If I allowed myself to think about what I'd seen and Jamie's death, I would dive into that abyss and never come out.

I shoved the knife back in the block.

Not today. Not yet. You haven't finished yet.

I pulled on some trainers, slammed the front door, and started running. It didn't matter where I was going, I just had to get rid of all the mad chaos in my head.

I ran along the streets and found myself in Veralamium Park, running through the grounds until my calves burned and my breath came in short, sharp bursts. My head pounded, and sweat poured down my face and back. I finally stopped when a stitch twisted knife-like into my side. I bent over, my hands on my waist, massaging the stitch and waiting for my breath to get back to normal.

A noise made my head jerk up. The crack of a twig.

I glanced about. It was dusk. No one else was around.

Or was there?

A sensation of being watched prickled at my scalp. The hairs on my arms stood on end. I spun around.

A shadow moved behind a tree in the distance, darting out of sight. Or were my eyes playing tricks on me?

I squinted. Was anyone there? It looked like someone bulky, but had I imagined it? Was the fear making me hallucinate?

Panic welled up in my throat. For a second, I couldn't move. Just stood and stared into the gloom.

Then my brain kicked in, and I took off running, away from the woods, expecting someone to grab me by the back of my top and attack. I kept glancing behind me as I ran up the hill towards the cathedral, towards people, and lights, and cars, in the middle of commuters walking home and lads and girls bundling into the pubs on an early night out. No dark shape was looming after me. No suspicious figures lurking in shop doorways.

When I got to St Peter's Street, I flopped onto a bench, my chest heaving in deep, unfit bursts as my eyes darted around me, taking in everyone's face.

Maybe I *had* imagined someone watching me after all.

The sweat chilled against my skin as I walked into a newsagent to buy a bottle of water. I queued up behind a grungy teenager and spotted a headline and photo on the front page of a newspaper on the stand by the till—one of the many newspapers owned by Felix Barron.

My heart stopped.

I fumbled in the zip of my jogging bottoms and shoved a five-pound note at the guy behind the till, then I walked out of the shop in a daze without waiting for my change.

Standing on the pavement, I read the story…

Chief Constable of Bedfordshire Police Discovered Dead

The former Chief Constable of Bedfordshire Police, Sir Colin Reed, was found dead at his home in Barton-le-Clay yesterday after taking his own life. A police spokesperson said that there were no suspicious circumstances.

Sir Colin was Chief Constable of Bedfordshire Police from 1994 – 2005, before retiring. In January, he was appointed to investigate Operation Target, an enquiry into alleged wrongdoing by the Metropolitan Police. His review of Operation Target was to be used as a case study to improve a new police complaints system.

The present Bedfordshire Chief Constable, Michael Fullerton, said, 'Sir Colin's death is a shock to his former colleagues. He was an outstanding police officer and will be sorely missed by all. As well as being a loving husband and father, his commitment to public service, both as a police officer and a senior member of numerous government reviews, spoke volumes about his values and integrity. My thoughts are with his wife and two daughters at this difficult time.'

I ran back home, ignoring the pain in my fatigued muscles. I didn't stop to change my clothes or have a shower. I just grabbed my bag and car keys and drove to Mitchell's house. When I knocked on his door, there was no answer. I tried to call him, but his mobile kept ringing until it went to voicemail. I left him a message and then sat on his doorstep, reading the story over and over again.

Had Colin Reed committed suicide because he knew he would now be under police investigation, or had he been bumped off to shut him up? To contain the fallout?

I phoned Alistair on the Samsung while I waited for Mitchell. 'Have you seen the story in the paper about Colin Reed?' I blurted out before he could even say hello.

'No. What story?'

I read it out to him.

'Jesus.' He exhaled a long breath. 'No one told me about this. I'm going to see what I can find out.'

'Do you think they murdered him, too? Kill the lesser offenders and any investigation gets squashed and covered up and then everyone can all live happily ever after?' I didn't give him the chance to reply and carried on, 'Not that they seem to be actually investigating anything, anyway. No arrests have been made. Nothing has been done. It's a farce. A smokescreen.'

'I agree. I'll make some calls and get back to you.'

'Thanks.'

I tapped my fingers on my knee manically, jigging my leg up and down, waiting for Mitchell to arrive. It was about an hour later when he pulled up on the drive.

He smiled as he got out of the car, picking up a couple of shopping bags from the passenger seat.

I leapt up. 'Were you in St Albans earlier? Following me again?'

He frowned. 'No.' He held up the bags. 'I've been to the

supermarket. Why, was someone following you?'

I thought about what I'd seen in the park. What I *thought* I'd seen? Of course there hadn't been anyone there. My imagination was going into overdrive.

'No, it's just me. I'm so stressed out and tired I'm seeing things that aren't there. Maybe I'm hallucinating.'

'Are you sure?'

'Yes.' I thrust the newspaper towards him. 'Read this. You won't bloody believe it.'

Frown lines appeared on his face the more he read. 'It says no suspicious circumstances? Yeah, right. This newspaper is owned by Felix Barron. It's just spin.'

'Exactly.'

Mitchell glanced around the street then swept his hand towards his front door. 'Come on. Let's go inside.'

I followed him into the kitchen.

'Do you want a brew or something stronger?'

'As strong as you've got.'

He nodded, poured out two shots of whisky, and handed one to me. I paced up and down the floor, taking hits of it in between my mind reeling.

Mitchell leant against the worktop, his arms folded, his biceps flexing, staring at a spot on the floor with narrowed eyes, as if deep in thought.

'I'm glad he's dead,' I said. 'Part of me thinks he deserved what he's got. But the other part of me knows there won't be any justice now. He won't be exposed. His reputation will stay intact. Everyone will say how wonderful he was, and no one will know the truth.'

'Yes, but there's also the alternative. If he's dead, maybe it *will* come out.'

'They can't expose him without exposing the rest of them, can they?'

He took a slow swallow of whisky. 'Maybe he'll be the fall guy now he's dead. The lions could be turning on themselves.'

I downed the last of my drink in one swift gulp, the alcohol burning my throat. 'I wonder who will be next.'

294

Chapter 41

A few weeks later, I returned home after having dinner with Ava and Jackson. Ava had been hassling me to come over and wouldn't take no for an answer. It was ten p.m. when I parked the Jeep on my drive. The street lamp outside Jamie's house had suddenly stopped working, plunging the front garden into shadowy darkness.

As I walked up the path, I again had that eerie feeling of being watched. I glanced around, up and down the street. A car parked at the top of the cul-de-sac switched its headlights on and drove off onto the main road, a young teenage couple were arguing on a doorstep three houses down—my neighbour's daughter and her boyfriend— but apart from that, I couldn't see anyone else around.

Then I noticed the light that I'd left on in the lounge when I went out at six was no longer alight. At first I though maybe the bulb had blown, but after I slid the key into the lock, warily opened the door, and turned on the hallway light, I knew something was wrong.

It was that same disturbance of air, the faint tang of cigarette smoke that I'd smelt in the house the day Jamie had been murdered.

From where I stood, frozen in the doorway, my gaze travelled down the hallway into the kitchen. I stayed there just long enough to register the drawers pulled out from the units and their contents scattered on the floor.

Then adrenaline hit me in a heart-pumping rush. I backed away from the door and stood in the middle of the street, fumbling in my bag for my iPhone.

I dropped it once. Misdialled three times. Then, finally, I was dialling 999.

My finger stopped on the second 9.

What was the point of calling the police? They wouldn't investigate. For all I knew, it could've been the police. Special Branch. Or one of the security services. And whoever had been inside would've been clever enough not to leave a trace of evidence.

I knew what they were looking for. Copies of the photos and videos I'd taken at Mitchell's. Which meant...somehow they'd found out what I knew.

I glanced back up the street. The teenage couple were sitting on the front wall of the house now. He had his arm around her, her head lolling against his shoulder.

I turned back to my front door, debating whether to go inside. They could still be in there, waiting for me. And then what would happen?

Another suicide? An accident in the home? A fire? Beaten to death by an intruder?

If I screamed, would those kids hear me? Would I even get the chance to scream?

I walked towards the teenagers. Safety in numbers. Hopefully.

When I reached them, they were having an argument about Justin Bieber. Now what?

In front of me, the entrance to the cul-de-sac fed into the main road. I spotted a young guy walking a Staffordshire bull terrier, wearing a hoodie, the hood pulled up, his face just a shadow in the dim street lights.

I stopped just after the teenagers, leaning against the wall of another neighbour's front garden. I thought about calling Ava, but a vision of Jackson giving me a cheeky smile swam into my head. I pictured Ava's kind, sympathetic face. A surge of love for them both squeezed my heart. I wanted to just pour the whole thing out to her, but I couldn't. I couldn't bring my troubles to her door. I'd been stupid enough to think that if Alistair knew about everything, then they'd be arrested and I'd be safe. Now I didn't think that would ever happen.

I stood on the path and dialled Mitchell, keeping one eye on the teenagers.

'You need to get away from there,' he said. 'Drive to my house.'

The dog-walker sauntered past with a cocky swagger, glanced at me, and gave me a leery smile.

I held my breath.

'Hello? Maya? You still there?'

I breathed out, my pulse hammering in my veins. 'I'm here. I want to get some things from the house. Some of Jamie's things. I can't leave them in there, Mitchell.'

He paused. 'Okay, but you're not going in there on your own. I'll come down, but it's going to take me a while to get there. Can you wait somewhere safe with lots of people around?'

'Yes. There's a pub called the Oak Tree in town. I'll drive there and meet you inside.'

'Okay. See you soon.'

I walked back towards my driveway, pulling from my bag the pepper spray Mitchell had given me a while back, clutching it in my sweaty palm as I reached the teenagers. They were arguing now about a girl called Sam who fancied the boy. Young love. I wanted to bang their heads together and scream at them that they didn't know how lucky they were to have each other. That they should make the most of every second of every day because they never knew when it would all be snatched away. They ignored me as I walked past, oblivious.

I got into the Jeep and backed out of the driveway. There was a quiet stream of traffic as I sat at the junction to the main road, carefully scanning the area. No cars that might attempt to follow me were parked suspiciously anywhere. I turned right without indicating and drove a circuitous route to the Oak Tree, regularly checking my mirrors for a tail of some kind, but no one was following me.

At least I didn't think so.

When I finally drove into the car park, a young couple were standing outside by a picnic table, smoking, laughing about something. I locked up the Jeep under a lamp and pushed open the pub's door with a final glance over my shoulder.

I stood in the entrance, surveying the interior. Inside was pretty quiet. Most people were in the beer garden at the rear, smoking under a pergola, visible through the windows. I ordered a vodka and Coke and sat at the bar.

I picked up the glass, my hand shaking so hard I spilled some onto the bar mat, and gulped it down, keeping one eye on the few people inside. An old man in the corner reading a paper. A group of thirty-something men in suits, shirt collars loosened, arguing good-naturedly about football scores.

The barman kept sneaking glances at me. I was starting to become suspicious about *why* he kept looking when I caught my reflection in a mirror behind the bar and thought it was someone else at first. I looked like a mad Medusa—my knotted hair all over the place, big, dark smudges under my sad, red eyes, my skin sickly and anaemic-looking, my cheekbones protruding sharply. I looked as if I was fading away.

Fading into nothing. How long would it be before I disappeared completely?

One of the football guys sidled up to the bar to order a round. He smiled at me and said something inane about the weather. I ignored him, pulled out the Samsung, and pretended to send a text, my fingers sliding over the keypad, writing the words *You're fucked!*

Before I could delete my own text to no one but myself, the phone beeped with an incoming text.

Expecting it to be Simon or Alistair on this phone, I clicked on the new message that didn't show a number and read: *I warned you to be careful!*

I dropped my phone on the bar as if it was a bomb, staring wide-eyed at the words on the screen. A face swam into my head. The guy who'd bumped into me when I was out shopping with Ava. What had he said?

You should be careful. You're going to get hurt if you don't watch out. Who was he?

And I knew, without any doubt then, that it wasn't a random burglary. My life was in danger.

The pub door opened, and I spotted Mitchell at the same time he saw me. In a few strides, he was next to me, his meaty hand on my shoulder, concern clouding his eyes. 'You okay?'

I blinked back tears. I *was* fucked. I shook my head. 'They know who I am.'

He took my hand and pulled me off the barstool. 'Let's go.' He led me out to the car park, where his pickup truck was parked next to my Jeep. 'I just checked over your car with a bit of kit I have, looking for any GPS transmitters or bugs they may have put on the Jeep, but it was clean. We'll leave it here, though, take my truck back to the house and get what you need, then we can pick up the Jeep again and you can follow me back to my place.' He held his hand out for my keys.

I handed them over. He unlocked his pick-up and wedged his bulk behind the steering wheel.

I slid in the passenger seat and glanced over at him. 'It's not a coincidence that they broke in,' I said, fighting the hysteria welling up inside. I showed him the anonymous text I'd just received on a number no one was supposed to know about except Alistair and Simon.

Mitchell hit the steering wheel with the palm of his hand. 'I knew we shouldn't have gone to Alistair. From the moment he handed over the evidence and dossier, they've been watching him, monitoring his communications. Whether intentional or not, he's led them straight to you!'

'I don't know what to do or where to go! I can't stay at Ava's. I can't put them in danger.'

'You can stay with me for as long as you need.'

'And then what!' My voice reached shrieking level. 'I can't stay with you forever.'

'It's not forever. Just until—'

'Nothing's happening, Mitchell. We've been fooling ourselves, haven't we? Nothing's *going* to happen. They're untouchable. How many more people will die over this?'

Mitchell put his arm around me and hugged me towards him. 'There's always a Plan B.'

'What's that?' I sniffed.

He evaded the question and leant over, wiping the tears on my cheeks with the back of his hand. 'Are you ready to go? We should get out of here as soon as we can.'

I nodded, my forehead throbbing and vibrating as if someone was attacking the inside of my skull with a sander.

When he pulled up on my drive, I wondered if this would be the last time I'd ever go inside the house. What about all my memories? The life Jamie and I had here? All the happiness? They'd stolen that from me now, too.

Mitchell grabbed an extendable baton from inside his jacket as we got out of the vehicle. The front door was open a little way, as I'd left it when I'd run out.

'Wait here until I come out and tell you it's safe. And when we go inside, no talking, okay?'

'Okay.'

With a flick of Mitchell's wrist, the baton extended to half a metre of lethal, hard metal. I watched him disappear inside. He flicked on lights as I clutched my pepper spray.

A few minutes later, he opened the door and strode to the car. 'It's all clear. It was a tidy entry. There's no sign of how they got in, but they made a hell of a mess afterwards.'

I followed him in and crunched over the kitchen floor, which was covered with everything from cornflakes to olive oil to broken mugs and glasses. Everything had been emptied from the drawers and cupboards and dumped on the floor. Even the garden hadn't escaped. The shed door hung open, the padlock bolt cropped off and lying on the floor, the contents ransacked, paint everywhere. The Buddha was upturned.

Nothing had been taken again. The TV and stereo were still in the lounge, along with Jamie's and my laptops. But pages of his books had been ripped out and scattered over the carpet. CDs and their cases smashed and broken.

In the spare room, Jamie's personal papers were ripped. The mattress hung half off the bed, slashed. Gutted like a fish. Pillows had been ripped open, spilling out the foam interior. My bedroom was the same, with the addition of clothes slashed and left in scattered heaps, drawers upturned, toiletries flung around.

But the worst thing was the photos of Jamie that had been on proud display. The glass in the frames had been smashed and ground into the floor. The photos inside had been ripped beyond recognition. All except the one which had taken pride of place on my bedside unit, of us at the picnic.

It was now on the plasterboard wall above my bed, held in place by a knife pierced through my face.

Chapter 42

'You can stay as long as you like,' Mitchell said after I'd put my car in his garage.

He let us in to his house, led me into his guest bedroom, and put my small suitcase on the floor.

'Thanks.' I slumped down on the edge of the king-sized bed.

'Do you want something to eat? Drink?' He hovered in the doorway.

As tempting as a drink sounded, I didn't think I had the energy to physically lift another glass of vodka and put it to my lips. 'No, thanks.' I leant forward, my forehead in my palms. 'I don't—'

'You're exhausted,' Mitchell butted in. 'Get a good night's sleep and let's talk in the morning.'

I nodded because it was the only thing I could do.

He closed the door, and I took off my boots and slid underneath the cool duvet fully clothed, knowing that even though I could hardly keep my eyes open, I wouldn't be able to sleep.

I turned over and over in my mind how far they were prepared to go to keep a lid on this. I knew the answer, of course. They were prepared to kill. They knew who I was now, what I knew, and it wouldn't be long before they came back to finish the job. How had they found out when we'd been so careful? Did it even matter now?

I needed to call Alistair. Get him to do something. Talk about my options. I wondered if I could get some kind of protection but then dismissed the thought. Any protection would be coming from the police. People who hadn't even launched an enquiry yet. If the people who'd broken in were from Special Branch, they *were* the police, so how could they protect me? And if it was the others, MI5, dealing with matters of national security, how did I stand a chance?

At some point, I must've finally succumbed to sleep because I was woken by a noise.

I sat bolt upright, wondering where the hell I was. My heart pounded as it took a second for my eyes to sift through the darkness, disorientated, reacting to shadows looming in the unfamiliar room.

Then it hit me. Mitchell's. Of course.

I gulped in some air.

The noise again. Shouting. No, more like whimpering yells.

It was Mitchell's voice, calling something I couldn't make out.

Oh, God. They're here. They've got him! It won't be long before they come for me, too.

Carefully, I slid out of bed and pulled on my boots with trembling fingers. I padded to the window and peeled back a small edge of the curtain, looking out onto the deserted, sleepy street. No one was out there. All the neighbours looked safely tucked up in bed. No strange men were walking up the path with *I'm going to kill you* T-shirts on.

I edged to the bedroom door.

Another shout. Louder this time. It sounded as though Mitchell was in pain. What the hell were they doing to him?

Icy fingers danced up my rigid spine. My hand grabbed the door handle, my mind desperately running through what to do. If they had Mitchell, a powerful, ex-elite soldier, I didn't stand a chance against them.

My gaze darted back to the window. Should I climb out of it? Run? Somewhere. Anywhere.

But no. I couldn't leave Mitchell here in their hands. Not when he'd opened up his home and given me the kind of strength and support I could never repay. Not when I owed him so much. I knew what the outcome would be. They were there because of me, so I couldn't abandon Mitchell to take the fall. But maybe I could cause a distraction of some kind.

I swallowed, headed back towards my handbag by the side of the bed, and pulled out the pepper spray.

Another cry then. I could just about make out Mitchell's words. 'No! Don't do it!'

I pressed down on the door handle. My teeth clenched tight as I opened it slowly, praying that it wouldn't make a sound.

Inching it open, I peered out into the hallway. A light was on downstairs, throwing a shadowy illumination up the stairs and into the end of the hall.

No one was there.

'I can't! I've tried! No. No, no, no!' Mitchell's voice cried out from behind his bedroom door dead ahead of me. 'I don't know. I don't know!'

I clutched the pepper spray tighter in my hand and tiptoed forwards.

I had no time to think about how many there were or what I'd do when I actually got inside, but I prayed I'd have the element of surprise.

Trying to ignore the pressure building in my chest, making it hard to breathe, I stretched my right hand out in front of me, my finger over the nozzle of the pepper spray.

My left hand shook so badly, I had trouble holding onto Mitchell's bedroom door handle as I eased it down slowly. Silently. In keeping with the element of surprise, I burst through the door, desperately trying to will my eyes to adjust to the pitch-blackness.

I swung my arm around wildly, waiting for a punch or kick or stranglehold from the intruders. But the only person there was Mitchell.

Asleep. Thrashing around in his nightmare.

I slumped against the wall, pressing a hand to my chest.

Mitchell suddenly jerked awake, and before I had the chance to assure him it was me, his hand disappeared underneath his pillow and reappeared in a lightning move with a handgun. I didn't know what kind it was, but it was pointed at my chest.

I could tell by his glazed expression that he didn't recognise me. 'Mitchell, it's *me! Maya!* I held up my left hand, palm up. 'It's just me. You were having a bad dream. A nightmare.'

His chest heaved, his breath coming out in heavy pants, but his trigger hand was completely steady.

The blood curdled in my veins.

'It's just me!' I cried.

He blinked furiously, his gaze darting around as if he was taking some kind of inventory of the room. 'Chair, wardrobe, floor. Chair, wardrobe, floor,' he muttered like some kind of mantra. He shook his head repeatedly. Then recognition seemed to spark in his eyes.

'You were…God, I'm sorry. I thought…'

He didn't speak for a while, the gun still pointing towards my chest. Then he fixed his gaze on me, and I couldn't read the expression in it. Anger? Embarrassment? Devastation? Pain? Hatred? I didn't stay to find out. I didn't know who Mitchell *really* was, and a horrible realisation hit me that I'd put my trust in the wrong person. For all I knew, he could be working for them, keeping me close, watching me from the very beginning, until they decided I should die, too.

I fled the room, ignoring my handbag in the bedroom and rushing down the stairs so fast I slid down the bottom two. I heard

Mitchell's footsteps behind me. Heard him calling my name as I tried to open the front door.

It was locked.

Fuck! Fuck! Fuck! I tugged on the door, and he was there.

Behind me.

Chapter 43

He grabbed me, his arms around my waist and chest so tight, locking me into him. I tried to struggle, but I couldn't move. Tried to gulp in enough oxygen, but my throat had closed and my head throbbed.

'I'm not going to hurt you, but you can't go anywhere.' He held on tight.

I managed to gurgle some kind of scream.

He held me tighter. 'Calm down. I'm *not* going to hurt you, okay?'

I nodded, whimpering, all the fight going out of me, surrendering to the inevitable. I was no match for him. He was *trained* to kill people. I wouldn't stand a chance.

Slowly, he relaxed his grip and let me go. I stumbled away, backing into the wall, starting to hyperventilate

He didn't make another move towards me. Just stood there, watching. 'If you go out there, they'll find you.'

I slowed my breathing, trying to take deep inhales and exhales. 'Who are you?' I cried, tears streaking down my cheeks.

'You know who I am.'

'No, I don't!' I yelled. 'Are you going to kill me? Are you working for them?'

'If I wanted to kill you, I would've done it by now.' He shook his head, his blue eyes boring into mine. 'Shit, I need a fucking drink.'

I watched him go into the kitchen. Looked back at the front door. That was true, wasn't it? He'd had plenty of opportunity to kill me by now.

I heard him banging around in the kitchen, opening cupboards. He made no attempt to come and get me. Silence me. Finish me off. *What the hell was all that, though?*

Mitchell obviously had his own demons. I thought about his angry outbursts, the strange reaction he'd had outside Simon's office. Was that a flashback? And he obviously had nightmares, too. Was Mitchell suffering from some kind of post-traumatic stress? He had to be, and I wasn't surprised, after everything he'd been through. He was probably wracked with survivor guilt, too, just like me. But was he unstable? Was he a danger to me? I couldn't decide, but it didn't matter now, anyway. He was all I had. The only other person close to me who could help.

Finally, when the panic subsided, I went into the kitchen. I definitely needed that bloody drink now, too.

Mitchell stood at the worktop, staring into a glass of brandy. He turned to face me. Ran a hand over his shaved head and left it there, his piercing blue eyes full of apology. 'Look, I'm sorry about that. I—'

'Can I have a drink?'

He poured me a shot of brandy and handed it over.

The adrenaline was wearing off, making me shivery. I grabbed my coat from the back of the chair where I'd left it when we'd come in last night and wrapped it around me as I sipped the drink.

'Sit down.' He waved a hand at the chair.

'I should leave. I was selfish, getting you involved in all this. You have your own life to—'

'You didn't get me involved. It was my choice.' He downed his drink in one go and poured himself another. 'And where else would you go, anyway? Like you said earlier, they know who gave Alistair that evidence now. Somehow, they've found that out. You should stay here, where no one will think to look for you. At least until it all comes out. And once it does, there will be no need to kill you anymore because the truth will be already out there.' His gaze wouldn't meet mine as he sat down at the kitchen table in his jogging bottoms and T-shirt.

'You don't believe that, though, do you?' I could tell by the tone of his voice.

'I don't know what to believe anymore.' He fingered the edge of the glass.

'The nightmares? Are they about the army? Or Alex?' I took another hit of brandy and pulled my coat tighter around me.

He stared into his glass and swilled the liquid around. 'Both. One of the times I was in Iraq, my squadron was part of the joint SAS/Delta Force team known as Task Force Black. We went out literally every night hitting al-Qaeda cells, and I lost count of the amount of contacts we had, but one in particular still scares the shit out of me now. We had good J2 intelligence, backed up by human intel from our source that a bomb-making factory in Fallujah was making sophisticated shaped charges which could penetrate the US Army armoured trucks. Lots of soldiers were getting hit by them, and casualties were mounting.

'When we eventually identified the right house, in one of the suburbs, we put a rapid plan together to assault it. Straight from the off, we knew it was going to be a hard takedown, and from the minute we stacked up outside the entry point and placed the door charges, we came under fire from across the street, which alerted the team inside the stronghold. As soon as the doors were blown, we pushed our two war dogs in through the breach and followed them up.

'The first few guys in were shot, and as we struggled to make our way into the building to secure it, a suicide bomber inside detonated, dropping an internal wall which crushed one of our guys. Eventually, we fought our way through, systematically shooting and grenading everything that moved before we cleared the building, but we lost two guys dead, three injured, and the poor bloody dogs as well.

'We killed three insurgents, and the suicide bomber made four, but there was one left still alive in the dust and the rubble, a young boy, no more than a kid about Alex's age. He'd been shot in the chest and in the side of the head but for some reason was still alive. I tried to stabilize him as we waited for the QRF to secure the outer perimeter and extract us, but he was never going to live. He died in my arms—there was nothing that could've saved him.

'It turned out that the young boy was being held by the terrorists as assurance for the cooperation of his father, who worked for the coalition as a building contractor and was being forced to provide information about troop movements in and out of the police station he was helping to renovate. It got worse, too, as we later found out that the suicide bomber had been the young boy's sister, a fourteen-year-old girl, again a hostage held against her will, who'd been remotely detonated by one of the bomb-makers as a sick human claymore mine. The young boy and his sister, his father and the rest of his family, they were the real victims of the war on terror. Innocent people just trying to survive—collateral damage—lives rendered worthless as part of a wider military strategy and a hidden plan that most people aren't even aware of.

'The war went on, and I went out on more operations, more assaults, night after night, but I couldn't stop seeing that boy's face all the time, the lights going out in his eyes, or imagining the sickening fear of his sister, as she trembled in her suicide vest waiting for the end. I saw him choking up foaming blood. Heard his never-ending screams. And in my mind, his face mingled with Alex's. In a way, he represented my son. Maybe it was even a message from Alex. I hadn't been there to save my boy. And I couldn't save this innocent child, either.' He drank the rest of his brandy. Stood and poured some more with his back to me, one hand gripping the granite worktop so hard his hand shook. 'That's when I knew I had to get out of the regiment. It was my wake-up call. My beliefs were changing, and I couldn't be a part of it. I couldn't justify the things I was doing in my country's name anymore.'

I rose from the table, wanting to comfort him. I stood beside him, took his hand in mine, and squeezed it. I didn't speak. Didn't think any words were good enough.

He squeezed my hand briefly then sat back at the table.

I leant against the worktop. 'Have you spoken to someone about it all? Someone professional, I mean? They could help. With the nightmares. The flashbacks. The guilt.'

He snorted. 'What's the point? I can't undo what I've done. In the end, it comes down to one thing. The powerful deciding who's going to live or die and why. No amount of talking is going to change that.'

'Why don't you have any photos of Alex around?' I'd noticed it before but hadn't wanted to bring it up. The photos I'd had of Jamie had become more precious to me than anything since his death, because one day I'd forget what he looked like. One day, I would close my eyes and be unable to see him clearly in my head. I needed those photos. And now even most of those had been stolen from me, too.

'My ex took them all when she left. She thought I didn't deserve to have them.'

'What? That's so...' I searched for a word. It was callous. No wonder Mitchell blamed himself so much. 'It's just unfair!'

'Is it?' He glanced at me with watery eyes. 'She was right. I couldn't keep Alex safe. I was a world away from here when it happened, fighting for other people's twisted agendas. *That's* what digs the knife in deeper.'

'You need to stop punishing yourself. You're only human. You were doing what you thought was right at the time.'

'Yes, and Alex and so many others paid the price for that misconception. They're still paying. I defended Queen and country because I was a patriot, because I wanted to make the world a better place, because I thought I was defending honour and integrity. How wrong was I? I'm just as culpable of committing war crimes now because I bought into it for too long. The cost of my actions in the name of loyalty is so high it can never be repaid.' His lips narrowed to a thin line.

'You don't really believe that, do you? You can't be held responsible for everything you did.'

'Who else can, then?' He stared at me as if I didn't have a clue what I was talking about before his gaze drifted towards his wallet next to the kettle. 'I kept one photo, though. It's there when I need it.'

'Where did you get the gun?'

'Iraq was brimming with weapons after the fall of Saddam Hussein. It's a gun culture over there, and every man of legal age was expected to own an AK, as a sort of stand-by militia. When I was down in Basra one time, we were working with the Iraqi Army, and one of them gave me this Glock. Ironically, it's a British-issued one, given to the Police Academy in Basra as part of a military training package. It wasn't hard to get it back to the UK.'

'So it's illegal?'

'Depends on your definition.' He shrugged. 'The law is set by the people in power and look how that's going so far for us. Lots of things are legal. Doesn't make them ethically or morally right, though.'

The dawn light began to creep in behind the curtains. I glanced at the clock, which read 6.12 a.m. A new day. The earlier shock and fear of the previous night had been replaced by rabid rage.

I wouldn't be beaten. They would not beat me.

Somehow I was going to stay alive long enough to see this through.

~~~~

As soon as it was 9.00 a.m., I called Alistair's private mobile phone number he'd given me. A number he'd assured me was secure and safe. Now I wasn't so sure.

'Hi, it's Jane. I've got a problem.'

'I'm sorry to hear that. What's happened?' His voice oozed genuine concern.

'My house was broken into yesterday. They made it look like a burglary, but it was more like a statement. I think someone was making sure I didn't have any copies of what I gave to you.'

He was silent for a moment, taking it in. 'Have you reported it to the police?'

I gave a hollow laugh. 'No. There's no point. They're not going to find any evidence, are they?' I told him about the anonymous text I'd received. 'So there's no doubt it was someone protecting those psychopaths. It's been months since the police launched Operation Highland to supposedly investigate that evidence. Why hasn't anything happened yet? I'm running out of time here, Alistair. They know I'm involved now. How long will it be before I'm killed, too?'

'I'm as frustrated as you. I've been trying to arrange a strategy meeting with top-ranking officers as a matter of urgency, but I'm being fobbed off. I'm not letting it go, though. I'm not giving up. I'll do some more chasing up today.'

'Isn't there anything else you can do? It's obvious an investigation is being stalled. These are serious offences! The police have undeniable evidence in their possession. The truth needs to come out!' My voice rose, and I tried to calm down. Shouting at one of my few allies wasn't going to help. I dug my fingernails into my palm. 'Why can't you name them using parliamentary privilege?' Simon had told me during one of our meetings that under British Constitutional Convention, comments made in Parliament were protected from any libel action. 'At least then their names will be out in the open and they can't hide anymore and I'll be safe!'

'I understand how you feel, believe me. I feel the same. But there are proper procedures in place that *must* be followed. I can't use parliamentary privilege at this stage, otherwise I'll be in serious danger of compromising or prejudicing any police investigation.'

'There *is* no investigation! And in the meantime, these people are swanning around Westminster. You know who they are. You see them regularly. You know what they've done. How can—'

'I'm well aware of that, and I don't like it any better than you, but we have to make sure the police have every opportunity to pursue evidence and track down witnesses. I'm not ruling out naming them in Parliament if nothing happens with an investigation, but I have to follow the rules and wait to see what happens.'

I rubbed at the angry, pulsing vein in my temple.

'I know you're upset, and you have every right to be. But getting angry isn't going to help matters.'

He was right. I knew he was right. I was letting my desperation get in the way. I had to stay calm and be objective. Try to detach myself from what these men had done and what they'd taken from me. From other innocent victims. But I was so scared now.

I took a panicked breath and held on to it, clenching my teeth.

'I'll do some chasing up today and get back to you as soon as I have some answers, okay?'

'Yes. Look, I'm sorry for losing my temper. I just hate the thought of them getting away with it all.'

'Believe me, neither can I. And I won't stand for it.'

Two hours later, when I was online in the chat rooms, posing as a ten-year-old boy and talking to disgusting perverts, Alistair called back and asked to meet.

Somewhere neutral. Somewhere walls couldn't have ears.

Chapter 44

We took the underground from Southgate to Wood Green, then we caught a bus to Alexandra Palace, rather than drive there. All the better to spot if someone was following us and shake them off.

'We just have to hope no one tailed Alistair,' Mitchell said as we walked to the pre-arranged meeting spot, taking random routes and doubling back again, our eyes alert and scanning the area.

Alistair was already on the bench in the surrounding parkland, nursing a cup of takeout coffee. His tie hung loosely around his neck, a weariness etched on his face. He looked as if he'd aged twenty years since I'd first met him. I knew the feeling.

We observed him for a while from the cover of some trees, watching to see if someone was watching him. Finally satisfied, Mitchell took one last glance around before pressing one hand between my shoulder blades and steering me towards the bench, indicating it was okay.

'Morning,' Alistair said as we sat down. 'I wish I could say it was a good one, but unfortunately, I have more disturbing news. Ted Byron is dead.'

I shook my head in angry disbelief. So the children's home inspector would escape justice, too, now. 'Let me guess. Another well-timed suicide?'

'No. A car accident this time. Apparently his brakes failed, and he ran head first into a tree.'

'God,' I said, unable to decide if I was glad or not. Yes, he was dead, which could only make the world a better place, but he'd escaped the weight of the law in the process.

'I don't think He can help us with this,' Alistair muttered.

Mitchell said something under his breath. Judging by his expression, I imagined it contained a few swear words. He jigged his leg up and down, blinking rapidly as he stared at the ground. 'So many people dead over this.' He ran his hands over his face.

Alistair shifted in his seat. 'I don't think this is ever going to see the light of day. The forces at the top want this buried deep. I believe this goes even higher than the people we're aware of, and they're protecting their assets. There's a network of very powerful people pulling strings here, and that's their impenetrable shield—their immunity. And it's entirely possible that the national security and intelligence services were always well aware of this VIP paedophile ring and are using their own evidence about The Friday Club and others to gain leverage over people in other positions of power. With this kind of information, they can blackmail and manipulate anyone involved to do whatever satisfies their own agendas. But if your evidence goes public, they can no longer use theirs to influence what they want, can they?'

I told him what Simon had found out about some of them being interlinked to a more powerful financial scheme that put them all in bed with each other, all looking after each other's backs.

'Good God. When you think you've heard the worst, more worms come out of the woodwork. I've reached the sad conclusion that they're beyond the law.' He rubbed at the pinched frown on his forehead. 'I've been receiving phone calls, threatening my children unless I let this lie. And yesterday, I was approached by a fellow MP, someone I thought was a friend, and warned in no uncertain terms not to proceed with any of this if I knew what was good for me. All my colleagues are concerned with is MPs turning up and voting the right way. They're not interested in tackling other issues with members of their party, especially when the issues are as rotten and indefensible as this is.' He shook his head. 'Do you know what the latest is with the police investigation?' He laughed humourlessly. 'They say the dossier I gave them, along with the videotape and the photos, has disappeared.' He waved a hand angrily in the air. 'They've apparently lost any evidence that could've secured successful prosecutions.'

I opened my mouth to tell him that there were copies, but Mitchell shot me a warning look, and I stopped myself at the last moment. That was our ace card, and I couldn't play it yet. 'So…so, what? That's the end of it?'

'We have no witnesses who will speak up and now no evidence.' He finished his coffee and crushed the cardboard cup in his hand. 'I'm fully prepared to use parliamentary privilege now to name them all. There is a cover-up at the highest level, and I won't let this be buried any longer. They have to be held to account.'

Alistair left before us. We gave it ten minutes, then we walked around the park, making sure no one was taking an unhealthy interest in us. We didn't speak on the nerve-wracking journey back to Mitchell's, taking a different route this time via public transport, our eyes alert for any possible signs of danger. I turned everything Alistair had said over and over in my mind. I felt sick. Sick to fucking death.

After we were safely inside Mitchell's hallway, I leant against the wall, a cold sweat breaking out over my forehead.

Mitchell dropped his keys onto a small table in the hallway. 'Like Alistair said, this probably goes deeper than we know. The guilty are protecting each other or silencing each other. We don't know the identity of the hooded man on the video. Maybe the Home Secretary is even involved himself.'

'So, what next then? We wait for Alistair to name them with parliamentary privilege?' I clenched my sweaty fists. 'But in the meantime, while it's still a secret, I'm not safe.' I took a deep breath and stared up at the ceiling.

'I don't think we should wait anymore. They'll find a way to silence Alistair, too. This has to end now.'

I closed my eyes and felt myself deflating. I slumped to the bottom stair before I collapsed and threw my head in my hands, tugging at my roots.

'There's only one way to stop them coming after you. As long as it stays in the shadows, you'll always be running and looking over your shoulder. But if you expose it, there's no percentage for them to eliminate you because the secret is already out there and there'll be no reason to come after you.'

'How?'

'Plan B.' He sat next to me on the stair. 'I've been speaking with Lee. Do you remember I told you he's got his own cyber intelligence company now? He's a world-class expert in cyber security and protection.'

I nodded. 'So how can that help?'

'We get him to set up a website and upload the video and photos onto it. Then everyone can see exactly what kind of vile deviants these people who are running the country are.'

'Won't they just find it and take it down?'

'That's why we need a cyber intelligence and security expert—to make sure if they try to take it offline, we're ready for it. It'll be our very own WikiLeaks page.'

'And how can he do that?'

'I don't know exactly. Lee was coming out with terms that are way over my head. DDOS counter-attacks, coding, threat protection, mirror backups, decoy servers.' Mitchell shrugged. 'But the bottom line is, even if they try to take it down, they won't succeed. He can keep the website up there in front of billions of people. And then we watch it all go viral.'

Chapter 45

'First, we need to eat.' Mitchell dumped his wallet on the kitchen worktop and banged around, opening the kitchen cupboards, looking for food. 'Then we get the copies of the evidence we hid. Lee's meeting us here at eight tonight to set up the website.' He pulled from the bread bin some bread that had seen better days.

'It's okay. I'm not hungry.' The last time I'd eaten was with Ava yesterday. Was it really only twenty-four hours ago? It seemed a lifetime ago. I hadn't been able to face breakfast and was light-headed with hunger, but I didn't think I could force anything down. Not until we'd done what we needed to do with Lee.

'You'll be no good flaking out before we see this through.'

I opened my mouth to protest. I just wanted to get the evidence from where I'd hidden it, get that website set up, and then I knew I'd be safe, but if Mitchell needed food, then I couldn't complain. Plus, we still had four hours to kill.

Unless those four hours killed me first.

Mitchell's mobile phone rang as he was buttering slices of bread. 'Hey,' he answered. 'What? Slow down.' His voice ratcheted up to an urgent notch. 'What do you mean, missing?' A pause. And then, 'Right. Okay, I'm coming over. Just...no, just wait there.' He hung up. 'Shit. Kelly's gone missing.'

'Your niece? Oh no.' My eyes widened. 'Do you think…do you think they found out about your involvement? Oh God, have they taken her to get to you?'

'I don't know. Maybe.' He slapped his hand hard on the worktop. 'Shit! I don't know what's going on yet. Just that Kelly was supposed to be home from college hours ago and she hasn't turned up. Neena phoned Kelly's friends, and they said she never arrived there this morning. This isn't like her at all. I've got to go.'

I thought back to the night of my anniversary, waiting for Jamie to come home, worrying why he was late. It sounded all too familiar.

'Shall I come with you?'

'No, it's better for you to lay up here. I'll call you as soon as I know what's going on.' He snatched his car keys up.

'Go.' I nodded urgently. 'Good luck. I hope you find her safe.'

I slumped onto the kitchen chair, rubbing my fingers against my forehead. No, no, no! I pictured them torturing and killing Kelly as revenge. An image of *The Friday Club* tape flashed into my head. Bile rose in my throat, but I swallowed it down and tried to breathe through it.

I watched the clock creeping around to 4.30 p.m. Three and a half hours until Lee arrived. Three and a half hours until we could upload the photos and video and wait for it to explode. Three and a half hours and they'd have no reason to kill us to cover their nasty secrets because they'd be exposed.

I paced the floor, chewing on my thumbnail. I licked my cracked lips. Drank a glass of water. Thought about drinking something stronger but dismissed it. I needed to be clear-headed for what was going to come later.

I glanced at the clock.

5.05 p.m.

5.30 p.m.

5.45 p.m.

Where was Kelly? Why hadn't Mitchell called?

Please let her be okay. Please don't let anyone else die.

But the phone call, when it came at 6.05 p.m., wasn't what I'd been expecting.

Chapter 46

'I take it you're not watching the news?' Simon said down the line.

'No. Why?'

'Turn it on. It's on all the channels at the moment. Take your pick.'

At his tone of voice, a sinking feeling of dread hit me. 'Hang on a sec.' I picked up the remote control in Mitchell's lounge and turned the TV on, flicking it to a news station.

A young female presenter was standing on the steps outside a police station, relaying a story which a ticker running along the bottom of the screen told me was *Breaking News.*

I turned up the volume.

'And tonight MP for Hendon Constituency Alistair Bromwyn was arrested for serious sexual offences following allegations from a thirteen-year-old girl.

'The Conservative MP was arrested at 12.30 p.m. at his home address and taken to the police station behind me, where he was questioned for many hours before being released on bail.

'Fifty-nine-year-old Bromwyn stopped to speak to reporters as he left the station, vehemently denying the allegation and reiterating his innocence. When asked if he could give us details of the alleged offences, he said, "Not at this stage. However, what I can say is that they're totally false and unfounded. My lawyers and I are doing everything we can to show categorically and conclusively that there is absolutely no truth to any of this".

'Bromwyn went on to add, "Anyone who knows me will have no doubt in their minds that I am not guilty of the accusations levelled at me. These allegations are very distressing for myself, my family, and my constituents. This is nothing more than a smear campaign to ruin my reputation". A police spokesperson said the investigation is still continuing…'

'Bloody hell.' The phone felt heavy in my hand.

'Quite.'

'Do you believe it?'

'Not for a second. I know him. He's a good guy. It's a witch-hunt, a hatchet job, pure and simple, to discredit anything he was about to say. They wanted him silenced before he could name them. I don't know where they've drummed up this girl from, but if Alistair is embroiled in a sexual abuse charge, there's no way he'll be able to name anyone with parliamentary privilege now. For a start, no one will believe him, and he'll be forced to resign as an MP, anyway, after they're through with him. And if the Crown Prosecution Service manage to convince a jury he's guilty, he'll also be looking at jail time.'

I sank to the floor, shaking violently. 'I don't believe it, either.' I imagined what would happen to Alistair if he was convicted. A sudden heart attack or suicide in prison? Attacked by another inmate? That was the most likely scenario. Alive or dead now, Alistair was being silenced.

'I also had a visit today from someone claiming to be a serving police officer. He's disgusted with the deep-rooted cover-up going on and was told there would be no investigation into this ever. He said the orders to scrap any enquiries came from a very senior officer who told them it would be a major catastrophe to national security if it came out. He can't go on record because he's been threatened with the Official Secrets Act. If he blows the whistle on Alistair's dossier he saw, he'll lose his job, face prosecution, and possibly worse.'

I thought about the message from the man who'd bumped into me. The anonymous text.

I warned you to be careful!

Was it the same guy?

I chewed on my bottom lip so hard I drew blood. 'They know about me. And they may know about Mitchell now, too. His niece has gone missing. All this time when they were supposed to be investigating, they were probably planning their attack.'

'I really hate to say this, but nothing will ever be exposed through normal channels. They're just too powerful to be touchable. You're never going to get the truth and justice you want. Instead, you should concentrate your energy on trying to find a way to expose this yourself. Before it's too late.'

It already was too late. Justice was a delusion. Laws didn't protect the innocent.

But I'd started this, and I was damn well going to finish it.

I glanced at the clock for the millionth time.

It was 6.16 p.m. and still no call from Mitchell.

I had to go and get the evidence right now before Lee arrived. Before anyone else was killed over this. I had just about enough time to get to St Albans and back before he arrived.

My car was in Mitchell's garage, where we'd stashed it after I'd followed him home the night my house had been broken into.

I picked up my handbag from the kitchen worktop and caught Mitchell's wallet with the corner of the bag, sending it flying to the floor. The wallet skittered into the edge of the fridge, landing with its fold wide open.

And that was when I saw it.

Chapter 47

I pulled out the small photo from the clear plastic protector slot in the centre of the wallet fold, and the world started spinning.

He was a beautiful boy. Curly brown hair, blue eyes, and a round face like Mitchell, staring into the camera lens with a gappy-toothed smile, holding a big red balloon.

Alex. And I'd seen him before.

The other photo of him flashed in my head, as if the camera was right there in my brain.

Alex was on the floor at 10 Crompton Place. Naked. Head lolling to one side, his eyes half open, his face slack, as if he was drugged. Straddling him, with his hands around his neck, was Eamonn Colby, the children's minister.

Alex was the other anonymous boy Jamie had heartbreakingly described in his diary. The boy sadistically raped and murdered in front of them all.

I fought the urge to be violently sick. I had no time for that. This had to end.

I wanted to call Mitchell and tell him I knew who had killed Alex, but I couldn't do it over the phone. I left the photo on the worktop and willed the tremor in my legs to stop so I could get moving.

It was dark when I left Mitchell's. I crawled through the rush hour traffic at a snail's pace, wanting to scream at everybody to get the hell out of my way.

Fighting to keep the steering wheel steady, I kept checking the rear-view mirror, but so many cars were around it was impossible to see if anyone was following me.

When I got onto the dual carriageway, I drove fast. Erratically. Weaving in and out of vehicles.

My Nokia rang. I picked it up from the centre cubby box. It was Mitchell. 'Thank God! What's going on?' I veered over to the kerb as I answered, quickly righting myself again with one hand on the steering wheel, one hand pressing the phone to my ear.

'It was a…alarm.'

'What? I didn't get that.'

'False…'

'False alarm?'

'Yes! She…bunked…college.'

'She bunked off college? So she's safe? It's nothing to do with any of this?'

'No…then…you?'

'You're breaking up! The signal's really bad. Say that again.' My hand clutched the steering wheel so hard my knuckles strained against the skin as I negotiated a roundabout.

'…going? Where…you?'

'I'm on my way to get the evidence and bring it back. I couldn't wait around. They got to Alistair!'

'…need to…a…copy!'

'What?'

'…get…'

A crackly burst of static sounded in my ear. 'I can't hear what you're saying. Look, I'll be back in about an hour. And there's something else you need to know, and it's…oh God, Mitchell.' I hadn't wanted to do this over the phone, but something made me blurt it all out. 'I found your photo of Alex and…you didn't look at all of the photos Jamie had in that box, did you? And you didn't read his diary when he described the other boy who was murdered. They did it. It was the same people. There was a photo of Alex at Crompton Place with the ones Jamie got from Dave. They killed Alex like they did Moses. They killed him and then dumped his body.'

I heard a strangled sound down the line. '…Alex?…king joking?…sure?'

'Yes, I'm positive. I can show you when I come back with the copies we made. I'm so sorry. So, so sorry.'

'…now!'

'What? I can't hear you.'

'…around…need…evidence.'

'I know we need it! I'm nearly there.' I turned off a slip road, onto a single carriageway, and spotted a marked police car in my rear-view mirror.

'Shit! The police are behind me.'

'…plates…marker…off…road!'

'What?'

'Your…plates…put…of marker…'

The number plates! Of course. Why hadn't I thought of that? They'd probably set up some kind of marker or alert on them in their databases to find me. If the police checked the plates, they would pull me over.

If they pulled me over, they'd arrest me.

If they arrested me, how long would it be before I had an accident in custody?

'…them…stop…'

'I can't hear you!' I yelled, panic flooding through me as I tried to drive sensibly.

The police car was three car lengths behind me. I threw the phone on the passenger seat and gripped the steering wheel with both hands, my gaze manically darting from the windscreen to the mirrors.

A four-way junction was ahead with traffic lights on green.

The police car edged closer.

'Go away! Go away!' I muttered repeatedly.

I sped up, towards the traffic lights.

And then their blue lights flashed on and their siren started.

I held onto the steering wheel fiercely, wondering whether I could outrun them. How was I going to get away in the built-up area of the town? There was no way I would pull over for them.

They edged closer behind me.

I kept my eyes on the rear-view mirror...

And watched the police car suddenly veer around me and speed off, through the traffic lights. Watched the blue flashing lights dancing in the air as it sailed away from me into the night.

Chapter 48

I took the quiet back roads towards the church, hyper alert for more police cars. Even though they hadn't been after me, I couldn't take any chances.

I was breathing so hard when I parked the car in the quiet residential street opposite the church that I thought I'd pass out.

I picked up my phone from the seat, suddenly remembering I hadn't hung up. I glanced at the screen, but Mitchell must've been cut off. I turned it to mute, tucked it in my jeans pocket, and crept out of the car, my head whipping around, checking for signs of anyone lurking nearby.

Warm lights glowed behind curtains in a few of the houses. The smell of wood smoke permeated the air from one of the chimneys. A cat fight erupted further down the road.

There were no gates to the church grounds, so I walked along the pathway, past the deserted building and around the back to the graveyard. In the distance, I heard a helicopter droning in the air. Was it a police helicopter? Who were they looking for?

It was a new moon. A thin crescent of white in an all-black sky that didn't throw off any light. My eyes scanned the dark patch of trees along the border fences and the shadows in front of me, waiting for someone to jump out.

An owl to my right screeched into the night, making me duck momentarily.

As I approached Jamie's grave, I turned on the small torch I kept in my bag. Maybe it was morbid, but my copies of the photos and video were stored on the flash drive inside a plastic, fake hollow stone buried under the earth at the base of his gravestone, the kind people often kept spare house keys in and left around their gardens. Here was the one place I was sure they would never think to look for it.

I sank to my knees, the cold, wet earth seeping through my jeans. I put the torch in my mouth and angled it towards the ground, digging with my fingers.

A memory hit me from nowhere then. It was disabling for a few moments, stopping me like a catatonic dummy. Jamie and I on my birthday, having a romantic dinner at Jamie Oliver's restaurant, which was something I'd always wanted to do. It had been a surprise for me, and we were slightly drunk on wine and love. I'd asked him one of those silly hypothetical questions: *If you were stuck on a desert island, what three things would you take?* He'd thought about it for a long time, and I'd expected him to say something funny or profound, but in the end, he'd just said, *You, you, and you. I don't need anything else.*

Then the helicopter blades chopped through the air, getting closer, pulling me back to the present. I carried on digging through the mist of tears.

The Nokia vibrated silently in my pocket with an incoming call. I ignored it and curled my fingers around the stone and drew it to the surface, turning it over and sliding the underneath section off. I retrieved the flash drive from a sealed bag inside and put it safely in my other pocket. Then I reversed the process, burying the stone and smoothing out the earth so it looked as good as new. Scattering a few leaves and twigs over it for good measure.

Another noise echoed into the night. Movement. Rustling. I whipped my head around. No one was there.

The wind. It's only the wind.

I power-walked back towards the entrance, around the building, towards the car, glancing up and down the deathly quiet street.

My phone buzzed again as I slid behind the wheel of the Jeep and started the engine. I pulled the phone out of my pocket and pressed the answer button.

'Mitchell, you got cut off. Are you okay? I'm so sorry I had to tell you about Alex.'

'I looked at the photos. I saw Alex!' he yelled at me. 'Those fucking cunts killed my boy. They were the ones.' I heard the tears and despair and raging fury vibrating through his voice. 'He was seven years old! Seven years old and he never hurt anyone! He didn't deserve it. Didn't deserve what they did.' The line was clearer now. I put the phone on loudspeaker and put it in the centre cubby box as I drove.

'I know. It's heartbreaking,' I said softly, tears springing into my own eyes. Tears which blurred my vision for a moment, so I didn't notice a black van appear behind me at first.

Mitchell sniffed. 'Where are you now? Are you okay?' I imagined his jaw clenched as he ran a hand over his shaved head, pulling himself together.

'Yes, I've got the flash drive, and I'm just leaving St Albans. I'll be there soon.' Rather than going through the town centre, I decided to take the smaller back roads and weave through residential streets.

'You didn't need to go there! I had my own copies.'

'What? How?'

'When we were making our duplicates, a copy of everything automatically got stored on my hard drive. I took them off that and hid them so we'd have another backup.'

'Why didn't you tell me?' I waited for a Mini to go past at a junction and navigated onto a quiet lane.

'It doesn't matter now,' he said impatiently. Angrily.

I glanced in the rear-view mirror as I manoeuvred onto a roundabout. That was when I realised my mistake. 'I'm heading towards the North Orbital Road. I think I'm being followed. There's a black van about four car lengths behind me.'

'Shit. Okay…okay, stay on the line. I'll look at Google Maps and try to work out a way you can shake them.'

Both sweating hands clutched the wheel as I sped up, my heart fluttering erratically in my chest.

The van sped up, too.

'Okay, when you get to the North Orbital Road roundabout, instead of going straight on like they're probably expecting, take the turn for the A414. Try to turn right there at the last possible moment without slowing down too much and giving away your next move. Then I'll work out a further route.'

I leant forward in the seat, my shoulders rigid with tension. There was the roundabout up ahead. 'I'm about to get to it.'

Five.

Four.

Three.

Two.

One.

As I lifted my foot off the accelerator and slowed a little onto the roundabout, I turned the steering wheel right.

But nothing happened. There was no response from the Jeep, and it carried on straight over the roundabout onto the dual carriageway of the North Orbital Road.

What?

I took my foot off the accelerator.

The Jeep didn't slow.

I turned the wheel slightly left and right. The wheels didn't follow. They just carried on driving, heading straight.

I tapped the brakes. The car still didn't slow down.

'What's going on?' Mitchell said. 'Did you make the turn?'

'No! Something's happening to the Jeep. It's not...' I tried the brakes again. Nothing. The Jeep carried on at a steady seventy miles per hour. There was no hard shoulder, but I tried to steer it towards the small verge on the left, but again, the steering wheel wasn't responsive. 'I don't know what's going on. I can't control the car! It's like...it's like it's driving itself!' I glanced in my rear-view mirror. The black van was still behind me. Tears sprang into my eyes as the hum of the wheels on tarmac vibrated into my bones.

'What do you mean you can't control it?'

I turned the wheel again, aiming for the outside lane.

Nothing happened.

Turned it towards the verge.

Nothing happened.

Slammed my foot on the brake.

Nothing.

Pumped the brakes.

Still no response.

The Jeep sailed at high speed over the next clear roundabout.

Except I wasn't driving it.

Panic hit me full throttle. My limbs turned to ice while my stomach lurched around as if I was caught at sea in a violent storm. 'The brakes don't work. Neither does the steering wheel or accelerator! And the black van's close behind me now.'

'What?'

'Should I turn off the engine?' My eyes darted to the button on the dashboard.

'I'm thinking, I'm thinking! If you turn off the engine, it might send you spinning out of control.'

The Jeep slowed slightly as I came up behind a Ford Focus driving sixty miles an hour in the slow lane.

Relief hit me. Maybe there was just some weird kind of electronic malfunction that was righting itself now. 'It's slowing down.' I pressed the brakes again, but the Jeep still didn't respond. Instead, it swerved out into the fast lane without me touching anything, then increased in speed back up to seventy miles per hour. 'Now it's speeding up again. Mitchell, what can I do? What's going on?'

'I think they've taken over the vehicle remotely and they're controlling the car.'

'How is that even possible?'

'I don't know, but I think they've hacked into your electronic system somehow.'

I glanced at the van behind. The driver and passenger were a featureless blur.

The traffic was light in front, and the Jeep swerved left into the slow lane, its speed gradually increasing.

I studied the road ahead. It was straight on this patch. If I took a chance and hit the ignition button to hopefully cut the engine, the best I could hope for was that the car might fishtail for a while before coming to a stop. The worst? Well, a deep embankment was running parallel with me now. After the embankment was a row of dense trees. The Jeep could lose control, hurtle down the embankment, possibly flipping over on the way, possibly hitting a tree at full speed, possibly breaking my neck.

Panic clawed at my stomach as the Jeep's speedometer crept higher.

73 MPH.

75 MPH.

78 MPH.

My heart drummed to the beat of a rock concert beneath my ribs. 'I need to do something! It's going faster. Tell me what to do! Shall I turn it off and see if that works?'

'Yes. Try to turn it off!' Mitchell yelled, the panic in his voice matching mine.

80 MPH.

I pressed the ignition switch and...

No response.

83 MPH.

The night sped past me, my pulse booming in my ears.

I pressed it again.

85 MPH.

I gripped the steering wheel, even though I wasn't in control, and stabbed at the switch repeatedly. The road curved in a sharp bend ahead of me.

87 MPH.

90 MPH.

And then one word flashed up on the digital display in the centre of the dashboard:

GOODBYE.

The Jeep veered sharply left, off the road.

It flew though the air. Weightless. Effortless. And it seemed as if the world slowed down and speeded up both at the same time.

When people say their life flashes before their eyes when staring death in the face, they're wrong. It wasn't my life I was aware of. Only thoughts, firing madly with each synapse of the cells in my body.

Maybe some people would ask questions. Be suspicious. But they would probably be labelled conspiracy theorists or smeared or killed. My death would probably be announced to the world as an accident.

Tired woman falls asleep at the wheel.

If only they knew.

Maybe I'd been naïve to believe the truth could ever come out. It was too much of a threat to too many people for too many reasons. And pretty soon I'd be yesterday's news. I think I'd probably known even from the very beginning that I couldn't win.

There was always Mitchell, though. They didn't know about him, I was sure. He'd expose them. He still had the evidence. He'd do what I couldn't. He'd see it through to the end.

Wouldn't he?

I said a silent goodbye to Ava. To Jackson and my parents.

I hit the embankment, and the Jeep bounced.

Once.

Twice.

The momentum smashed my head into the roof, against the window. The car flipped over. There was crunching and smashing and shattering and tearing and searing pain. Jerking and ripping and darkness and shadows. The world was up and down and everything in between as the Jeep rolled over and over.

And the final thought. The one before the huge tree embedded itself into the bonnet was…

At least I'll see Jamie again now.

PART 3

SELLING THE LIE

"My silence is not weakness but the beginning of my revenge."

~ Author Unknown

MITCHELL

Chapter 49

What if you ever found out who'd murdered Alex? What would you do then?

Maya's words echoed in my head constantly. Every second of every day.

Over the years, I'd fantasised about dishing out the same treatment to them. What father wouldn't? It had consumed me, like a writhing, hungry monster living inside my belly, its fangs and claws ripping me apart. And now the monster would be unleashed—a wild, angry beast. It was all about balance. Righting the wrong. Tipping the scales in favour of good, not evil. Creating order from chaos. Reinstating light from the deepest depths of depraved darkness.

The bottom line was, child rapists and murderers didn't deserve to live. We should bring back the death penalty.

Which is exactly what I was about to do.

I slid Alex's photo out of my wallet. His innocent, trusting face smiled back at me. His bright eyes crinkling at the corners, so full of happiness and promise for the future. He should've grown up to be a complicated, moody teenager. A determined, principled young man. A well-balanced, fulfilled adult with everything to live for. He could've had his own kids by now.

Alex. My greatest gift. The only thing I almost did right. And my biggest failure.

I was supposed to protect him. Keep him safe. Watch over him.

But I'd failed. Just as I'd failed so many helpless people. Hundreds of men, women, and children. Jamie and Maya, too. I couldn't protect Alex, but I'd thought I could protect Maya. I couldn't even do that right. There was so much blood on my hands.

I was culpable in mass murder. Saturated with guilt. A fraud. A failure. A fake.

Guilty as hell. And maybe that was where I was heading. Eventually. And maybe when I got there, I'd get rid of the ghost town in my heart and stop the shadows calling out to me from those desolate places.

But first I had to get this done. First came atonement. Vengeance. Vendetta. Call it what you like. Only a thin, sometimes invisible strand separated it all.

I rested my head in my hands and tried to breathe. I needed to stay focused. To plan. There were so many possibilities. It would take time to work them all out. To prepare. Make sure everything ran with precision. No slip-ups. No mistakes. Nothing to point back at me.

But that was all I had left now, anyway. Time.

I sat up. Slapped my cheeks. Shook myself like an animal shedding water from its fur.

Focus.

My gaze strayed to the newspaper article again…

Woman Suspected of Trying to Take Her Own Life after Boyfriend Commits Suicide

Emergency services were called to the North Orbital Road, St Albans, last night after what is being tragically described as a suspected suicide attempt.

Maya Morgan, 37, was seen driving erratically by several eyewitnesses before appearing to drive her Jeep Cherokee purposely off the main road, down an embankment, and into a heavily tree-lined area. A female witness in a vehicle behind Ms Morgan stopped after the impact and dragged her unconscious body from the Jeep and alerted paramedics, fire brigade, and police. No other vehicles were involved.

Ms Morgan's sister, Ava Potter, said, 'Maya was left devastated by the suicide of her boyfriend, Jamie, nine months earlier and was struggling to cope'. Mrs Potter described Ms Morgan as being depressed, preoccupied, and unwilling to seek help. Ms Morgan had been secretive and distant from her sister since her boyfriend's death, and Mrs Potter believed that she had secretly been considering suicide for a long time. 'The whole family is obviously devastated,' Mrs Potter added. Ms Morgan suffered multiple broken bones, serious internal injuries, and is now in a coma. Doctors treating Ms Morgan have described her condition as critical.'

Lee had told me it was possible to hack into her Jeep. They'd inserted code inside her electronic system and remotely controlled it. She hadn't stood a chance.

I'd called in some big favours and had a few good men I trusted watching Maya at all times. Lee had put a covert camera in her hospital room when it wasn't possible to have a physical presence to protect her. It was a precaution, because I didn't think they'd make another attempt on her life unless she woke up. For now, they'd leave her to suffer, trapped inside her own battered body. Alive and dead at the same time. They would've found out the doctors weren't optimistic she'd ever come out of the coma. But I knew she was stronger than that. She was a fighter. She'd pull through. She had to. And by the time she did, the person who ordered the hit would be dead, and it would all be over.

Apparently, it was good to talk to coma patients, and I spent as much time as I could with her, reading, talking, playing music. So far there had been no response. I'd introduced myself to Ava and her parents as an old friend of Jamie's, and whenever they arrived to visit Maya, we made polite small talk and I left them to it. They were grateful I was there when they couldn't be to try to stimulate Maya. One day, when this was all over, maybe Maya would tell her family who I really was.

In between visiting Maya, I was perfecting the little details in my mind. The hunters would now be the hunted. Plan B had turned into Plan C.

The evil bastards behind everything still didn't know about me. They didn't know I was coming. They thought they were safe now. Thought they'd silenced everyone who knew the truth.

Suicide. Accident. Natural causes. There were so many ways to do it. And they weren't the only ones who could sell a lie.

When I found out who really took my son's life, I was way past wanting justice and truth. Now it was a necessary ending. Now it was all about revenge. It was personal.

Vigilante or protector? Who was to say?

If justice wasn't done by the legal system, then it was my responsibility to be judge and jury. I could save the world one person at a time.

There was a time to follow rules and orders. A time to think outside of the box and start to question the bullshit. A time to wake up and take action.

And then there was a time to kill.

It was time to start a war of my own.

Chapter 50

Geoff Barker – Crossfield Head – DEAD
Howard Sebastian – High Court Judge – DEAD
Colin Reed – Chief Constable of Bedfordshire Police – DEAD
Ted Byron – Children's Home Inspector – DEAD
Keith Scholes – Crossfield Deputy Head
Eamonn Colby – Children's Minister
Douglas Talbot – Defence Secretary
Felix Barron – Owner of Barron Private Banking Group, etc
Hooded Man in dungeon at 10 Crompton Place?

Four dead, five to go. Eeny meeny miny moe.

I decided on Keith Scholes first for several reasons, but mostly because he was the weakest link, the easiest and lowliest target, and I wanted to start from the bottom up to take out as many as I could before their alarm bells started ringing.

He'd retired to a small cottage on a quiet road that backed onto Epping Forest. Pretty handy, really. The nearest houses were half a mile away in a tiny village, and the occupants wouldn't hear a thing.

I established a small, one-man covert observation post to the rear of Scholes's cottage. A thick bramble hedge ran along the fence at the bottom of his twenty-five-metre-long garden, which I had burrowed into via the rear of the hedge itself. Firstly, I made sure I had a good field of view towards the cottage. Once satisfied I had good eyes on, I set to work constructing the hide. Using secateurs to hollow out a small but manoeuvrable working space inside, I pushed out some chicken wire to hold the brambles and nettles in position, and then I covered the lot in a small individual camouflage net. Lastly, I laid out a green foam mat for insulation, and the OP was ready. In my daysack I had the various optics I needed for observation of the target—a good set of binoculars, a Tasco scope, mounted on a small tripod, a high quality set of AN/PSV-7 night-vision goggles, US-issued kit, which was another illegal souvenir from my operational days in the regiment, and a small Dictaphone, to note down timings and anything relating to his routine that was worth recording.

For more routine tasks inside the OP, I carried in some cold scoff to eat and a flask of tea. For ablutions, I had an empty two-litre plastic bottle to piss in and some baby wipes, cling film, and plastic bags for anything else, because once inside the OP, I didn't want to move unnecessarily. Keeping as still as possible and remaining quiet would reduce the likelihood of compromise, either from the target or by any passing ramblers. All would be carried out with me when I exited after each stint.

I also had the business end of the equipment inventory, my Glock 19 pistol, safely tucked into a pancake holster on my waist, along with a double mag carrier holding two further sixteen-round mags, giving me forty-eight rounds in total. My expanding hasp baton was held in a small pouch on my belt. Inside my daysack, I had a large roll of black masking tape, a dozen heavy-duty plasticuffs, spare high-durability latex gloves, a Maglite torch with an IR filter, and some sedatives, just in case. To keep out the cold and the rain, I had a one-piece Gore-Tex camouflaged sniper suit with detachable hood. Encased in this, I was both protected from the elements and afforded a high degree of cover.

At the rear of Scholes's house was a small kitchen with an archway that led into a lounge at the front of the property, next to a downstairs toilet. Upstairs, a small bathroom, and next to that a spare bedroom at the front. The rear bedroom that overlooked the garden was used by Scholes. He had a single garage attached to the side of the house with an internal door that led into the kitchen.

Over the next few weeks, I learned several things that allowed me to build up a tactical picture in my head, familiarising myself with his routine. Scholes woke up between seven and eight every morning. After a cup of tea, he left the house and walked to the small shop just past the nearest house. One newspaper later, he walked back and ate breakfast. Usually two slices of toast. Sometimes cereal. After that he left the house again in his classic old Ford Cortina that he kept parked in the garage when not in use. After observing which direction he always seemed to be heading in, I followed covertly in a beat-up old VW Golf I'd bought for five hundred pounds and would never register. A small price to pay. Scholes regularly drove to a park five miles away. A park that had a large pond in the middle of it, frequented by ducks.

Scholes walked around the pond clockwise, carrying his bag of birdseed. He sat on the third bench he came to, opened his bag, and began to scatter his seed to the ducks. But Scholes wasn't an avian fan. I could tell that by the way he flinched every time the ducks got too near his feet and the way his lip curled in disgust. No, Scholes wasn't there for the birds. His gaze was firmly fixed on the children's play area near the large gravel car park, directly in his sight line from the bench, watching with his tongue protruding from his moist lips like a reptile tasting the air, his eyes filled with glassy longing.

But not for long, eh, Scholes? Not much longer.

He usually spent about an hour in the park. Anymore time and it would've been hard to justify why an old man was sitting there with no bird food left, in the coldest November we'd had for twenty years, watching a kiddies' play area.

So back home it was for Scholes, where he spent the rest of the morning reading in a saggy brown armchair, stained with dark patches on each arm. Then a light lunch before turning on his laptop, probably intimately enjoying his private collection of child porn, which I'd discovered when I'd been inside the house when Scholes was out one day. It was all carefully hidden behind other images stored on his device.

His medicine cabinet in the bathroom had a half-empty packet of Ambien, ten-milligram tablets prescribed to Scholes.

Have trouble sleeping, do you? Is there any conscience inside you? Any remorse?

It would happen at night-time, that was a given. When it got dark around four thirty, Scholes shut the curtains at the front of the property that faced the quiet country lane but not the rear ones. After all, who could possibly want to be looking into his house from the woods after dark?

He pottered around in the kitchen every night about six, making dinner. Sometimes beans on toast. Sometimes a frozen microwave meal. After dinner he had a bath, before heading back downstairs to read again in his armchair, with a glass of whisky, which he refilled several times before retiring to bed, presumably with a sleeping tablet, too. I wondered if he had nightmares.

I hoped so.

I waited until Scholes went up for his nightly bath before making my move. *Nothing like being nice and squeaky-clean before you kill yourself.* It was a perfectly normal ritual, they'd say. He still had some dignity left and didn't want to be found in a filthy state. Wanted to make it as pleasant as possible for whoever discovered him. Even though he was a lonely retiree, who appeared to have no friends— apart from the ones online, in secret chat rooms, who shared his evil predilections—he was still thinking of others until the end.

Bless him.

The man in the small shop and the nearest neighbour would say he was just a nice old man who kept to himself and couldn't cope with it all anymore.

I checked the plastic shoe covers on my steel toe–capped boots. Clenched and unclenched my latex-gloved hands. Adjusted the balaclava I wore a millimetre to the right.

My Glock felt snug in my hand as I emerged from the cover of the woods. It was a new moon, and what little moonlight that should've been glowing was hidden by a thick band of cloud.

Even the weather gods were on my side. The side of the righteous. It was a message, a sign. Of course it was.

I climbed over the three-foot wooden post and rail fence just past the hedge and my OP, my eyes scanning the night, my ears alert to every sound.

Nothing. Silence.

The rear door that led into the kitchen was locked, but it was an old, single-glazed wooden door with an old, useless lock. It took about thirty seconds for me to get inside again. Upstairs, the radio was tuned in to a play. I heard a slosh of water as Scholes settled into the bath, and I shut the door slowly behind me. There were no creaks, no squeaks of wood to give me away.

As I said, a sign. Or maybe the fact that I'd been in the house yesterday to hide what I needed and had added a little lubrication to the hinges. Vaseline was a wonderful invention. I'd had plenty of time to familiarise myself with the layout of his house, scouting for any signs that might give me away before I was ready.

I sat in Scholes's armchair, the Glock like an old friend in my right hand resting on my knee. My left hand casually placed on my left thigh.

And I waited.

Chapter 51

Scholes shuffled into the lounge, his head down, picking at a piece of fluff on his cardigan. The years hadn't been kind to him. His once black hair was now grey and thinning. His face was saggy and criss-crossed with drinker's veins.

He was halfway into the room before he glanced up. Saw me. Froze.

His eyes widened. His lips fell open.

A gun had that effect on people.

I pointed the Glock at his centre mass. I could've pointed it at his head. The idea of treating the sadistic Scholes to a third eye in the middle of his forehead was tempting. But this wasn't a murder scene. This was a suicide. Of course, Scholes didn't know that.

Yet.

'Wha-what…do you want?' Scholes stammered. 'I have a few pounds upstairs. About a hundred. J-just take it. I don't have much else.'

I smiled. 'I have some questions for you.' I trained my gun arm lower, lower. His balls were a perfect shot from here. 'If you give me the right answers, I'll let you live. If not…' I paused and raised my eyebrows. 'I'll shoot you in the bollocks. It'll be messy, of course. There'll be a *lot* of blood. Not to mention the pain. Agony, in fact.

You could bleed out, which would take a while. Or someone might find you before that, if you're lucky. Or unlucky, depending on how you look at it. Then there'll be a lot of reconstructive operations. Excruciating surgery to repair the damage.' I nodded at his crotch. Smiled again. 'Your choice, of course.'

'But…but I don't know what…' His hands trembled at his sides. 'Who are you? I don't know anything. I'm just a retiree. I…I can't answer any questions.'

'Oh, but I think you can.' I stood up and kept the Glock steady on him. 'Like I said. If you answer my questions truthfully, I'll be gone before you know it, and you can get back to having a nice quiet evening by the fire, reading *Story of O*.'

His forehead crinkled with confusion. 'How did you know—'

'Doesn't matter.' I tilted my head. 'So? You ready for a little Q and A session?'

Scholes's mouth flapped open and closed, a little rush of air exhaling as he did so.

'I'll take that as a yes.' I inclined my head towards the archway that led into the kitchen. 'We're going to the garage.'

'W-why?' Dread settled over his face.

'You'll see.' I stood and stepped towards him. 'Come on. The quicker we do this, the quicker it's over and you'll never have to set eyes on me again. That's a promise.'

He took a step back and held his palms up. 'Okay, okay, just, please…don't shoot me.' He turned around and shuffled forward in his navy-checked slippers. 'I don't know what I can possibly—'

'Shut up.' I pressed the gun under his left shoulder blade. Metal on fabric on skin on bone on heart. 'Get in the garage.'

Scholes moved unsteadily through the kitchen to the internal plywood door painted white that led into the single garage.

'Open the door.'

He nodded incessantly, like one of those stupid nodding dogs people had on their dashboards. He turned the key. Then hesitated.

I dug the gun harder into his back.

In response, Scholes quickly swung open the door and took a step forward.

'Turn the light on.'

Scholes flipped the switch on the wall just inside the doorway. A yellow fluorescent strip light sparked on. The old external garage doors were wooden and opened outwards onto his driveway and were locked from the outside with a bolt and padlock. There was no way he was getting out of them.

'I don't know what you want,' Scholes whined. 'There's nothing in here.'

'I told you, I don't want money. I want answers.'

His neck began shaking, causing it to nod rapidly again. 'But I don't…I don't know anything.'

The old Ford Cortina was parked in the middle of the garage, with just enough space to walk around the doors. Along the wall to the left of the kitchen doorway we stood in was a hip-height metal workbench with junk dumped underneath it. Pots of paint, tubes of silicone, old curtains, two folded deckchairs, boxes of junk.

'There's a roll of flexible hose, duct tape, and a pair of scissors hidden underneath that pile of red curtains under the bench. There's also a bottle of your favourite whisky. Get them out.'

Scholes's head turned, trying to look at me over his shoulder, but I nudged him forward with the barrel of the gun. 'Chop, chop.'

He bent down, an old man's stooped hunch, pulled a few paint pots out of the way to get to the curtains, and then tossed them to the side. He hesitated again when he saw the length of black hose and duct tape, realisation kicking in. 'I don't know anything. I don't understand. I'm just a simple man. I keep myself to myself. You've got the wrong person,' he whined.

'I don't think so. Get the whisky.'

He retrieved the full seventy-centilitre whisky bottle. Glenfiddich, laced with Ambien. Just a little something to make things go more smoothly. I pointed my gun at the whisky. 'This interrogation is going to be nice and relaxed, as long as you tell me the truth, okay? What's that look for? It's your favourite brand, isn't it? You can't say I'm not thoughtful. So, go on, have a drink. Then we'll talk.'

Under the unwavering barrel of my gun, Scholes unscrewed the cap and warily took a swig. He swallowed. Licked his lips.

'Nice blend, eh?'

He nodded warily.

'Well, have some more. Nothing like two people having a pleasant chat over a few drinks, is there?'

Scholes took a bigger swig.

I waited. Smiled. He got the message and drank again.

'Keep going.'

Scholes obliged, dribbling some of the amber liquid down his stained grey cardigan as he watched me cautiously. 'Look, I really don't know wh—'

I jerked my head towards the car. 'The outcome is all up to you.'

He nodded again, but this time it was as if he was convincing himself. 'Okay,' he said, his voice a meek, compliant whisper. I pictured him when he was younger, how Jamie had described him in the diary I finally read after Maya's attempted murder. I wanted to pistol-whip him right there and then. The urge was so fucking strong that my Glock hand started to shake as I gripped the handle. I couldn't slip up, though. Scholes's prints had to be all over this to make it look authentic.

'Now, I want you to put the whisky in the car and open the rear offside passenger window, just enough to slip one end of the hose through. Then wind the window up again to secure it.'

He rested the bottle on the front seat, opened the rear door behind the driver's seat, and unwound the window. He slid one end of the hose through until about fifteen inches dangled inside the vehicle. Then he wound it up again so the glass held the hose in place, leaving an open gap of a couple of inches wide at the top of the window.

'Now duct tape over the gap from outside of the car.' We couldn't leave any leaks anywhere, could we? Not when I would be in close proximity to the vehicle.

Scholes pulled off pieces of tape and overlapped them until the opening was sealed. He looked at me for the next instruction and swallowed hard, his Adam's apple bobbing up and down. He knew what was coming.

'Secure the other end of the hose into the exhaust and wrap it with duct tape.'

He picked up the hose and pushed it up inside the exhaust pipe. His hands trembled so much it took four attempts before the hose stayed in the pipe. Then he taped it up so the hose wouldn't fall out.

'Nice cars, these old classics, aren't they?'

Scholes looked at me but didn't reply, as if he didn't know what the right answer should be.

I examined the pipe and hose, smiling. 'Good. Don't worry. It will be over soon as long as you behave.'

'I'll tell you anything you want to know. Anything!' he snivelled.

'Sit in the driver's seat.'

Scholes opened the driver's door and slid behind the wheel, staring down the barrel of the Glock.

'Drink the whisky.'

Scholes swallowed more.

I waited.

He drank. The dosage of tablets wouldn't take much longer to kick in and make him drowsy.

'Okay, so here's what's going to happen. If you tell me the truth, I'll let you go. No harm done. I'll be on my way, and you can forget I was ever here. But if you lie...' I stood in the kitchen doorway, facing the front of the Cortina, and took his car keys from my pocket, dangling them in the air. 'If you lie, you'll start the engine and close the doors and I won't let you out until you tell me the truth. Got it?'

He nodded, his neck wobbling again involuntarily.

'Good. Have a drink.'

He swallowed more whisky. A quarter of the bottle had gone now.

'Crossfield Children's Home,' I said slowly.

Scholes's eyes bulged with surprise. With terror.

'You were supposed to be looking after those kids. You had a duty of care to protect them. And yet you subjected them to the most unimaginable abuse and torture. You were also complicit in their murder. What you and the others did is way over the edge of human depravity.'

'It wasn't me! I didn't know anything about it at the time. It was...it was only after I found out some of the staff did—'

'Don't insult my intelligence. Do you want to live?' I tilted my head and jingled the keys.

'Yes, of c-course I do. I—' His eyes were wet now, glistening in the harsh strip light filtering through the windscreen.

'Take a drink.'

He nodded vigorously and gulped the whisky.

'Let's try again. Crossfield Children's Home. You and Barker abused those boys. And then you procured them for sadistic VIPs to rape and torture and murder at 10 Crompton Place.'

Scholes closed his eyes briefly, tears slipping down his cheeks.

'Didn't you?'

The tone of my voice made his eyelids snap open.

He nodded pathetically. 'They made me. I had to do it. I had to.'

'The only thing you *have* to do in life is die. The rest is all up to you. Your choice. Your actions.'

'I'm sorry, I'm sorry.'

'It's too late for sorry.' I narrowed my eyes. 'Who was the masked man at the parties?'

'Wha-what do you mean?'

'Crompton Place. Judge Sebastian's house. There was a hooded, masked man there on several occasions. Who was he?'

'I don't know.'

I raised my gun, aiming it directly through the windscreen at his forehead. 'Who was he?'

'I don't know! I don't *know!*' Scholes's head shook violently, tears and snot dribbling down his pathetic face.

'Have a drink.'

He gulped more whisky.

'You must know. You knew those children were being trafficked there, to be tortured, to be *murdered!*' I spoke slowly again. 'Who. Was. The. Man. In. The. Mask?'

Scholes's breath came in short, choppy pants as he stared down the barrel of my Glock. 'I don't know. I swear, I don't. I never went to the parties. I only knew the judge owned the house, but I never knew who went there. I swear! Honestly, you have to believe me. I'm telling the truth.'

I took a moment to push the sickening, violent anger down. Inhaled a deep breath. Held it. Made my mind up.

'You're lying to me. Barker had a scouting party at his quarters at Crossfield. Want to tell me who the guests were?'

'I...I can't remember. It was a long time ago. I wasn't even there!'

This time Scholes desperately glugged more alcohol without being prompted, as if it was his saviour.

'Okay, then. Time's up.'

I walked forward, around the open driver's door, and held out the ignition key to him. 'You're going to start the engine and shut the door. I'm going to stand in the kitchen doorway and ask you some more questions until I'm satisfied you're telling the truth. If I am, you can get out before the carbon monoxide renders you unconscious and you die. Is that all clear, or do you want some further instructions?'

He snivelled some kind of reply that didn't make sense.

'I'll take that as a yes.' I wiggled the key in my left hand and kept my Glock trained on him with my right.

Scholes stared at me, but I wasn't sure whether he was actually seeing me or looking straight through me.

'Take the key. Now.'

He blinked, his eyelids growing heavier, but didn't make a move to take them. 'You'll kill me anyway.'

'Well, now, there's a big dilemma. And the choice is entirely yours, of course.' I gave him a crooked smile. 'One, you can have your cock and bollocks shot off and I'll leave you to die in agony. Two, I might leave you in the car until the carbon monoxide kills you. Or three, and this is probably the clincher, you can tell me the truth and I'll let you turn off the engine and get out before any of the above happens. How does that sound?'

Scholes stared down into the whisky bottle in his lap, his lips moving with no sound coming out, occasionally sniffing and snorting like a pig. Which, actually, when I thought about it, was offensive to pigs.

'What's it going to be, Scholes? Only I have to wash my hair tonight so…' I shrugged. 'I need to run along soon.'

'I'm sorry,' he mumbled before swallowing some more whisky. 'I loved those children.'

'You're sorry?' I snorted. 'Take the key, and this will be over soon.' I stepped closer. Aimed the gun at his crotch.

Defeated, Scholes held out a trembling hand.

I dropped the key fob into it. 'Start the car. If you turn the engine off or try to get out, I *will* shoot you.'

He was docile now, compliant, as he started the engine.

I took a step back. 'Now shut the door.'

Scholes pulled on the door handle and slammed it shut.

I took up my position in the kitchen doorway again. Scholes would be the marker. Even if any carbon monoxide leaked out of the vehicle, it would render him unconscious first, and that was my cue to leave him to it.

I stared through the windscreen and shouted over the noise of the engine. 'Okay, let me refresh your memory. Howard Sebastian, Colin Reed, Douglas Talbot, and Felix Barron all came to the party Barker held at Crossfield. You knew what was going on, so you must've known who the people from The Friday Club were. You were involved in it all, too.'

'I was never at the parties.' Scholes swayed a little in his seat. He downed some more whisky. The bottle was just over half full.

'Let's try again. Who was the masked man?'

Scholes clenched the steering wheel with one hand, as if it could save him. 'I don't know! Really, you have to believe me.'

'That's a lie, Scholes!'

'I don't, I don't,' he said, his eyelids drooping for a moment before he jerked upright again, trying to stay alert, but the tablets were taking effect, enhanced by the alcohol. A trail of grey smoke swirled inside the car. It almost looked as if it was something alive, dancing on the air. Fascinating to watch.

'Who was he?'

'They'll…kill me. They'll all kill me.' His chin drifted down towards his chest.

'I hate to point out the obvious, but you can't be killed twice, can you? And it looks like I've got there first. Scholes! Stay awake now!'

His eyelids snapped open.

'Who is he?'

'What? I can't hear you!' he whimpered, his face contorted with panic.

'You know who he is. You know what he did. I want a name. I want a name and I'll let you out.'

'He…no…he…' He mumbled something incoherent.

I cupped a hand to my ear. 'Who is he?'

'They knew I had…had the same…' He trailed off, coughing with the exhaust fumes. I waited for him to carry on, watching the smoke.

Tears streamed down his face. Could've been from the fumes. Could've been from fear. Could've been with remorse. Although that seemed unlikely. And it didn't matter, anyway. It was far too late for that.

'They…'—he coughed—'knew about Barker and me. They said… I…they'—he coughed again—'would.' He stopped mid-sentence, confused. 'Wurl we wit not,' he slurred. 'Exp…expo…expose—' He broke off in a fit of coughing, deep hacking that sounded as if his lungs were being hurled out of his mouth.

'Give me his name.'

Scholes blinked quickly, his head swaying from one side to the other, as if he was having trouble keeping it upright. 'I don't know. I don't…' he slurred, his eyes fluttering closed, his chin lolling onto his chest.

I believed him. Scholes had never been to the parties. I was hoping

Barker might have known and told Scholes but apparently not. He really didn't know.

I watched until he finally lost consciousness, succumbing to the drugs and alcohol and carbon monoxide.

'By the way, I lied,' I said before letting myself out of the house and stealing through the rear garden the way I'd come.

Five dead, four to go.

Chapter 52

Ben Scree.

Not a person but a seven-hundred-metre cone-shaped mountain in Scotland. From the summit, the views were breathtaking. Breathtaking literally for the next hit on my list.

Ben Scree was a 4.75-mile hill walk with a mostly pleasant terrain. Slightly boggy at the bottom, but once I was past that, a handy narrow track snaked up through heather and grass to the summit. The rocky shingle-and-flint path could be a little treacherous in a few spots, where it ran along the very edge of the mountainside. One wouldn't want to slip off at one of those points. If someone were unlucky enough to fall there, they would be battered against the rocks on the sharp drop down. The very best they could expect would be a broken neck or spine or both. The worst unfortunate outcome would be all of the above, plus having the internal organs liquefied to soup and the soft tissue and bones pulped to raw hamburger meat. And what a tragically sad accident that would be.

Ben Scree was also interesting because, four miles away, Eamonn Colby, the children's minister, had a holiday home he liked to frequent. A spacious and rustic log cabin, although it was more like a mansion than a cabin. Probably funded by an expenses scam. Definitely paid for by the taxpayers. Eamonn Colby's main recreational activity whenever he was in residence in the cabin was walking Ben Scree and drinking the best Scottish Highland malt whisky. The media reported hill walking helped Colby relax and clear his mind of the daily stresses of Westminster, and kept him fit. Which all served to refocus him, so he could return to Parliament reenergised and raring to go from his weekend or week-long Scottish breaks. And the best part was that Ben Scree was relatively unknown in walking circles. I was told by reliable sources that someone could be on that mountain a hundred times and not see a soul. And also, that he liked to walk it alone. It was the place where I'd find, fix, and finish Colby.

Scholes's suicide had been reported in the media, correctly predicted, as the suicide of a lonely old man. Not surprisingly, there was no mention of the repulsive, sickening images and films on Scholes's laptop. Maybe it had been covered up by the remaining members of The Friday Club. Or maybe the police or coroner's officer hadn't even bothered to check it hard enough to find the hidden images. It didn't matter much to me. The only thing that mattered was that Scholes was on the lower rung of the chain. Not in the same league as the rest of them. So his suicide would probably go unquestioned. From what I could tell, Scholes hadn't been in contact with any of them since Crossfield was closed in the '90s and he retired. They didn't care about him. He was merely a pawn.

But when it came to the others—Colby, Douglas Talbot, Felix Barron, and the Masked Man—then someone would definitely start to sit up and pay attention. Which meant it would be increasingly harder to get close to them.

But who dares wins, eh?

And this was one war I *would* win.

The passage in Jamie's diary of Alex's last moments was burned into my brain…

The children's minister grabbed an empty whisky bottle from the table in the corner of the room and strode towards the boy. 'Hold him down,' he said to the banker.

The banker kneeled on the boy's back, pushing his head into the carpet. The boy struggled, crying, pleading.

I turned towards the door, wanting to escape but frozen in place with shaking legs. The boy's screams were louder but muffled by the carpet. And then there was an agonising cry and I knew what was happening, as he'd done it to me and the others before. My guts churned. I was light-headed, floating. I huddled on the floor, my knees drawn into my body, and buried my face into my thighs, pressing my hands over my ears to block it all out, but I could still hear it.

Gradually the screams stopped and were replaced by a thumping sound on the floor. Inexplicably, I was drawn back to look at him. The boy was sprawled on his back with the children's minister straddling his chest, a demonic look in his eyes. His hands were round the boy's throat, and the boy's arms and legs slapped the carpet, terror in every gasped breath. He struggled as he fought for his life, his eyes bulging, before sinking back into his head, staring blankly, and his body slackened into stillness.

Of course, when Maya had told me there were photos of Alex at Crompton Place in amongst the ones Jamie had got from Dave, I'd forced myself to look. Forced myself to see the brutal images that Jamie spoke about as they unfolded that night. From what I could work out, it must've been Douglas Talbot behind the Polaroid camera, recording the savage and ruthless murder of my son for them all to laugh about later, as if pondering over something completely inconsequential, like the death of an ant they'd squashed under their shoe.

So, inevitably, it had to be Eamonn Colby next.

Chapter 53

I'd visited the mountain numerous times in the last few weeks while Colby was in London, scouting for the perfect spot, working out which was the best place to stage it. And I'd found it. Again, it was *so* perfect, it had to be a message or sign from some higher force up above that was on my side. From Alex.

Almost at the summit, the track turned into a narrow ridge before a bend that would hide me from view until the last minute. Over the years, the battering winds and weather had loosened the shingle and unstable rocks underfoot there. The ridge also sloped away from the body of the mountain, towards the deadly drop. Looking down from the precipice to the craggy rocks far below, I was reminded of the top of Pen y Fan, the fabled mountain in the Brecon Beacons that I'd climbed up and down so many times during the punishingly hard Hills Phase of SAS selection all those years before. If only I'd known then what I knew now.

In normal circumstances, the ridge could test a nervous hill walker, particularly during strong winds. It was wide enough for one person to pass along comfortably. But when two people met at that point? Well, accidents could happen, couldn't they?

I left the blend-in-with-the-world white Vauxhall Astra parked a mile away. There was a small shingle car park at the base of the mountain, but that was far too close. The Astra was twenty years old with false number plates. I'd bought it for two hundred quid in a private sale and wouldn't be registering it either—surprise, surprise. It would be torched in a remote location, just like the Golf I'd used when tailing Scholes.

It took three and a half hours to reach my surveillance point just shy of the summit, merging into the mountain in my army-green camo trousers and Gore-Tex jacket. I'd rolled the camo balaclava up onto my head so it looked like a beanie hat.

I sat on an outcrop of rocks and admired the view. The guidebooks were right about this place. It was pretty fantastic. And I had a perfect vantage point of the car park at the base of the mountain, watching for Eamonn Colby's black Mercedes E-Class Coupe.

The sun had been out when I started my ascent, but after a while it disappeared behind a ribbon of low clouds the colour of slate. The wind was a wild, roaring voice in my ear.

It was 10.00 a.m.

I waited.

Chapter 54

I saw Eamonn Colby a whole four hours before he saw me. I knew it would happen today as he was staying at his cabin for only two nights before heading back to London, and he'd arrived late afternoon the day before.

I sat with my back against the mountain, watching him make a steady pace up towards the ridge. My ridge, as I thought of it now. Or Alex's Ridge.

When he got closer, I headed slowly back up nearer the summit, around the bend, so that he wouldn't see me until the last minute, when we were both finally face-to-face.

I heard Alex's voice in my head, whispering, *Daddy, save me.* I heard Maya, saying, *I want to get them, Mitchell.* And the words in Jamie's diary reverberated in my gut.

I stood with my back pressed into the rocks, clenching and unclenching my fists. And waited some more.

Until I heard Colby, panting, his walking boots crunching over shingle and stones. It was time.

I rounded the rock, onto the narrow ridge, and there he was, a few metres ahead of me, dressed in lightweight North Face waterproof trousers and jacket, sturdy boots, and carrying a water bottle. His face was red from exertion and wind.

The plan in my head had been to strike without warning and simply push Colby off the ridge. He would've been floating through the air on a downward trajectory quicker than one could say *child killer*. He wouldn't have known what had hit him. A simple and unfortunate hiking accident. A terrible, terrible shame.

But as he stopped suddenly, his chin jerking up, startled at the sight of another person, the plan changed.

'Oh, hello.' He smiled. 'I wasn't expecting anyone else up here.'

I smiled back, pushing down the swelling darkness inside. 'No. I'm told not many people come up here.' I glanced to my right, out over the sheer drop, to the wide expanse of Scottish lakes and glens. 'It's a shame, really. The view is stunning.'

Colby followed my gaze. 'Yes, it is. It's a great place to get away from everything and clear your head.'

I gritted my teeth and nodded.

The children's minister grabbed an empty whisky bottle from the table in the corner of the room.

'Aren't you Eamonn Colby?' I tilted my head, an interested and affable smile fixed to my face.

'Yes.' He gave me that practised politician's smile. A lizard smile. 'Have we met?' His forehead furrowed slightly as he tried to place me. God forbid he should forget a potential voter.

'Hold him down,' he said to the banker.

'No. But you've met someone I know, Alex Butler.'

The banker kneeled on the boy's back, pushing his head into the carpet.

'Alex Butler?' Colby pursed his lips. 'I don't seem to recall that name.'

'You met him in London.'

He smiled. 'Ah, well, I meet a lot of people in London, of course.' He chuckled conspiratorially.

The boy struggled, crying, pleading.

'You probably didn't even know his name, actually,' I said.

The boy was sprawled on his back with the children's minister straddling his chest, a demonic look in his eyes.

Colby's eyebrow quirked up. 'Oh? Was Mr Butler one of my constituents?'

I took a deep breath. Kept my gaze fixed firmly on him, watching for the tell to come. 'No. You met him at 10 Crompton Place.'

His hands were round the boy's throat, and the boy's arms and legs slapped the carpet, terror in every gasped breath.

Something flickered in Colby's eyes for a fraction of a second before he recovered. 'Sorry, I'm not familiar with that address. I think you must have me mixed up with someone else.' He took a swig of water.

'I don't think so.' I took a step closer towards him. 'You must remember Crompton Place.'

He struggled as he fought for his life, his eyes bulging, before sinking back into his head, staring blankly, and his body slackened into stillness.

'I've never heard of it,' Colby said uncertainly, taking a small step backwards along the ridge. 'I'm sorry, but I think there's been some kind of mistake.' He glanced at his watch. 'Damn. I didn't realise how late it was getting. I really need to get going if I'm going to get back in time for a conference call later.' He smiled that smile again, his eyes devoid of emotion, like a shark's, and turned around, about to walk back down the ridge. Down the mountain.

And that was when everything I'd been holding together inside snapped.

I strode towards him, pivoted on my right foot, and kicked out with my left. My boot connected with the back of his knee, and I heard a snapping sound. It sounded like sweet music to me.

The impact propelled Colby forwards. He fell to the ground on his hands and knees in a crumpled heap, dangerously close to the edge of the ridge, his water bottle skittering over the edge of the mountain. He scrambled around onto his backside, away from the edge, facing me, his face emblazoned with arrogant indignation and pain. 'Get your hands off me! How dare you! That's assault.' He clutched his knee with both hands and cried out, wincing. 'Well, you've done it now, haven't you? I'll have you arrested for that, you thug.' He pulled his mobile phone out of his pocket and pressed a few buttons.

I was the thug? Ha! Good one, Colby.

I kicked out at his hand, my foot connecting with bone and plastic with a satisfying *crack!* The phone flew from his grip in an arc, over the side of the ridge off the mountain. 'You won't be calling anyone.'

Colby slithered backwards, like the snake he was, trying to ignore the obvious pain in his knee and his hand with the thumb that was now sticking out at an unnatural angle. Beads of sweat pricked his forehead. His face had turned from red to sickly white. The adrenaline suddenly surging through him would probably be masking the worst of the agony for a while. He glanced up at me. 'You're making a big mistake. I have powerful friends, you know. You're not going to get away with this.' His voice was filled with defiance.

'Really? Because from where I'm standing, you're on the top of a mountain, with a suspected torn ligament in your knee, a broken thumb, no mobile phone, and no one else around for miles.'

Colby swallowed hard, the arrogance wearing off as he saw what was in my eyes and it dawned on him exactly what kind of situation he was in. Confusion filtered through his body language, trying to register what was happening and why. 'What do you want? I've got money. I can pay you money! Lots of it.'

I snorted. 'Let's talk about Alex.'

'I told you, I don't know any Alex!'

'Wrong answer. 10 Crompton Place. The Friday Club.'

Colby shook his head vigorously. 'I have absolutely no idea what you're talking about. Please stop this nonsense. If you let me go now, I won't press charges.'

I plucked the photo of Alex from the inside pocket of my jacket and threw it towards him. It landed face down on the shingle.

'Pick it up,' I said.

Colby glanced at the photo cautiously, breathing hard.

'Pick. It. Up.'

Colby reached out with his uninjured hand. Picked it up. Turned it over. His eyes widened for a fraction of a second. His lips twitched, but the rest of him went very still.

'Remember him now?'

'It's a fake! Someone's trying to ruin my reputation. That isn't me. I absolutely deny it!' he blustered.

'Okay. Let me get this straight. That's not you with your hands around Alex's neck, strangling him?'

'It's doctored. It's obviously been fabricated for some kind of smear campaign against me. It's a fake. A pack of lies.'

'Uh-huh.' I nodded. 'And what about the rest of them?'

Colby licked his lips. Swallowed. 'The...rest?'

I gave him a cold smile. 'Hundreds of them. All taken at The Friday Club. And the videotape? The snuff film which shows you all torturing and murdering Moses, like you tortured and murdered Alex. Like you and your psychopathic cronies sadistically abused all the others for your own decayed self-gratification. Are they all fake, too?'

Colby blinked rapidly. His lips moved, but no sound came out at first. Finally, he said. 'I can make you rich. Whatever you want, I can give you.'

'Really?'

'Everyone wants money! Everyone can be bought. They won't let this come out—you know that, don't you?' The fear was replaced once again with arrogance. 'You don't know who you're dealing with here. I'm protected.'

'Oh, I think I do. How can you sick perverts even think about doing those kinds of things to innocent children?'

'Why do you even care about a couple of retarded, worthless brats from children's homes? They were all expendable! They deserved what they got. No one cared about them! Where were their parents, eh? They obviously didn't care about them, so why should you?' he shouted.

I locked my eyes on his and saw the viciousness in them, his words setting off a grenade in my head. Ribbons of red exploded at the edge of my vision.

With a primal rage, I threw myself at Colby on the ground, straddling him, my bulky weight locking him down, just as he'd done to Alex. My fists pummelled Colby's face as his arms flailed around, trying to protect himself, his nails catching the skin on my cheek. 'I'll tell you where one of the parents is right now. Alex was my *son*! He was kidnapped off the street by you bastards!' I spat into his face.

Colby yelled, 'Stop! Stop!' as he squirmed beneath me, trying to avoid my raining fists to no avail.

I grabbed the collar of his jacket with both hands and smacked the back of his head against the rocky ridge. 'I was in the military when you were killing my son! I was defending my country for bastards like you. Fighting bullshit wars for traitors who'd sell any*one* or any*thing* out to get what they want!'

'Please! Wait! I'll give you money! Anything!' His voice was nasally, distorted through his now broken nose.

I got to my feet and yanked the dazed Colby up by the scruff of his jacket, twisting around so my back was against the mountain and his feet rested precariously near to the edge of the ridge, my hands gripping onto his collar.

Colby's eyes met mine, one already closing with swelling, blood from his nose dripping down his chin. He glanced over the edge with terror. Glanced back at me. 'How much do you want? Whatever the amount, I'll give you.'

'How much is your life worth, Colby?' I sneered.

'Fifty thousand! I'll give you fifty grand if you let me go.'

'Is that all?'

'A hundred! How much do you want?'

'It's not all about money. I want a name. I want to know who the Masked Man was.' I gripped his collar tighter. Pushed him a little further back, his heels now hanging slightly off the ridge over the long drop.

'I can't tell you that!' Colby panted hard, taking in the drop. He tried to dig into the ground with the toes of his boots, sending chunks of shingle over the edge. An animalistic howl escaped his lips.

'Who is he? Give me a name or you're going over.'

Through his good eye, Colby's darting gaze dropped down the side of the mountain again. His lips trembled, saliva pooling at the corners, mixing with the blood.

I pushed him back further. 'Tell me or you're a dead man.'

'Okay! But you can't let anyone know it came from me!' Colby desperately shouted out a name.

I inhaled sharply as those two words hurtled through the air and slammed into me.

Fuck. No wonder.

'Take a look down, Colby. You wanted to be rich and powerful, eh? King of the world?' I pushed him further back. 'Now you're at the top, was it worth it?'

'You can let me go now. I...I've told you what you wanted. I'll get you the money!' The fear rolled off him in almost tangible waves.

I narrowed my eyes. 'How does it feel knowing you're going to die? You ever wondered about that? You ever wondered how those boys felt? Trapped? With nowhere to go and nowhere to turn? Treated like nothing more than a piece of dirt? Living a hell on earth because you think you can just take what you want, from who you want?'

'Look...I—'

'And you think there are no consequences for killing my son? You really think you're all untouchable?'

'Please...I...'

Not so arrogant now, are you, Colby?

'Well, I've got a message for you, from Alex. And from Jamie and Maya and Dave and Sean and Moses and all the others out there, too.'

'Let me go. We had a deal. I'll get your hundred grand. I—'

'Fuck you and fuck your money!' I unclenched my hands and let go of his jacket, the sudden shift in my hold making him teeter backwards slightly.

I swung my right arm back and down. Brought it forward and up with all the force of a worthless father. A guilty soldier. A haunted failure.

The uppercut hit Colby underneath the jaw, and two things happened.

One, his head shot back as his jaw shattered.

And two, the force of the blow lifted him off his feet.

For a brief moment, it seemed as if he was suspended in thin air, perfectly weightless, hanging in stillness. In nothingness.

And then he fell backwards, and gravity took care of everything.

I peered over the rocky edge at what had once been Colby's body and was now reduced to a bloody, broken pulp on its sharp bounce and tumble during the long drop.

But I'd messed up. I'd failed to keep it a professional hit. I'd lost it in an intense storm of unleashed emotions.

When they recovered Colby's messy remains and pieced it all together, and worked out the points of impact on his body on the way down—the shattered jaw, broken finger, and torn knee ligament—it would just be put down to normal trauma. They were all reasonably sustained injuries, considering the fall. But would they find any of my skin under his nails from the scratches on my cheek? Would they find on the ridge any traces of Colby's blood that I missed after cleaning up? Would they suspect murder or would it be classed as a simple walking accident, just as I'd planned?

And would I get them all before they took me out?

Only time would tell.

I unrolled the balaclava and pulled it over my face. Great protection from the chilly winter wind that any hill walker should have in their kit. Even better for keeping me anonymous on the trek down.

I took one last look at my son's murderer and spoke into the silence, finally delivering to Colby the message from Alex. 'Touchable.'

I started walking down the mountain.

Six dead, three to go…

Chapter 55

As I walked into the hospital, Ava was coming out, carrying a crying Jackson in her arms. His face was red, his eyes puffy, wet tears streaking down his chubby cheeks. Ava was so engrossed in running a hand over his head to try to calm him down that she didn't notice me at first.

'Hi,' I said.

'Oh, hi!' She gave me a harassed and tired smile. 'I haven't seen you for a few days. You look like you've caught the sun—have you been away?'

'Just a short business trip. I'm looking forward to telling Maya all about it.'

'I've got to get this one home for a nap. He's been screaming the place down. If that didn't wake Maya up, I don't know what will. Mum and Dad are exhausted, and they've gone back to my place for a little sleep. We'll all be back later on.'

'There's no change with her, then?'

She smiled sadly, tears brimming to the surface. 'We had a meeting this morning with the doctors. They say she's deteriorating. They…' She blinked and looked away for a moment.

I put my hand on her shoulder, and she turned back to me, unable to hold the tears inside any longer.

'They don't think she's ever going to wake up. They think she's giving up.' Her face twisted with anguish. 'I just want her to get better again. I want her to see this little one grow up. See her laugh again. It's so unfair. I'm not ready to say goodbye.'

'Neither am I. There are plenty of cases where people wake up from comas. The mind is a powerful thing, you know, and people still aren't sure of the complexities of how it works. Doctors aren't always right. You just need to hold onto that thought.'

'You think miracles can really happen?'

I thought that the ending was up to Maya, but I was pretty sure that wasn't what Ava wanted to hear. Instead, I said, 'She's stronger than you think.' I dropped my hand, holding out the newspaper I was carrying. 'I'm just going up to read to her now. There's a story in here I think Maya will love to hear.'

She repositioned Jackson onto one hip and touched my arm. 'Thank you again for visiting her. It's so kind of you. I can't get here as much as I'd like with this little one, and they do say that any kind of stimulation can help pull her out of it.'

'It's no trouble, honestly. I want to. Just don't give up hope yet.'

Jackson let out an ear-piercing scream.

Ava adjusted his weight and said, 'Thanks again. I'll probably see you soon.' She walked towards the car park, muttering words to Jackson and kissing the top of his head.

I got in the lift and rode to the Intensive Care Unit. Standing in the doorway of Maya's room for a moment, I watched the machines that breathed for her, beeping and flickering with lights. The bruises were beginning to fade, but she looked so frail and small. If she did recover, she had a long way to go. Intensive physiotherapy was just the start. They said she might have some damage to her brain, but no one would know for certain until she woke up. If she woke up. She might have to learn to walk and talk again.

I sat in the chair next to her bed, put the newspaper on top of her blanket, and took her hand in mine. It was warm and dry and unresponsive.

I held onto it as I spoke. 'How are you today? Sorry I haven't been in for a little while. I had something important to do that I couldn't put off. There's another really interesting story in the paper, Maya. I'll read it to you, shall I?'

I glanced briefly at her face. No sign of anything behind the closed eyelids. '"Defence Secretary Douglas Talbot and Owner of Barron Private Banking Group Felix Barron are both missing, presumed dead, following the discovery of Barron's Yacht, *Invincible Storm*, floating abandoned in the waters off Corsica two days ago. Talbot's wife, Melissa, reported that Talbot was taking a short weekend break with close friend Barron aboard his yacht to do some fishing before returning to government duties. Mrs Talbot became increasingly worried when she was unable to reach her husband by mobile phone and alerted the authorities.

'According to the Coast Guard, the engine of *Invincible Storm* was still running when it was discovered, although no one was on board. Barron's family stated both he and Talbot were experienced sailors, and there were no other crew on the yacht at the time. They are shocked and confused as to exactly what could've happened. The search for both men continues".'

I watched her carefully, hoping for some kind of recognition that my words had penetrated her sleeping mind. It hadn't worked before, when I'd read out the news reports of Scholes's and Colby's deaths to her. I stared up at the ceiling, trying to think of what to say to pull her back to the land of the living. 'The doctors are giving up on you, but Ava, your parents, they want you back. And I know you can hear me, Maya. I know you're still in there.'

I blew out a frustrated breath when there was no reaction, leant closer, and whispered in her ear. 'There's one more left. The masked man is Xavier Wentworth. Part of the richest, most powerful family in the world, the most influential puppetmasters who manipulate everything from behind the scenes. Pulling the strings of the world's heads of states and captains of industry. They're worth several trillion dollars, controlling everything from global finance to energy, mining, defence companies, pharmaceuticals, healthcare, media, real estate, and a lot more via hundreds of different banks and corporations. You don't get that rich without having your fingers in every pie. They have a major involvement in world politics and affairs and can create a war or orchestrate a supreme global change to suit themselves at the drop of a hat. But a plan is in action. It won't be much longer. Will you hang in there until then? You can't give up now. Just one more to go and you'll be safe.'

I squeezed her hand softly and pictured the final hit in my head again. Lee had hacked into Wentworth's emails, medical records, business schedules, travel arrangements, and all manner of other things that helped build up a picture of how I could do it. Xavier Wentworth had recently been diagnosed with a B12 deficiency—had seen a doctor who'd prescribed a course of ten intramuscular B12 injections for the next three months. But Wentworth didn't have much time for doctors. He was far too busy with his role of managing hedge funds and raping boys to get the shots from someone else, so after being shown how to do them, he'd elected to inject himself in the privacy of his own company. He'd recently been in London for a meeting with some top executives from one of the many banks his family owned and had stayed at Claridge's in the penthouse suite he always graced his presence with whenever he was in town. He'd never married—hardly surprising given his tastes were so far away from the standard wife and 2.4 kids—so he was travelling alone, apart from a few bodyguards who travelled with him whenever he went out and were stationed outside his penthouse when he returned. Apparently, he liked his privacy too much for his men to be in the same room while he was in residence. I didn't need three guesses as to why. The stuff on his laptop was a repeat of *The Friday Club* tape and worse.

For Lee, manufacturing a card key for Wentworth's suite was piss easy. Lee had rented the suite previously under an assumed identity and hidden cameras in it prior to Wentworth's arrival. When I knew Wentworth was at a board meeting, I secured an entry and switched his syringe with the B12 inside for a fast-acting, strong dose of insulin. He took it at night, just before going to bed, so by the time he started feeling ill, it would be too late. He'd fall into a hypoglycaemic coma and then die. Shame. The best bit? Although any pathologist would see the needle marks on his skin, he'd assume they were from the self-inflicted B12 shots. And even if they detected insulin during his post-mortem, there was no trace I'd ever been in his suite, and Lee had deleted all hotel and nearby CCTV footage.

Wentworth was already a dead man walking. He just didn't know it yet.

I was so lost in thought that I didn't notice it for a moment, but when I did, my heartbeat quickened with hope.

Maya's eyes were still closed but moving rapidly now beneath her lids, as if she was in the REM stage of sleep. It was the first time I'd ever seen any kind of change in her. Surely that had to be a good sign, so I carried on talking as I rubbed her palm gently with my thumb.

'I know you're tired. And I guess you have to decide if you want to see this through to the end with me or if you're going to let go and be with Jamie now. But whatever you choose, I won't judge you, I promise. What I do promise is that justice does exist, even if it's what we make it.' I lightly kissed her forehead.

When I pulled back and studied her face, her eyes were still again. No sign of movement. The machine made the usual steady *beep, beep, beep.*

Had I been mistaken? Imagined something that wasn't there? Was she making a choice? I held my breath, waiting for her to wake up. For her to make a sound. A movement. *Do* something else.

And then her hand gently squeezed mine.

Epilogue

I'm walking down a long hospital corridor. I know I'm in pain, but I can't feel it, so I don't know how that's true. I remember some things. Like, I know my name's Maya. But my brain feels as if it's been replaced with something itchy and spongy.

The harsh strip lights above me are flashing *on-off, on-off,* casting pulsing shadows everywhere. It's slow going. Hard to breathe. I'm walking and walking and getting nowhere. And I don't even know *where* I'm actually going anyway. I keep looking behind me because I think someone might be following me, but no one's there. Just an endless, empty corridor from where I've come. I don't know whether to stop and turn back or keep going. I get the feeling that if I go back, the corridor will collapse in on me while I'm walking, and the only way I can avoid it is to keep moving in the direction I've been going.

Sometimes I feel things on my skin, a light touch, gentle pressure, but I must be imagining it. I can hear voices, too, but they're not in the corridor. They're further away. I know the voice belongs to someone called Mitchell, but I don't know how I recognise it or why the name's familiar. And there's another woman's voice, but it's nothing I've ever heard before. I don't know that woman. Not sure what she wants with me, but she's talking fast.

I carry on walking, but the corridor in front is getting darker now, and the lights down there are fading. It's scary. Eerie. I can smell something decaying and rancid. And I don't think I want to go down there anymore, but I'm not sure if I can turn back, either.

Is anyone here?

Hello?

HELLO?

The words form in my mouth but go no further. I can't speak. Letters are tangled together. My lips don't work.

A little way up, I see another corridor that branches to the right. It's long, too. But at the end is a doorway that looks tiny from here. The door is open slightly, with sunny light spilling through underneath and at the edges. It looks warm behind the door, and I'm cold. Shivering.

I stand still, looking from one corridor to the next, wondering which is the right way. I think if I make a mistake, there's no going back. And if I don't choose, I know I'll be wandering these corridors for a long time. I just don't know how I know.

I can't make a decision, so I listen to Mitchell's voice from the place that's far away. I can hear happiness in it, excitement. I'm sure I used to know what that felt like.

'Wait a minute, Maya. It's coming on. I'll turn up the volume now so you can hear the TV.'

I wait. I can do that. I'm not going anywhere just yet. And the other woman's voice is louder, talking from this TV, but I'm not sure what a TV is.

She says words that jumble together too quickly. Xavier. Wentworth. Died suddenly. Found by his secretary. Richest family. Businesses. Legacy.

Suddenly something clicks together inside, like the interlocking pieces of a jigsaw. *Snap. Snap!*

I feel something warm in my heart. Like the sunlight from that doorway is reaching out to me all the way from over there. I turn to look at the dark, endless corridor, then back at the sunny one.

I can hear Jamie's voice now. I think I know which way he is, but I don't know whether to go and see him yet or wait. I wish someone would make a decision for me because it hurts my head to try to think.

I lean against the wall, but the more I try to make the right choice, the more impossible it seems.

And then Mitchell says hello to someone. Another woman. Ava answers him. She's my sister, right? How do I know that but not other things? I hear a baby crying and feel a kiss on my forehead.

As if someone has just flipped a switch on in my head, now the choice is so clear. I know for certain which way I'm going.

I take a step forward...

A Note from the Author

Although all events and characters in this book are entirely fictional, *Untouchable* was inspired by many horrific allegations surrounding the following UK police investigations: Operation Midland, Operation Yewtree, Operation Hydrant, Operation Fairbank, Operation Fernbridge, and Operation Rectangle, to name a few, which involve deep-rooted historical and institutional child abuse allegations, including murder, by VIP paedophiles.

Firstly, I'd like to say a huge thanks to my readers from the bottom of my heart for choosing my books! *Untouchable* was a very difficult book to write, for many reasons—after all, a book about child abuse isn't going to be light reading. Many people doubted the horrific subject matter would work in a novel, and there were *so* many times when I doubted myself. As I did a lot of research in preparation, the sheer scale of institutional child abuse, the physical and mental effects on survivors, the quashed investigations, inquiries, cover-ups and the lack of prosecutions, insanely light sentencing, and low number of convictions for offenders was mind-blowingly devastating and heartbreaking. So I had to follow my heart, and my intention was to raise awareness, because making child abuse taboo takes the power away from survivors and gives it to the perpetrators. Silence and denial makes the vulnerable even more voiceless. I really hope I managed to give the subject the justice it deserves, and this book is dedicated to survivors everywhere. If you did enjoy it, I would be so grateful if you could leave a review or recommend it to family and friends. I always love to hear from readers so please keep your emails and Facebook messages coming (contact details are on my website: www.sibelhodge.com). They make my day!

A massive thanks goes out to my husband Brad for supporting me, being my chief beta reader, fleshing out ideas with me, and helping me see the light when my brain was exploding with this book!

Thanks SO much to JY for all your SAS advice and input, and for bringing Jamie's and Mitchell's military background to life. You know who you are!

Big thank you hugs to my beta readers Karen Lloyd, Sue Ward, Tom Elder, K'Tee Bee, Dianne Wallace, Joo, and Joseph Calleja for all your feedback. It's so much appreciated.

To Angela and Jill and Red Adept Editing for catching the things I missed.

Huge thanks to Emilie Marneur for all your editing advice, along with Sammia. Sorry for being such a nightmare with this one!

And finally, thanks to all my author friends. Writing is such a solitary existence that it's great to know you're not going mad sometimes!

Sibel xx

About the Author

Sibel Hodge's No. 1 Bestseller *Look Behind You* has now sold over ¼ million copies. Her books are International Bestsellers in UK, USA, Australia, France, and Germany. She writes an eclectic mix of genres, and she's a passionate human and animal rights advocate.

Her work has been nominated and shortlisted for numerous prizes, including the Harry Bowling Prize, the Yeovil Literary Prize, the Chapter One Promotions Novel Competition, The Romance Reviews' prize for Best Novel with Romantic Elements, and Indie Book Bargains' Best Indie Books of 2012. She was the Winner of Best Children's Book by eFestival of Words 2013, Nominated for the 2015 BigAl's Books and Pals Young Adult Readers' Choice Award, Winner of Crime, Thrillers & Mystery | Book from a Series in the SpaSpa Book Awards 2013, Readers' Favourite Young Adult - Coming of Age Honourable Award Winner 2015, and New Adult Finalist in the Oklahoma Romance Writers of America's International Digital Awards 2015. Her novella Trafficked: The Diary of a Sex Slave has been listed as one of the top 40 books about human rights by Accredited Online Colleges.

For Sibel's latest book releases, giveaways and gossip, sign up to her newsletter at: www.sibelhodge.com

Also by Sibel Hodge

Fiction

Duplicity
Where the Memories Lie
Look Behind You
Butterfly
Trafficked: The Diary of a Sex Slave
Fashion, Lies, and Murder (Amber Fox Mystery No 1)
Money, Lies, and Murder (Amber Fox Mystery No 2)
Voodoo, Lies, and Murder (Amber Fox Mystery No 3)
Chocolate, Lies, and Murder (Amber Fox Mystery No 4)
Santa Claus, Lies, and Murder (Amber Fox Mystery No 4.5)
Vegas, Lies, and Murder (Amber Fox Mystery No 5)
Murder and Mai Tais (Danger Cove Cocktail Mystery No 1)
Killer Colada (Danger Cove Cocktail Mystery No 2)
The See-Through Leopard
Fourteen Days Later
My Perfect Wedding
The Baby Trap
It's a Catastrophe

Non-Fiction

A Gluten Free Taste of Turkey
A Gluten Free Soup Opera
Healing Meditations for Surviving Grief and Loss

CPSIA information can be obtained
at www.ICGtesting.com
Printed in the USA
BVHW03s0141300318
512029BV00001B/44/P